ANAKI
MC SHIFTER ROMANCE
VERA FOXX

FOXX FANTASY PUBLISHING

Publisher: Foxx Fantasy Publishing

Editing by: MarcEdits, Alease_Reads

Sensitivity Reading by: Alease_Reads, Emm E. Goshald

DEDICATION

To all the thirsty readers who have been waiting for this double peened dragon to slide into your laps.

His human form might be a 100% a cinnamon roll but his dragon side is not...

"Scream for me."

CONTENTS

ANAKI

The always cheerful, bar-dancing, bartending dragon shifter hides dark secrets beneath his lively personality.

His time is slipping away faster than anyone suspects,

ticking down with an urgency that gnaws at his very soul.

When offered a chance to help the future Luna's family

He jumps at the chance to forget the darkness that lurks inside.

Anything to keep his mind from slipping.

Then, he meets the stubborn Luna's sister, Elena

He hears his dragon roar within him for the first time in years.

She's feisty and wants to protect her family, especially her son.

He wants all of her and the new family he has just gained.

But will she accept his past with the secrets and desires he hides?

DEAR READER

Anaki's book timeline is the same as Locke's book. Locke may show up in parts of Anaki's book that weren't mentioned in his book because it wasn't relevant to Locke's story. It would have been repetitive, and we didn't need that.

Anaki's story begins where Locke is in the early stages of shifting back into a human. He has just given the order to retrieve Emm's family to use them as leverage to keep her as his mate if he has to. Just after the scene where Emm was at the park.

(Gah, Locke was such a drama llama.)

BEFORE READING

E vents that happen in the book worth mentioning.
This could also be a list of spoilers.

Anal Play (both MCs receiving)

Rimming

Edging

Double Peen/Special Equipment

Some Edging

Breeding

Brief Mentions of Murder

Depression

Thoughts of Suicide

Rejection

Domestic Violence from FMC's past, talked about in passing

Feelings of unworthiness

Fighting

Gore

Graphic Violence (mentions)

Obsessive/Aggressive (MMC's inner dragon)

CHAPTER ONE

Anaki

I used to stay down in the water for days. Hide in the vegetation, among the fish and other creatures that lived here. They didn't bother me; they stood by me.

They didn't see me as a threat because they knew I only fed when I really needed to.

I took only what I needed. That was what I was taught. I never forgot my mother's lessons when she told me never to kill for the sport, only to feed. Preferably, I should only take the lives of the animals that can no longer contribute to the ecosystem.

The murky water surrounded my body, blocking any visibility except for a faint glow of light trying to penetrate the darkness. My hair floated around my face, tangled and wild, as the final bubbles escaped my lips and rose to the surface.

Light won't reach this far down. Too cloudy a day.

My lungs burned, and my throat constricted.

I can only stay down here for minutes, unlike I used to.

I never was the strongest dragon, but I'd like to think my swiftness and lungs were beyond superior. I breathed air and water. Not that anyone knew at the club.

Everyone was worried about themselves. Which they should be all of us were slowly dying. To talk about our problems wasn't for the faint of heart.

There were the few who talked to me about their better days, how their mates rejected them for no other reason but stability, higher ranks in packs, or just plain cruelty. It swung both ways. Males rejected females, too, but this group... well we were different. Ready to help each other, and we believed in something better.

Once I heard there was such a group, the Iron Fang, I knew I had to get here fast. Being around souls like me, kindred spirits and all, it brought a spring back into my step. I think it made me better, at least for a while.

My body settled into the muck. My chest tightened, and I could feel the sting of the icy water seeping into my bones. I gritted my teeth against the numbing cold, and I could no longer feel my fingers or toes. Each second became more of a motivational struggle to move, but I allowed myself to feel it all.

It was almost as if it were a form of punishment or penance.

Not good enough.

What a weak dragon I was.

I couldn't keep the cold away, I couldn't breathe in the water, I couldn't swim as quickly.

I wanted to feel something other than the hopeless feeling of loneliness. I'd rather feel the pain.

I squeezed my eyes tight and opened them again. An ugly catfish was staring right at me.

I could stay here. Let the waters that once soothed me and my dragon take away the ache in my soul. I didn't want to deteriorate in front of my brothers. I wanted to be remembered as the lively one who made their lives brighter, even for a time.

People have given me sideways glances lately.

I couldn't even carry a keg over my shoulder. I could barely roll it to the front of the bar without becoming winded.

Locke was getting better. Never thought his wolf would ever return. Thank the goddess, Journey told everyone to leave the mangy wolf alone. After not even a month's time, he came crawling back and can shift into human form for short periods.

Locke was psychotic, his methods questionable, brutal, but he brought this club together, and he was going to make it a pack again. I had that much faith in him.

It gave everyone hope. I had hope for them, too.

I let out a low groan in my throat.

Useless, weak, unworthy. Those words chanted in my head.

If my mate strode in the bar tonight and if I somehow could get their attention, would they stay? Or would they reject me?

Staying down here would be for the best. The easiest way, so I did not have to face it.

The club wouldn't miss me that much. They would move on, try to save as many other souls as they could because that is what this club was about.

It wasn't uncommon to put shifters down. I've seen it with my own eyes. I'd rather go out my way, not be held down, like an animal.

I had my fun with everyone. Made the jokes, the drinks, and danced on the bar. It was all in good fun, just to see everyone smile for at least a little while. I wanted to make them laugh, make them all laugh, to forget the pain of yesterday and today.

But mine was consuming me, and I didn't know how much longer I could hide it.

Black spots clouded my vision. How long had I been under? Just a few more minutes, that's all I needed. Or just stay?

I felt the fish surround me, wrapping me in a cocoon.

A little longer, yes, maybe a nap.

A shout from above had me sitting up in an instant. It was deep, rumbling, a shout so loud I instantly knew who it was. Splashes from the surface, more shouting.

I tilted my head and forced back a smile. If I stayed down here, the stubborn bear would dive in after me if I did not resurface soon.

I pushed my feet into the mud and propelled myself forward. I let my body move and slither, gyrating my hips, legs and body. I tried my best to mimic my dragon's movements, to feel alive, to find the remnants of him within me.

My lungs burned, and black spots came across my vision. When the light was brighter, I reached out my hand to break the surface, and a strong hand gripped it, pulling me from the waters.

"Damn it, Anaki!" Bear growled when I landed in the dirt.

I took in big gasps of air, starved of the oxygen I needed.

"What the fuck do you think you are doing? Your lips are blue and... you're naked!" He pulled at his beard and turned away.

When I was done coughing, I broke out into laughter and slung my hair back. "Not that it has bothered you before. Why are you bringing it up now?"

Bear scowled, his hands on his hips like a fussy mother hen. "Nadia is on her way here. I don't need her to see this." He pointed to my lower half.

I couldn't help but lie back, put my hands behind my head and prop up one foot so he could get a full view. "You mean this pose? Why, are you jealous she might find me more attractive?"

Bear and Nadia had a sweet mating. It took Bear long enough to claim her, but with a little pushing of my own, a little makeover for the female, and fattening her up, they did just fine.

At first, I was afraid my relationship with Bear would change. He would want to spend more time with his mate, which he should. However, I was surprised at how they embraced me.

With Bear being a... well, a bear, and me being a dragon, we have similar animal dynamics. We didn't need a pack to survive, as our animals did well enough on their own. Bears didn't need packs, so they only came together with other bears to find mates, to trade and hunt with.

Dragons enjoyed their solitude as well. We didn't have a pack, but there was a hierarchy, with meetings and flocks. We liked social interactions, but also enjoyed our time alone.

Bear lived in a cabin near to the cave I had claimed, which was far from looking like a cave on the inside. Bear had never come inside, so he and Nadia thought I slept on rocks.

While I appreciated Bear and Nadia wanting me to live with them, even going as far as adding an additional bedroom for me, a newly mated couple should not be taking on a lonely dragon.

Especially one that could go rabid soon.

I just wanted someone for myself.

My bruised hearts thumped long and slow. Bear made sure that our friendly, brotherly relationship remained the same, even when I tried to give them space. They both demanded I come to dinners with them and stay in their home often.

They also let me do cuddle piles and sleepovers.

That isn't normal, and if the bar got hold of that information, it would be the end for all of us.

"Where are your pants?" Bear looked everywhere but me and found them thrown against a tree. He stomped over, picked them up, and threw them in my face.

My body shivered, and I held back a wince when I did. I didn't want him to see me like this.

"Anaki?" His voice grew softer, and he sat on the ground next to me. "Have you seen Bones lately?"

Right, Bones. If I went to Bones, he would suggest checking in every day. He would put me on a 'watch list' for everyone to stare at me. Then he would test me, see how much I can lift, ask how long I can hold my breath, and if I can maintain my body heat while in the water.

I did not need that. I'd been successful at not having to get a physical in a while by giving him free beers.

"Nah, don't need to." I shrugged his hand off my shoulder. The act was cold, and Bear's body stiffened beside me.

"Anaki, this isn't something to joke around about."

"Yeah?" I snapped, my eyes darting to him. "And what did you do when you were having problems? Did you run to Bones?"

Bear snorted and played with his beard on his face. "No, and when I got my physical for my supposedly last mission, I told him where he could shove his stethoscope."

I chuckled and threw on the woolen, tan sweater that had been closer to the water's edge. I knew I would freeze when I got out, and I wasn't about to make myself look worse in front of my friend. I didn't need him to be worrying more than he already was.

"You ready?" Bear asked, talking about covering myself, when we heard footsteps coming through the forest.

I couldn't smell very well anymore, but the person was prancing and from the rhythm of their steps, I immediately knew who it was.

"Anaki!" Nadia scolded when she approached. "You shouldn't be swimming. You are going to catch a cold." She came up behind me and ruffled my hair.

I smiled, enjoying the contact she brought me, and let out a contented growl.

Bear nudged me and looked much more at ease when his mate sat down on his lap and her feet landed in mine. "You aren't supposed to be swimming when it's this cold, you know?" Nadia raised a brow.

I huffed and leaned back on my elbows. "You know, just because you are becoming a certified nurse, doctor, whatever under Bones, doesn't mean you can sass me. I still make your drinks. What if I spike it with something not so nice?"

Nadia gasped. "You wouldn't dare!"

Bear deeply laughed and stroked his mate's cheek. "I don't know, we've talked about sleep fucking before."

"Bear!" Nadia screamed and covered her face. "You can't—" Then she looked at me with a twinkle in her eye. "I guess you can tell Anaki. He knows everything." She wiggled her feet in my lap.

We all broke out into laughter, and I watched as Bear placed a kiss on Nadia's forehead. I knew they were trying to make me feel welcome, a part of their family, but I wanted one of my own.

I moved to stand, and they followed. Bear cleared his throat and rubbed his hand behind his neck.

"Anaki, there is something I needed to tell you. But after seeing you—"

"Don't." I cut him off.

"What you were doing—"

"I wasn't doing anything!" I feigned innocence. "I went for a swim. I needed to feel the water on my scales." I gritted my teeth together. "Skin. I needed to remember, just like how you used to go for hikes in the forest."

Bear took Nadia off his lap and stood. He stomped away and smashed his fist into a tree. "But I wasn't bare ass naked. I wasn't freezing to death!" he snarled.

Nadia's head bounced from us both, and I hated the way she looked so sad, how Bear was upset.

"It's really nothing." I pulled on the string of my sweater. "It was colder today, that's all. If it upsets you so much, I won't do it anymore, alright? Come on, why are you both out here?"

I gave them both a big smile and patted them on the back to lead them back up the pathway in the forest. My cave leads down by the lake, but I didn't want them to have access to it. Not that I didn't trust them, but even dragons had to have their secrets.

Nadia leaned into me, and her arm wrapped around my waist. "We were inviting you to dinner."

"Nadia," Bear growled and pulled on one of her space buns that looked more like fake bear ears.

Nadia rolled her eyes. "Well, we are inviting you to dinner, but Bear was at a meeting last night, and he was supposed to tell you that you have important orders."

"Orders?" I stopped along the path. Even the squirrels stopped chattering to listen in.

I didn't get orders from Locke or anyone from the inner circle. Orders were for special missions, duties to perform in the club. The inner circle met at the church for deeper discussions that I wanted no part of.

I'll stay behind the bar, thanks.

"What sort of orders?" I jerked my head back and forth.

Bear sighed deeply enough for his bear to come through with a heavy growl. I patted him on the head and made a cooing noise. "Easy there. Let's not get our berries in a twist."

Nadia snorted behind me and grabbed my hand. Instantly, my nerves were relaxed, and Bear shook his head dramatically.

"I don't know why I like you so much," he grunted and put his hand around the back of my neck to pull me closer to him.

I hummed when his enormous chest warmed my face. The connection of a brother and sister, in both of them, kept my sleeping dragon calm while I was near. I wondered if Bear and Nadia could feel the change in me when we were apart for a time, and when we were close.

"Let's get some food in you, then we will explain. After the act you pulled down by the lake, I don't think you should go," he muttered the last part under his breath.

I whipped my head at him. "Go? Go where? And I am the one who is supposed to be feeding the both of you tonight. Not the other way around."

At least, I thought it was my turn to cook dinner.

Nadia snorted. "Way to withhold information for less than ten seconds."

We all walked up the steps, and Bear pressed his fingers into his eyes. "A mission, Anaki. But you are getting a physical first."

CHAPTER TWO

Anaki

I kept quiet as we walked into the dimly lit cabin, the only sound the gentle ticking of a grandfather clock.

I didn't have an appetite as I helped plate the food. A large roast cooked in the crock pot where I had put it that morning, in the their kitchen. Surprise crossed their faces, and I shrugged my shoulders.

The meat was tender and the vegetables steamed to Nadia's preference of slightly crunchy. She was originally half fae before turning into a full bear by Bear's bite.

Nadia winked at me, a mischievous glint in her eyes, before we sat down, a silent thank you passing between us. My prior dark thoughts turned to a guilt that hung over me like a storm cloud.

How dare I think such things when I have such great friends? They would miss me, hell, if I were gone and could look back, I would miss them, too.

I wiped my hand over my face, trying to school my expression. No one wanted a depressed dragon at their table. No one wanted to see a bartender with more baggage than the drinker.

With a sigh, I extracted the crumpled, grease-stained napkin from my lap and twisted it between my fingers, the texture strangely comforting as Bear attacked his third helping of roast. With the speed of a starving bear, he ate the food, smearing it across his beard; Nadia giggled as she stood to wipe away the mess.

I coughed to break the intimacy between the two. Not that I didn't adore watching them. It brought hope that I might have what they have one day, but I was still raw from my earlier near-drowning.

"Can you tell me what the mangy mutt wants me to do?" I took my fork, stabbed it into the meat, swirled the sauce around the plate and stuck it into my mouth.

Even the flavor was dull, and the roast was my favorite. Did it need more salt? More seasoning?

Bear ignored me and licked the corners of his mouth.

"This taste alright to you?" I pointed at the dull, colorless slop on my plate.

Nadia licked her lips and took another bite. "Yes, same as always. Are you sure you are alright?"

I chuckled and took another bite of the flavorless meat. "Just making sure it is to your liking. I couldn't remember if I put in everything. Mind was wandering today."

"As it should," Bear interrupted. "Locke being back has put everyone on edge. Especially since he's found his mate."

I nodded, and a bubble of laughter escaped. "Yeah, a real firecracker she is. She's perfect. Absolutely perfect for him. She'll test him at every turn. Their sex is going to be damn explosive."

Nadia shoved a russet potato in her mouth to cover her laughter. "Yes, she said she works at a paper company. Can you believe that?" she said with her mouth full.

Bear huffed, his big shoulders rose and fell. "Yeah, like anyone believed that. Locke's got his hands full. Tajah doesn't like her, though. That is reason for concern." He narrowed his eyes on the plate. "She's in charge of getting Emm's family here. Nadia and I are going. We all agreed you should be on the team, too."

The fork I was about to force into my mouth fell back to the table. They wanted me to go? In my state? I didn't think I was capable. While I didn't need a pack to survive, to gain strength from like the wolves, I didn't think I was strong enough with no dragon. There wasn't much left. I wouldn't be worth it to the team.

"Locke agrees. You have a knack to handle women, make them feel at ease and not a threat. I'm the muscle. Beretta is the weapons specialist. The Moonlight Outcasts are our cover. You and Nadia are the care team."

I didn't know if I should take what Bear said about me as a joke or an insult. I had a way of *talking* to women. It was a matter of understanding, being sympathetic. Mostly when they were drunk, scared, or vulnerable was when I really shone. I wanted them to feel comfortable and not see me as a threat, that not all guys are assholes.

A lot of men didn't know how to *not be an asshole*.

Example one... Hawke.

I didn't carry a big alpha vibe like a lot of the males at the bar. That wasn't me, as much as I wanted it to be, so long ago.

I had accepted that I wasn't going to be Mr. Macho. I wasn't going to be a part of a mission because of it, and I was fine with that because I didn't want to get blood on my hands unless I had to.

But this? They wanted me?

"Why do you need me, exactly? Why do I need to be part of this 'care team'? You guys have done fine before?"

Bear and Nadia shared a look. Bear put his hand on Nadia's. "We are worried that Tajah might show some hostility toward Emm's family because she doesn't trust them. While there are females on this trip, we need gentle voices and bodies that will make this not... a hostile environment."

I quirked a brow, and Bear stood and walked to the living room. He brought back a manila folder, thick with papers inside. Some of us were still living twenty years behind technology and still stuck on ink and paper.

Bear slung the folder onto the table. When the folder opened it was like the divine power of the goddess that the folder opened up to a grainy photo of a woman. The picture was taken from at least forty yards away, but zoomed to the max. The woman was bending over, pointing to a piece of paper on the table with a young boy underneath her. She was smiling, and her shoulder length hair was tucked behind her ear.

I pulled the paper closer; the grainy picture didn't do her justice. I knew that. I slid it aside and went to the next papers in the piles. More pictures, but none of them where I could get a good look at her face.

"That is Emm's sister, Elena," Bear said, his voice fading as I continued to stare at Elena's picture. "There are more pictures of the rest of the family in there. Their grandmother, whom we can't seem to find a name for, and Elena's son, Luis. He attends a private school. We are in the process of getting all his school records. He's extremely bright..."

I heard a low buzzing in my head as I glanced over the pictures. I entirely ignored the older woman who kept popping up. She was older, had pepper-spiced looking hair, nothing out of the ordinary from what I saw.

No, I concentrated on the younger woman. She was spellbinding, capturing my full attention. I couldn't put my finger on why. Maybe it was because of how her brow pinched together in some of them. Even with the grainy picture, it pulled at my heartstrings when she sat in a rocking chair or even used a cane to walk to her living room.

Why would she need to use a cane?

"She had her son, Luis, at twenty-two—"

"Why the fuck is she walking with a cane?" I gritted out, my hand crumpling the extra pieces of paper that didn't have her face on.

With a frown pulling at her lips, Nadia scooted closer, the movement a quiet, almost hesitant shuffle. "T-that's what we wanted to talk about. It's sort of the reason why Emm has kept them all hidden. Her grandmother is old, her sister has a son. Elena, she also has a chronic disease. She has trouble walking, with numbness in her hands and feet. It can cause pain…"

My throat tightened, a lump forming as my fingers clenched the paper, the texture rough beneath my nails. For anyone to go through such a disease sounded terrible, but for her specifically? To have a child to raise, too?

"What of her male? Does he not take care of her?"

My heart pounded in my chest. For a sick, twisted reason, I didn't want her to have one. If we brought the family here, we would protect them all. They were family. The president's family and we would give our lives to protect the future Luna's blood, but hell, my dragon wanted to take care of this specific family.

Bear shook his head. "No, there is no male. The only male in her life left her and Luis years ago. Dead from an overdose. Switch checked into it."

I didn't realize how tense my shoulders were until I heard that information.

Bear put his hand on my back. "Do you feel something for this woman?" He pointed to the picture. "You know how it was for Nadia and me, when I first saw her—"

I shook my head and got up from the table. The chair screeched and echoed throughout the kitchen. "No, nothing like that. You know how I get wound up when anyone has to go through any sort of pain, rejection like that. No one should have to be abandoned and suffer alone."

Bear grunted and patted me on the back again. "That's why we want you to come with us, Anaki. You've got a kind soul, and how you helped Nadia, we think we can talk them into coming with us rather than forcing them. With Elena's condition, we don't want to trigger a flare-up."

"Flare-up?"

Nadia stood up and rounded the table. "Yes, happens to people with this disease she has. Her condition could worsen. It will be difficult for her to walk, and she could have pain. The Moonlight Outcasts are already down there, scoping out the place, seeing if we can bring them back here when she's on a good day. When she arrives here, the cabin will be prepared for her to rest. She's likely to have a flare-up afterwards, I'm sure, from all of the stress."

I ran my hands through my hair. Right, if I was part of the care team, I would need to be able to help her and her kid in any way that I could.

"Don't stress, Anaki. Just be you, that's all we ask. You know how to make the ladies feel comfortable. Just, not too comfortable." Bear winked.

I rolled my eyes, pulled up my sleeves, and headed to the sink to do the dishes. No, there wouldn't be getting too comfortable with Elena. I was there to do a job, and Nadia and Bear thought I could help. Be a part of the Iron Fang. Be wanted, be useful.

I liked the sound of that. It would help get rid of the dark thoughts that clouded my head.

"The only thing left to do is a physical." Nadia sang as she stepped next to me.

I groaned and leaned on my forearm. "Please don't make me," I whined.

"Bones said he hasn't seen you in a while, anyway." Nadia nudged me. "Besides, don't you miss the whole turn your head and cough?"

My groan quickly turned into a laugh. "Oh, Bones doesn't do that for me. Dragons are special."

Nadia blinked several times innocently.

I gasped mockingly. "You mean, you don't know? Bear hasn't told you?" I placed my hand on my chest. "Why, the reason Bones doesn't like to give hernia checks is because—"

"Anaki!!! There are a few things I don't let you tell my female, and that is one of them! Now get out and go get it done!"

I took the terry cloth towel from the drying rack and flung it over my shoulder. "If you insist, but if she is going to be a full-blown doctor for the club soon, she's going to have to know basic reptilian anatomy."

Bear growled and crossed his arms over his chest. "And, I will let that be the last thing she learns."

CHAPTER THREE

Elena

While my abuela worries about my health, apparently I'm not sick enough for her not to throw a chancel at me. She can whip that chancla off, throw it around the corner, and somehow, still hit me in the face.

While I give her a hard time playing with her rocks—*crystals*—and her mushroom eating habits, she is good to me and Luis. Better than I deserve, after going out with a man who did not deserve my time and attention.

She's more than my abuela. She was Emm's and my mama. She taught us how to be strong and independent women when our father became what he is, a cold-blooded bastard.

We needed to be strong women, but along with that independence I decided to have a rebellious streak, while Emm was trying to take care of us.

My selfishness got me in trouble and the universe was now kicking my ass for it. I'm in more trouble now since having Luis. Being pregnant with him sped up my condition, but there isn't one day that I regret having him. He will be my one and only, and I thank the stars he's mine.

The only man in my life.

I gripped my cane and leaned on my left side. I hated the thing, but it was a necessity when I had a flare-up. As long as I didn't have to use the wheelchair, I didn't feel completely defeated. I am my abuela's granddaughter. I held my head high. I have a full-time job and can take care of myself, most days.

Wheelchair be damned!

Unless Luis wanted to go to Parque El Agua; the little booger was smart, and if I brought my wheelchair, we would have perfect parking.

I bent over and picked up both the chanclas from the floor. I could hear Abuela blabbering to Emm about finding a man on the phone. *Dios Mio.* Emmie needed a man to calm herself down. She had enough money to take care of us for at least the next ten years.

Now that I had my online editing business, a job where I could work from home and was getting steady money, I could take care of Luis by myself. From living frugally and the money I've saved from Emm's line of work, which none of us approve of, we would sit comfortably for a long, long time.

Firing the in-home nurse will also help save us money.

Emm would just need to learn to stay hidden and not flaunt her butt all over Venezuela.

I stood up and stretched my back, hearing it pop a few times. I winced when I heard my back pop two more times, and I let out a long sigh.

"Get in here, Elena. I need to talk to you." I heard Abuela's voice carry through the small house.

I swiftly entered Luis' room, just a stone's throw from where I stood. The sight of him engrossed in a book, with its content far beyond his tender years, filled me with a mixture of awe and disbelief. With a gentle shake of my head, I reluctantly tore my gaze away.

It keeps him occupied. I just wish the school would understand that if they gave him more challenging classes, he wouldn't be such a nuisance to them.

I could homeschool, but then that would take away time from work.

And what about a flare-up?

"Elena!" Abuela shouted. "Are you dreaming about your *dream* man?"

I scoffed and entered the room. Abuela was putting suitcases by the door. They were all lined up in perfect order from the largest to the smallest.

My eyes bugged out of my head as I walked closer. Abuela was humming a song and stepped away from the door. She headed to the kitchen, put *two* kettles on and hit the gas. The flames ignited as she smiled. The crinkles around her eyes got deeper by the second.

Slowly, I opened my mouth, afraid of what might come out of it. "What is going on? Why are there suitcases by the door?" I lifted my hand to point at the problem, and Abuela shrugged her shoulders.

"We are moving. Don't worry, I packed all the necessities." She waved her hand like it was no big deal. "We won't need the furniture, everything will be provided. I won't need much at all. I won't be knitting anymore. I did bring your computer, because I know how much you want your independence. Your medication is in your purse, along with your medical history. Oh…" Abuela walked to the coffee table and grabbed a clear plastic bag.

I groaned when I realized what it was. Magic *Mushrooms.*

"I told Emm you stopped those."

"Liar." Abuela hissed. "I could be an alcoholic. Now let your abuela have her herbs. I rub it on my joints."

I rubbed one of my temples with my index finger, trying to figure out what to do with her. I could put her in a home, but then I would have to give the place her real identity. I couldn't do that because somehow the cartel would find out.

We weren't stupid, they weren't stupid. I'm sure they could find a way to have someone hunt us down if they thought we were even in Venezuela. "Abuela, are you high right—"

Loud, heavy knocks landed on the door, and I jumped, causing a sharp pain in my hip. I groaned and sat in Abuela's favorite cushioned rocking chair.

Abuela ran toward me and patted me down. "Now, don't get stressed. You are having a good day, right?" I nodded, but it appeared she was telling herself that more than me. "Here, let us brush your hair. Make you look presentable. It isn't every day you, you know, meet... people."

Maybe she was having a stroke.

"You want to put some gloss on? Make your lips shiny?"

The hell?

"Abuela, open the door!"

Three more raps on the door shook the tiny house and made my chest shake. She went to the door and blocked my view. In a sickly sweet voice I'd never heard before, she said, "We've been waiting for you. Please, come in, come in."

Two people stepped into the room, their slightly confused faces evident. As they entered, the air filled with the scent of trepidation.

The shorter woman, with two buns adorning the top of her head, dropped her perplexed expression and replaced it with a warm smile. Her steps echoed softly on the polished floor, a subtle sound that blended with the hum of the low-quality appliances in our home. I noticed her attire, which surprised me, given her angelic face. She was clad in sleek black tactical gear, her black boots making a soft thud with each step. A bullet-proof vest hugged her torso, adding a weighty presence to her small figure. A walkie-talkie was securely strapped to her chest, its faint static adding to my mini-freak-out.

As soon as my eyes landed on the man next to her, my senses heightened, and I felt a surge of adrenaline coursing through me. The world around me seemed to sharpen, every sight becoming more vivid, every sound more pronounced. I could almost taste the electrical charge in the air, as my heart pounded in my chest, and the scent of anticipation filled my nostrils.

I gripped my cane, unsure if it was something in my coffee, maybe I was drugged, or my body was finally giving out. But it never stopped, especially when I took my fill of the man next to the woman.

Tall, clean-shaven, lips parted as if shocked he was even here. He was dressed similarly to the woman, overloaded with technical gear, yet his face strove for a non-threatening appearance. His dirty blonde hair was messy, like he ran his fingers through it too many times, and a sheen of sweat glistened on his forehead. And wow, those cheekbones were something.

The man straightened his back, and his eyes widened. His hand touched the woman beside him, and he leaned over and whispered something in her ear.

I don't know what possessed me, but I felt jealous that he touched her. He was a man, and I hated them myself. The only male who was allowed near me was my son.

I stood up, holding onto my cane, and pulled back my shoulders. "Abuela, what is the meaning of this? Who are these people?"

While the elders are supposed to be the leaders of the home, mine was crazier than a squirrel hoarding nuts for winter.

Abuela cleared her throat and nodded for them to introduce themselves.

"I'm Nadia, and this is Anaki. We are here to collect you and take you to your sister."

I narrowed my eyes. The audacity of these people. "We just spoke to my sister, and she mentioned nothing about us leaving."

I stepped toward the side table where my gun nestled safely in the drawer. Luis knew about the gun, and had been told many times never to open it. The fingerprint safety device was a necessity since he was a curious child, but would I be able to get to it in time while these two were here?

Neither had guns on them, that I could see, but that didn't mean they didn't have a knife or a taser, and I wasn't fast.

"I suggest you leave," I said. "We have already activated the security monitors and the silent alarm."

Heavy footsteps came from the open doorway. A man, no, a freaking bear of a man stepped up behind the woman. He pushed her until she was behind him. I looked up at him, and my heart raced when I saw the gun holsters at his side.

"We do this the easy way, Elena. We mean no harm. Security camera lines have been cut, you have no panic button, and you will never reach the gun in that drawer fast enough."

I was absolutely raging.

They had been watching us.

Instead of taking my anger out on them, I whipped my head around to my abuela. "What have you done?" I hissed. "Did you give us away? They are going to take us all to get to Emmie. It's your fault!" I took my cane and threw it to the other side of the room.

I ground my teeth, knowing full well we were absolutely screwed. I promised to keep them both safe, especially since Abuela had been acting strange. My legs felt weak, and my body fatigued. I let my arm settle on the stand beside the rocking chair when I felt two arms come behind me and save me from falling over.

"Hey, it's going to be alright," he whispered in my ear.

My heart slowed. I didn't have the nerve to look up at him, but I knew it was the dirty blonde who stood in the doorway. What was his name?

Anaki?

He gently put me in the chair and grabbed the blanket behind me, putting it over my legs. He tucked the blanket under my knees and kneeled down to see me eye to eye. "Believe it or not, we are the good guys. Emm just doesn't know it yet. You look just like her. Pretty stubborn, too." He gave me a crooked smile that could have made me fall into his arms, all over again.

Damn it, stop!

A whistle from the stove broke the trance, and he stood up. "Tea? Don't mind if I do. Nadia? Bear?"

The bear of a man shook his head and went toward the side table drawer. He pulled out the gun and grabbed my wrist, using my finger to unlock it. He promptly emptied the bullets and stuffed them in his tool belt, then he handed the gun back to me. "Just so you think you are in charge. You know, like your sister."

I narrowed my eyes at him and ripped the gun away from him.

"Easy, Bear." Nadia tapped his butt to move him over.

His name is actually Bear?

"You are in charge here, Elena, as well as the woman over there." Nadia hitched her thumb over her shoulder at Abuela. She had a chancla in her hand, pointing at me.

The only reason Abuela hadn't thrown it was because there were guests.

"I'm not sure how she knew we were coming. In fact, why do you have suitcases by the door?" Nadia asked her.

Abuela threw her chancla to the floor to put her foot in and fixed her hair. "Because we are leaving with you, are we not? That is why all the vampires have been hanging around outside."

I slapped the side of my face and groaned. "Abuela, did you chew on some rocks this morning, too?"

Anaki ran to my side and pulled my hand away from my face. "Don't be hurting yourself like that, love."

As his palm connected with my skin, a gentle warmth enveloped my body, sending tingles down my arm. The sensation flowed seamlessly, cascading towards my side and settling in my hip, relieving the dull ache. It felt akin to a soothing, heated compress encircling the entire joint, easing the pain. In response, a contented sigh escaped my lips, a sign of immense relief.

As I fixed my gaze on him, I jerked away, realizing I was letting him touch me for far too long. The sharp twinge of pain shot through my hip, bringing back the ache once again.

Once I had let go, the sight of his eyes resembled a wounded puppy, and it weighed heavily on my heart, as if aching in tandem with my physical discomfort.

"Hey! You got some sharp teeth! You really are a vampire!" Luis' voice screams excitedly from the bedroom. I stood up quickly, forgetting about the pain, and only concentrating on my son.

"Luis!" I let out a piercing shout, my voice reverberating off the walls as I clung tightly to the sturdy table, my fingers digging into the cool, smooth surface. The sound echoed in my ears, the intensity of it causing a slight ringing sensation. In a desperate attempt to navigate the sharp turn, I gripped the table with all my strength, my muscles straining under the weight of my fear.

Suddenly, Anaki seized my arm with a firm grasp. His touch sent a surge of electricity through my body, heightening my senses and fueling my determination. With newfound strength, I propelled myself towards the doorway, my feet pounding against the hard, cold floor. Each step reverberated throughout the room, creating a rhythmic thud that matched the pounding of my heart.

As I reached the entrance, a chilling sight greeted me. There, standing before me, was a mysterious, dark figure. The dim lighting cast eerie shadows across his face, accentuating the sinister smile that curved his lips. The corners of his mouth curled upward, revealing menacing fangs that glinted in the faint glow from the dark hallway. The air grew heavy with a sense of foreboding, as if danger itself had materialized in front of me.

And Luis had no idea.

There was no doubt about what I saw in front of me. It *was* a damn vampire. He had pale skin with a set of fangs. I've seen *Twilight*, I've seen *The Originals*. The presence of him was too much, too overpowering and made me feel utterly small.

The vampire smirked, showing off not just one set of fangs but two.

Abuela was right; this was a vampire. Does that mean the other people in the room were something? Are they even human?

CHAPTER FOUR

Anaki

For the entire flight, I studied Elena's condition to give her the best possible care. If I was going to be on a care team for our future Luna's family, I was going to be the best. It gave me something to concentrate on and made the darkness fade inside me. Pouring drinks and listening to everyone else can drag you down. Not that I didn't love my job, I was just lost in my own darkness now.

This change of scenery was good. Not to mention helping Locke and Emm. I was glad to help and be a part of a specific team. It was long overdue, because our president and the rest of the guys lacked finesse when saving humans. They didn't have a personal touch and could have trouble rounding up frightened humans.

It was obvious that Emm hid her family for a reason, and until we knew why, we needed them with us. Our club and territory were a fortress. Along with Bones and Nadia being medical personnel, they should all be well taken care of. I'm not sure why they needed me that much, unless they think I will go mother hen, like I did Nadia when she first arrived.

Which I rather enjoyed.

As I crossed the threshold, a celestial force seemed to guide me forward.

It couldn't be that easy, could it?

This had to be the will of the powerful goddess or the intervention of fate itself that brought me here.

Or Journey…

Upon my entry to the small home, a veil lifted from my mind, dispelling the clouds of despair that had plagued me for years. It was as if the sun itself had come out after decades of darkness, illuminating a path before me with newfound clarity and purpose.

She stood with her head held high, her brown eyes narrowed at us, the people who had come to turn her world upside down. She showed strength and stubbornness in her stance, even with the burdens she carried.

I knew she had a son, with a male who had treated her poorly. Thank the goddess he's dead, so I didn't have to hunt him down myself, because she was worth everything.

In that split second, I knew she was worth more than my previous mate ever was, in all the years I stood there pining for them.

She would be worth it. She would be worth pursuing because someone had broken her heart, just like mine had been. I would be the one who would heal her because she was already healing me.

I could feel the exhilarating sensation of my dragon stirring within me, its scales pulsating with energy. The sight of its shimmering blue and white hues danced vividly in my mind's eye. Suppressing the urge to fixate on the majestic creature unfurling within, I redirected my focus to the captivating woman standing in front of me.

I laid my hand on Nadia's shoulder to steady myself and lowered myself to her ear. "Please do the introductions."

Nadia's back stiffened. This wasn't how it was supposed to go. I was supposed to speak; we had this thought out, but damnit, I couldn't. I was stunned into silence.

I could hear Elena's heart fluttering in her chest; she reacted to me. I puffed out my chest in pride at that.

I focused my gaze on her face, capturing the intricate details of her velvety skin, the delicate freckles sprinkled across her nose, and the faint scar gracefully etched on her lip. A symphony of colors and textures danced before my eyes, as if my vision had heightened.

Elena was shorter in stature than her sister, but still very much of perfect height to have her bury her nose into my throat, to…

Elena threw the cane in her grandmother's direction. My heart jumped in my chest when I saw her screaming at her. Her grandmother, unphased, grabbed her shoe and was ready to throw it at Elena. My heart leapt in fear when I saw she was about to be struck.

While it was only a shoe, I would allow nothing to strike her. Nothing!

I stepped around Bear, who had blocked half my body, and strode over to Elena, who had no way to hold herself up securely, now.

Elena wobbled and grabbed the table before I arrived. With the gear on my body, I could not touch her with my skin. Curse these fucking gloves.

I carefully scooped her up and settled her into the cozy rocking chair. As I held her, I could hear the soft rhythm of her heartbeat gradually calming, a soothing melody to my ears. The air was filled with the delicate fragrance of fresh, clean linen, wafting through my nostrils and filling me with a sense of comfort.

I suppressed a low groan as I took a deep breath, the scent of anticipation filling my nostrils. I could feel the front of my pants constricting, my muscles tensing as my jaw clenched tightly.

Gods above, she was healing me, while she had to sit there in pain.

Hang on, love, I'm going to heal you. Take away all your pain.

I tucked the blanket under her legs and tried to recall all the information I read on the plane about her sickness. Dragons don't get sick like this, unless it is with magic or when pertaining to a bond.

I felt the heat of her stare while I tried to make her comfortable.

She won't reject me, will she? She won't... do what they did to me... will she? No, I refuse to believe that. They were heartless. So far, no second chances have done that, but no other shifter has been in my predicament.

Will she be as accepting of my past? Of what I am?

A trickle of my sweat beaded enough to drip down my temple.

The whistle blew from the kettle, and it was a perfect time to break away. The gear was getting too hot. I craved to get into the water, to feel the coolness against my skin once again.

It was all happening too fast, I couldn't believe I'd found her.

While my dragon stirred beneath my skin, I asked, as calmly as I could, if anyone wanted any tea. No one seemed to be the wiser as I pulled mugs down from the shelves like I owned the place.

I was good at that, making myself at home. A quirk not everyone appreciated, but I was trying to make the mood light.

I shrugged off my vest and gloves and glanced at Elena, who was staring at everyone else warily.

Pay attention to me.

My dragon lifted his head and yawned. He had full rows of teeth, all appearing to be intact, his tail was swishing, and his long ears were pulled back and twitching, urging me to put my eyes back on the prize. He hadn't claimed her, hadn't seen her yet, but by the gods and the universe, he was pushing.

We were both overwhelmed. It was too good to be true. There had to be a mistake. Was that what Bear felt like when he met Nadia?

I watched as Bear took Elena's wrist.

I suppressed a guttural, cavernous rasp that was hovering in my throat. My dragon hadn't seen her eyes yet; once he did, it would be all over. We would have leaped over that chair and taken Bear out for touching what was ours.

I shook my head. Surely not. It was Bear, just making sure she didn't shoot us. Because if she were anything like her sister, she would.

Which was hot, but I could die right now in my weakened state. So, it was a good idea to take it away.

I swallowed and listened while Elena argued with her abuela in the corner about eating rocks. Secretly, I hope she looked toward me while I poured the hot water into the mugs.

"There is no way you are a vampire," Luis' voice said, full of skepticism.

"Yes, they are real. Why don't you touch my fangs?" A smooth voice came from the back of the house. "Come see, don't be shy."

I rolled my eyes and pressed my fingers into my eyes. Quillion was going to overstep. The Moonlight Outcasts didn't kill anyone on this mission, so they were going to toy around with the boy to make Elena make a fuss.

It sounds like they already talked to the grandmother, who is very open to the idea of us being here. Or she found them. She appears to be in everyone's business.

I'd read her file, she had to be part Wiccan; a human with some magical power, and very in tune with the understanding of bonds. Quillion had already infiltrated the home and rummaged through her books, and had piles of ancient texts on bonds.

At least, the grandmother approved.

It was Elena I would have trouble with. She and the Luna seemed oblivious.

And right now, Quillian was making this more difficult for me, upsetting my mate's child. This will not bode well for me in the future. Especially, if it will make her body physically hurt.

"Hey! You got some sharp teeth! You really are a vampire!"

This time, the ruckus was loud enough for Elena to hear.

I heard her suck in a breath, her heart beating fast. She stood up, unsteady on her feet, and I grabbed her arm with my ungloved hand. She was trembling in rage, but once my hand connected to hers, I felt the jolt of connection I was looking for. My dragon reared back his head, his bright eyes glowing in the dark recesses of my mind. He let out a powerful roar, demanding that she pay attention to us.

Her steady footsteps echoed through the room, the sound reverberating against the walls. As she made her way towards the doorway, the soft glow of the hallway beckoned her forward.

Suddenly, a gasp escaped her lips, a mix of astonishment and fear, as Quillion materialized before her. The air seemed to hold a faint scent of musky cologne and dried blood. My nose wrinkled in disgust, remembering the scent from so long ago.

Quillion's flawless complexion glowed under the dim lighting, casting a radiant aura around him. A sinister smile stretched across his face, revealing his sharp, predatory fangs.

"Hello Elena," he mused as he draped his arm lazily over Luis' shoulder.

"Get your arm off of him," she growled and leaned into me.

She leaned into me.

His eyebrows raised. "Huh, she acts like her sister. Good luck to the lot of you, you are going to need it." He took his arm off of Luis and patted his head. Luis frowned slightly, but he went and hugged his mother after he saw her distraught state.

"Mama, did you see that? A real vampire? Do you think werewolves are real? Do you think Abuela is a witch too, now?"

I kept my arm around Elena. She didn't request me to stop, so I would not let go. I didn't want her to fall. I felt it was me who was holding her up, keeping her strong. At least, I hoped it was me.

Luis leaned away from Elena, who was still speechless. "Hola, who are you? Your eyes! They are like a snake's. Ey! What are you?"

I shook my head, and I coughed into my fist. I willed them back to my human ones. Elena turned and saw that I was still holding her steady. I reluctantly pulled my hand away and stared down at Luis.

"Name's Anaki. You must be Luis?" I held out my hand for him to shake. He grabbed it and shook it firmly. "Excellent handshake, firm grip. Your mother has taught you well."

Luis shrugged his shoulders. "Have to be. I'm the man of the house." He said with a thick Mexican accent. "Why are you all here? Why are there so many of you?" He gazed around the room, not with fear but with pure wonder.

Elena's piercing gaze locked onto me, its intensity searing through my body like a scorching flame. The heat it emitted made me squirm uncomfortably, feeling as if I were trapped in a sweltering furnace. My longing to meet her eyes, to immerse myself in their depths, was palpable, but I couldn't predict how my inner dragon would respond to this encounter - a sensation that left me unsettled and unsure.

I can't look, not yet.

Nadia and Bear took off their vests, relieving themselves of the heavy-weight gear that might frighten the boy. The grandmother was sitting on the couch, taking sips of the tea I had left on the counter.

Nothing bothered this female at all. She was patting the seat next to her, telling Nadia to sit.

"How about everyone sit down?" Nadia said cheerfully. "Since everyone is handling Quillion so well." She narrowed her eyes at the vampire in the corner. He had his arms crossed, his eyes rolling into the back of his head.

"Abuela over here is a low-level witch." He waved his hand. "She would not die of a heart attack due to her knowledge, and human children have a vivid imagination. The only one we had to worry about was Elena."

Elena was still silent beside me. I kept waiting for her to pass out, ready to catch her if she fell, but she continued to assess the room.

"I'm processing," she said slowly. "*Really* processing."

I put my hand on her lower back. "I'm going to guide you to the chair, have you sit down."

She jerked away from me. "I don't need help! I'm not fragile!" she snapped.

I pulled my hands away, and my hearts felt like daggers had shot through them. She didn't want help? Didn't want me to touch her?

My eyes met hers, and that was all it took for my dragon to snap.

A torrent of water engulfed my dragon. He relished in the waters that kept him hydrated within my mind. He reared back his head, let out a roar that surpassed all wolves, bears, vampires or any other supernatural creature.

Dragons were the ancient ones, and while I was not the most powerful of my kind, I still held enough power near water that could destroy cities. I clutched my chest. Elena stared at me wide-eyed.

"Your eyes, they're glowing."

Our eyes locked.

She took a step back. My dragon was furious that our mate would step away. Did she not know that we would take care of her? Why would she be afraid? While we couldn't shift, yet, we would do everything within our power to protect her.

My dragon tried to push through the forefront of my mind. I shook my head, pulling on the loose strands.

"Anaki!" Bear barked at me. He swiftly moved forward, his long strides echoing through the empty space. I could feel the rush of wind as he reached out, his fingertips brushing against the back of my neck.

In my weakened state, I was acutely aware of my dragon's heightened senses, which seemed to be ten times more perceptive. The scene unfolded before me, revealing Bear's unsuspecting wrist, which my dragon seized with a vice-like grip. I could almost feel the pulsating strength on Bear's wrist.

"Shit!" He pulled back and grabbed his wrist. "Nadia, get a dart!" Nadia rummaged through her tool belt. They think I'm gone, think I'm going rabid, but I'm far from it.

I backed away from Elena with great effort. I didn't want her to be frightened, didn't want to mess this up, but of course, reptilian instincts weren't going to play nice after being asleep for so many years.

I doubled over, crossing my arms around my stomach to keep my vision away from her. I took in large deep breaths and waited for the dart so they could put me to sleep. Take me back to the club and put me in a cage.

"Got it," Nadia announced, and I heard it slip into the gun.

I let out guttural growls, deep enough to alert people outside.

Just knock me out, I'm putting everyone in danger.

I fell to my knees, opening my eyes on feeling a contact. When I did, I saw a pair of feet.

Mine. My dragon hissed.

Fingers threaded through my hair. I gasped, tears threatening to fall. Why was she touching me? Why was she not afraid of me?

Strong, because she is so strong.

My dragon puffed out his chest, his head nudging me to respond.

I groaned and leaned into her touch, seeking more.

I relished the sensation of her delicate hand gently gliding through my hair, savoring the softness against my scalp. As she tenderly lowered her other hand towards my face, I could feel the warmth radiating from her touch. A shuddering sigh escaped my lips, causing a slight tremor to ripple through my body.

Touch. I craved her touch, her body, her love.

She did not know that she held my hearts in her hand. She could break me so easily, and that scared the absolute shit out of me.

CHAPTER FIVE

Elena

A dart? A damn dart?

They dart their own kind?

Whatever Anaki was, whatever everyone else in the room was, they were insane.

This was when we needed Emm. Not when she was out gallivanting all over the states while she tried to catch bounties on this Locke guy. We needed her here to keep us safe from these crazies... whatever they are.

Because we all knew I was too weak.

I swallowed the bitterness that built in my throat.

I checked on Luis, tucked under Abuela's arm. Everything was in slow motion as I watched Nadia reach into her bag for a dart and a gun.

I'm nothing like my sister, as much as I try. I might have a mouth like a Latina, but that was all I possessed. I never stood up for myself, but like hell, I stood up for others who couldn't stand up for themselves.

While I didn't know Anaki, the thought of him being shot didn't sit well with me. He helped me stand, kept me calm. He had a gentle hand.

He was part of the kidnapping team here, but that didn't matter.

I didn't have time to think; I stepped forward and shouted a resounding *No* as soon as Anaki's knees hit the floor. I blocked the dart's path, my hands instinctively reaching for his hair.

Anaki's forehead gently pressed against my stomach, his hands instinctively reaching for the back of my legs, tightly gripping them as if the weight of the world threatened to snatch him away. The room was filled with a hushed silence, broken only by the sound of our steady breaths.

The air carried a faint scent of sweat and anticipation, mingling with the warmth of our intertwined bodies. In that moment, I could feel the intensity of Anaki's emotions, his grip conveying a mixture of fear, longing, and a desperate need for... I couldn't put my finger on it. Despite the carefree attitude he had earlier, this was different.

"Do not shoot him," I nearly begged. I turned to look at the shocked faces in the room. Nadia hadn't even placed the dart in the gun.

"What just happened?" Bear said as he stepped forward. "What the fu—"

Anaki cleared his throat, let go of my legs and stood. "I'm alright. I apologize." He rubbed his throat with his hand. "I got out of control there for a second. Please forgive me if I startled you."

I eyed him up and down and shook my head. "It's fine." I mentally shook off the effect his touch had on me, the growls and the odd behavior. Rather, I concentrated on the fact that there was, in fact, a vampire in our living room, who was cleaning underneath his sharp nails with a dagger in the corner.

And he touched my son.

"¡Dios Mio!" I rubbed my forehead with my finger. What would Emm say about all of this? She was the tough one. I tried to toughen up over the years, to be the head of this family since Abuela's mind had gone, but I could only do so much.

Always too soft, wishing to see the best in people.

Damnit, I saved my kidnapper.

"As lovely as this all is—" while talking, the vampire stashed the dagger in his suit pocket. He didn't look like a kidnapper, more like a businessman who never sees the sun. Could he even go out in the sun?

"Isn't he just swoon-worthy," Abuela said as she took another sip of her tea. "Just how I imagined they would be. I'm so glad I got to see one before I died. Think he will let me make him some of my tamales once we arrive where we are going? I assume you are not allergic to garlic."

The vampire smiled.

Emm is going to shit herself.

The vampire gave a fanged smile. "We should head to the plane. I've got an angry sorceress, with an equally angry panther, ready to fly while you all play tea party."

I sat down in the chair, suddenly feeling dizzy.

Luis bounded toward me and gave me a hug. "Please, can we go with them?"

My eyes widened. "You realize they are taking us without consent. We don't have a choice. This isn't a vacation, Luis. They have guns, there is a vampire, and who knows what else these people are?"

Nadia and Bear gave each other a look.

Luis shrugged his shoulders. "They haven't hurt us. They didn't shoot Lizard-eyes over there when you said not to. Don't think they are very good kidnappers."

Why was everyone trying to convince me we should go with them?

"Emm is in trouble, obviously. Are you taking us to make her compliant?" Instead of looking at the vampire guy and Nadia, I dared to look at Anaki. The one who was making my stomach flutter in ways it shouldn't.

I haven't found any man attractive for a long time. Especially after what

Luis' father had done to me. Men were just… off the table. I have a son and a medical condition that would annoy most men.

Who wanted a broken woman to take care of?

I gritted my teeth and looked away from his handsome face.

Anaki had kind eyes that I could get lost in now that I've really seen them. Pretty, cerulean-blue with hints of green around his pupils.

He *was* swoon-worthy. I would remember him in my personal time with myself.

"Emm doesn't know that we came to take you with us. It is imperative that she doesn't know, yet. Under direct orders of our president," Bear said from the other side of the room.

I crossed my arms. *I wouldn't be soft, I wouldn't be the pushover anymore.*

"No." I ground out. "We are fine here, no matter your intentions. We have been for years. I am not uprooting mi familia, because of Emm and her hunt for one of your members who supposedly has done something. She will make sure they are innocent before she does anything, she doesn't kill innocent people, she—"

The men in the room barked out a laugh.

Bear shook his head and possessively put his hand on the back of Nadia's neck. "We aren't worried about Locke getting killed. It's you, Emm's family, that we are worried for. There have been… complications." Bear's eyes flicked to Luis, who was stealing cookies someone had placed on the table.

"What sort of complications?" Emm had told me she was being stalked and wouldn't be able to call for a few days. She called a few days later and told me she was fine and not to worry about it.

Had she been lying?

Bear cleared his throat. "Complications that involve Emm's past, along with yours. *They* are hunting her, *they* know where she is, and *they* are trying to find her family."

Instinctively, I put my hand over my heart as my face paled.

Shit. I knew she had gone too far. She'd played this game long enough.

"And why doesn't she know you are coming for us?"

Anaki stepped closer. His hand had a tremor, but it landed on my arm like it steadied the both of us.

Why did the gentle warmth of his touch soothe me? As his hand connected with mine, the aches in my body gradually faded, and I could feel the tension in my muscles melting away.

Everything didn't seem so overwhelming, which it should have. All of it should have me screaming and crying, but everyone was acting like it was normal.

Abuela was having tea with one of our captors for Christ's sake!

"Because Locke likes to take care of things in his own way. Think of this as his present to your sister." Anaki gently guided my arm down intertwining our fingers. The touch sent a wave of warmth through me, leaving me momentarily breathless. The air felt heavy with anticipation as I stood rooted in place, unable to react to the audacious act he had just pulled off.

"By the time this is all over, your whole family will be safe, with the MC by your side. We protect what's ours."

I heaved out a breath. "An MC? A motorcycle club? That has a kidnapping team?" I raised a brow.

Anaki shrugged his shoulders. "We're specialists. Not just an MC."

"Obviously," I retorted. I waved my hand around, "especially with the whole vampire, witch and—"

Nadia stood up. "Bears!" She hugged the big man's arm.

That tiny thing was a bear?

"There are also wolves, a lot of wolves." Anaki bobbed his head back and forth. "Even some dragons." He tilted his head toward me playfully.

"Woah, cool!" Luis jumped off the couch and ran over. "Is that what you are? With the way your eyes went loco." Luis pointed to his eyes and swirled his fingers around.

Anaki puffed out his chest. "Aye, that I am."

That explained the deep, guttural growl that came from him. I've never heard such a growl before. It reminded me of Smaug, when we had a 'Lord of the Rings' weekend.

I covered my mouth and closed my eyes.

"Hey." Anaki pulled my hand away. "I know it doesn't seem like it, but we are the good guys. I promise you with my life." He put his hand over his chest and bowed.

I stared at him strangely as he did the gesture. Butterflies erupted in my stomach as he did, especially when he looked up at me with those eyes that shifted from human to dragon.

"Careful, watch your step," Nadia said at the door of the private plane. It was luxurious, far better than I thought we were going to be led to. Plush, leather seats with TVs in the backs.

Luis was bouncing on his toes as he ran down the aisle, looking out at the different windows. He'd ran his mouth a-mile-a-minute in the SUV that brought us to the tarmac. He wanted to know everything about The Iron Fang MC and shifters.

Thankfully, Bear and Nadia kept him occupied, answering questions vaguely so I could ask my own later, because right now, I needed to process.

We were leaving with people who could be lying to us, to go to the United States, to an MC club and hiding out in a remote cabin until the coast is clear.

Once Luis learned that there was a naga, or a snake shifter, at the club, his eyes lit up even more. With his love for fantasy, magic and reptiles, he was going to be one happy child.

Meanwhile, I was having a mini panic attack. We were going on a plane—

None of us had flown before, and for good reason. We were in hiding. We didn't need our legal names to pop up for anyone to find us. Mainly for Emm's sake, but we were linked to her, and if they wanted to get to her, hurting us would be their way to do it.

The first few seats with tables held folders, laptops, guns and ammo. Quillian and several other vampires sat by them. None of them attempted to move them when we walked by while he flipped through his phone.

Because he trusted us?

Or would he slit our throats if we tried?

"Ah, there you all are," Abuela said, and put her hand on the table. "Nice to see you all again. Winter, how is the blood lust coming along?"

I made a horrified face when I checked the woman nestled in the lap of a male. "She's much better after your donation, Abuela. We owe you. She isn't ready for cold, stored blood yet. I don't know why your blood called to her so much."

"No worries," Abuela waved her hand. "Any time she needs more, you let me know, Cyran."

Winter cuddled up to Cyran more. She pursed her lips together and nodded. "Yes, many thanks."

We had a blood-lusting vampire on the plane, and there were three humans on it. My breath picked up as Abuela pushed me in the back, and I almost stumbled over my cane. "Keep going, Elena. They can smell fear. You might get them wound up."

I quickly took my seat. My heart raced, and I could feel the sweat building on my forehead. Meanwhile, Luis took a seat beside me, his eyes glued to the scene outside. He watched the other planes landing and taking off.

"Mama?" he asked, and I tried to put on a brave face. I had been quiet for the ride over. I needed to be strong.

"Yeah, what is it, mijo?"

"Why are the other planes getting checked and not ours?"

I leaned out the window, and Luis was right. A plane beside us had a team checking the wings and the tires. When we arrived, there was no one filling our plane with fuel, no one checking the outside. Our plane was already moving and backing out of our parking space.

While I hadn't been on a plane, I would have thought an engine so large would make noise. I turned in my seat, seeing the rest of the passengers walking around, getting comfortable. Nadia sat on Bear's lap, his arm wrapped around her.

What was up with these people sitting on laps? Were they couples?

I unbuckled my seat belt and stood, still not feeling the vibrations of the plane. Something was off.

"Need something, Elena?" Anaki's smooth voice asked. He had appeared before me, and those eyes dug deep into me. How dare he make me freeze in my tracks like that?

"Ah, well. I just, I've never flown before and..."

"Are you scared? Don't worry, I'll protect you." He sat across from me. The table in front of us gave us enough space. "Don't forget to buckle up. I can do it for you if you like." He sent me a wink that made my tanned face flush. I quickly buckled so he wouldn't dare come over.

"They didn't check the plane!" Luis panicked. "They checked the others. Why not ours?"

Anaki chuckled and leaned his head back on the cushion. "Don't need to. Ours is a special plane," he said in an excited, childlike voice.

Luis narrowed his eyes. "How is it special?"

Anaki rolled his eyes. "Magic, duh." He bit his lip to suppress a smile.

Luis scoffed. He was a smart child. While he had seen a vampire and Anaki's pupil-changing eyes, none of us had yet to see any magic.

Even that felt far-fetched.

Abuela held onto her purse, nudged Anaki, and shook her head. "They are non-believers. I've been telling them for years."

Anaki gasped in mock horror. "I think we need to bring in the pilot, Tajah, the club sorceress. She will be very disappointed in both of you."

CHAPTER SIX

Anaki

I took another SUV rather than staying close to Elena. I needed time to calm my dragon, but that proved to be the worst decision.

As soon as I shut the door, my dragon went to work on the black leather. He clawed the back seat and tried to open the side door while we were in motion. Quillian wanted to pull over, but that would have been worse. I didn't want to run after Elena's vehicle because then too many humans would see me.

We didn't need the Royal Council popping up to dispose of me.

So instead, the inside of the vehicle was slashed to leathery shreds. The material was ripped so fast, I swore I saw smoke from the fabric.

Cyran held onto Winter, his eyes narrowed as I growled and held my head to contain the beast inside.

Be still, you idiot. She's safe.

He reared back his ugly head, we let out a roar, and the vamps covered their ears.

"Fucking hell!" Quillion swerved on the bumpy road.

Great, I've got vampires pissed and my phone kept vibrating.

I pulled out my phone to see it was Nadia and Bear. They were worried, of course. The string of texts kept coming, asking what the hell was going on behind them.

Little Bear- Is she your mate?

One text said.

Big Bear- Damnit, Anaki, answer. Why aren't you in this car, then?

It was hard to text with my claws out as I tried to keep my dragon calm. Cyran ripped the phone out of my hand to text back a quick, "*Yeah, she's mine. Keep her safe,*" and chucked the phone right back at me.

Nadia and Bear sent a picture of Elena staring out the window, and instantly, my dragon calmed. Just seeing her, knowing she was safe in my friend's presence, was enough to get him under control.

I'd have to thank Bear later. He knew what it was like when your animal came back out to bite you in the ass, literally when you got your second chance. He would make sure I got my space. He obviously knew I needed a picture of Elena to calm my stubborn dragon.

My dragon was strong and relentless, everything I wasn't. He pressed against my mind and searched for everything he had missed over the years. Sweat trickled down my brow, mingling with the cool scales that had protruded down my neck, creating an odd sensation against my skin. The world around me seemed to blur, sounds becoming distant echoes as I teetered on the edge of consciousness, like a fragile glass ready to be shattered.

We did not need Elena seeing that. Didn't need her to see us break.

My dragon sensed this. His persistence calmed, and fell back into my mind. Thank the goddess for that. I wiped my forehead again. I could not let my mate see me lose control. I knew what her previous male did to her—

My dragon snarled. The spines on his back stood on end.

I took a deep breath. Calm. Remain calm.

While my human form was slimmer than most wolves, I was big in my shifted form. Shifting in the car or a plane would be bad news for everyone. I knew he wanted to wrap our tail around Elena to keep her safe. He was unpredictable, unstable, and I had to remain in control. I don't know what he would do if he grew strong enough, took over my body, and snapped.

Especially after what happened when we were rejected.

He would not let Elena out of his sight.

Like every other stubborn member at the Iron Fang.

I calmed him on the hour-long drive. We stared at her picture, while I mentally prepared what we needed to do for our mate, or soulkin as the dragon clans called them.

I have never felt so underprepared, especially for Elena. While my cave was comfortable, dry and everything a comfortable home should be for her, she needed a nest.

I couldn't bring her there right away. We had to win her, woo her. Even the dragons had to do that; we couldn't just steal our soulkin.

My dragon huffed in annoyance. He didn't want to take any chances. Take her, make her love us.

"Yes, Elena, please come with me to my lair. It's a cave. It looks dark, cold and damp on the outside. I know we just took you away from everything you have ever known, but my dragon wants to keep you inside and not let you go until we have rutted and marked you as our own, to make sure we always know where you are."

Yeah, that isn't creepy at all, you son of a bitch.

I pulled out my phone and tried to will him to put the claws away. My fingers were blue on the tips and I shook my head while I explained we were shopping, preparing for our mate. He'd been asleep for ages, he was groggy, a grumpy piece of shit and when he saw all that we are buying our mate, he allowed my claws to retract and my heart stops racing.

Blankets and pillows, the softest and highest quality I could find. In my cave, I needed to provide her a nest. While furred females create the nests in their pairs, male reptiles create them in ours, and Elena would need to approve.

My hand shook. I've never made a nest before. .

Why haven't I even prepared one? Everyone in the club were getting mates left and right, even this vampire over here had a female! Why did I not think that I could? Why have I been so...?

I pinched the bridge of my nose, feeling the slight pressure against my skin. The weight of my despair was suffocating, like a thick fog enveloping me. The darkness crept in, seeping into every corner of my mind, shrouding me in its cold embrace. I couldn't help but wonder how much longer I would have endured this torment if I hadn't seen her. My physical strength had faded, along with my mind, like a flickering flame on the verge of extinguishing.

I don't think I would have gone rabid. My dragon wouldn't have woken up, ever. I just would have faded into the darkness of the lake.

I balled my free hand at my side. That darkness was still there. I still had to convince Elena and, most of all, her son, who was now my son.

My dragon rumbled in agreement. He was on board with that. We were ahead of most males at the club. We had a son, a five-year-old, who could take care of himself, and a smart one, too. He was ahead of his class. I would make sure he was taken care of and had the best teachers.

My head perked up. Taking care of Elena and Luis was my calling, my ultimate desire. I could do this. A little longer, to see if she would have me.

As I glanced at Elena, her weary eyes spoke volumes, mirroring the weight she carried as she boarded the plane. The cabin was filled with the palpable scent of her anxiety, mingling with the stale air. A sense of unease settled upon me, as if I could almost taste her fear. It was clear that she was in desperate need of rest.

While the plane was still taxiing onto the runway, I explained to Luis and a very intrigued grandmother the logistics of how this plane was under a magical enchantment by Tajah.

"It's glamoured. To everyone else outside the plane, it appears to be running, but in fact, it isn't. Tajah is going to use her power of levitation and take us home."

"But why not just use the..." Luis paused, as if searching for the word.

"Engine?" I asked while I secured the table to the side of the wall. "Because, simply, she cannot fly a plane."

Elena's eyes went wide, and she clutched the invisible necklace around her neck.

Well, fucked that up.

I reached overhead to the storage compartments and opened them. I found pillows, blankets, a sleeping mask, even noise-canceling headphones. *Bingo!*

"Hang on, love, I've got you," I told her. I directed Luis to my side and handed him a blanket to hold, then pressed a button to recline her seat. Little did she know, with no takeoff, we could have her reclining and resting in no time.

Luis smiled, placed the blanket on his mom and motioned for her to sit up. She stared at me wide-eyed while I fluffed her pillow and put the eye mask just over her forehead.

I kneeled beside her, and because I could not resist her, I put my hand on her arm. She let out a sigh of relief, and I tilted my head as I watched her. Did she like my touch? She hasn't pulled away, not yet, at least.

Luis tapped my shoulder. "What else?"

I shook my head and pulled the noise-canceling headphones from my lap. "Mama is going to take a nap while we visit the cockpit. I'll tell you all about the magic there."

Luis nodded excitedly.

Elena tried to sit up, but I squeezed her arm. "Love, nothing is going to happen to you or your son on this plane. He can't go anywhere while we are up in the sky."

"W-what?" she breathed and gazed out the window.

We were already in the air, the clouds rushing past us. By the way, Tajah was using her magic, we would be home in a few hours.

"H-how?"

"Magic." I simply stated and urged her to lie back down. "Here is what I want you to do. I want you to sleep for me, okay? I don't want to see any more dark circles under those pretty amber eyes of yours. I'm going to take care of you and your family."

Her eyes went soft, and her hand clutched the armrest. "Why would you do that?"

Because I protect what is mine.

"That's what the club does. Protects those who need it. Now, lie back. Put those on. I'll take care of everything."

Elena looked over at her grandmother, who nodded. She was smiling lovingly at her granddaughter. Silent words passed between them until my mate put on the sleep mask and headphones.

While my body ached to be near Elena, I stayed true to my word and took Luis to the cockpit. Beretta, Tajah's mate, was inside, flipping through a magazine, and with an amused smirk on her face, beckoned us inside.

Tajah was in a mood. She didn't particularly like Emm because she knew Emm had been hiding her true self all along. Emm was a bounty hunter and lied about who she was, but everyone in the club trusted Locke. Tajah wanted the club and everyone in it protected, and I could see her going against his word to protect what we have built.

Tajah's face softened when she saw the young boy, however. She waved him over to the captain's chair to let him think he was flying the plane. Tajah's power was so strong now because of her bonding to Beretta that there was nothing that would take this plane down.

"How are you so strong to hold up an entire plane?" he asked her.

Tajah smirked and got to his eye level. "I've practiced for many, many years. I grew up in a coven that demanded strict studies. However, no matter how much you practice, your power will never reach full potential until you have a bond." Tajah glanced back at Beretta.

"A bond?" Luis blinked and stared up at her. "What's that?"

"Have you heard of a soul mate?" Tajah asked.

Luis rolled his eyes. "Yeah, Abuela talked about it all the time. She took me out in the woods and did this naked dance on a full moon. She said I was going to have one, one day."

Tajah stared at him and held onto the necklaces on her chest. "She did what now?"

Luis sighed dramatically. "She got naked and danced around a big fire. She held up some of her rocks—crystals. Chanted from a book that has spells?" Luis rubbed his eyes. "I am not meant to see Abuela naked. I can still see her." He gave us a terrified look.

Tajah sat up straight. "Where is his grandmother's file?"

I crossed my arms and leaned against the doorway. "You mean you didn't read any of the files?"

Tajah scoffed. "My job was to fly the plane, pick them up, and bring them back. I saw we had an old woman, a five-year-old and a cripple, I didn't think—"

I snarled, and my hand darted out to grab Tajah's throat. Streams of purple shadows came from behind her back to catch my hand. My dragon, already sensing the magic in the room, was on alert. The low guttural growl shook our body, and absorbed the magic through our skin.

Tajah gasped when my fingers wrapped around her neck.

Beretta growled and stood next to me, but I kept my eyes on Tajah.

"Back away, Beretta. Don't want me to crush her neck."

Beretta's black fur filtered down her arm. "Crush her neck and you kill us all. What a plan that is. Let her go." Beretta's sharp claws flashed in the light.

Tajah chuckled and brought up her hand to wave Beretta away. "I was too blinded by my anger to notice."

Luis' head bounced from Tajah to me. I couldn't smell fear, just amusement while he sat cross-legged in the captain's chair, leaning in like we were his favorite TV show.

"You've found your dragon again, and it's her that has awakened him?" Tajah mused.

I raised an eyebrow in warning.

"I apologize then for calling her—"

"A cripple." Luis deadpanned. "You called Mama a cripple. She won't like that." Luis stood up from the chair and stood by me. "And you are the first man to stand up for her."

I released my grip on Tajah, and she took a deep breath while I knelt down to Luis.

"I'll always stand up for your mama."

"Because she is your... soulmate?" His voice rose.

I rubbed the back of my neck, suddenly feeling nervous about talking about this to a child. My child. I guess I should ask permission from her son if I could even date his mother.

My dragon rolled his eyes.

"She is. I'm not ready to tell her that, though. I want her to trust me first. Show her I'm a good male and dragon."

Luis stood, mimicking my mannerisms by scratching the back of his neck. "Mama doesn't date. Says they wouldn't want her anyway. It isn't true." He yelled and narrowed his eyes at Tajah.

Tajah's face flushed.

"You're right, it isn't true. I want your mama. I want to take care of her, you, and your grandmother. What do you say to that?"

Luis crossed his arms. "It's going to be tough. She doesn't think she deserves to be happy. She only looks out for me and Abuela."

I hummed in acknowledgement. "I am up for a challenge. I might need your help, if you are willing."

Luis thought for a moment. "I'll help if you let me see your dragon. Nadia and Bear said I can see their bears when we get to the cabin."

"Did they now? Well, mine is still healing from being asleep for so long. I was very sick before I met your mom."

Luis frowned. "You were? So, Mama healed you?"

"Yes, and now it is my turn to heal her."

CHAPTER SEVEN

Elena

"The town is down there. After eliminating the threat, you will be able to walk around more freely. There is a grocery store, flower shop, even a witchy store." Nadia directed that last part toward Abuela, pointing toward the quaint town before them.

We were coming down a mountain in a convoy of SUVs. These were a little older, owned by the MC to be less conspicuous and melt in with the rest of the scenery.

This time, Bear drove while Nadia sat beside him. Bear then went on about the typical upper Pacific Northwest weather. Cloudy, rainy. Much different from where we had spent most of our years.

I'm somehow still holding it all together while Abuela asked questions like: Are there farmers' markets in the summers, because "Elena loves buying fresh, home-grown vegetables?—asked somewhat mockingly.

I wasn't able to go as much last year. Not when my muscle weakness had gotten worse. I found it not worthwhile loading a wheelchair into a car, and being exhausted before I got there.

She acted like we were staying here forever. While Emm might make friends here, she was a nomad and never stayed in one place for long. It would have been nice for our whole family to live in one place, but it wasn't going to work. Our enemies knew where Emm was now, which was here, and we had a lot of enemies.

A whole cartel.

I wouldn't keep Luis here. I couldn't. Especially when I couldn't physically protect him.

There was also the matter of getting a citizenship. Emm made a lot of money, but not that much to get us here without the constant worry of being deported.

I peered out from the second row of our colossal vehicle, my eyes scanning the surroundings eagerly. Towering trees stretched towards the sky, their branches swaying gently in the cool breeze. The evergreens stood proud and vibrant, their emerald hues captivating my gaze.

The air hung heavy with the smell of damp earth. There must have been recent rainfall; Bear had mentioned that happens a lot here. The overcast sky blanketed a somber tone over the town. It felt as if I had stepped into a scene from a Twilight movie.

Considering the vampires trailing us, I recognized the irony.

I thought that was why I hadn't completely lost it. It was because I'd been raised around Abuela's crazy antics, as she tried to make me believe that there was *more out there...* and there was my son's vivid, creative imagination. It also helped that I read my fair share of paranormal romance novels.

Had I become immune?

At least I had not become the fainting, screaming heroine. Just the numb, dumb woman that couldn't do jack to save her family.

Emm, where are you when we need you?

Crap, I couldn't believe this was real. Vampires, shifters, witches? Not to mention, there was a dragon in the back seat playing Go Fish with my son.

I turned my head, to see Anaki and Luis whispering to each other. They were both animated, talking, and laughing like they had some sort of secret. Luis saw me watching and waved his hand for me to turn around.

I stuck my tongue out at him, and he returned the gesture.

They continued their card game, but instead of watching Luis, my attention was on Anaki.

A long sigh escaped my lips when I realized he was part of the club's care team. He was only there to make sure we were comfortable and to make sure that Luis was adjusting.

When he comforted me on the plane, it was the most delicate care I had ever received from a man in my life. He tucked me into a chair, made me a bed, and ordered me to sleep. I should have fought back, but something in his gentle voice, the soft touch of his hand... he took the physical pain away.

He called me *love.*

No one had called me anything like that. Babe, baby, *love?* Was it an endearment he used with the other women he helped take care of?

Part of me hoped it was only for me. I decided then and there, I wasn't going to believe it was only for me. Because a handsome man like that wouldn't want a woman with a condition like mine, and a son.

I'll keep that fantasy to myself.

It was selfish to even have such a fantasy when I have a son to look after.

I looked away and faced the front while we drove through the town. The first man to show me a bit of kindness for the first time in my life, and I get the warm fuzzies. What was wrong with me?

Why couldn't I be like Emm? I needed to toughen up, for Luis' sake. We wouldn't be here for long. Once the threat was under control, we would talk to Emm and figure out what to do next. Find another place to hide, because we would never truly be rid of the problem.

This was just an MC. Magic or not, they couldn't be that strong.

I felt my breath rise and fall faster and faster. I had tried to remain calm the whole time, but damn it, it all came to a head. Stress made my disease worse, and here I was, falling apart in front of all these strangers.

My heart sped up, and my body shook.

I should have called Emm. I should have told her what was happening. Why didn't I fight more? They could be lying. Why did I just let them take us?

Abuela squeezed my hand. "Mija, look at me." I shook my head, then screwed my eyes shut.

You're weak. What do you mean, you're tired? Can't you do anything?

"Mija, come back to me. These people are not bad. Emm is safe. She's with her soul mate—"

I blocked her out. I tightened my jaw, and my body tensed. The ache in my hips came back in full force. There she goes on about her *soul mate* again.

She always rambled on about that. She was *insane.*

The seat belt popped, and I was suddenly lifted. I tried to steady myself with my arms, and my eyes opened wide, but I was seeing double.

"Hey, hey, easy there, love. I've got you."

That voice. Anaki had me on his lap, his arms wrapped around me, tightly, almost too tightly, but it was an embrace that caused instant ease.

"I don't need your help," I hissed. "I'm fine, I was just having a moment of clarity—"

"Yeah, that there are a bunch of scary monsters in the car, and now you are sitting on a dragon's lap."

My face turned six shades of red.

Anaki's hand went up to pet my hair. My eyes focused more clearly. I was damn embarrassed sitting on his lap, but when I looked around the car no one was paying attention to us. Abuela gazed out the window, Nadia held Bear's hand, and Luis?

"Luis is fine, Mama. He's reading," Anaki whispered in my ear.

My eyes went wide, and I nestled further into his hold.

He did not just call me that.

"You can let go now," I muttered and tried to pull away. "I'm fine."

Anaki hummed, and I felt his head bob back and forth. "Don't think you are, and that's okay. I'm here for you. You aren't alone anymore. No one in your family is. And you can say you don't need a good hug right now. That's fine, but really, I'm the one who needs a hug." He sighed dramatically.

His tight hold loosened enough so I could get a good look at his face. His eyes weren't glowing or shape-shifting into strange slits like a reptile. He appeared to be a regular man with that pantie-dropping smile.

I still didn't know if I wanted to trust it or not, but I wouldn't lie to myself and say being held by him wasn't nice.

"Why would you need a hug?"

Anaki frowned and placed his hand on Nadia's chair. "Nadia knows all about it. It's a terrible condition I have, really." Nadia looked over her shoulder and rolled her eyes.

"Here we go," she said.

Anaki held his head in shame. "I am... a cuddle slut."

The car erupted into a fit of laughter, and automatically, I did the same. By the time the laughter was over, I didn't feel the pain in my hips anymore, just the warmth where he held me.

"A cuddle slut?" I asked incredulously.

Anaki leaned back into the seat, getting comfortable. "When Nadia first came to the club, she was pretty sick. I'm Bear's bestie, so of course we had movie nights, and *of course,* I was invited."

Bear scoffed, and I saw he shook his enormous head in front of me as he drove. "More like inserted himself, but it was welcomed."

Anaki smirked. "Anyway, I like my cuddles. And Bear, being a bear, he was fun to curl up to, and Nadia, needing the warmth because at the time she was human and so small and fragile—"

"Hey!" Nadia glared at Anaki. They both stared-off at each other. "I liked it. I'm not gonna argue."

I held back my laughter with a smile.

"As you see, I am a cuddle slut. Now that they are official, I don't get the cuddles much anymore. I don't need to piss off Bear's bear."

"Wait!" Luis unbuckled his seatbelt and sat on Abuela's lap. "Nadia wasn't a bear. You were a human before?"

Nadia turned around in her seat. "Yup, I was."

"So cool," Luis said. "Could I turn into a bear? Wait, I want to be a dragon!"

Anaki's smile grew so wide, I thought his face would break.

I sat up straight when reality hit me that my son wanted to become a dragon. There was no way that was happening. How did it happen anyway? With a bite? Was it like legends of vampires?

"I don't think so, mijo, you go sit back in your seat and buckle up!"

Luis groaned. "No fun, Mama."

There was no way my son was getting a bite from a dragon. Before my body could tense again, I felt Anaki's thumb run over my cheek.

I froze, feeling his hand so close to my face. I should have pushed him away. He was too close, touched too much, but the little fantasy in my head ate this up.

I couldn't resist as his touch enveloped my sore muscles in his warmth, it eased the ache and relaxed me.

Anaki chuckled. "Don't worry. Luis isn't going to get changed by a shifter or a vampire. Doesn't work like that. Nadia and Bear fell in love, they are committed to each other, that's why she changed."

I didn't ask any questions about that. I was still having a hard time wrapping my head around everything else. I didn't want to know what that process was like for someone to change into a shifter. It'd been less than 12 hours. We traveled at an alarming speed to get from Venezuela to our final destination, which was just a few minutes away, and I'd had my brain fried for the day.

He leaned in closer, his warm breath sending shivers down my spine. "You can trust me, you know," he whispered softly, his voice like a soothing melody amid chaos. "I may be a cuddle slut, but I'm also someone who cares deeply for those around me."

I felt my heart race as his words resonated within me. Despite the uncertainty and fear that lingered in the air, there was something about Anaki that made me want to believe in him. Maybe it was the way he held me so gently, or the sincerity in his eyes.

I pursed my lips. "You don't know a damn thing about me. Why would you care?" I was shocked by the bitterness in my tone. He's been nice despite the whole kidnapping my family thing.

His smile dropped, and he leaned in closer. Conversation flowed in the car while Nadia pointed out the sights to Abuela.

Anaki's forehead was almost touching mine. His breath fanned my cheek, and I swallowed nervously. "Let's just say, I know we are kindred spirits. I can see you aren't just hurting physically, Elena. You hurt here, too." His hand reached up and pressed at the top of my chest. It wasn't sexual, it was just below my throat.

I couldn't tear my gaze away from his intense eyes, a myriad of emotions swirling within them. His touch, though gentle, seemed to reach into the depths of my soul, stirring up feelings I had long tried to bury.

A lump formed in my throat as I struggled to find the right words, to make sense of the conflicting thoughts and sensations that coursed through me. "I... I don't understand," I whispered, my voice barely audible above the hum of the car engine.

Anaki's expression softened, a hint of sadness flickering across his features. "You don't have to understand everything right now, Elena. Sometimes, things are felt rather than explained." His thumb traced a soothing pattern on my chest, a silent reassurance amidst the chaos surrounding us.

I closed my eyes briefly, allowing myself to lean into his touch, seeking solace in the warmth he offered. Despite the uncertainty of our situation, there was a strange comfort in Anaki's presence, a sense of belonging that tugged at the walls I had built around my heart.

What the hell was happening?

Anaki broke the serious tension when the car turned. "This is home," he announced and waved for Luis to get out of his seat and stand beside him.

I opened my mouth to protest.

"This is the safest area in town, trust me. No one is gonna be speeding or messing with us."

I made a noise of disagreement, and he hugged me tighter as he pointed out the sights.

I didn't squirm in Anaki's hold, but I was very aware of every movement he made. He brushed his thumb over my thigh. His nose was in my hair while he explained.

The apartments were first. He explained that a lot of men and women who stayed there were survivors who wanted to stay close to the MC, to get back on their feet after they had been saved. Just because they had been rescued, didn't mean they had a strong support system where they came from, so the club helped them find jobs in the town until they wanted to leave. Most of them stayed and even made families of their own.

My heart softened at how an MC would want to take that extra step to help in the aftermath of helping victims of sex trafficking, slavery, and forced marriages. While I hadn't had the chance to prove if it was true, the smiles from the people coming from the apartment complex and the waves from the MC across the street were a good sign.

The club on the outside was everything I thought it would be. The dimly lit street was lined with motorcycles, their engines purring like contented beasts. The bar itself, with its weathered wooden door, had the rustic charm of an old tavern.

Engines rumbled, and a faint smell of gasoline filled the air. Rough-looking bikers strutted down the sidewalk, their heavy boots echoing against the pavement, asserting their dominance over the town.

As we drove by, the bar appeared to be even larger, the double-story building making me tilt my head in question.

"At the top there," Anaki said as he pointed. "Are apartments for a lot of the guys. Wolves need to be in close spaces. Like a pack, just like real animals."

My eyes stayed on the bar as we drove by. There was even a mechanic shop at the back of it. It was huge compared to a lot of the buildings in town.

"The MC has more wolves than any other supernaturals. I live there some of the time because I work there, but I have my own place. So do Bear and Nadia. They have a cabin in the forest that the MC owns. That's where we are going. It's quiet there, Luis, you'll like it. You get plenty of places to run without getting into trouble."

Luis rolled his eyes. "I don't get into trouble. Not that much."

Abuela scoffed. "When he gets bored, he does."

After a few more minutes, we left the bustling town behind, going down a narrow, curvy, gravel road. The dense forest enveloped us, casting darkness as nightfall took hold.

As we approached the clearing, quietness enveloped us. The crunching of gravel beneath the tires was all I could hear besides the distant chirping of crickets and the rustling of leaves. The scent of clean air was refreshing as they rolled down the windows.

Along the gravel road, cabins stood in a neat row, some in the midst of construction, while others remained silent and unoccupied, their windows devoid of light. At the culmination of the driveway stood the grandest dwelling of them all, an imposing structure that commanded attention. Vines crawled up the mansion, making it look part of the forest. It was still being built. Some parts still had fresh stone being laid at the steps, but it was gorgeous.

"That's the pack house," Anaki said and opened the door. "A lot of wolves will live there eventually, instead of at the bar."

I nodded, and Anaki helped steady me as we climbed out of the car. The cabin before us was quaint, with beautiful vines, flowers and bushes already grown around it. The cabin looked brand new but settled so beautifully into the forest.

"This is where we are staying?"

Anaki laughed nervously. "Yeah? What did you think we were gonna do, put you in a tent? Or wait, is it not good enough? I could find somewhere better?" Anaki ran his fingers through his hair and nervously looked over to find Bear. "Hang on, I can find something else."

Before Anaki ran off, I grabbed his arm. It was the first time I took the initiative to reach out to him. He froze and turned back to me, surprise on his face. "This is great. I'm just surprised. I didn't think our kidnappers would set us up with something like this."

Anaki put his hand over his chest. "You wound me yet again. You really think we are that bad of people?"

"Still deciding." My lip curled into a small smile. "No one does this for free. There is always a catch."

Anaki frowned. "While we were told to come get you by orders of our president, Locke, it was for good reason. He cares about your sister."

I shook my head. "Don't see how. She's supposed to be hunting him, catching a bounty on his head. She isn't romantic either. She's more of a one-night stand kind of woman." I never did that. While I dated, I looked for *the one*. I didn't give out the goods like Emm and Abuela thought. A few stolen kisses here or there to find a spark, and when I thought I had found him...

He turned out to be a dud.

"Locke doesn't give up so easily. You'll find that out. He's very... persistent."

She's gonna put up a fight. Hope he's ready for that.

Anaki put his hand on my lower back. "Come on." He jerked his head to the cabin. "Let's get you settled. You've had a long day."

That was certainly an understatement.

CHAPTER EIGHT

Anaki

As I reached out to guide Elena towards the cabin, my hand brushed against the soft fabric of her dress. "Anaki?" The deep, rumbled timbre of Bear's voice jolted me from my thoughts. A mixture of surprise and irritation curled my lip into a snarl, but Bear remained steadfast on the porch, his presence unwavering. Nadia swiftly motioned Elena inside, and left me cold in the doorway as she shut the door.

The deafening chorus of crickets and buzzing insects engulfed our surroundings, their relentless noise assaulted my healed ears. The noise was at an almost unbearable level. Between Bear and me, the silence was heavy, a thick fog suffocating any possibility of conversation.

The relationship we had with each other was brotherly, but our inner turmoil was left alone. We didn't have deep-rooted talks about our pasts, as it hurt too much.

I had witnessed his past before my eyes; it tore him apart. I had felt his pain. In some ways, I felt I was partly an empath because of how deeply it had hurt me as I watched him suffer the bond break with his first mate.

He was a big, cuddly bear under all that meat, and I was glad he received Nadia, even if it was before me. He needed a mate quickly. Most mammal shifters did.

Why had I lived so long without dying or going crazy? I'm not sure why. Maybe it was because I...

I scoffed internally. Yeah, not going there.

Bear's heavy footsteps in his silver-toed boots echoed across the porch. To others they would find it intimidating and downright frightening, making them piss their pants before he even reached halfway to them but not me.

I've never felt more comfortable with another man besides him, in my life.

Bear pulled me into his famous bear hugs, which were only meant for Nadia and me, and rubbed his big hand on top of my head.

My dragon scowled. He hadn't had time to filter through our memories to even know this male, but he felt my comfort in my best friend's presence, so he let it go.

"You doing alright?"

I shook my head on his chest. "No."

I wasn't.

Goddess, I wasn't okay. While I knew Bear's past, had saved him, and brought him with me to the Iron Fang, he didn't know mine. He never asked, not that he didn't want to know. He left me plenty of opportunities when we both had too much to drink, but even in a drunken stupor, I wouldn't open my mouth.

"I'm scared." I finally admitted. I backed away from him and leaned up against the railing. "I'm not like you, Grim, or Hawke. Being big, bad, tough, that just isn't who I am. I'd rather sit back and laugh. I fight when I need to, protect the club when called, who I care for and love... but I'm not some big, bad biker like the rest of you."

I was far from it. If anything, I was the joke of the bar. Not that I minded.

I'd rather see the girls smile and the guys shake their heads to keep their minds off their pain.

"What if she rejects me, too?"

Bear let out a long sigh and stood beside me. The crickets continued to sing, and the moon was far too bright for my mood. I'd like to think it was the goddess telling me that brighter nights were coming my way, that I should be optimistic, but that darkness lurking inside, the hurt and betrayal, still felt like yesterday.

My dragon constantly moved inside me. His serpentine body rolled, curled in on himself. He was ready to strike, ready to lurch his body into any imposing enemy. He, too, could still feel the sting of rejection.

Bear huffed in annoyance. "You don't let her. You don't give her a choice."

I turned to him, dumbfounded. "Is that what you did? Just told Nadia: 'Hey, just so you know, you're mine.'"

Bear shrugged his shoulders. "Basically."

Of course, Bear would do that. He isn't the most talkative person. Plus, he's built like a massive tree. No one would say no to him.

"What I did learn was that the bond made Nadia very... receptive." I turned to face Bear, who continued to stare up at the moon. "While I didn't know my first mate very well, didn't talk to her... with Nadia, I felt an overwhelming need to keep her near my bear and protect her in the state she was in. While I healed her, she healed me. Just like every other couple that is coming together at the club.

Bear continued. "And you would have to be blind not to see that you have a hold on Elena already. She's been compliant every time you touch her. The way you normally touch people. Simple gestures, not like the way the rest of us took our mates."

That was an understatement. Every other male that had a mate had picked them up right away and had them in their arms within minutes. Hawke took a while because he was a stubborn ass, but once it finally clicked...

And Locke... once he had arms again, I'm sure he would do something with Emm.

I stared down at my hands and rubbed them together. I liked to touch Elena. Too much. I wasn't lying when I said I was a cuddle slut. Touch was my damn love language. If I could hold her hand for the rest of my life, I would be one happy dragon.

But I wasn't about to throw her over my shoulder and demand it. No, I wanted her to want me, too.

I cleared my throat. "She could be calm because of the bond. You know the goddess can put two people together, but they still have the choice to reject the bond. That is why we are in this situation." I scratched the back of my neck. "She could get rid of me once I tell her..."

I stood up and walked away from Bear. I couldn't tell him *that* now.

"Anaki, for fuck's sake, spit it out. What the hell are you so worried about? She already knows you are a dragon, that there are shifters. You jumped the biggest damn hurdle of them all today. She accepted all of it. All of this." He waved his hand around us. "She's in our territory. She ain't going anywhere. And that bag of bones in there is okay with all of it! She knows shit!"

"I heard that!" The grandmother shouted from the inside.

Bear slapped his hand to his face.

"It's not just that. I can't do the dominance stuff like you can. I'm not very in charge like that. And—I just, I can't tell you." I pulled at my hair. "If I told you," I pointed between us. "We'd never be the same. You wouldn't look at me the same. You might—"

Would he think of me differently if he knew the mate that rejected me was a male?

The Elysian Realm heavily frowned upon same-sex relationships. People frowned upon it, much like in most areas on Earth; surprisingly, however, it was more accepted here than in Elysian.

With Bear being one of the more stoic males, the manliest of males, I feared I would lose him as a friend. Would he think of me differently?

Bear rubbed his hand down his beard and hummed.

"That right? You think, after all that we have been through, that would change what we have? I'm hurt."

My mouth dropped. "No, no, that isn't what I meant!"

Bear sighed, defeatedly. "You think, after the many years we have been together, that I would throw away everything we have because of something in your past? After you have rescued me? Helped my mate?"

I let out a pathetic whimper. "No, I just..."

"Anaki, are you attracted to males?" Bear murmured so no one could hear.

I blinked several times and rubbed my hand up and down my arm. Warmth filled behind my eyes, tears threatening to fall. Was it obvious? Was I that obvious that I would be into males? I appreciated the male body as I do with females. But, I'd only sleep with someone if I was bonded to them.

For obvious reasons.

Nothing worked down there anyway, not without a connection.

My mouth opened and closed several times. I didn't even hear Bear as he walked towards me in those heavy boots and put both hands on my shoulders. "Anaki, Nadia and I had a feeling. In fact, I think some members think it is a possibility. Some might be in the same boat. Look at Tajah and Beretta? Why in this realm would you think I care? None of us do. If your mate rejected you because of that, that is on them, and I hope he's dead."

He knew I might be like this? Yet he still let me stay in their nest and be with them?

I nodded. "He is very much dead." I swallowed heavily. "So, movie nights are...?"

"Still on. Elena and Luis can even jump into the cuddle pile if they're into it. That will be something you need to talk to her about, though."

I cleared my throat. That was much easier than I expected, but it was still awkward. I didn't find Bear attractive in that sort of way. Did I need to tell him that? Did he already know?

Bear growled and pushed on my shoulder. "You reek of anxiety. You think too much. How can you stand it?"

I let out a bark of laughter. "Sorry, I wanted nothing to change between us."

"And it won't, you skinny fucker. Just don't think so hard. You're still my best friend. I'd trust you with my life, and I'd better be one of the first people to see your dragon, or I'm gonna be pissed. Never seen a dragon before."

I smiled. "Yeah, well. Not gonna get my hopes up yet. Elena has to accept all of me first."

Bear narrowed his eyes. "She will. Don't know why you are pessimistic about it. That is not the Anaki I know."

"Careful, Bear, that's a big word. Better not choke on it."

Bear growled and leaned toward me to wrap his arms around me. I darted out of the way, laughing at him.

He huffed in annoyance and pulled down his cut. "You know Locke is coming by. He needs to know their scents. He'll be in animal form, most likely." He grabbed my upper arm and pulled me into a hug.

I could see my eyes glow against Bear's chest. My dragon must have already known Locke, by just skimming briefly through our memories. The president, while a good leader and meant well, was an unhinged psychopath who had no control over his wolf.

Bear leaned up against the post and crossed his arms. "There are guards around the perimeter, extra prospects, too."

Locke's wolf would rip them to pieces to get to humans not meant to be on the club's land. He'd better be stable.

My dragon let out a guttural growl, which resonated so deeply the porch shook.

Bear's eyebrows went up. "Damn, you even got my bear impressed."

"I am quite large and not just in my pa-"

"Shut up," Bear snapped. "I swear to the goddess, Anaki."

I chuckled, and Nadia stepped out onto the porch. She gave me a thumbs up, and wrapped her arm around Bear. "Sorry, Anaki. I had to get you to talk to Bear real quick." She gave a small smile.

The corner of my lip curled into a smile. I was getting pretty obsessed with my woman.

We all said our goodbyes, and I stepped into the cabin.

My mate and her family's luggage had already been brought inside, and each person had their own bedroom, except for me, because I wasn't supposed to be there. The couch was for me, but soon I'll make my way into Elena's bed.

You know, if she said I could.

My dragon snorted and licked his lips.

I let out a shaky breath. I really hoped Bear was right, and she really was into me like I was into her. I couldn't go into detail about just how much I wasn't at all dominant. Although I was a dragon, I was very—soft.

I looked around the cabin. Luis' bedroom door was already closed, and I could hear light snores coming from the other side. My hearing had already improved so much, I could even hear Elena in her room. Was she getting undressed? Was she going to think of me? Did she bring any battery-operated friends?

My mind wandered to when she sat on my lap in the car. I haven't had a hard-on in ages. While I didn't lose my erection capabilities for a few years after my mate rejected me, unlike most mammal shifters, I still haven't had an erection in some time.

Hiding mine will be troublesome.

I felt them rouse when she sat so nicely on my lap. Luckily, my position prevented her from feeling them. At least I hope she didn't. There was a lot to unpack today, and adding *that* was not going to go so well.

You really think she is going to accept your past, your dragon anatomy? Look how quickly she dismissed the idea her son could become one.

I was staring off into space when I felt a touch on my shoulder. The old woman stared up at me and narrowed her eyes. "Not giving up on her yet, are you?" She put her hands on her hips.

"What, no, of course not!" I stepped away from her. She was like a silent ninja walking around the cabin in those slippers. "I'm just getting started."

The old woman chuckled, her eyes twinkling mischievously. "Good, good. Persistence is key." She patted my arm before shuffling away to the kitchen. "I knew when *she* showed you to me that you would be perfect. You both are kindred spirits, I told her."

I stared at her in confusion.

Strange woman. She couldn't possibly be talking about the Moon Goddess, could she?

I shook my head, wandered over to the window and gazed out at the moonlit forest. The night was alive with the sounds of nature, a soothing backdrop to my racing thoughts. Could Elena truly accept all of me, the man, the dragon with certain wants and desires? Would she be willing to look past the secrets I carried, the weight of centuries on my shoulders?

As I stood there, lost in contemplation, a rapid scratch on the cabin door broke through my reverie. I approached cautiously. It could only be one person. Opening the door revealed a familiar furred face, Locke, in his wolf form, his eyes holding a glint of intelligence that spoke of his dual nature.

Locke bumped past me into the cabin, his presence a reminder of the delicate balance we all walked between human and beast. His wolf form padded silently across the room. He still had patches of hair missing, his teeth were sharp and still looked menacing.

I glanced at the old woman. She didn't seem a bit frightened.

"I take it you haven't won my Emmie over, since you still look like shit?" she smirked.

I snorted and stared at them both with horror. What was this woman thinking? How did she know who this wolf was?

Locke huffed in annoyance, and he padded to the woman. He took in her scent as she stood there with her arms folded. "I'm Abuela. You and the rest of your people can call me that."

Locke stared at her, then turned his head and, without another glance, went to the other closed doors. First to Luis'.

Together, we moved through the cabin, Locke committing each scent to memory with a focused intensity. When he got to Elena's door, I stiffened and growled. I felt my fangs descending. The burn from my gums brought tears to my eyes.

Locke stared at me and stomped his paw in annoyance. I pushed the door open only because I knew Elena was already fast asleep.

She slept soundly, her chest rising and falling in a steady rhythm. Locke approached her bedside, his wolf form emanating a protective energy that both comforted and unnerved me. He lowered his head to gently nuzzle Elena's hand, a gesture that seemed surprisingly tender coming from the formidable wolf.

I watched in silence, my heart pounding in my chest. Locke turned to me with a piercing gaze before padding back towards the door. As he passed me, I caught a glimpse of understanding in his eyes.

"Hope you got what you came for, 'cause you can't get near her any-more," I muttered as he stepped out the door.

Locke's wolfish form didn't look back when I shut the front door and locked us in for the rest of the night.

CHAPTER NINE

Elena

The sun was bright and shining through the curtains by the time I woke up. Yesterday was a whirlwind, and I had wished, to the greater part of the universe, it was all just a dream. When I opened my eyes and saw the cedar planks above me, I knew that was all hopeful thinking.

I sat up, waiting for the aches in my bones to hit. Mornings were the worst. I think that was why I dreaded getting out of bed. I felt like my muscles were worn and heavy. I tried to move them just enough to lessen the pain.

My face already twinged in anticipation as I sat up, but the inevitable pain didn't come, at least not as strongly. I sat up and turned my body, still waiting, but the pain wasn't as great.

I frowned, and my eyes went from side to side in confusion. It was a dull ache, but nothing that would warrant me to use a cane today.

With the events that happened yesterday, I knew I would be in pain because of the stress. I took my regular dosage of medicine, took some pain relievers, but I knew full well today would be a bedridden day.

I stood up, still waiting for the inevitable pain to hit. When my feet hit the ground, I let out the breath that I'd held in my lungs and let go.

Nothing.

Perhaps there was some magic to this place. I mean, we flew on a magical airplane. Could this cabin could have some properties that could help?

Or just dumb luck.

I flipped open my suitcase, which I had haphazardly tossed on the bench at the end of the bed. I grabbed only what I needed last night and quickly got into bed. Yesterday, I was ready for sleep and to forget about the blue-eyed dragon and the mess Emm had gotten us into.

When I flipped through all the clothes I had, which were mostly shorts and dresses for the tropical climate where we lived, I gasped loudly, mortified that Abuela had packed all my electric boyfriends.

And extra stuff.

She packed the lube. *Mierda*, what was wrong with this woman?

It had been a long time since I've been with a man. She often joked that I didn't need to go find one, that she would take care of finding me a soul mate later on. Did she think my coochie was so dried up now I needed *lube?*

The door rattled under a sudden, forceful knock, the sound reverberating through the room. With an ear-splitting crack, it swung open violently. The door collided with the wall with a resounding thud. My heart raced, and I instinctively raised my hands in front of me, bracing for the imminent impact of Luis barreling into my body.

To my surprise, it wasn't Luis, but Anaki. He panted, his hair and eyes wild as he took in my form. While I wasn't naked, I felt utterly exposed in my short knit shorts and camisole. I folded my arms to cover what little dignity I had left.

That embarrassment completely went away once I realized what he was wearing. Gray sweatpants and no shirt. Every girl's wet dream. And he was standing in my bedroom.

He looked way better than that Viking-looking guy on social media, who likes to come out in his pajama pants holding a cup of coffee, does his morning stretches and tells us all to have a glorious morning.

Anaki was ripped. Every single ab was carved out of stone. Even his sides had abs. How was that possible?

He was a dragon shifter, and could have different muscles, right?

Oh, he's got nipple rings. Does he play with those when he gets himself off? Does he let people lick them? Suck them? My tongue slipped out of my mouth at the thought and I sucked it back in quickly.

My mind was whirling with excitement, as I uncovered my breasts to ogle him more, because Dios Mio, we were both getting something out of this.

I could see that sweet looking V-line traveling lower, lower, until it disappeared right down into the soft texture of his pants. The bulge in his pants was growing. There was no denying he liked what he saw of me.

Why? I didn't know, because I had a soft belly, stretch marks on my stomach, hips, thighs and boobs from having Luis.

Anaki was just... perfection.

"Mama, come see what food Anaki made! He gave me a food baby!"

I blinked several times and took my eyes off his crotch. That was when I saw that sweet smile, not a cocky one that would fill me with embarrassment. He looked so excited, so proud that I was looking at him. Like a proud little puppy. I swore if he had a tail, it would have been wagging behind him.

"You can still look." Anaki came forward. "I don't mind." Again, it wasn't cocky, it was more of a validation he was looking for as he cautiously came forward.

Jesus, Mary and Joseph, he was cute! He looked so innocent, and cautious.

And I wanted to do terrible things to him.

Dirty, depraved, naughty things to him.

I quickly pulled my frayed camisole down over my hips, covering myself as best as I could. My heart was pounding in my chest, and I knew there was no way I could pretend nothing was happening. He had seen me in a state of undress, and I had seen him aroused.

"I... I'll come see what you made for food in a minute," I stammered, trying to regain some semblance of composure. "Just give me a minute."

Anaki's eyes were still wide with anticipation, and he nodded slowly, giving me a small, reassuring smile. "Of course. I understand. It's still early."

Anaki turned and walked out the door, and gave me one more glance before he shut it.

What. Was. That.

You cannot be having feelings like that, not with what's going on around you.

I hurriedly grabbed new clothes to wear and smoothed out the wrinkles as best as I could, hoping to appear more presentable, and then washed up in the attached bathroom. As I emerged from the bedroom, I noticed that Anaki had prepared breakfast on the little table near the window.

There were plates piled high with fresh fruit, sweet pastries, and steaming cups of coffee. The sight filled me with hunger, but also a sense of dread, as I wondered if we could pretend nothing had happened just minutes ago.

"Wow," I said as I approached the table. "This looks amazing." I've never seen so much food in one sitting. It was like a massive buffet.

Anaki beamed with pride. "Elena!" He jumped up enthusiastically and offered his chair. Abuela smiled into her coffee.

That crone was holding back her laughter. I didn't shy away from Anaki, not when he was still shirtless, in those sinful gray sweatpants, and being such a gentleman.

Are the sweatpants part of being a dragon uniform or something?

"Thanks." I sat down in my seat, and before I could make my plate, Anaki already was. He didn't ask what I wanted. He piled on the plate with all my favorites. I watched in shock at how he added fruit, sausages, and waffles, then covered it all in maple syrup.

He didn't stop there. Once he set it down in front of me, he began to cut my food! I stared in shock, while Abuela took another sip of her coffee and did not bat an eye.

"Anaki made me dragon pancakes!" Luis picked up one of his pancakes and showed me it. Sure enough, it was in the shape of a dragon, and it was even dyed blue.

"Wow," I remarked and watched him take a large bite out of the head.

Anaki cleared his throat. "Open." I opened my mouth automatically, and an explosion of flavor erupted into my mouth.

Damn, these waffles were amazing.

Once I swallowed, he fed me another forkful. I wasn't even protesting. These waffles were the shit!

All the while, Anaki was grinning like I made him the happiest person in the world. Is this part of a care team promotion thing? He has to feed everyone here? Literally with his hands?

"Did you feed Luis and Abuela, too?" I asked with my mouth half full.

He shook his head. "Nope, just you." He grinned wildly and shoved another piece of waffle into my mouth.

Once I swallowed, I grabbed his wrist before he could shove another piece of food into my mouth. "I can feed myself, thanks. Why don't you eat? You already fed everyone else."

Anaki's brows furrowed. "I already ate. I want to make sure you get enough." He pushed the fork closer to my lips. I noticed Abuela scowling at me.

What the hell was going on?

I opened my mouth reluctantly and Anaki's eyes brightened as he continued to feed me, until I was on the verge of being overly stuffed.

"I see you aren't using your cane today," Abuela said when she stood up from the table. "How do you feel?"

I cleared my throat and reached for a napkin, but Anaki was already there, dabbing the corners of my mouth. I giggled and pushed his hand away. While I wasn't used to someone taking care of me so closely because I liked my independence, he was doing it in such a heartwarming way.

"I'm feeling really good today," I admitted. "Just dull aches. Maybe it was the bed. The mattress was top notch."

Anaki stood and grabbed the empty plates. "I'm glad you liked them. The club will be happy to hear. Most of us have particular tastes with sleeping quarters, so money was no object when buying good mattresses."

The dishes clattered in the sink. I grabbed the plates filled with fruit and brought them to the kitchen. I opened up several drawers to find storage, so we could eat it later. "Do shifters get cold or something? I saw so many blankets in the closets. And pillows, so many pillows." I opened the cabinet and saw the plastic containers far too high for me to reach. I stood up on my tiptoes, trying my best to use my fingers to flip the contents toward me.

Anaki stood behind me, his body flush with mine. I was very aware of his body brushing up against my ass. He leaned in and whispered in my ear, "Elena, you don't have to reach that high. I can help you." His breath was warm on my skin, sending shivers down my spine.

I blushed at the feel of his breath on my skin and his closeness, but I managed to keep my wits about me.

With a small smile, Anaki reached up, his hand on my hip, and grabbed the containers to hand to me.

As I carefully placed the plastic containers on the counter, I felt his eyes on me. His presence was both comforting and irritating. I couldn't like him. Not what he was, not what he had done to my family.

"The extra blankets and pillows are meant for shifters. They make nests for their... partners."

Luis' head popped up. "Wow, do the wolf shifters have litters of puppies?"

Abuela gasped and nearly dropped one of the crystals from her luggage, which she rolled out of her bedroom. She was in the process of setting them up on the coffee table. It was her own way of helping. Something about protection and wards or whatnot.

Anaki laughed. "No, that would be pretty awesome if they had a lot of pups. A lot of mammal shifters like to feel warm and safe. Like in a den."

"Do you make a nest?" Luis asked. "You're a dragon, like a reptile. Would it be different?"

Anaki's face turned a pretty shade of pink as he stuttered and rubbed his hand over his mouth.

"If you don't want to answer, you don't have to." I blurted. "Luis is curious, but he doesn't need to ask all these questions. That sounds private."

Anaki shook his head, his eyes widening. "No, it's not private. It's just... there are only two dragons in the club. No one has ever really asked. I'm not sure how to describe it." He rubbed his hand up and down his face.

Why was he so cute when he was nervous? I wanted to walk over and just give him a big hug, and not let him go.

"Well, it can't be that strange. Not after all we've faced in twenty-four hours," I chuckled. "I doubt you are like the legends of actual dragons. You know, that has an actual cave along with hoards of gold, and it's tucked away in a mountain somewhere where no one can find it." Luis and I laughed, and I picked up a dish as I began to wash it.

"Like Smaug!" Luis added, and I nodded.

Anaki went quiet, and I turned to face him. His face was pale while he stroked his arm nervously. "Right, that would be crazy. Absolutely crazy."

I dropped the dish in the sink, and my mouth dropped in a surprised 'oh'. "Wait, do you have a hoard? Or a cave?"

Anaki bobbed his head back and forth. "More or less."

Luis gasped. "Cool! Can I see it?"

"You can't ask a dragon to see his hoard. That's private," Abuela scolded. "Any sort of nest or home to these supernaturals is very sacred. It is where they sleep, where they are comfortable. It brings them a sense of security."

Abuela sat back on the couch and laced her fingers together over her stomach. I leaned back on the counter and assessed her. How did she know so much, while I knew none of this? Was it those books?

As a child, we would go to flea markets and old bookstores, and she would request the oddest books and scrolls. A lot of them were in Latin, special books that were out of print. Some cost more than we could afford, but somehow she would get her hands on them.

She knew a lot, while Emm and I secretly made fun of her.

She always took care of us. This was just a hobby of hers on the side, and we left her be.

An unsettling feeling formed in the pit of my stomach. How much of the warning signs have I ignored over the years, while thinking she was crazy or insane? All this time, I blamed mushrooms, fancy rocks and dementia.

"Hey, you alright?" Anaki was beside me in an instant, his hand touching my arm. The calmness of his touch made the worry go away. The ache in my body vanished.

Perhaps Abuela wasn't so crazy after all. There was magic out there. I haven't seen Anaki shift into some dragon, have seen no wolves or bears yet, but there was no denying the pain I usually had was down to a mere two on the pain scale.

"I'm fine." I gave Anaki a small smile. "Just came to terms with everything that's happening around me. That this is real." I let out a breath as I watched Luis jump on the couch next to Abuela. She pulled out her phone, so they could scroll funny cat videos.

What kidnappers were they if they let us have our phones? We were told not to tell Emm we were here. Of course, they had to be here for the phone call.

"That's a good thing, right?" Anaki whispered.

I hummed. "I guess so. I can't think with you not wearing a shirt, though. You should put one on." I eyed him up and down.

Anaki smirked and puffed up his chest. "Yeah, I did that on purpose. You seemed to like it earlier."

I smacked his stomach with my hand.

Yep. Nice, hard washboard abs.

I blushed and looked away from him. "You are part of the care team. You are just making sure we don't all flip our shit with what's going on."

Anger bubbled inside of me. That's all this flirting was... to keep my mind off being stuck in a cabin and unable to go anywhere. He was here to keep me occupied.

Because who would want someone who was broken, tired, sick... and who had a son from a previous relationship? Anaki was a dragon. Supposedly. A hot, caring man who could have a girlfriend, or boyfriend, for that matter.

It could all just be an act.

Because men lie.

"It doesn't matter." I schooled my face. "You should put a shirt on. It *is* distracting, and I don't have time for games. I need to take care of my son and get some work done, so we have money once this is all over."

Anaki's playful face fell, and it felt like a stab to my heart. But I couldn't get close to him, not when this was all over, things would go back to normal. We would move away and make sure we hid from the cartel that would still be chasing Emm.

I don't need to be healing a broken heart during any of that.

CHAPTER TEN

Anaki

What was the saying?

Two steps forward? One step back?

One step forward, two steps back?

Whatever the human saying was, I was behind where I wanted to be with Elena. I thought things were going well. She approved of my body; it was clear when she eyed me up and down in her bedroom.

I know humans have preferences when selecting their males. With the bond that we shared, and my dragon lineage, I would sweep her off her feet. It had worked well with others when I danced on the bar.

Once dragon soulkins find each other, it was natural to show off our bodies. We were presenting ourselves, showing off the bodies that we had worked so hard for. I knew I couldn't show all of myself to Elena, not when her elder and son were in the cabin. Dragons usually strode around naked when they found their mates, giving them a full view of their bodies.

Goddess, I don't think I would have done that. Not with her being human and the whole situation between my legs.

Even I knew that would have been a step too far.

My torso, I knew, was appropriate enough to show to everyone in the cabin. While I didn't have my soulkin chains clipped on my nipple rings to enhance my broad chest and bring her attention to my body, she still had her fill.

Her arousal that gathered near her thighs was a testament to that.

And goddess, when I fed her! She let me feed her. It was all I could do to keep my dragon's rumblings of satisfaction quiet enough to not scare her off. She was still hesitant, worried; the anxiety rolled off her in waves, but her elder made no attempts to keep me away from her.

Unfortunately, it was Elena who pushed me away, and she stayed away from me for the rest of the day. It hurt that she wanted me clothed and to not look at my body. If I was a fire dragon, smoke would have filled the cabin. Instead, our blood boiled when we longed for her from afar.

"Come on, Anaki." He waved his hand up and down my body. *"You don't think this is serious, right? Go put your robe back on."*

My eyes burned.

At least she did not cast me out of the cabin, because I would not have abided by that request. I could default by saying she was my charge, still part of the care team, even if it was a lie.

I was here for her. The security team outside were the ones truly watching over them.

I just couldn't stay away from her—not now.

I thought we got somewhere this morning, but obviously not. I would stay, to see if she would change her mind.

Even if the rejection wounded me more than she would ever know.

I strode up to the cabin. There was no longer pep in my step. It had been two days since Elena had told me to put on a shirt and to stay away from her. I was no closer to having her look at me.

She purposefully stayed away.

While I took her son out into the forest for walks, showed him where to climb the best trees, she stayed inside and worked on her computer. She said she needed to work and provide income for her family.

I wanted to tell her that was my job. I was to provide for her. I had enough money to take care of all of her family, and her sister had Locke.

I let out a low, guttural snarl, and the sound reverberated throughout the forest. With a swift movement, I extended my razor-sharp claws and forcefully swiped at the nearby tree, the rough bark splintering under the weight of my power. As I withdrew my hand, a surge of frustration swept over me when I saw the bark healed itself, causing me to curse under my breath.

Even the fae that lived in the forest, close to here, healed everything I destroyed. I couldn't even show my frustration. I wanted something to show off my efforts, and I couldn't even do that.

"You don't even have the urge to fight."

I had to get away from the cabin, away from her. I was succumbing to the darkness again, even with her in my presence. It was like I was being rejected all over again. Only this time, she was right in front of me, and I couldn't do a damn thing about it.

I had gone up to clean myself and make sure I had enough clothes, so I didn't have to return for a few days. I needed to stay with her to get my dragon stronger. Do I push her more? How did I know what was too far or not?

"I never liked your affection. You were always too much."

I could do it to a certain point with my friends. I knew them; I didn't know Elena that well, and her past male wasn't good.

After texting Switch to dig up more information about Elena's past, which I shouldn't have, but I was desperate, I found out the bastard beat her. It was one police report, a hit to the face. While it was just one report, I knew damn well it happened multiple times.

I couldn't force her to talk to me. I couldn't force her to do anything because I didn't want to cause a flashback, cause her stress.

I pinched the bridge of my nose and felt the heaviness of the bag I carried at my side. The walk back to the cabin should have brought me joy to see her, but it brought dread.

I was failing.

My dragon scowled at me in the darkness. He wanted me to take her from day one. He's the darker side I've only ever let out once. Just once and it damn near killed me when I did.

Not this time. I would not let him take over.

It isn't like he could anyway; we haven't gotten any stronger because she won't get near us.

A stick snapped to the right of me. My nose jutted toward the sound, and I took a deep breath. It was Abuela, her citrus and patchouli scent hit me. She lowered herself to the ground a few yards away and moved the leaves in front of her.

"Never seen moss like this. It's got sparkles in it."

I lowered my shoulders to change my direction toward her. "That's because it's a fae moss. Don't ask me what it's called, I'm not a fae botanist. It helps heal trees from damage."

Abuela hummed. "Yes, like the one you took your anger out on over there." She nodded her head toward the once-sliced tree.

"Yeah." I scratched the back of my head. "What are you doing out here? I thought I told you it isn't safe." While the club was out watching, they must have thought it was okay when I was close enough to the cabin.

However, I'd warned everyone that they had to stay in the cabin if I wasn't there. Locke was still out roaming. His wolf was still unpredictable, even if he said he was the one with more control. I wouldn't risk Elena and her family getting hurt. It seemed that Abuela didn't listen to anyone.

Abuela waved her hand in dismissal. "My time isn't up yet. I know how I'm going to go, and it's not by a wolf." She put her hands on her knees and stood up. "I came out here to talk to you before you came back in. Needed a break from Tajah. She wanted to know my life story." She rolled her eyes.

I ran my hand through my hair. "What do you want to talk about? When we get back, I can get Luis outside and have him burn off some energy—"

"Stop it." Abuela stepped toward me. She came chest to chest with me and showed no fear.

Not that she would. She was a formidable woman.

"For a dragon, you sure are a little chickenshit!"

Ouch.

I stepped back to give us space. My dragon huffed in frustration. He couldn't do anything to this woman because it would upset Elena, and he knew very well I was a—*chicken shit*.

"You gave up on her right away. Just one time she told you to stay away, and you gave up." Abuela threw her hands up in the air. "You haven't even taken off your shirt again. If you did, you would have her in the palm of your hand."

I ran my hand down my chest.

"She said she didn't want to see it." I pouted. I wouldn't say I'd been doing pushups and crunches ever since that night.

Abuela rolled her eyes. "Because she liked it. She liked it too much. I'm sure your dragon nose could smell it. Thank the gods I didn't. She hasn't so much looked at another man since what happened to her so long ago, because she is worried about Luis and me. She needs this, needs you."

"I haven't seen her look at me. I haven't so much as smelled any arousal since that day." I winced. Probably should not have told her I could smell her granddaughter's arousal.

Abuela scoffed. "She looks at you when you aren't looking. It is the most sickening puppy love I have ever seen. I swear, Luis and I want to throw up every time it happens. And as for not smelling her, maybe you don't want to smell it because you are so self-defeating. I know, I hear that stupid vibration noise between those walls myself, and I'm half deaf." She stuck her finger in her ear and gave it a jiggle.

My dragon lifted his head from his resting stance, in my head. She had been... pleasing herself?

And I missed it?

"Wait, what? Why didn't I hear?" I stepped toward her and grabbed hold of her arm.

"Because you don't listen, or smell, obviously. Too self-destructing. You don't give yourself enough credit. That bond is there to pull you together, and you are sitting in the living room like a floppy fish, feeling sorry for yourself." She pulled her arm away. "Fight for her." She put her fist in my face. "Tip her over the edge."

"How do you know so much about a bond? You're a human, you—"

"I know more than you, obviously! *She* told me. The Moon Goddess told me all I needed to know. She said you would need a push, and then once Elena takes that step... you will be fine." Abuela patted my arm like all was well.

I shook my head in disbelief and walked away from her. She stayed behind me as we drew closer to the cabin. "How do you know about the Moon Goddess? About any of this? How are you even a witch?"

Abuela chuckled to herself and brushed her long, salt and pepper colored hair behind her ear. "I come from a long line of witches. Well, humans who wanted to be witches. I believe my blood holds some witch blood, with some things I've been able to do and conjure." Her lips curled into a smile. "Along with being able to hide my name, I have also conjured up small protection spells for our home in Venezuela to hide us from blood relatives who are hunting us." She sighed. "I'm not as strong as I once was, though."

We ascended the creaking wooden steps, each one emitting a soft groan under our weight, until we reached the weathered porch, where she settled into the worn rocking chair. Leaning against the rough railing, I felt its coolness seep through my clothing. Crossing my arms, I embraced the comforting late afternoon breeze, mingling with the scent of fresh forest air and blooming flowers that wove up the post.

"I spent most of my magic on my two granddaughters and great grandson. I came across a text when Emmie was young about the Moon Goddess's gift of soul mates. I wanted my descendants to have that. The only way for them to receive such a gift was to be mated to a supernatural."

I tilted my head curiously.

"There was a ritual, an ancient one. My daughters bring it up every so often, making fun of me for it, but they will see why I did it." She laughed solemnly. "I bore myself to the goddess, begged for her mercy to shine her light on my family, to bless them with lovers that would protect them. Love them. Treat them right."

Abuela's eyes warmed with unshed tears. "And she did. She promised me so. She gave me a vision of their future pairings. A wolf and a dragon." She shook her head in disbelief. "Took me a while to accept it. Your dragon is beautiful, by the way." She smiled and looked out over the forest.

I wiped a hand down my face. "I still don't—"

"You don't have to know everything. You don't have to know my history; how I came to know shifters, packs. I know Elysian is real. Just know that I know. The goddess promised my granddaughters soulmates, even before I asked. Their souls were destined to be yours and Locke's in repayment for what has happened to both of you. This entire club—they will get their repayment in this life or the next." She stood up and walked toward me.

If I could have backed away from her, I would. If she knew so much, did she know of my past? Did she know every detail?

A smile played across her lips. "And you think she would care what happened to you?"

Fuck!

I turned away from her, and my chest rose and fell rapidly.

"She won't care. You don't know her yet, but she won't. Because you both share pain, you will heal each other. You just need to make the first move."

My dragon purred in my chest. His soothing vibrations calmed me despite the anxiety thrumming through my body. I gripped hold of the post, and my head rested on the wood. I took in a deep breath, smelling the flowers.

"And what about Luis? You said that he will get a mate, too?" She was at the railing, looking out over the trees, a sad look on her face.

"He will, in time. His future is still uncertain. The right pieces have to fall into place. I will be gone and won't be a part of seeing it through."

I shook my head. "You are a vibrant woman, I don't see you passing anytime soon."

She hummed appreciatively. "My time is short. It is time to pay the price for using so much magic. As long as the people I love are cared for, I will gladly go into the stars with a willful heart."

With that, I heard her footsteps fall away from me. She opened, then closed, the door with a light click. I could hear Luis's sounds of amazement through the door.

A purple light exploded on the inside. I stepped to the window and saw Elena, who sat in a chair. She was holding her cane again, a strained smile on her face.

While Abuela's words hung heavy, my mate was at the forefront of my mind.

Was she hurting because I wasn't there?

My dragon reared up his head, his claws scraped inside me to pay attention.

How dare you not try harder? he thought.

I put my forehead against the glass.

Why was dealing with a mate so much harder than dealing with my friends? I couldn't control my emotions around her.

It hurt too much when she rejected me, and now I must face the fact that I needed to step up first. I needed to force my hand. Show her that I would not go anywhere.

My dragon's deep chuckle reverberated inside me. While he never spoke to me before, I could understand his intentions and wants.

A playful thought came to mind.

If Abuela was right, and Elena wanted me as much as I wanted her, I could put her to the test. If she resembled her sister, and someone provoked her, she would take the bait.

Was the plan slightly evil? *Yes.*

Would it pull her out of her shell? Most definitely.

I rolled my lips together and chuckled. This would be a night I would tell our little fledglings of... one day.

CHAPTER ELEVEN

Elena

I knew it was too good to be true. The lack of pain from the past few days came back with a vengeance.

I watched Tajah show a series of magic tricks to Luis for a few hours. Tajah's magic tricks captivated Luis the whole time. They started small, but grew bigger over time.

Tajah flickered the lights on and off at first, then moved Abuela's crystals around the room. She even had Luis levitate, but I think none of it was as impressive as moving the plane across the sky while we were inside of it.

It took time for Luis to warm up to Tajah. Which was odd because Luis was always friendly with everyone he first met. When I excused myself to use the restroom, the awkwardness had vanished by the time I returned. By the time the afternoon wore on, they were thick as thieves.

Tajah brought up my ailments and said she would check her spell books for a numbing potion to help with my pain. I told her not to bother. While it may numb my pain, it wasn't a cure.

Tajah still waved me off like it was not a problem for her to look. I didn't have any hope for much of anything in return.

In a few years, I would be indefinitely confined to a wheelchair.

The door opened, and Abuela walked back in. She immediately came to sit beside me and rested her hand on my back. She could tell when I wasn't feeling my best, despite the smile I put on my face for Luis. I didn't want him to know I was in pain this afternoon.

Tajah's feminine hand wielded a sphere in the air, conjuring a luminous ball of vibrant purple light that hung weightlessly before her. Luis, his eyes widening in awe, leaned closer, his breath catching in anticipation. Beretta, a mischievous grin played on her lips, nudged Luis towards the enchanted ball. He let out a high-pitched scream when he touched it. In an instant, the ball erupted into a dazzling ball of lights, engulfing the entire space with a kaleidoscope of shimmering colors that danced and flickered, transforming the cabin surroundings into a rainbow of colors.

Had I not watched all the dazzling magic earlier, I would have been worried about Luis getting hurt. But, as I observed how they had treated and watched over Luis throughout the afternoon, I felt comfortable enough.

I had assumed they were part of the care team when they first arrived to relieve Anaki. Only to find out that they were there of their own accord to ask Abuela questions. Anaki only left to grab more clothes, and more likely, to get away from me.

Tajah took some of Abuela's blood to test, to help find out more about our ancestors. She was very interested in why Abuela understood and wielded as much magic as she did.

Meanwhile, I felt like a terrible granddaughter because I didn't have any idea she was using magic to keep us safe.

"I knew Abuela was special," Luis said. "Abuela could always put me to sleep as a baby when I had colic and Mama couldn't stand. Abuela said she used a magic song."

Abuela laughed and shook her head.

Now I'm wondering if that was true.

The door creaked open, and Anaki strode in. My body instantly responded, especially since he didn't have a shirt on.

Dios Mio, what the mierda is this man doing to me?

It was all I could do not to look at him. Just his presence alone would make my heart race. To show indifference to him was difficult, especially when he showed so much care to Luis.

Made my ovaries want to release all the eggs.

I groaned and rolled my eyes. Do not go there.

He stepped deeper into the room, a bag in his hand. As he set it down, Luis went barreling toward him to give him a hug. "Anaki! I missed you!"

Anaki smiled. "I was only gone a couple of hours. I'm sure Beretta and Tajah kept you occupied."

"The boy is mine now." Tajah leaned back in her chair. "Magic is way cooler than dragons."

Anaki scoffed. "Sure. Whatever you say."

"She has shown me magic, and you haven't shown me your dragon. Even Bear and Nadia have shown me their animals," Luis confessed.

Anaki placed his hand on his heart. "You wound me. I'm still healing. Soon, I will shift, and you will be so jealous of me."

And why did I find that idea so hot? When we saw Nadia' and Bear's animals, they were cute and fuzzy. Sure, they were dangerous, but a dragon? They were known to be fierce in legends.

I couldn't see Anaki as fierce. He was everything light and happy.

I needed someone calm, sweet. Just like him.

He was everything I wanted but couldn't have.

I bit my tongue. It wasn't like he was into me anyway; he was just part of the care team. His flirting hadn't gone unnoticed, but it was just part of his personality, that's all.

Anaki patted Luis on the head. "Sorry to say, but you will have to deal with Tajah longer. I have to work tonight."

My ears perked up. He won't be around?

I internally scoffed at myself. Why should I care? This is what I wanted, right? To stay as far away from him as possible? Who cares if he was the center of my fantasies with those gray sweatpants, those tight muscle shirts he wore, and how he doted on me even when I gave him the evil eye?

It was so hard to stay away from him, even if I wanted to touch him. Feel that warmth spread across my body and made my aches and pains go away.

Luis hung his head. "But we were going to play Uno tonight."

Abuela chastised from her seat on the couch. "He has other jobs than watching us, Luis. Besides, you're going to hurt Tajah and Beretta's feelings."

Beretta let out a soft cry. She curled up her hand, resembling a kitten, to wipe away an imaginary tear. "I thought we had become friends. I was going to show you my panther."

Luis' eyes widened. "You'd show me your panther?"

Luis stepped away, his young squirrel brain taking him elsewhere.

Their conversation faded into the background while my panic rose.

Anaki wouldn't be here tonight. I had comfort knowing he was close in just the few days I've known him. I wasn't sure why. He had a way of calming me when no one else could.

Maybe it was because it was the first time I've had trust in a man. One that didn't look so imposing and looked like I was a pebble in his shoe. One I didn't have to prove my worth to.

He knew I had a son and a sickness I couldn't control. A sister who was a pain in everyone's ass and a grandmother who claims she is a witch.

He accepted me, but I couldn't accept myself.

The conversations rose, and when I came back to my senses, I saw that Anaki no longer stood at the door. My eyes bulged and I rose to go to the kitchen. I acted as calmly as I could, since I didn't want to show my panic.

Was he gone? Did he leave already? I glanced out the window as I tried to see his fading figure. There wasn't anything there, and then I felt the heat of a body behind me.

I knew who it was. The aches in my body faded away in an instant. His warm breath tickled my ear as he whispered, "Looking for me?"

I jumped in surprise anyway, spinning around to face him. His eyes bore into mine, a mischievous glint dancing within them. The proximity of his body sent a wave of warmth through me, and I struggled to maintain my composure.

"What are you doing?" I stammered, trying to sound nonchalant.

Anaki flashed a charming smile, his dimples deepening. "Couldn't stay away, could I? Especially when someone was missing me so much."

I rolled my eyes, attempting to mask the rapid beating of my heart at his words. "Don't flatter yourself. I just... noticed you were gone."

His gaze softened, a hint of understanding in his eyes. "You missed me," he stated simply.

Before I could protest further, Anaki closed the distance between us, his hand reaching out to tuck a loose strand of hair behind my ear. The tender gesture tugged at my heartstrings, and I found myself leaning into his touch despite my better judgment.

"I missed you, too," he confessed softly, his voice barely above a whisper. "Earlier, and the past few days, you've been pushing me away."

My heart felt like it was about to burst out of my chest as I searched his eyes for any sign of deceit. But all I found was sincerity and something more... something that mirrored the unspoken emotions swirling within me.

As if drawn by an invisible force, our faces inched closer until our lips were mere inches apart.

"You are part of a care team. You are here to keep us quiet. That's all." I managed to say.

Anaki chuckled, both hands landed on either side of my hips to pin me. There was no way out. His body was flush with mine, and I felt the large prominent thickness between his legs that had been the focus of all my fantasies.

How does it even fit in those jeans?

Anaki chuckled. "Don't think I would call just anyone *love*, feed them, make sure they take their medicine, kiss their forehead when they are scared. Even a care team has limits, Mama."

My heart raced.

"And you really think I was supposed to stay in the cabin all this time?" He shook his head. He leaned forward and whispered in my ear. "Nah, I was supposed to rotate. Take turns. But I just couldn't stay away from you."

My face turned six shades of red as I pushed him away, which did nothing to make him move. He stepped back and rubbed the back of his head. He was nervous, and I instantly felt my heart ache for doing what I did.

I was such a prick!

But Anaki smiled and nodded to the two bottles of medication on the counter. "Make sure you take those. You almost forgot last night." He gave a knowing look.

I bit my lip and drank him in one last time. He was now wearing a black meshed shirt, and I could see his nipple rings through it. I felt myself become hot with pleasure, and I immediately put both hands to my face to try to rub the picture out of my head.

Why did he have to look so damn delicious? He was so tempting, and I don't think I could handle much more of him without breaking.

"I'll see you later tonight." Anaki bent over to grab his bag. I got a magnificent view of his ass. Thoughts of doing taboo things to that tight, muscular hunk of meat popped into my head, and had my thighs squeezing together. My breasts felt heavy, at the idea of ordering him to suck my nipples until they hurt, and to tell him what a good dragon he was for taking care of me. It made my breath hitch, and I swore a tear ran down my leg.

Anaki paused. His back tensed and he glanced back at me, clearing his throat. "Right, uh. I'll see you later."

Tajah let out an evil laugh and tossed her phone onto the coffee table littered with Abuela's crystals. "Well not for the foreseeable future, Anaki. It appears you are off the hook, watching everyone in the cabin. Not that I see it as punishment, I prefer my time here, with my future sorcerer." She threw a wink at Luis.

Anaki and I both darted our heads in Tajah's direction.

"I may have had Switch spy on your sister." Tajah smiled at me. "He got caught, and Locke was in the crossfire," she cackled. "Your sister is quite the woman. I cannot wait to see what she does for the club in the future." Tajah wrapped her fingers around Beretta's arm and nuzzled into her.

I didn't have any idea what was going on with Emm and this Switch guy. I was more worried that Anaki wasn't coming back. My head darted between the two.

Anaki straightened his back. Giving no signs of worry. "That's great. I'll stop by every once in a while and take Luis out for some adventures. Sound good?"

Wait a second, he was just going to give up on me?

Well, you pushed him away, multiple times. What did you expect?

My mouth opened and closed, with the protest on the tip of my tongue.

"Have fun at ladies' night," Beretta purred. "I heard they will be extra ravenous." Her smile gleamed predatorily.

"Ladies night?" I questioned as Anaki put his hand on the doorknob. He twisted it, the click echoing into the cabin.

"Yeah, it's when the ladies are in charge. They can ask the men to dance, bartenders can dance on the bar..."

Beretta let out a bark of laughter. "Anaki is their favorite. I've never seen someone meant for a pole more than him."

My eyes widened. "You p-pole dance?" I stuttered. "Wait, cover Luis' ears!" Abuela already had his ears covered and was smiling wildly as she listened.

Anaki puffed out his chest. "Yeah, I do. Water dragons are known for their seduction dances. If you had engaged in more conversation, perhaps I would have shown you." He wiggled his eyebrows. Anaki opened the door to step outside.

Beretta shouted before he stepped out the door. "Do you give lap dances as well?"

Red hot anger and jealousy surged through me. Did he?

Anaki stared at me, a smile playing across his lips.

"Only for those I find, extra special." He winked and shut the door.

I stood there, staring at the door, waiting for my brain to reboot, until I turned and a chancla hit me in the back of the head.

"¡Dios Mio! Mierda! What is wrong with you! He has thrown everything at you! Is your pussy broken! Ay!" Abuela lay back on the sofa, my son's ears covered by Tajah, who held back a smile.

"I'm going to die without seeing my daughters with their soul mates. I've given you everything on a silver platter, and none of you will accept it. Are you trying to bring dishonor to me? Why? Why was I cursed with ungrateful granddaughters?" she wailed. "I danced naked for nothing."

"Abuela!" I screamed. "You stop this nonsense right now! I have stayed quiet and gone along with all this!" I waved my arms around the cabin.

"I have done quite well not freaking out about this supernatural shit, leaving our home, being here and now you are upset I am not flirting with a supposed dragon? What is wrong with you? I have a son! I have a debilitating illness! I have a family to look after! Our future—"

"Bullshit!" Abuela stood up and marched toward me, the other chancla in hand. She shoved it close to my face. "Anaki is perfect for you! In every way, he is your match."

I gritted my teeth. "Why would he want someone as broken as me? With the past I have? The doubt, the pain, the suffering. When he is so perfect?"

The room fell silent. Darkness threatened to swallow it whole. Not even my son's quiet footsteps could be heard as I felt him hug my side. He knew his biological dad was a wicked man. I never told him the extent because he didn't need to know. He knew he was safe from him, that he was gone, and I had no intention of giving him a fatherly figure because I worried about his safety and mine.

"I like Anaki," he whispered into my leg. "He's a good man."

I let out a shuddering breath. "It isn't so simple, mijo." I rubbed my hand into his soft hair. He was too young to understand.

"If I may," Tajah interrupted. "While I am not your sister's biggest fan, right now, I like you very much. You are much stronger than I expected, and I know some of Anaki's past. You feel you are broken; most of the Iron Fang members are broken, too. Terrible pasts, heartbreaking, worth dying, they're so terrible."

Beretta squeezed Tajah's hand in comfort.

"Anaki's pain is deep, I sense it. He's as scared as you are, but unlike you, he will fight and give what he feels for you a chance."

Tears stung my eyes. He shouldn't. I wasn't worth it.

"Elena," Abuela whispered. I shook my head, not wanting to listen. "I know you don't want to hear me out. I hope you will. All those years telling you that you have a soul mate; you have one. Anaki is your soul mate. Your fated mate."

I shook my head again. "You're crazy."

"Do you feel a pull toward him?" Beretta asked. "Can't stay away, need him, he consumes your thoughts?"

I stared at her. That was lust. That is all it was.

"Why would we lie? This club full of misfits is real, yet you won't believe this? When he touches you, what do you feel?"

"Stop," I whispered. "This is insane."

Abuela smirked. "You don't have to believe it now. But be nicer to the boy. He's trying hard. And watching him pine over you is damn near painful."

My mouth dropped.

Beretta slapped her arms down on the chair she sat in. We all winced in surprise. "That's it. Let's go."

"Go, go where?" I asked incredulously.

"Go get dressed, dolled up. We are heading out. You get to go watch Anaki at work. Let's get the bond at work here. We haven't been here to see the tension, but just those few minutes of witnessing it, I bet it's stifling."

Abuela nodded. "It is. Makes me hot and bothered." She pulled on her blouse several times to get the air circulating. "If it wasn't about my granddaughter getting laid, I might get a little turned on."

I groaned and rolled my head back. This wasn't happening, it couldn't be happening. "I need to watch after Luis. We were going to play Uno, right, mijo?"

Luis shook his head. "No, you go ahead. I see you all the time. Some time apart would be nice."

Shot to the heart.

Tajah played with her hair. "Ah, what comes out of the mouth of babes.

I suggest you get ready. Put on something sexy. You won't be able to get on the main floor with him, on account your sister will be there, but I'm sure he will smell you from afar. Dragon noses are powerful, and I'm sure he knows your scent."

"M-my scent? He can smell me from far away?"

Beretta stepped toward me, her yellow eyes flashed. "Yes, your scent and your arousal. Tajah and I smelled it when you were both in the kitchen, and when Anaki bent over to pick up his bag. What were you thinking when you were staring at his ass?"

I gasped and stepped away from her. "He-he didn't smell me. He couldn't—"

"He did," Tajah said, still holding my son's ears. "I could smell his arousal, too. You are going to just love dragon--"

"Stop! Enough!" I covered my ears. "I'll get dressed! None of you say another word!"

CHAPTER TWELVE

Anaki

"You aren't supposed to worry about what's going on with the cartel. You are supposed to keep your mate and her family safe," Bear said as I jumped over the bar.

"Yeah, but what if my mate asks? I want to give her all the answers. I don't want to seem less than—"

As I turned around, the deafening sound of Bear's fist slamming on the bar echoed through the dimly lit room, causing a collective flinch from the patrons. The acrid smell of spilled drinks and stale beer wafted in the air, mixing with the faint aroma of cigarette smoke. The sudden tension was there, but my dragon scoffed at him. Ignoring Bear's narrowed, piercing gaze, I defiantly puffed out my chest, feeling the coolness of the body oil on my bare skin and the slickness beneath my fingertips.

I was all prepared for the excitement of Ladies' Night, but Bear, seeing me all greased up, always made him uncomfortable.

Bear sighed and shook his head. "I've got nothing to tell you. Even from the inner circle, I know nothing about the cartel right now. Keep your phone on you. Once I know something, I'll let you know."

"What about Idris?" I leaned across the bar and grabbed his hand. "Anything with him? Are the two connected?"

Bear growled and ran his hand through his beard. "Not a hundred percent sure. It is still too early to tell. I wouldn't be surprised if they were. Not the way things are lining up so perfectly." He scowled.

Bear went to turn away but stopped, half-turned. "Your packages are by the cave. Figured you would want them there instead of the cabin. Tajah even teleported your mate's suitcase. I guess they have high hopes for you tonight."

My smile widened drastically. Bear shook his head and stomped off, ready to open the doors to the bar. This was going to be the most memorable night of my life, and Locke's.

Anytime there were men dancing on the bar—ladies in control—and alcohol was involved, you knew it was going to be a good time.

Tonight, my mate was going to be here and I couldn't wait to stir some emotions out of her. She's kept to herself, holding herself back for too long, and seeing that flash of jealousy in the cabin was enough to make my confidence soar.

Her arousal really showed that she wanted me. I just had to fucking pay attention and not seep back into the dark recesses of my mind. That sweet scent of sea-salted caramel called to me now that I knew her scent so well. My dragon and I salivated for a taste. I couldn't wait to stay buried between her thighs for hours, if she would let me. That image alone could have made me come right behind the bar.

Would she order me to lick her pussy? Demand that I pleasure her in front of these females to stake a claim?

I could feel a shimmer of pleasure race down my spine. My tail demanded to make an appearance. I let out a groan and forced myself to hold back any sort of shift.

I was not a male who hunted as thoroughly as my brothers here in the

MC. I did not have a dominant personality in the slightest. I liked to play and flirt. I did not care to pin my mate down and order her submissiveness.

I would not mind if the roles were reversed.

I trusted the goddess wholeheartedly, even though I'd been hurt in the past, because of Journey. She had told the club, countless times, that the goddess was trying to right her wrongs.

Please, Goddess, let her choose me.

Accept me.

Want me.

I surveyed the dimly lit bar, it was already filled with a lively atmosphere. The sound of laughter mixed with the rhythmic beats of the music pounded my sensitive ears. The energy in the room grew, making me feel alive and eager for Elena to arrive.

The Moonlight Outcasts opted to start out with their DJ equipment before they switched over to live music.. They switched on the strobe lights, the music blared and thrummed through the floors. I could feel the rhythm pumping through my body as I pulled out my phone for the last time tonight, to check for any last messages.

Beretta: Your mate's dolled up. Don't fuck it up.

Right, thanks.

I chuckled and threw my phone under the bar where we kept our stuff. The other two bartenders who enjoyed dancing on the bar for tips nodded to let me know they were ready. Pulling off their shirts to signal our start, I leapt onto the bar top with more confidence than I'd ever had before.

The crowd roared with excitement as the music pulsed, filling the room with energy. Women hooted and hollered, reaching out to slip dollar bills into our waistbands as we danced. The lights flashed and sparkled, casting a kaleidoscope of colors across the walls and ceiling.

I moved with a fluid grace, letting my body sway and twist to the beat. The scent of alcohol and perfume mingled around me, adding to the heady atmosphere of the bar. As I scanned the crowd, my heart raced with anticipation, searching for a familiar face.

My dragon instantly felt her when she entered the building. It wasn't through the front door, but the back. I could smell her from here, and I heard her footsteps. While the movements around me were fast, everything else was in slow motion.

Would she like my body, my movements? It was for her, not for the people here. Sweat dripped down my brow, my body contorting around the pole, and when I looked up, feeling the heat of her gaze, I nearly collapsed, seeing her staring at me with wide eyes and her lips parted.

The music reached its peak, and the women screamed when I landed with a thud on my knees. The glasses shook, and some fell over, covering the bar with liquids. I laughed, seeing Emm on the same side of the bar where Elena, her sister, sat upstairs.

How fucking ironic.

"Well, hello there, sugar. You made it." I told her, giving her a wink.

Emm glanced away from me. Now that my dragon was strengthening and my mate was so close, I would release a massive amount of pheromones since I was dancing for her. It wouldn't affect Emm so much because she had her own mate in the bar. It would still make her uncomfortable.

"Aw, come on, can't handle me at my worst. You don't deserve me at my best!" I rubbed my hand down my abs. "But, really, I think this is my best."

Emm snorted and pushed on my bare shoulder. "Just get me my drink, you perv."

In a few short minutes, I returned to her side of the bar and held out a Pina Colada. Emm raised her eyebrow and took the fruity drink. "I know you have more than one drink. It depends on your mood."

She was a whisky drinker, but tonight she needed something sweeter. Well, sweeter tasting anyway. Especially with what Locke wanted me to do for him. He'd appreciate her tasting like his personal favorite.

Emm stared at me dumbly, and I tapped on the bar with my hand before I hopped back on it again and rubbed my body up and down the pole.

Time passed, and I got the signal to start the body shot portion of the evening.

"Alright, ladies and gentlemen, time for some body shots!" I called out. My voice was strong, my aura exuded across the bar. The members who knew me well enough understood that I was not a threat.

Several couples came and went. Only mated or soon-to-be mated couples were allowed.

The auction was rigged. Only the males who were destined to be mated to the woman on the bar were allowed to be up there. If we knew a woman didn't have a mate in-house, she was refused politely, and told there was a sign-up list and would have to try another night.

But now was the best part: our president would claim his mate, then I could go claim mine.

Piece of cake.

I grabbed the tequila and took a small swig. Not that it would help with any liquid courage since my dragon was becoming stronger by the second. I felt the heat of Elena's gaze on me the entire time. I did my best to ignore her. She needed to see me in my element, lust after me like I have lusted after her.

Nadia and Delilah urged Emm to step on the stool and sit on the bar. I tilted Emm's head back and dripped the tequila into her mouth. She giggled, some running down her mouth and neck.

Yep, Locke was going to have a field day with Emm.

The girls continued to tell Emm she had a choice to stop, but she was all for it. She was brave, just like her sister. She took it all in. That was when I had to do the next step, as requested by the president.

Man, he had some balls.

I pulled the blindfold out of my back pocket. "Let's make it interesting," I announced. "Let's make her blind!"

Once the blindfold was settled, the bidding began. The money went to the bar, not to the woman on stage. Everyone was aware of that, including the women who signed up.

Technically, Emm didn't sign up. We just threw her into it, but who cared? She was the future Luna, anyway.

I started at the normal number, twenty bucks, because we were supposed to be a low-class biker bar. For the show, members would throw out numbers, and when the supposed mate called out the agreed number, we would stop.

Before anyone could bid, Locke threw out a grand, and the room went silent.

Show off.

While I acted completely shocked by the whole act, I knew damn well where this was going. Locke was going to eat his Luna out on the bar while everyone watched. Well, if they dared to watch. I wasn't going to, because that was my future sister-in-law, and I had a little more respect than that.

As I continued to pour the tequila slowly over Emm's leg so it would dribble down to her toes and Locke could lick it up to her pussy, I glanced up at the second-floor balcony where Elena stood wide eyed.

Was she staring at her sister or me?

Hopefully me, because seeing your sister getting eaten out by her boyfriend would have been weird.

Elena's face heated when I put two of my fingers into the stream of alcohol. I brought them to my lips and spread my fingers, sensually licking between them.

She bit on her bottom lip, her fingers digging into the banister. I tried to hold back a smile, trying to be sexy as hell and hold back the massive erections in my pants.

Compression shorts don't fail me now.

A fellow bartender tapped my shoulder, handing me a lime. "Open." I barked at Emm and she opened her mouth so I could place the lime in it for Locke to suck the juices from her lips.

My pants felt bearably tight while I waited for my president to finish their weird courting ritual.

I kept my leg up against Emm's back while Locke put more pressure into her body and ravished her. I dared to look back up at Elena, smelling her scent above all others in the bar.

I didn't want anyone to have smelled her, to know she was there, an unclaimed human above the bar watching the debauchery below.

My dragon's pheromones grew without my permission, and I snarled at the men beside me.

It didn't affect Locke, he was powerful even if he hadn't mated Emm yet.

My dragon was on his last thread of patience to go feral for her.

Claim.

It felt like ages passed until Locke took Emm off the bar. Elena disappeared from sight, and that was when I knew I needed to leave.

I patted the bartender on the shoulder next to me. He jumped away in fear. My brow furrowed, and my dragon roared inside me.

Shit, I forgot he gets pissy.

I grabbed my phone and got out of there, ready to meet Elena at the spiral staircase. Beretta blocked her to keep her out of sight from her sister and pushed her down a hallway.

"Have fun," Beretta smirked and walked into the bar. Elena grabbed me by the arm and pushed me against the wall.

Holy shit!

"What was that?" Fire blazed in her eyes when she looked at me.

Was she mad? She was hot when she was mad.

"I was working." I shrugged my shoulders. "Like what I do?"

She growled at me and crossed her arms. "I don't like you dancing in front of other girls. I don't like you being all…" She waved her arms in front of me and grunted.

"Sweaty? Oily?" I rubbed my hands up and down my body, flexing my muscles as I did.

"You oiled?" she gasped.

I shrugged my shoulders. "Yeah, makes me shiny. It's more appealing. The women like it."

Elena growled again.

"Aw, are you jealous, Mama?" I cooed and stepped forward. I brushed a pretty, brown tendril of hair behind her ear.

"Er, uh, no! I'm not jealous." She shook her head. "Why would I be jealous? I could never be—"

"Well, I smelled you," I interrupted. "I could smell your arousal all the way down at the bar."

Her eyes widened. "You didn't, there is no way—"

"I did, because my body is completely in tune with yours." I cautiously stepped forward. As I approached, she instinctively stepped back, her shoes scraping against the cold surface. I could see the uncertainty in her eyes as she slowly retreated. Her scent bloomed, and my nostrils flared, taking it in.

I cupped her cheek. "I know you want me, love. Just know I want you, too." I ran a finger down her chin, then across her lips. It still smelled of tequila and I had an urge to stick it into her mouth and ask, no, beg her to suck. But I didn't.

Her chest heaved, her breasts rising and falling within the little black dress she wore. We stood there in silence as I waited for her to reply.

She cleared her throat. "Ah, fuck it!" She pushed her hands into my chest and took me by surprise. I grunted, hitting the other wall. She grabbed the back of my hair and pulled me into the most electrifying kiss I'd ever had.

CHAPTER THIRTEEN

Elena

He drove me mad.

When I saw him dancing on a bar, moving his hips and straddling the pole, I wanted nothing more than to be *that pole*. I wanted him to dance around me, lick the sweat off my body. I wanted to trail my finger down every crevice of his body while he made me the center of his world.

Was I crazy?

Jealousy rose its ugly head as I watched the other women at the bar stuff money into his tight black jeans. He was mine, he wanted me, right?

But you pushed him away. Several times.

Not anymore. Not the way my body was responding. I could feel his presence, like he was standing beside me, even from across the room. I wanted him.

After much pushing and insisting from Abuela that I go have some fun and not worry about Luis, I put on my only nice dress, and Abuela rushed me out the door. Even Luis looked excited when he waved Beretta and me off.

I remembered to take my medication. Luckily, my pain had gone down to a dull ache. The excitement must have made my body forget I was in pain this afternoon. When I rushed with Beretta to the second floor of the bar, seeing Anaki glistening under the cheap strobing lights from the dance floor, my pain was long gone.

It was like I could feel him, as if he was right next to me the entire time.

I didn't even pay attention to my sister and Locke, and the debauchery they were doing in front of the entire bar. She was a big girl and could handle herself. Once they finished and left to have their good times, it was my turn. It had been too long since I had a man want me the way Anaki did.

Not just wanted me, but cared about my family, too.

I didn't want to give in so easily, so when I stood in front of him, I had planned to give him a hard time, but what a pointless endeavor that was.

I wanted him and not just for the night, and maybe that's why I was fighting so hard.

My body and my heart were falling for him so hard and fast, and I couldn't explain why.

It was the softness in his eyes, the tender way he looked at me. I wanted to care for him the way he did for me when we first met. I was lost, but he found me. Now it was my turn to take care of him.

"Ah, fuck it!"

I wrapped my arms around him, and I was completely done. D-O-N-E. I claimed him and I would not let him go.

My fingers dove into his hair, and I pulled him into a searing kiss.

His lips were warm and eager against mine, and I felt a surge of electricity shoot through me as our bodies pressed together. In that moment, every-thing else faded away. It was just him and me, lost in the whirlwind of heat.

I pressed my body closer to his until he finally wrapped his arms around me and pulled my hips closer to his so I could feel his large erection dig into my stomach.

Dios Mio, he was large. I didn't know which way his dick was facing, up or down but I knew I wanted it right then and there.

I parted my mouth and traced my tongue across his lips. He whimpered, and that spurred me on to pull his hair.

He deepened the kiss, his tongue sweeping into my mouth and tangling with mine. The taste of him made my head spin, and I felt my knees weaken.

As he held me tightly, his hands roaming all over my body, I melted into him. He led me to a private corner, where the passion between us intensified. He lifted me off the ground and pressed me against the wall, our bodies undulating in a frenzy of need. My nails scratched the bare muscles of his back, feeling the heat radiating from his skin.

"Shit," he whispered and pressed his cock against me while one of his hands dove into my hair.

I reached down and gripped his erection through his pants, marveling at its size and girth. As I pressed against it, he groaned into my mouth, his hand tightening in my hair as his lips devoured mine.

I didn't know where his cock began and ended. It was everywhere. I felt around the front of his pants. He groaned and grabbed my wrist. He broke the kiss and laid his forehead on mine. "Don't want to go too fast yet."

I groaned. "Why not? If you edge me, I will not be a happy girl."

He hummed thoughtfully. His kisses traced down the side of my neck and into the hollow of my throat. "Trust me, you do not want to go down there yet, but I can certainly make you come."

He turned me around, my dress flaring out around me. The music was blaring, the beat rose, and I was highly aware that anyone could walk around the corner.

"I want you to let loose, love. It's just me and you. No one would dare come back here." He whispered huskily in my ear. "I won't let them."

We swayed to the music, my ass grinding against his crotch. While his hot breath fanned my neck, his hand trailed up my thigh and moved the free-flowing dress to the side. He roamed closer to my underwear and cupped my mound. He hummed appreciatively. "I could smell you when you first walked into the club." He nuzzled my ear. "Why have you fought me so much?"

I panted. My body swayed with his as we danced. I raised my arm over my head, my fingers threaded through his hair. "Trying to save you the trouble. I'm not worth it."

Anaki clicked his tongue. His warm hand rubbed my damp underwear. "Oh, Mama, you are definitely worth the trouble." He bit down on my ear and moved my underwear to the side. My body instantly melted when I felt two hot fingers rub across my clit. "Fuck you are wet, been wet for a while, did you like me dancing for you?"

I moaned and leaned my head back on his shoulder. "Was it for me, or those women out there?" I gritted my teeth.

Anaki huffed. "That was all for you. Once we are in private, I can really show you what me and my dragon can do. I've got a special one that involves a lot of touching."

He shoved two fingers inside me. There was no warming up with just one. He stuck them both inside with eagerness. I cried out, and his hand went over my mouth.

"Now, now, can't have my brothers hearing those cries. Those are for me. My dragon and I can get very jealous, and we can't have him causing a ruckus."

Anaki smirked, his eyes darkening with desire. "You don't have any idea how much I want to take you right here and now." His fingers sped up, and I felt my orgasm building, an electric charge running through my entire body. "But we have all night, and I intend to make it one you'll never forget."

Good, I had hoped for a good dicking.

"More," I demanded. I wasn't at the point of begging, I wanted it and if he even dared tried to pull away, I would grab his wrist and fuck *myself* with his fingers.

His head landed on my shoulder, took in a large breath of my scent, and curled his fingers to rub on my G-spot.

Holy fuck!

"Tight and wet, I'm not sure if you can take it all," he mumbled.

My head leaned back, as his sharp teeth grazed across my neck. I was in utter bliss, falling into the dark ocean of desire. I had no control over my body, as waves of pleasure crashed over me, pulling me under. My mind fogged while I tugged on the back of his hair. All I could focus on was the feeling of his fingers inside of me, each movement causing a new wave of pleasure to crash through me.

Anaki's lips trailed down my neck, leaving a trail of fire in their wake. He whispered something in a language I didn't recognize, but the words were music to my ears. His breath was hot against my skin, and I could feel his desire growing with every passing moment.

He pulled his fingers from my body and brought them to his nose. My stomach lurched with embarrassment, but he smiled at me in reassurance. "This scent will have to do." He rubbed it on one side of his neck, and I saw my arousal glisten there.

"Hold still." His voice was deep and gravely, not like the tenor, playful voice he usually carried. Anaki leaned forward and rubbed his cheek against mine. "No male will touch you, not after this."

I felt warmth cover my muscles. After a good orgasm, I would usually feel tightness in my bones and muscles, and my body would ache because of the tension I created. I knew I would hurt after, but there was none to be found. I never hurt when he was near.

"You're mine, you're stuck with me." Anaki's eyes flickered back and forth from dragon to human several times. Small slits appeared and my pussy fluttered.

A dragon. I let a dragon finger me in the hallway.

"What did you just do?" I snapped back to reality.

Anaki grabbed my hand and pulled me further back into the shadows. He took one last look at the bar behind us and pulled me closer to his body.

"My dragon marked you and, well, used your slick to mark us." He smirked and pulled me further into the dark.

My eyes bulged as I processed what he said, and he laughed as we got closer to the back. An exit illuminated, and he pushed on the door to the alley outside.

"Where are we going?"

Anaki continued to lead me around the corner, where bikes were lined up in a gravel parking space. It was an overflow of bikes, and I noticed some bikes still had their keys in the ignition, which astonished me.

"Come here. As much as I'd like to have you on the back of my bike, we can't take it where we are going."

He grabbed my wrist and pulled me forward to some trucks and SUVs in the lot. He opened the passenger door to the truck, which, of course, was unlocked and pulled me around, pinning me to the car. "You ready for this?"

"Do I have a choice?" I replied playfully.

"Always, with me anyway." He cleared his throat. "If my dragon comes out, I don't know what he'll do. He's kind of obsessed with you."

I jutted out my chin. "And what about you? Do you want me? Kid, chronic illness, baggage and all? I'm a lot to handle, and I can't take the heartbreak. If you don't think you can do this," I waved my hand up and down my body, "I suggest we break it off now, or I'll break your face."

His smile was contagious because I began smiling, too. "I won over Abuela and Luis. Don't think I did that just for a one-night stand, Elena."

I crossed my arms. "We'll see."

Anaki pulled me in by the hips and placed a sweet kiss on my lips.

Just then, we heard the roar of an engine and tires skidding on the road. We both paused and looked around, unable to see anything with the back of the bar blocking our view.

Anaki held me to his body as if to protect me from the sounds. I stared up at him, his jaw tensed, his ears took shape into something pointed, light blue, and topped with silver. Tiny scales traveled up the side of his neck for a brief moment until they were gone.

Holy shit!

His nose flared. "Your sister. She just left. Locke isn't happy about it."

My shoulders dropped. "Your president is trying to woo my sister while she is trying to hunt him... I knew that wouldn't go well."

"He's a good man, Elena... he's done so much—"

"I'm sure he is." I patted his shoulder. "While your methods are unconventional, she's briefly told me about the town. She likes the bar and the people in it. After seeing it for myself, I believe you."

Anaki's eyes brightened.

"And what about me? You believe in me?"

I rolled my eyes. "I don't know, depends on what you got planned for the rest of the night."

Anaki bit his lip and picked me up behind my legs, forcing me to wrap them around his waist, and pinned me to the car. "Is that so?"

I nodded.

"Then, I guess we better get a move on. I'm going to need the rest of the night to prove my worth."

CHAPTER FOURTEEN

Anaki

My dragon demanded to keep her on my lap for the truck ride up the mountain, but the more sensible part of me—the human side—had buckled her up in the passenger seat. That didn't make me keep my hands to myself.

My hand wrapped around her luscious thigh. I perhaps inched further up as the ride went along. She was in a fit of giggles. The walls that once stood tall around her heart were slowly falling. At least, at that moment, they were. Later, when she came to her senses and realized I would never let her go after this, she might change her tune.

Once my dragon had her in our cave, I worried he wouldn't let her go, and the closer we got, the more his tail slashed about in the back of my mind. It reminded me of the documentaries of those alligators and crocodiles of Earth, barrel-rolling their prey before they submerged them under the water.

Only with this, Elena was my prey. She would roll in the sheets from pleasure, and would only surface when my dragon and I had completely consumed her.

It terrified me of what she would think afterward. I had to keep my dragon under control, at least not claim her until I had her permission, which I knew I did not have—yet. I just got her to accept me.

Accept me for what? I'm not sure. For this one-night stand? The date? I don't know what I would do if she just fucked me and left. That would be worse than the rejection when she wouldn't even touch me.

The more I thought, the more my dragon lashed inside me. Elena reached over the console and wrapped her hand around my arm. "Are you alright? You're sweating?"

I didn't have a shirt, too excited to even find my discarded clothes. I cracked the windows to remove some of her scent. Her arousal that I had marked my skin with was the stupidest thing I could do. While my dragon roared with pride that we wore her perfume, it drove me mad.

I swallowed deeply, the taste of nervous anticipation lingering on my tongue, and turned down Bear's driveway. The wheels skidded on the loose gravel, the sound of their friction filling the air with a sharp, gritty scrape. My heart pounded in my chest, its rhythmic thumping resonating in my ears as I hit the turn too hard. In that moment, Elena let out a surprised yelp, her voice echoing through the stillness of the surroundings. "Just excited," I said.

I wasn't going to let her go. No matter what she thought or said.

Elena licked her lips, biting down on the bottom one. Goddess, did she have any idea what she was doing to me? She spread her legs wider. My hand went up higher as we bounced over several holes in the road. Her breasts bounced, and while I had to keep my eyes on the road, they kept wandering to her side of the cab.

"You're stunning, you know that?" I rasped. "Not just your body, but you?"

Her playful seduction turned to a look of surprise. "W-what?"

We pulled up to the cabin, and the lights were on inside. Nadia didn't care for the loud sounds at the bar and was currently babysitting Delilah's pup. I saw her form as she pulled the curtain away to check who was outside, as she held the baby in the crook of her arms. Her vision having improved significantly, she smiled and waved.

I turned my attention back to Elena. "You, Elena. Just you. Just want you to know this isn't just a... fun time for me. I'm serious about this."

Her mouth opened and closed, her arm loosened around mine. Panic set in, and I braced myself for a rejection. She'd rejected me before, so why wouldn't she do it now? I'd have to just try harder.

"You hardly know me." Her touch didn't leave my arm, but I missed how she was wrapped around it like a lifeline. "What you said earlier." She shook her head. "You don't actually want—"

My grip grew stronger around the softness of her thigh. "I absolutely meant everything I said back there." I jerked my head toward the bed of the truck."\ "You are stunning. You raised a child, helped your elder, worked, and took care of yourself. You are sweet and kind and think of others before yourself. My dragon can see your heart, and I can see"—I traced a finger down her cheek—"you. I see you, not the flaws you think your body has."

Why would I say such sweet words to sleep with her? Who would ever do such a thing?

"I—"

I released my grip on her trembling leg, twisting the key and pulling it out of the ignition. As I forcefully kicked open the stubborn door, it swung wide, colliding with the nearby tree, causing a resounding thud and a shower of leaves. My heart pounded in my chest as I hurriedly dashed around to the other side of the truck.

I took in the dazed expression on Elena's face, her eyes lost in a haze after the weight of my words settled upon her.

She was about to get another earful.

I opened the door and put my arm across her body to unbuckle her, then backed away and held out my hand.

"If you take this hand…" she looked down at it, and then back at me. "I will take you. Not just your body, Elena. I will take all of you. Your body, your mind, your soul. Maybe not right away, because I will give you time to process. I can be reasonable. My dragon, not so much," I muttered under my breath. "I'll do my best to keep him under control, though!" I quickly added, my face heated with embarrassment. "I want the complete package. All of you. Not one night, not a couple of days." I waved a finger back and forth between us. "We are a *thing.*"

My dragon roared enough for it to rumble in my chest.

I couldn't say mate, not even soulmate, for her to understand because Abuela had said it before, and she became very upset. I would do the best I could to skip around the word, until I needed to.

My chest continued to vibrate. She stared at it and tilted her head in curiosity.

Elena rubbed her lips together as I waited. Seconds passed that felt like an eternity. Her eyes danced between mine, searching for the truth in my words. In that moment, I could see her weighing her options, considering the gravity of my proposition. I held my breath, waiting for her decision.

Finally, she took a deep breath and placed her small hand in mine. "Okay," she whispered, a hint of vulnerability in her voice.

My smile widened when I pulled her out of the cab and into my arms. She made an "oomph" sound when she landed on my chest, and I twirled her in my arms.

I set her on the ground, grabbed her hand, and pulled her to the trail at the side of the cabin. She looked around her as the cabin began to grow distant. "Wait, wasn't that your place?"

I shook my head. "No, what gave you that idea?" I chuckled and gave her a little pull.

I saw the tiny wrinkle between her brows furrow, and I pressed my thumb between them to straighten it. "I'm a dragon, remember? I have a cave."

Her eyes widened in shock. "Wait, so it's true? I thought it was a joke." She playfully smacked my bare chest.

I rubbed the back of my neck. "No? When I shift, I need somewhere big to stay. My dragon can be sort of a dick and not change back into my human form, so I need a big place. A cave is the best place."

Her hands went to her mouth as she gasped. "You really are a dragon?!"

Isn't that what I have been telling her all this time?

"I mean, I have seen Bear and Nadia shift, so I know they are bears. That was more believable because there are actually bears you see in real life and in zoos, but... a dragon? You don't just see a dragon; they are in fairy tales! Luis will be—oh, he will be so excited." Her eyes beamed.

I puffed out my chest. "Yes, well, what about you? Will you be impressed?"

Why did I have to be so desperate for her affections? I was like one of those wolves that always sought to do anything and everything for their mate. I was just glad my dragon's tail hadn't yet emerged, because it wagged incessantly when she complimented me.

If she gave me pets through my hair, I would be done for.

"I'll have to see first," she said coyly as she approached me. "Depends on the shade of blue."

Compliment denial. I don't know if I liked that or not.

I cleared my throat when she put her hand on my chest. My dragon grumbled, wanting more of her touch on us. Elena's eyes widened, and she placed her palm flat. "Is that your dragon?" she asked.

I nodded and gripped her wrist. "Does he like me touching?" She fluttered her eyelashes.

I nodded again and cleared my throat. "Very much."

She smiled and her hand rubbed down my stomach and to the edge of my pants.

Nope, nope. She cannot go there.

But she's going to in a minute, and that is another conversation.

Fuck!

I pulled her hand away from my raging erections and had her follow me on the trail. Her infectious laughter reverberated through the dense forest, filling the air with joy. Each step she took seemed to resonate like thunder to my healing ears. She gracefully pranced ahead of me, as the leaves rustled and twigs snapped under her feet. The sweet scent of moss and damp earth wafted through the air, immersing us in the lushness of nature. I could feel the cool breeze against my skin, its gentle touch a reminder of the freedom she embraced, daring to let go of my hand and dance with abandon.

"Elena!" I called out as I realized she was getting further and further away from me.

"Sorry, I just don't hurt, and I don't remember the last time I ran." She turned around, and her dress flew around her hips. Her lace thong caught my eye.

My dragon's sharp teeth glistened as drool dripped from his mouth, fixated on her graceful twirling as her lacy thong peeked through. The soft moonlight bathed her face, illuminating the strands of her rich, dark brown hair. Her radiant smile and laughter had lured me in like a siren's song,

"And tonight, I will not think of tomorrow's repercussions since you promised me a good time."

I huffed out a laugh. No pressure, absolutely no pressure at all. My dicks were painfully pressed against the seam of my pants and I had to adjust them just so. She couldn't see this far away from the cabin's light and the moon was only so bright with the trees overhead.

Elena pranced away from me, unaware of where she would run to. I let out a growl, my dragon surfacing as she fled.

Damnit. Don't run away from a dragon.

My dragon roared for me to follow, and immediately I answered so he wouldn't dare rear his ugly head and force his way out. He was a silent fucker, but I knew every emotion he had.

Once I caught up to her, I grabbed her hand. She squealed in excitement when I pulled her down a smaller path. The foliage hid us further from the moon and stars; now only the fireflies lit our way. She held onto my arm, as her human sight was now dull, and she would have to rely on me to take her where she needed to go.

"Are you alright, are you in pain?" I asked.

While I knew she could be in pain, I tried not to ask her about it. It seemed to irritate her when Abuela did. I couldn't help but do it now since she just ran half a mile through the forest.

She panted, still catching her breath. "No. And I'm sorry that I ran. I wanted to feel the air in my face. I felt free." She laughed. "It's the magic around here, don't you think? The forest seems more magical. Not that I was really looking at the plants, I concentrated on Luis most of the time to make sure he wasn't getting hurt." She waved her hands around excitedly, not at all bothered I had asked her.

I couldn't wait to tell her it was the bond that we shared that made the pain fall away. I watched how Journey healed. She was a timid thing when she first came here, but as her and Grim's bond grew, she had become so much stronger. I believed Elena was the same. I was healing her.

That was why I hadn't had Bones come around to do a checkup. I was the one who would take care of her. Her pain would be gone permanently once we bonded.

"This way." I pulled her in the direction of the entrance of the cave. It was twelve feet high and fifteen feet wide. When I originally found the cave, it was much smaller, but I took my time carving it out because on the inside, it was much larger.

Since the spring and summer fae have taken over several spots of the forest, their vegetation has run rampant. The front of the cave was covered in a thick tangle of vines, each with vibrant green leaves and delicate flowers in shades of pink and purple. The vines climbed up the sides of the cave, obscuring the entrance and creating a natural barrier to protect it from outsiders. Thick moss and lichen cover the rocks. It was home, much better in appearance than when I first arrived here.

I don't know if the goddess planned this, but it has worked in my favor because now my home was warm and dry, and would continue to be so as long as the vines continued to grow here.

The boxes I had ordered to ensure my mate's comfort and her suitcase were placed just to the right of the cave. They were just behind the vines, keeping them out of sight. Bear and Nadia never went inside my cave. I've never invited them in.

Dragons were a rare species, our numbers low even in the Elysian Realm. No one knew what would happen if an outsider came into my territory and my dragon suddenly appeared. It was best they never entered.

Elena, being my mate, I was sure was okay.

I went to bend down to grab her suitcase, but I felt her push me against the stone of the cave. As her arousal enveloped me, the air seemed to crackle with electricity. I couldn't help but release a breathless sigh of anticipation as her delicate hands glided up the contours of my body, sending a delightful heat straight to my cocks.

She hummed delightedly. "You are still slick with this body oil. You don't know how much I wanted to run my hands all over you when you were dancing."

My body snapped up, and I wrapped my arms around her. The entire time I danced, I thought of her. Each movement calculated to seduce her, to have her want me, let me touch her in ways I have always wanted to touch my mate. Goddess, I wanted her to be that pole, rubbing myself all over her, drowning her in my scent, letting my precum wash all over her body to mark her.

She rained kisses up my chest as far as her height would allow, I lowered myself so she could kiss the side of my neck and immediately my cocks filled thick with blood.

Fuck.

I unbuttoned my pants to let them breathe. If I didn't come now, I would explode. It had been years since I had let out any seed, too afraid she would hear me in the cabin. I could only get it up around her, and I wasn't about to get caught by our son.

"Damnit, Elena, we need to talk first."

"You talk too much," she replied, annoyed. "Take me to bed."

I fisted her hair, my fingers twirled into her hair to have her lips meet mine. Then, we strode through the vines and I forgot all about the boxes and suitcases. They would be fine until morning.

I fumbled at the side of the cave wall for the makeshift switch, to light up the large tent that sat inside the cave. My home was inside the cave.

The tent glowed in muted light, with shades of deep colors adorning the inside of the tent. The navy, purples, and greens blended together in the dimness with the blankets and silks that hung from the top of the cavern. Gold colored lanterns dangled from holes strategically cut into the tent above, casting a gentle glow on the makeshift interior. The area was filled with soft mattresses, plush pillows, and thick blankets that were all covered in my scent. Soon my mate would cover it with her own.

Elena mewled, and I picked her up by her thighs as we approached the monstrosity of my home. Large enough to house my dragon so he could sleep in peace. Elena paid no attention, her mind on one thing. Well, two things that were very much to attention now.

The compression underwear I had to wear now couldn't cope, my cocks had pushed the material down, and now they rested just under my mate's ass.

"Anaki," she whined. "I think you are going to be too big."

I rolled my head back at the compliment.

I've got a praise kink, oh yes, I do.

"Elena, we need to talk." I groaned when she rubbed her wet, delectable pussy on the top of my first dick. My lower dick wanted to cry that it wasn't being touched.

Can a dick cry?

It was certainly leaking everywhere.

"I actually want to taste it first. Can I taste you?" She panted as she looked at me. Her lips were red and pouty from me sucking on the soft skin. I grabbed the back of her neck and pulled her forward to touch my forehead.

"I am not human, love. I need to tell you something."

"You're gonna be rough? That's ok." She put both hands on my face. "I'm down with that, if you are okay with me being bossy with you some-times. I'd like to bite and maybe spank your tight ass."

I stared at her in shock. *Goddess, she was perfect.*

She wiggled out of my arms, my body buzzing with electricity as her wet thong slid down my cock. I whined when the heat of her body left me, and then a gasp rang in my ears.

Whoops.

"There's two!" she gasped and placed a hand on her chest, backing away. Her mouth was agape in shock, and all I could do was shrug my shoulders sheepishly.

"Told you, I need to talk to you first."

I waited for the scream, the humiliation of being rejected. I should have brought this up back at the bar, in fact, before I even pursued her.

But how does one tell a human female that a dragon has two dicks?

I rubbed over my chest painfully, ready for it to break in two. I couldn't even look at her while I tried to form the words.

And then I felt it. Her hand wrapped around my wrist, pulling it away from my chest to her own.

She stared at me as if she bore into my soul, like the first time I saw her. Instead of me seeing her, she saw me. I felt utterly naked, which I partially was, but my insides were raw, still burned from my previous rejection.

I could not take another.

Her other free hand reached up and cupped my face. I jerked in surprise but leaned into her touch.

"If you think I'm upset about this, I'm not," she whispered as though the room was full of people, a secret that we needed to keep between ourselves. "Surprised. Delightfully so, and let me just say, wow! How have you kept all that hidden in your pants?"

She didn't look down to inspect it. While I think she wanted to, she was bouncing on the balls of her feet, and the dread and embarrassment that had built up suddenly vanished.

"There is a story to that, actually." I pulled up my pants, but not buttoning them. "Depends on if you want to hear that story or if you just want to, uh..." I smiled and gave her a wink.

She bit her lip playfully and tugged on my waistband. "You say this isn't a one-night stand, that you want this to work," she said, more to herself than to me. "I think I'll deal with stories later."

CHAPTER FIFTEEN

Elena

Two. *Two!*

Anaki had two of them, and they weren't short, by any means due to there being multiple. They were both good sizes. While I haven't been around the block *that* many times, I knew what the average size looked like.

The top protruded out more, maybe a fraction of an inch. The way it was positioned may have played a part, but I focused on not staring after that initial brief glimpse of his whole package. It wasn't a normal human dick. It was blue, maybe silver, and shone in the golden light of the cave.

I had kept my sight on Anaki's face instead, despite my curiosity. He was nervous and waited for my reaction. His multiple attempts at trying to tell me *something* I'd brushed off without a care because of my eagerness.

Now I'd made this really awkward.

I bit my lip to calm myself. I haven't felt this good in years. The fatigue, the depression from my illness and ex had floated away since meeting Ana-ki. I'm not sure what it was, but since meeting him, there was something that pulled me closer to him that I couldn't put my finger on.

I had sworn off men five years ago, and I was doing great until he came barging into my life. Accepting everything about who I was.

I craved him more than flan, and that was a pretty big deal.

I gently tugged on his waistband, noticing how his cheeks were still flushed with a delicate, rosy hue. I was surprised to discover that men like him could blush so intensely, but it was evident in the way his cheeks glowed. The warmth of his embarrassment seemed to radiate and reach all the way to the tips of his ears.

Once we reached the bed, the back of his heels touched it, since it was so low to the floor, and he fell backwards into the lush blankets and pillows. The mattresses had to be at least three California Kings. It looked so comfortable, I almost felt bad that we were going to mess it up.

Anaki, with a surprised look on his face, lifted himself up using his elbows. As I moved along his body, crawling up towards his hips, I could feel the heat radiating from his skin. With each kiss I placed on his lean, muscled physique, I could sense his tension melting away, his body sinking deeper into the plush comfort of the bed.

His body was thrumming, a deep vibration coming from his chest, and I reveled in it. It was a warm caress that let me know that what I was doing pleased him.

As I reached his neck, I took in his scent; it had a hint of sweetness but also smelled like fresh water you would find at a lake, right after a good rain. Cool, crisp, and enticing me to take a large sip. My breasts felt heavy as they brushed against his chest, and I lowered my body over his. My pussy ground into his erections and he moaned as he wrapped his arms around my waist.

While I peppered kisses over his collarbone, I had to think about how this was going to work. Was this a double penetration thing, one hole? Because, for one, I didn't think I could do that until I had trained myself. There was just no way that was going to happen. And two, if I were just going to use one of them, which one did I use?

There were so many fun possibilities with this. I couldn't believe Anaki thought I would be afraid!

Then again, he could have scared off a few humans in his time, which reminded me...

"Anaki?" I kissed his neck. He groaned as his hands palmed my ass. "Do you have any protection?" I continued to kiss him up his neck to his strong jawline, and he tensed.

He immediately sat up and hugged my biceps. "What protection. I'll protect you!"

I blinked several times at him, and realization hit me. "Ah, no. Protection for, ah, us." I waved a finger between the two of us. "You know, from any diseases or anything."

Anaki's eyebrows shot up. "I don't have any diseases! And I can't catch human ones."

I put my hands on my hips. "Well, I don't know that. You've been dancing on the bar and women stuffing money in your pants." I crossed my arms and huffed.

Anaki opened and closed his mouth. "Elena, I... shit." He ran a hand through his hair. "Elena, this is really embarrassing, but I haven't. Fuck!"

This was so much talking. Way more talking than I wanted to be doing, but the more he blubbered in front of me, the more I realized he was not as experienced as I thought. The gyrating hips, the sensual movements, and the sexual appeal of him were there, but the actual act?

"I haven't technically had sex," he whispered and turned his head away in shame.

"Technically?" My voice rose.

"Okay, not at all!" He threw his hands up in the air, fell back on the bed, and covered his eyes with his arms.

This sex beacon of a man that was humping a stripper pole at a bar had never had sex before.

I felt the truth and the weight of his words. He wasn't lying. He had no reason to. I knew when a man lied. I felt it. I knew it when I looked at them. I've been gaslit, beaten and lived with a narcissist for years.

Anaki was none of those things.

He was a sweet, tender little puppy who was trying to make me happy.

No guy had ever done that for me.

His face was red down to his neck and chest now. His cocks were still hard beneath my underwear and to be quite honest, I was utterly turned on.

I wanted this man more than ever.

I pulled on his arm, but it wouldn't budge, so I pulled a little harder. "Little dragon!" I sang as I tried to pull his arm away. "Come out, little dragon, do not be afraid."

"Goddess, no, you are treating me like a child."

"But you are a cute little dragon. Such a good dragon telling me this before we got started!"

He moved his arm down and peeked over it to look at me.

"Yes, a good boy. Come on out," I coaxed. Finally, he put his arm down, and I smiled widely, pulling him up by his arms. "Why didn't you tell me?" I cupped his face. "I was about to ride you into the night and not consider your feelings. If we are going to be in a relationship, you should be honest with me."

I felt Anaki's heart beat wildly in his chest. I placed my hand on it and gasped.

"I have two. Two hearts." He held up two fingers.

Wow, okay, that's good to know.

"My dragon is large, so I need to sustain it."

I nodded slowly. I didn't understand shifter and dragon biology, so I was going to roll with it.

Anaki sat in silence. His hands rested on my thighs while his thumb ran soothing circles around my skin. I don't think it was for me, but for him. He enjoyed touching me, and to be honest, his touch calmed me as well.

"Why haven't you?" I tilted my head so I could see his eyes. "You're so handsome. I thought you would be with so many women."

Anaki chuckled. "No. I only get hard or want to have sex if I have a connection with someone. Someone I can see myself having a future with."

My heart stuttered in my chest.

"You mean never? Not even when you went through puberty did your dick get hard?"

He tilted his head. "Puberty?"

I ran my hand down my face. "You know, when you go from being an adolescent to an adult.

Anaki ran his hands up and down my legs. "Shifters go through a process. Shifters are considered adults when they can shift into their animal forms. That's when we can... get hard. I mean, I can do stuff to myself, but with someone else I need to... have a connection," he stuttered bashfully.

Dios Mio, can he get any cuter?

I ran my hands up his arms and then around his neck. I didn't know what I should do with this information, but I didn't want to make him feel uncomfortable anymore. It was embarrassing him, making the night worse, when we both should be feeling good.

He'd already made me come. He was a grown adult, and he knew what he was doing. I was going to just hope he has watched some porn, so he knew what I was about to do next.

I gently tilted his head up with my hand, feeling the soft brush of his hair against my fingertips. The air was filled with a faint scent of his home, mixing with the warmth of our breath as our lips met. My hands instinctively cupped both sides of his face, the warmth of his skin warming me. As I leaned in closer, I could hear the soft sound of our breaths mingling, the tender brush of our lips parting.

He tasted so good; he was better than any expensive tequila.

He huffed in relief, and his hands rose up my back. His fingers dug into my flesh, sending waves of pleasure and comfort throughout my body. I deepened the kiss, wanting to taste every inch of his mouth, every part of him. I wanted him to know that he was safe with me, that he could let go of any inhibitions or fears that I might have caused.

As our kiss grew heated, his cocks strained against his pants. I gently guided him onto his back, still keeping our lips locked, then trailed kisses down his neck, savoring the smell of his skin and the taste of his sweat. His heartbeats thundered beneath me, echoing the desire that coursed through me like wildfire.

I reached down, feeling his cocks strain against his pants. I undid his fly and slid the material aside, freeing him from the confines of clothing. Anaki was fucking glorious!

His cocks were one on top of the other. Both were the same in color and size. The top part of his shafts were blue, and the bulbous head was as well. The underside appeared to have thick, dripping scales, which looked silver.

My clit throbbed thinking about which ways to have sex with him.

Anaki gasped as I wrapped my hand around both shafts, marveling at the firmness and warmth of his lengths. A pearl of precum formed on one while the other dripped down to the base, which appeared to have empty pockets on either side.

Hmmm.

His eyes fluttered shut as I stroked him gently, watching as he arched his back and moaned softly from the pleasure I was giving him. Now and then,

I would look up at his face, relishing in the pleasure etched on his features.

As much as I wanted to continue exploring more of Anaki's body, to feel every muscle and curve beneath my fingertips, I knew we needed to take this slow. This was something new for both of us, and we needed to make sure we were both comfortable and enjoying ourselves.

A virgin. He was a virgin.

I moved down his legs to straddle his thighs to get more comfortable. "You are doing so good, Anaki. You like me stroking your cocks?" I took the precum that now leaked profusely, covering my hand and his shafts. He whined, and his hands fisted the blankets beside him.

"Yes," he breathed, his voice barely audible over the sound of his hearts pounding in his chest. I could hear a rumble coming from his throat, which grew louder by the second.

Tremors rippled through his body as I continued to stroke him, exploring the unique texture of his shafts. I couldn't wait to guide my clit over them. Rub his cock inside me.

What would it feel like to have one in my pussy and one in my ass?

I bit my cheek to keep my own moans at bay, but of course they escaped me. This was turning me on from just watching him, thinking of all the dirty, vile things I wanted to do to him. I was going to make him my little plaything, and we were going to have so much fun together.

The best part about all of this was the trust I had in him. The first time I actually ever trusted any man in my life.

His eyes flicked open to meet mine, and I saw a mix of apprehension and excitement in his gaze.

Slowly, I leaned down, brushing my lips against the head of one of his cocks. Anaki let out a soft moan, pushing himself closer to me, and I felt my desire flare up at the sound. Gently, I took one of his cocks into my mouth, savoring the taste of his precum and feeling the throb of his shaft against my lips.

Anaki's fingers pulled on the blankets beside him. His breath hitched as I continued this exploration. As much as I wanted to give him pleasure, I knew it was important for both of us to communicate openly about our desires and boundaries.

"Tell me if you need me to stop or change anything," I murmured against his length, looking up at him with concern. Anaki nodded, his face a picture of mixed emotions: apprehension, desire, trust.

With a gentle smile, I pulled away from his cocks and sat back on my heels, offering him a reassuring look. "We're both learning this together, okay? If something feels uncomfortable or wrong, let's talk about it."

Anaki nodded again, looking more at ease now that we had established some ground rules. As much as I wanted to pounce on him, I would not force him to do anything if he wasn't comfortable. Even if he expected sex tonight.

I watched his face light up as I wrapped my mouth around one of his cocks while I fisted the other.

"Goddess!" He gasped, his hand reaching for my head.

He shivered beneath my touch and bucked his hips.

Anaki seemed to have found his voice now. His moans and cries of pleasure filled the room, urging me on. I could feel my own desire growing with each passing moment, but I didn't have another hand to take care of myself.

But watching Anaki through my lustful eyes was more than worth it. Anaki's lower cock dripped come on my dress, I felt it cover my breasts and the warmth of it made me go through a sickly haze of lust.

I wanted more of him; I craved him. The feeling of his arousal against my skin sent a wave of longing throughout my entire body.

Anaki grunted. His hand squeezed a fistful of my hair. "I'm going to—"

His release cut him off. He roared, more powerful than I thought his lungs could carry such a noise. It was monstrous, just as if a dragon were in the room.

I jumped in surprise, but I kept my mouth securely on Anaki's cock. It swelled as it burst inside my mouth. The lower cock doing just the same. While I drank him down, my dress was covered in light blue semen from the other cock I was jerking off.

Once Anaki let go of my hair, I came off him with a pop. I licked my lips for any remnants, and before I could turn to him to give a snarky remark, he attacked and pinned me to the mattress.

CHAPTER SIXTEEN

Anaki

I pinned Elena to the mattress. My dragon growled within me. I couldn't hold back, and I allowed his primal urges to be heard. His guttural growl came up and out of my throat, the heat of my breath fanned her face and displaced her hair.

My seed had splattered all over the front of her black dress, it was soaking through, but I could see the light blue tinge to it. I snarled, watching it seep through the material as it touched her skin. It smelled of me. I wanted her to be covered in it.

"Anaki?" Elena breathed and placed her hand on my face. She did that a lot. She liked to touch my face and let her hand wander down my chest.

She didn't know how much I enjoyed it. The tenderness she held was comforting, just as her voice was as she told me how *good* I was.

"Sorry, I don't know what came over me." I panted and lowered my body to hers. It was a lie, but I wasn't about to freak her out that I had lost control.

While I was stark naked, her body remained covered. I wanted to rip the damn dress off and press my whole body against hers, but was that too far? I had only felt her between her legs and not yet touched her breasts.

Fuck, they would make good pillows.

Elena smiled, and her arms wrapped around my back. Her nails scratched down my skin, and I stretched my body out like a cat over her.

"That's okay. I liked it. Was that you, or was that your dragon? Does he take over sometimes?"

"Yes." I gritted out. He does, but I try to hold him back.

"If you are worried you are going to scare me, you won't. I can take it." She licked her lips, and her finger traced down my jaw. "You know, it is getting rather warm in here." She tapped my nose. "Did you want to see anything? You don't have to get me off or anything, but if you wanted to explore..."

My eyes trailed down her neck and to the top of her dress. Her cleavage was inviting as her deep breaths made her breasts strain against the fabric.

I don't think I have ever been this close to breasts in all my life.

"You can touch them, you know. Unless you are too scared to touch your come," she laughed.

I didn't waste time. My hands swept up her side, and I cupped her breast. She was so damn soft and squishy. Now I knew what all the mated pairs were talking about. Breasts were awesome.

She moaned, her head rolling back. I saw her nipple harden beneath my touch, and I used my fingers to pinch it. She gasped. Her hand reached around my head.

"I bet it would feel even better if you took my clothes off."

Don't have to tell me twice.

My dragon lengthened our claws and swiped down the middle. She gasped when we ripped the dress into shreds, and I found more material there.

I growled in frustration. "Ugh, how many layers?"

"It's a bra. Don't you dare tell me you don't know what a bra is. You aren't that innocent." She snapped playfully.

I wasn't. I've seen porn. I know how the body works. As soon as Grim mated to Journey, I went to town. Then I heard a lot of it wasn't realistic there weren't pizza guys that would come to your door to have sex with women. Their dicks were rather small, too.

Elena covered her stomach, for the first time, vulnerability laced her face.

"Hey, what's wrong?" I hovered over her. "You said I could take it off. And I'm quite happy you did." I wiggled my eyebrows.

"Well, I've had a baby—"

I gave her an exaggerated nod. "Yes, and I see your breasts filled out nicely." I stared at them, and my dragon's tongue licked across my lips.

Her mouth parted, and her arousal seeped around us. So, she liked my tongue? I wondered if she would like if I—

"I have stretch marks. I don't look like a young woman. I don't have a beautiful fit body. My stomach and boobs sag a little." She pouted. "Just so you know."

I reared my head back. "Are you serious? That is what you are worried about?" I pulled her hands away to inspect her stomach. Tiny little stretch marks coated her stomach and thighs. She still looked perfect to me. I enjoyed having her stomach soft. She was perfect to cuddle. "You know what?" I said. "This has to be the best stomach I have ever seen."

Elena scoffed and rolled her eyes.

"Yes, because you see, this is a tummy that carried a child. An amazing, smart, loving boy who cares about his mama very much. A boy that's my son, too now."

Elena gasped. "Anaki, you can't say—"

I placed my finger on her lips. "If you're mine, he's mine. Simple as that. And I'm keeping the both of you, no matter what you think about all this."

Even if that meant keeping her glued to my side until she was fully mated to me. My dragon wouldn't allow her to leave our side until we do.

Elena's eyes filled with tears.

"And these stretch marks..." I traced my finger across one, "are the evidence of how strong you are. Your battle scars of how you held him inside you, created him and kept him healthy."

"Anaki—"

"And these stretch marks show me just how wonderful of a mother you are—and how much I want to fill your belly with our own child."

Elena's eyes widened.

"Yes, Elena, I want to do that." My dragon growled, and I felt my teeth lengthening. From the top of my mouth and the bottom, my jaws elongated and my tongue thickened into its long dragon form.

I tried to push my dragon back, I shook my head in annoyance, but he was rising to the surface. Smelling our mate covered in our scent, seeing how breedable she was, there was no stopping him.

"Elena," my voice deepened.

Her arousal grew, her eyes hooded as she stared up at me. "Oh, wow!" she gasped.

I grabbed both sides of her hips and pulled her toward me. The scent between her thighs was driving me wild. I wanted to taste her, every inch of her.

"Rip those off!" she ordered, and just like with her dress, I tore it to shreds, and immediately my face went between her luscious thighs.

I licked her folds, savoring the salty-sweet taste of her essence. Her aroma was intoxicating, and I couldn't help but bury my face deeper, teasing her folds with my tongue. She moaned in pleasure, her hands gripping the sheets as she arched her back, offering herself to me completely.

Elena's body trembled under my touch, and I could feel the heat generated by our bond as it grew stronger. Her arousal was filling the air with her scent, driving me feverishly wild. I wanted to possess her completely, to feel her shiver beneath me as I took her.

As I tongued her swollen clit, she moaned and cried out my name. Her hips bucked against my face, and I felt the warmth of her climax building within her.

She was warm, so hot and wet inside. I wanted to sheath myself into her channel and let my cock take over.

Both! I wanted both inside her so I could impregnate her. Breed her.

"Anaki," she panted, "I'm close."

Her words sent a surge of pride through me. My mate was mine to pleasure and claim. I continued to tease and lick at the bundle of nerves on her clit until she cried out in ecstasy.

Her hands fisted my hair, and I growled, sending vibrations between her legs. She moaned and pulled me further into her pussy.

How had I ever lived without this taste? How did I ever live without her? She has given me a life I never knew had existed.

"Mine," my voice rumbled into her body. I pushed her legs further apart and let my dragon's tongue push inside her.

"Holy fuck!" she screamed as I tongue fucked her. "It's too much! Argg!"

Her body released a tidal wave of liquid, splattering me across the face. I snarled hungrily, drinking her down greedily as she cried out. My fingers dug into her thighs while she lay lifeless on the mattress. My cocks were at full attention, but I made no attempt to take care of them.

I needed to tend to my mate and her arousal, which covered me, satisfying me enough.

I hummed eagerly as I cleaned her. My jaw relaxed and went back to its more humanoid form. She rolled her head back and forth on the bedding. I licked my lips and crawled back over her, and she pulled me in for a kiss.

She sighed happily, her legs wrapped around me, her pussy rubbing on my lowest cock.

"Dios Mio, you are good at that." Her hand went up into my hair and grabbed at my scalp. "I think I might die of orgasms by the end of the night."

I snarled. "Not allowed. I just found you and I'm not gonna let you go."

She hummed playfully, not scared of my angry voice.

Elena bopped my nose with her free hand and forced me to roll on my back. She straddled me, my cocks grazing her ass. "Do you want more?" She reached behind her back, and I heard a click. The straps of her bra fell down her arms. Elena grabbed the middle of it and tossed it away from her. "Because we don't—"

"Yes," my voice quivered. "Yes, please. I can't stand it not being inside you." My once loud voice was now but a whimper, as my hands roamed up her thighs.

I wanted this so bad. If she made me wait, I'd have to go fist my cocks on my own while she slept. Fuck, I might even sleep fuck her if I had to. She was my mate, and it was allowed right?

Hawke does it.

Didn't mean it was right, but—I'm a dragon. I've got needs!

Shit, I'm as bad as the rest of the club.

My dicks had already leaked come down the shafts. Dragons always had good lubrication, especially in our dragon forms. Not that my mate needed any lubrication, she was soaked.

So perfect for me.

My body shuddered for what was to come. Ready to sheath myself inside her. Would she take both? She was so small when I used my fingers and tongue, there was no way—

"You are thinking too much." Elena grabbed my hand as she scooted down my body and had me hold one of her breasts. She hummed when I flicked her nipple and gave the supple part of her body a squeeze. "I'm going to take care of you, give you what you need. Be a good dragon and let me do all the work."

I let out a whimper when she dragged her pussy down my first cock. She gasped as her clit rubbed against the underside of the ridges of my shaft. Elena closed her eyes and trailed herself up my second dick, this time, leaving the head right at her entrance.

She looked absolutely stunning, holding my cock at her dripping cunt, ready to take all of me.

My mate took in the head and swallowed it with her pussy. I gritted my teeth and gripped her breast as she lowered herself. So hot, warm. She let out noises of pleasure, and my hips bucked, wanting her to swallow me whole.

"Nah, ah." She smiled wickedly. "We are going at my pace right now. You're huge and we aren't going to rip my cervix open."

Slowly, she slid herself down my shaft.

Don't come, don't come.

"You are doing so good, Anaki. You are all the way inside me and didn't come." She grabbed the cock in front of her. She rubbed it up and down slowly, getting her hand wet with my come, then gave it a tug. I gasped and gripped her hips, my nails poking into her skin.

"While I ride you like this, I want you to keep your eyes on me."

I let out a half-cough, half-laugh. "What?" I was barely keeping it together, and she wanted me to watch her? Why was she ordering me around?

"I want to watch you come inside me."

My mate was the hottest creature to walk the realm.

I nodded enthusiastically as she rose on her knees, then I watched as she slowly went up and down on my cock. I groaned as I held her waist. She didn't leave my other cock cold and alone, she had it in her hand, squeezing it tightly, working it to the same rhythm as her thrusts.

Fuck, it was too much. I was going to come too fast.

"Anaki, damnit, you feel so good. So thick." She grabbed her breast and pinched her nipple. "Am I wet enough for you? Am I strangling your cock enough?"

"Elena, you're going to be the death of me," I groaned, my hands tightening on her hips. She grinned seductively, her eyes locked onto mine as she sped up.

I thrust up to meet her, my hips bucking in time with her movements. The pleasure built rapidly, my body arching with the intensity of it all.

"I'm close," I warned, my voice hoarse with arousal. "So close, love..."

I grabbed my cock from her hand so she could continue to ride me with my lower one. She watched as I jacked myself in front of her, and her mouth opened in awe.

"I love watching you do that. Seeing you get off while I'm riding your other dick. We are going to have so much fun together." Her breasts bounced, and I whimpered as I sat up. I needed her close, needed her face near mine.

She grabbed the back of my head, tightening her hold on my hair.

I gritted my teeth. "Elena, please."

"You need to come, sweetheart?" She bounced harder, her pussy tightening around me.

"I'm going to come," I panted, my free hand tightened on her hip even more. "Inside you... I'm going to come inside you."

Elena's eyes flashed open wide, her face a picture of pure lust. "Yes," she hissed, her grip on my hips becoming more possessive. "Fill this pussy up!"

At that moment, I lost all control. My body convulsed, bucking up into Elena as wave after wave of pleasure crashed over me. I felt ropes of my come fill her while my other cock splattered between us.

Her breasts were covered in my scent, again.

The primal part of me was utterly satisfied. I wanted to cover her in it. Maybe one day she will let me stand over her and cover her entire body..

My cock drove into her with relentless power, pouring everything I had into her depths as I finished. Her pussy gripped me fiercely, demanding every last drop with intensity. I thrust up into her one final time, feeling the electric charge that came from my spine, before wrapping my arms around her already collapsed body.

I gently lay us to the side of the bed, both panting, utterly drained and consumed by overwhelming satisfaction.

CHAPTER SEVENTEEN

Elena

I hummed into the pillow. My legs and thighs were achingly sore. Not the typical soreness that I usually have, but more from exertion. I didn't dare open my eyes because I didn't want to wake up from this dream.

I slept with Anaki, a dragon. And he was for sure a dragon because he had two dicks, crazy lizard eyes and a magic tongue. I moaned and stretched. The blankets and pillows piled around kept me warm.

Throughout the night, Anaki woke me two more times, once with his head between my legs and another time with my stomach resting on pillows, and he plowed me from behind. I didn't mind it, didn't say a word. Nope, I screamed his name over and over again.

He had some stamina, and I think he would have gone for a third time, but exhaustion took over when he tried to spoon fuck me. I groaned and begged for five more minutes' rest.

While I didn't have the usual chronic pain, my fatigue had taken over. I don't normally stay up late or have rigorous sex.

Not until him.

I just hoped my pain stays away, and hopefully, the fatigue would get better soon.

Birds chirped outside, and a soft breeze brushed my face. I groaned again, wishing I could purr like a cat at how comfortable I was. This bed was nice, even though it was huge. I felt myself wrapped up in my own little cocoon.

I fluttered my eyes open, my hair was a wild mess on the pillows. I lifted myself up on my arm and gazed around the room, or tent rather, and finally took it in. I never had a moment to check my surroundings in Anaki's home, because all my thoughts, desires and wants were on him last night.

The bed was massive. It was several California King mattresses pushed together. Layers upon layers of plush pillows and luxurious blankets covered them. Expensive materials, silk, cashmere, and other soft fabrics in rich hues of navy, purple, and blue, adorned every inch of its surface. When I looked around, I realized we were in a large tent inside the cave. It felt like a cozy home nestled within the cold stone walls.

Ornate golden lanterns brightened the space. They were suspended from the ceiling with delicate gold chains and cast a warm golden glow throughout. The mood of the room was romantic and well-lived in.

On the other side, there was furniture; old, expensive-looking furniture with fancy wood carvings and velvet cushions. It all made it look like a sitting area. I sat up fully, smelling something wonderful coming deeper within the cave. I grabbed the blanket next to me, feeling the soft texture under my fingertips, and wrapped it around me.

I didn't even want to find my clothing. There was no point with all the blankets strewn across the massive bed. *I'm pretty sure he ripped them up anyway.*

As I wrapped the blanket around my body, I took in a deep breath. I don't know what I was looking for, detergent? His scent?

Anaki didn't have on cologne, but his own wonderfully crisp, clean scent that I wanted to drink. It was embedded in the blanket I held, and I kept it to my nose. My lungs expanded to take it in, and I felt the tingle in my body, which went straight down to my toes.

I was in such big trouble with this dragon. He wanted to raise my kid as his own. He said that Luis was his *son*. Who does that a few days after meeting them?

Did he know I would become a pile of goo for him? I almost completely accepted him after saying such things. Because no man would have ever accepted me. *People talk*. I got from the outside that my life looked like a handful, and I guess it was.

Since choosing the wrong guy, given what Luis' father did to me, I haven't wanted to take the risk. The men here, though, they seemed nice despite most of their appearances.

Anaki was the best-looking one. He would always be the better-looking one. It was his kind eyes that drew me in.

I think that was why I caved when he looked down at me at the bar. They were so pleading, begging me to accept him. I knew that same feeling. I'd wanted to be accepted for so long, for someone to love me, and to find my place.

I had just made some mistakes in my youth.

But, because of those mistakes, should I make Anaki suffer for it?

I stepped off the bed, and my foot landed on the patterned carpets. The entire room had a bohemian vibe I absolutely loved. All it needed was some music playing in the background to complete the vibe.

I trailed back to the back of the cave, and it curved to the right where the scent was coming from. The tent followed the curve, as though Anaki had tried to create walls within the cave, instead of looking at the bare rock.

I called out, "Anaki?" and tilted my head to the side before I rounded the corner.

The sounds of pots and pans clanged, and I jumped at the sound. "I'm okay!" he said in a panic. He came around the corner with four plates, all balanced on his arms. It was impressive and I stared at him in shock, with all the food that sat on them. "I made breakfast!"

Anaki was bare-chested, and around his waist was the equivalent of a male sarong. It was navy blue with gold chains around his hips. My gaze fell upon the chain around his waist, the dips and curves of his Adonis belt, and his very defined abs.

I wanted to hide my stomach right away because I knew I was less than perfect, but after he said he wanted to breed me last night, it made me turn my mind around real quick.

My pussy was gonna cry.

I cleared my throat. "Are you feeding a small army?"

Sausages, eggs, bacon, fruit, biscuits, and pancakes littered the plates. I knew *I* wouldn't eat that much, but I'm pretty sure I knew who might. *I mean, I might eat a sausage later.*

Anaki's nostrils flared, and he looked down at my body. I was only wearing a blanket, no way to see the curves of my body, but that didn't stop him from looking.

"Sorry to leave you in bed. I know you wanted to rest. My dragon was restless, so I thought preparing you breakfast would calm him." His shoulder brushed by me, just to touch me, and like a helpless puppy, I followed him to the massive bed on the floor.

"We are going to eat here? Not at a table?"

He juggled the plates in his arms and set them down on trays by the corner of the bed. He did it so effortlessly. One thing I found drastically different about Anaki, and the rest of the Iron Fang that I'd had met so far, was that he was graceful. His movements were fluid, purposeful, and calculated. Not once have I seen him trip or drop anything. It made him an excellent dancer and bartender.

Once Anaki was finished arranging the food, he reached up, waiting to grab my hand.

"Come on, mama, let's get you fed. I wore you out last night." The corners of his lips twitched, and I groaned when I finally took his hand to sit down beside him. Instead of sitting down on the mattress, he pulled me into his lap, and I squeaked when he nestled my backside right near his already hard dicks.

"Do those things ever go down?" I asked.

"Not since finding you. Now hush and let me feed you."

I rubbed my forehead with my hand. "Why do you need to feed me? I can do it myself." I tried to take the fork away from him, but he wouldn't let me. "Nuh, huh. I do it. My dragon demands it. It shows that we can provide for our female."

My nipples hardened when his other arm wrapped around my waist. Why did this primitive talk sound so hot? "E-excuse me?"

"Listen, love. Now that you are understanding how serious I am about us," —he waved the fork with the half-cut strawberry between us— "you are going to have to let me take care of you. My dragon is an animal, with courting rituals, he has to do certain things to keep his claws in you, just like if you were another dragon shifter."

My mouth dropped. "What?"

He took his hand and pressed my mouth closed. "Love, there is a lot to explain."

Anaki

I didn't know where to begin with Elena. I wanted to do everything with her. She was my soulkin, she was my heart, my light out of the darkness.

While I still had nightmares of my past, they weren't so bad when I woke because she was there in the dim light of the overhead lanterns. When I wrapped my arm around her, my body stirred with desire, and I had to take her then and there.

She didn't seem to mind when I spread her thighs and woke her with pleasure. I didn't know what I had been missing all those years. I had taken myself in hand many times before I had lost my first mate, but having it sheathed in Elena was... fucking earth-shattering.

Even with the romps of pleasure through the night, I was still stuck in memories of my past. I don't know if the brothers of the club experience the same; we don't talk about our dreams, but mine used to be so vivid, full of the rejection, and felt like it was just yesterday. Even if it has been close to a hundred years.

His tanned skin, bright, white hair, and blue eyes made him different, a rare gem that every dragon wanted to behold. I thought I was so lucky to have found him and that he was mine. I used to think he was stunningly beautiful. And his dragon? Magnificent!

After seeing Elena, and her being in my arms, he was just a faded gem now. A pebble not worth having in the hoard. The nightmares I still had weren't of him rejecting me, but what I had done after, where I still held my guilt.

When I was close to Elena, I could fall back to sleep, when normally I could not. When I was inside her, she granted me the euphoria that I had always craved. To be near my soulkin, to be wanted, cared for. I craved touch, and having been denied for so long, I just wanted to soak myself in her, bathe in her scent and arousal, so that I would always have it with me.

I wasn't blind. I knew I'd taken things too far when she waved her hand and said she was too tired. My dragon was annoyed and prodded me to at least sheath myself inside her while she slept, to be connected to her.

He would be a problem. He felt the same pain I felt when we lost *him,* and he didn't want to experience it again.

Elena wasn't like *him* at all. Elena was kind and thoughtful. She taught us things we didn't know and was understanding about it. She gave us praise and let us touch her. So far, she hadn't said I was annoying or too touchy.

However, Elena was human. She didn't understand my dragon's needs and my culture, like the small things, such as feeding her.

Elena sat in my lap, her blanket covering her perfect breasts. I wanted to demand she drop the blanket, but I had already told her she was mine, that I claimed her and her son, so I would try to take it slow.

The keyword was *try,* because after waiting so long, I wasn't sure how long I would hold out.

"Dragons have a need to take care of their females. We need to feed, clothe, and shelter. All the basic needs that our females should have."

Elena's eyes widened, and I could see the faintness of her nipples poke through the thin blanket.

"When you fed me at the cabin…" Elena trailed off, her hand pointing to the entrance of the cave.

I nodded, took the fork, and placed it in front of her. "Yes, that officially started my courting. As soon as I saw you, Elena, I knew you were mine. My dragon instantly awoke inside of me, no longer in an endless slumber. You woke him, brought him back to life as you have done to me."

Her lips parted.

"When I fell to the ground and made all those growling noises, I was trying to keep him under control, so I didn't scare you. I couldn't very well just tell you that you were mine then because, well, you had just found out about vampires and shifters. I couldn't scare you off just yet."

Elena's face turned a beautiful, glowing pink. The tips of her ears even turned. "What? You did not claim me—"

"I did, now open." I shoved another piece of food in her mouth. My dragon hummed, vibrating her body in my lap. Instead of holding the blanket so it wouldn't fall, she nestled herself closer to me. "The entire club knows not to bother you. I've staked my claim."

Elena did a dramatic swallow. My mate let out a half-cough, half-laugh. Her arousal scent was thickening, and I grabbed her thigh and squeezed. "That's barbaric."

I huffed and shrugged my shoulders. "That's the way things are done around here. Technically, at any MC really. If you want, I can throw you over my shoulder, if you wanna get barbaric." I wiggled my eyebrows playfully.

Elena slapped my shoulder. "Love at first sight isn't real." She shook her head. Her dark, messy hair swung around her bare shoulders. "Maybe lust." Elena fluttered her eyes playfully.

I shoved another plump, crimson strawberry between her swollen lips. She eagerly accepted it, her tongue swirling around the ripe fruit before pulling it off the fork with slow, deliberate movements. My dick pulsed at the sight, my thoughts being consumed by desire as I struggled to remember the purpose of our conversation.

I chortled and looked away from her beauty. "It wasn't lust, love. My broken soul awakened, healed because of yours calling to me."

This could have been a step too far, but I was an impatient dragon. I could feel Elena's emotional pain through the bond we shared. She was lonely, she was tired of being *tired.* I wanted to alleviate that for her, show her I could be the male she could lean on. To protect her and her family.

My dragon's strength had grown just by lying next to her through the night. While the darkness of my past was there, I knew it would only be eased by telling her who I really was, what the Iron Fang was at its core, but would I ever truly get rid of it?

It was her past that was stopping her. That fucking bastard. I was lucky she was willing to touch me, for everything he did.

It didn't help that she has a resentment about soulmates because she thinks her abuela is crazy.

Elena's pout deepened, her fingers digging into the soft fabric of her blanket, as if it were a lifeline. It took all my willpower not to tear it from her, exposing her bare chest to me. I craved the closeness of skin on skin, not just for sexual pleasure, but to simply hold her close and feel her warmth against my own.

"You are so needy. I can't deal with it." His words came flooding back.

I opened my mouth to take back what I said, to tell her to forget everything and get back to a playful, fun morning, but she stopped me.

"You really mean that?" she whispered. "Is that how you feel?"

I ripped the blanket from her body, and her eyes widened in surprise. I pulled her into my embrace and had her head tucked under my chin. My dragon let out a loud humming vibration, similar to a cat's purr. It was a sound I heard my parents give each other when I was a young fledgling. A sound I could never replicate on my own.

"I will tell you every day, until our last breaths, that my soul belongs to you." I closed my eyes. "I know this is fast, but I can't help but speak from the heart. I've always been honest. It's gotten me in trouble a lot. Might have gotten punched in the face one too many times, but... it's just who I am." I sniffed.

Tears threatened to spill from my eyes, but I quickly forced them back. I couldn't let her see me like this. As the man in our relationship, it was my duty to be strong and hide my emotions. But deep down, my dragon was roaring with the same pain, struggling to keep me from breaking down completely.

I had wanted to show her how much she meant to me, but now all I could think about was how I had screwed everything up. My mind was a jumbled mess of guilt and regret, and I didn't know how to fix it.

Elena abruptly withdrew from my hold, leaving me feeling exposed and vulnerable. I could feel her eyes scanning me, judging every inch of my appearance. My cheeks burned with embarrassment as I attempted to hide the tear that had escaped. But Elena reached out and gently brushed it away, leaving me conflicted between wanting to push her away and craving her touch

"You said your soul was broken and your dragon was asleep. What do you mean by that? Are they connected?"

I nodded. "Yeah, but that isn't important right now. I just want you to know that I care for you, and I mean it."

My mate didn't look convinced, but what could I have said? My late mate rejected me, broke me, and if you reject me, too, I have no hope? I wanted her to choose me, but not for her pity.

Elena leaned forward, her forehead meeting mine. I let out a sigh of relief, feeling her touch. "Oh baby, who hurt you?" she whispered to me. Elena rubbed her face along my cheek, across my nose, and met the other side of my face. My dragon purred, reveling that our mate touched us, felt us, comforted us.

Her warm hands pressed to my chest, and her lips landed on mine for a precious kiss. "You are the sweetest person I have ever met. Thank you for being honest with me."

I held my breath as I waited for the rejection.

"And I am falling for you far faster than I should."

My breath caught, and my hearts pounded in my chest. Relief suddenly flooded my entire body.

CHAPTER EIGHTEEN

Elena

Anaki and I walked up to the bar, our fingers intertwined. The streets were busy with people doing their usual shopping, and cars driving by. As the end of spring approached and summer was around the corner, it was still unusually chilly for my taste. When a gentle breeze blew by, I would feel the cool air nip at my nose. The light sweater I brought did little to shield my usually toasty skin.

My nose ran, and I wiggled my nose several times with the back of my hand. Anaki was observant and immediately thought the worst.

I knew it was the weather because I was used to the scorching sun, but Anaki thought the world was ending, because apparently 'humans had terrible immune systems.' He demanded that I see Nadia and have her check on me. She was studying to be a doctor for the club and was also his good friend. The way he worried was so damn cute I couldn't say no.

Not when his words from earlier this morning hung heavily on my heart.

If this were an ordinary man, a human, I would have reservations about all these emotions. He could twist his words, play at my emotions, and use coercion to make me stay with him. This was Anaki, though, and this strange connection that I felt with him was strong. I felt the truth in his words that I was his world.

Behind those tearful eyes, however, I saw something much, much deeper.

Someone had caused him immense pain, someone vile and evil had crushed his soul. My heart burned with a deep desire to seek this person and bring them to justice, to make them pay for the harm they had inflicted on such a kind soul. Though I had only known Anaki for a few days, I could never imagine this sweet, gentle person hurting anyone.

Anaki possessed an amazing humor and a caring nature, showing genuine concern for Luis and treating me as though I were the most precious woman in the world. Our time together felt like a dream, one that I never wanted to wake up from.

Despite my overwhelming adoration for him, I couldn't deny the fear that coursed through me. This was too much, too fast. A dragon had declared his love for me mere days after meeting me, claiming his very soul belonged to me. It was a whirlwind of emotions, and I wasn't sure if I was ready to handle the weight of it all.

He said his soul belonged to me. Who says that? That should be in a damn proposal. It made me melt, made me want to take it and cherish it so no one would ever hurt him again.

Did I really want that?

I did, I really did.

I couldn't shake off the memories of Abuela's words about soul mates. They had always seemed silly to me, but now they were haunting me. Emm would scoff at Abuela's tangents. I was young and naive and wanted to be just like my big, bad ass sister, so I ignored Abuela, too. But now, I couldn't help but wonder if there was some truth to it all.

Was I missing out on something by being closed off to the idea of a soul mate? My mind was torn between embracing and rejecting the concept.

If I thought hard enough, I could remember Abuela dancing naked in the woods. She told us as we walked out into the woods that she would ask someone for a blessing. I was thinking it would be a priest. Obviously, that didn't happen. She had an enormous pile of wood set up for a fire, lit it, and stripped down. Then there was a prayer. She threw her hands up, powder going into the fire. She called out to the... Moon Goddess. She stood still, staring up into the sky, unmoving.

Emm took me to a tent to sleep after that.

I rubbed my head. I could just ask Abuela about what had happened. She could have had a stroke while she stared up into the sky, and that was why she did that.

Was it worth looking into now?

Probably, because she knew more about these people than Luis and I did.

I popped my lips together when Anaki opened the front door of the club. It was a way to rid myself of all the thoughts in my head and bring me to the now. The old door creaked, and the bar was much quieter than the night before.

The bar was covered in a thick haze of smoke, creating a hazy atmosphere that made it difficult to see across the room. The clinking of glasses and murmurs of conversations created a calm atmosphere. Anaki winced and put his finger inside his ear to shake it.

"You alright?" I asked, squeezing his hand.

Anaki nodded, giving me a smirk that hid all that pain behind his heart. "Of course, Mama. My hearing is just getting better, so I have to learn to block out the higher-pitched sounds."

Since his soul was healing–because of me–his dragon must be recovering. But how did his dragon get so damaged in the first place? We never talked about that this morning. Was it a family member, a friend? Another lover?

I didn't like the idea that he could have had someone else, but Anaki was handsome and sensual. He could get anyone he wanted. What was it that caused his soul to crush like that? Anaki loved with his whole being, and to hurt him was damn cruel.

I gave him a small smile and rubbed my hand up his arm. "I have some earplugs back in my suitcase. Maybe that could help."

Anaki's smirk grew to a grin. "Maybe I'll try that. We could give some to Bear and Nadia, too, so they don't hear you screaming tonight."

I gasped, my face burning as I snuggled into his arm. "You're terrible."

"Not as terrible as when I take two of your holes," he whispered low into my ear.

My mouth dropped when I looked up at him. "You talk a big game, but can you deliver?" I raised a brow.

It was Anaki's turn to blush and shuffle his feet when we went past the bar. "When you order me to, I will."

Christ, this dragon was going to kill me.

A burst of childish laughter echoed through the dimly lit bar, followed by a joyful cry of "Mama!" The customers didn't even look up from their drinks to watch the small figure darting through the small group of bikers, who stood with beers in their hands.

Luis, with his mop of dark hair and bright smile, came bounding toward me at full speed. I had to prepare myself for the battering ram that was about to knock me over.

I let go of Anaki's hand to try and grab him, but it was Anaki who scooped him up and held him to my height on his arm. "Hey there, we don't need to hurt Mama's back, do we?"

Luis shook his head and smiled. "Wow, we're high!"

I pressed a kiss to Luis' cheek. "I was going to come to the cabin soon.

Why are you here?"

Ignoring me completely, too absorbed in Anaki's attention, Luis petted Anaki's cheek. "Look, dragon, uh..., what is the word, Mama?"

I leaned over to see what Luis was pointing at on Anaki's face, and I saw light blue, shimmering scales near his ears. His ears were also pointed, as they were last night when Emm left the bar. "Your ears. They are pointed and have scales on them."

"*Scales*," Luis repeated. "Muy bonito. I want to have scales."

Anaki rubbed his fingers against them, then grabbed Luis' wrist. "Here, want to touch them?" He grabbed two of Luis' fingers and had him rub them on the scales. "These are impenetrable. That means bullets can't get in, and I can reflect magic."

Luis' eyes grew wide. "You mean Tajah and Bram can't use magic on you? Ever?"

Anaki chuckled. "They can when I am like this." He waved his hand down his body. "If I concentrate hard enough and pay attention, I can absorb less harmful magic. When I am in my dragon form, no magic can touch me."

"Wow, so cool."

Anaki chuckled. "It is. Just wait until I can fully shift, we can go swimming in the lake this summer."

"Yes!" Luis fist-pumped the air.

Abuela stepped out of the hallway where Anaki and I had escaped last night. Her large bag hung on her arm. It probably held her crystals and those cursed mushrooms. Beretta was beside her, with her hand on her shoulder. "There she is. We weren't expecting you for at least a few days. Why are you here?" Abuela narrowed her eyes at me.

Anaki stood up straight and wrapped his arm around me, still holding Luis. "Elena said she felt cold before I took her on a walk. I wanted to make sure she was alright."

"I'm fine." I nudged him. "He's being a little overprotective."

Abuela's wrinkles around her eyes deepened when she smiled. "Good. He needs to be. Bones is busy, but Nadia is upstairs in the clinic."

Anaki cocked his head. "Bones? Busy? He's never busy."

Beretta shook her head. "Best not ask questions, Anaki. It's tense between him and Locke right now."

Anaki pursed his lips and nodded. "That's not what I need. We'll go see Nadia then. Luis, you wanna come?"

Warmth filled me because Anaki wanted to include Luis. Then again, this was Anaki we were talking about.

Luis shook his head. "Nope, we are going to Tajah's shop. She's got witchy stuff in there, and I get to finally meet a warlock!"

Beretta half-laughed, half-purred and pulled Luis from Anaki's arms. Her golden cat eyes twinkled. "Don't worry, we will take good care of him. Have fun, you two."

As Luis waved and blew me a kiss, his smile stretched from ear to ear, radiating pure joy. Beretta's footsteps were light and carefree as she walked him to the door.

Abuela, on the other hand, moved slowly and deliberately, her gaze lingering on each of us before she passed by with a gentle touch on my shoulder. I leaned into her warmth, comforted by her presence. Even if she was crazy, she was familiar.

When I opened my mouth to ask if soul mates were truly real, she quickly shut it with her hand.

"Yes, mija." She snickered and laughed. She laughed and laughed until she cackled and strode out the door like a crazed lunatic.

"I missed that. What just happened?" Anaki asked.

I sighed dramatically and shook my head. "I should have put her in a home."

The clinic was just a small room, with a simple bed beside a sink, and cabinets filled with medical supplies lining the walls. The air was thick with the sharp, sterile smell of ozone, a metallic tang that prickled my nostrils. A few pieces of medical equipment sat in the dimly lit room; an ultrasound machine dominated one corner, while other unfamiliar devices cluttered the space.

I didn't go to doctors' offices often, only to manage my pain. Even then, we paid cash. I held onto paper records, which was easy in Venezuela at the time, to keep myself out of any electronic system.

Not that it didn't help with their club hacker.

Nadia flipped through the paperwork that Abuela had already given her. Abuela needed a good scolding for just giving up information about ourselves. While I did believe these people were good at heart, mostly, you just don't give everyone your private medical records.

"You've had this awhile, and it says you have had to use a cane for several years. Some days you need a wheelchair?"

Anaki was outside. He wanted to come into the room, but Nadia saw the hesitation before I could even answer. Bear appeared out of nowhere in the hallway and pulled him to the side, saying he needed to talk to him, thankfully. I didn't want to reject Anaki, but I didn't want Anaki to feel like I was more fragile than I already was.

I still needed that good dicking later.

"I do have relapses. I have constant pain, but with the medications I am on, it keeps the pain down to a minimum. I'm not sure how much you know about it. After I had Luis, it progressed more, and with the way it's going, I thought I might be in a wheelchair sooner."

Not going to school functions, such as sports, would be heartbreaking when the time came. I didn't want Luis to grow up without a mother being present in his life. Abuela was getting older, so who was going to look after him?

"And now?" Nadia asked as she looked up from the clipboard.

I folded my arms over my lap. "To be honest, the past couple of days, I haven't hurt."

Nadia raised an eyebrow. "You don't hurt? Like, at all?"

I tilted my head in thought. "A few times I did. It wasn't horrible, but I noticed... and this might sound crazy, but when Anaki is around, I don't feel pain. It may be because of adrenaline or something, you know? Just the excitement."

Nadia flipped a few pages and took notes. "I don't find that crazy at all, actually. Did you notice any pain if he left your side?"

I tapped my fingers on my lap. "He left for an afternoon to go get some clothes, and my pain returned, but when he came back"—my eyes widened just a bit—"it went back to a dull ache, then faded when I was by his side later that night."

Nadia pressed her lips together as she tried to hide a smile.

"Does Anaki have magic? Is that why I am feeling better around him?"

Nadia bobbed her head back and forth. "Not the magic you are thinking. It has something to do with Anaki, though." She put her pen down.

"Then, what is it? If he is making me better, then I need to know how he's doing it. I don't want to hurt him in the process. It doesn't hurt him, does it? I'm not sucking his energy or whatever, am I?"

Nadia scrunched up her nose and let out a burst of laughter. "No, no. It isn't anything like that. Anaki's dragon is helping you, that's all. Both he and his dragon care for you very much. He claimed you in front of the entire bar last night when he took off with you. It was even more obvious when you walked in this afternoon with his scent all over you."

I opened and closed my mouth. "Wait, his scent? His body scent?"

"Amongst other things." Nadia smiled.

I groaned and placed my face in my hands. So much for being like Emm and not having any embarrassment about her sexuality. I was nothing like her. She would have laughed and told her man to take her in a closet, to make other men jealous.

I heard Nadia's wheels on her chair scoot across the room until she was next to me. Her small hand patted my back. "Hey, are you okay? I know this has to be a lot."

I sighed and kept my face buried. "I don't know, honestly." I sat up straight. "I'm finally accepting things for what they are, and I'm scared. I am supposed to be mean and tough, not believe in happiness, because that's just not what happens in life."

Nadia scoffed. "You are not your sister at all. We love your sister to pieces, but that isn't the vibe I get. You are like an orange. Soft but durable on the outside and bright, sweet and tangy inside. But Emm's like a pineapple. Tough and prickly on the outside, slightly acidic and a sweet tartness on the inside."

I covered my mouth to laugh.

"I know I'm not her, but I try to be more like her. Stronger, better for everyone. I feel weak because of my illness, of my past, of what I fell for then. I feel like I have to be tough up here." I pointed to my head.

"Yeah, and how is that going for you?" Nadia crossed her arms. "You've been fighting since you got here. Not in the physical sense, but here." She laid her hand on her heart.

I huffed. "Everything is going so perfectly. I'm just worried something terrible is going to happen. It just all seems too good." I sniffed and felt the sting of tears filling my eyes.

Nadia reached over to the counter and pulled out some tissues for me to take. "Elena, you've had it rough so far. Everyone who has ended up here has been kicked when they were down, their hearts shattered, their life permanently altered by someone else. Each member is here looking for something, and that is usually a someone. You are meant to be here, with us."

A guttural sob escaped my throat, catching me off guard. My eyes welled up with tears, blurring my vision as I struggled to hold back the emotions that threatened to consume me. I tried to remind myself that I am strong, that I have always been strong. But in that moment, the facade of toughness crumbled, and all that was left was a fragile shell, shattered by overwhelming pain and vulnerability.

I didn't even know Nadia, and here I was, bare and raw, just as Anaki was this morning.

"I don't know if I'm good enough for him. What if I have a relapse? What if I can't be strong enough? I'm only human. He doesn't want someone who might end up in a wheelchair."

What if all of this was temporary? What if the pain comes back full force?

Nadia stood up and wrapped her arms around me. "Anaki knows you are human, and you two are so perfect for each other. It's almost gross." She giggled into my hair.

"What do you mean?" I sniffed.

"Because he thinks he isn't worthy of you." She ran her fingers through my hair. "You are his sun to take him out of the darkness that he lives in. All that happiness he shows on the outside is just a front, but you knew that already, didn't you?"

I did. I could look into his eyes and see it.

"It's because you can see his soul, Elena. You can feel his pain, you can feel the suffering. You don't pity him, you want to take it away. I do the same with Bear."

"You do?" I whispered.

Nadia nodded. "Of course. When you are soulmates, you want to carry each other's burdens."

CHAPTER NINETEEN

Anaki

With my arms crossed, I gripped my biceps. The pain throbbed when I let my claws pierce the skin in irritation.

"Fuck, you smell like fish," Bear groaned. "Is that what your dragon smells like? No more cuddle piles for you."

I curled my lip in a snarl and leaned in, catching a whiff of his scent. "You smell like a wet teddy bear dipped in sour honey," I remarked, scrunching my nose in distaste. I rolled my eyes, my gaze drifting longingly toward the door that held my mate inside.

"I don't think I've ever seen you in such a mood." Bear chuckled. "Not saying I blame you for it, I was the same before I claimed Nadia."

Elena didn't want me inside. I could see by the look on her face. I could read emotions fairly well; I swore there was a little empath in me. I didn't fight her. I let her go with one of my most trusted friends, but it still stung.

Silent words were spoken between her and Abuela before we arrived. I didn't know what they were, but it snapped something inside her that made me believe she wanted more information about... I wasn't sure what.

I rubbed my hand down my face, my claws coming close to my eye. I winced when it scratched the corner of my brow.

Shit, this was going to be hard getting used to again.

"You both moved fast, too. That's good. I smell her all over you."

I lifted my lip into a smirk. "Yeah, we did. I was surprised myself. The physical part of us is not a problem, it's the emotional part that is still rocky. I fucking love bombed her." I pressed my thumb and forefinger into my eyes.

Bear was leaning up against the wall, and he tapped the back of his head against it. "Not following. What does that mean?"

"Told her she was mine, wasn't letting her go. I was giving her my broken soul, and I'd do anything to keep her."

Bear chuckled and pulled on his beard. "Well, I did that—"

"Then I cried."

Bear gave a horrified look and backed away from me. "You... you cried? In front of her? Did she run away?"

I ran my fingers through my hair and shook my head. "No, she held me and we cuddled for a few hours, then we were going to go on a walk until I brought her here, because I thought she'd got sick. I thought things were fine, but she didn't let me inside."

Bear ran his hand down his face. "You fucking cried? Men don't cry around their women. You let the women cry on you." He wagged his finger at me.

Damnit, did she think of me as weak now? I couldn't help all the emotion that swirled inside of me. All the pain that had settled there for years. I haven't told anyone about it. Elena felt safe.

"What's done is done. You know I'm not like the rest of you." I leaned my body on the door and tried to listen to the conversation inside. Was eavesdropping on a private conversation bad? Yes, and Nadia knew that. That didn't stop Nadia from speaking in a normal tone, and Elena matched it. Elena's voice would stutter and come in hushed tones when she seemed upset. Still, I couldn't quite hear them. My hearing would come and go.

I wanted to break down the door.

Bear shuffled himself until his shoulder leaned against the wall so he could look at me. "That's not what I meant. I just mean, fuck. You know how I am. I don't like to talk all that mushy shit."

"Man of action, little talk or thought. Yeah, I know who you are." My smile widened. "Nadia likes the strong, silent type, but I'm going with my gut on this one. The goddess is trying to make it right. Give me a mate who would understand. I'm showing her all of me, even if it terrifies me."

Bear hummed, his bear rumbling deep within his chest. "Proud of you." was all he said, and that was all I needed to hear. He put his large hand on my shoulder, and before I could really let the praise sink in, I heard a near-silent sob from my mate. Sniffles, and then the salty tears invaded my nose.

I was done standing on the other side of the door.

My back straightened, and my hand landed on the doorknob. I shook it several times, but it wouldn't open.

"They are in the middle of an exam. Nadia always locks the door," Bear said as he tried to pull me back.

I growled, my lip pulled back showing my long, serrated teeth. Bear backed away, his hands in the air. "Fuck! Your face, man." He stared at it with concern.

Not caring, I pushed the door in with my shoulder. It didn't budge at first because all the doors in this place were reinforced. Locke had a thing for protection for those who needed it, and if anyone went rabid, we could temporarily lock them in their rooms, or members could lock themselves in their rooms.

My dragon didn't like it.

I snarled, my voice turned into a low, feral growl, and I shoved forward with an urgent force. My dragon compelled me to get inside quickly. The possibilities that flashed through my mind were terrifying: was Elena injured, distraught, or had someone from the cartel managed to find us? Or worse, could it be Idris?

The mere thought sent a fresh surge of adrenaline coursing through my veins as I hurled myself against the door once more. Bear stepped back, allowing the door to swing open with a creaking protest. Inside, Nadia stood motionless, her expression blank. She knew that if she showed emotion, a shifter could become worse. Meanwhile, Elena was on the far side of the bed, her body trembling like a leaf caught in a storm.

"Way to go, Anaki. You scared her," Nadia said calmly.

My hearts thundered as I ran into the room. Elena screamed and threw her hands out to protect her head. "No, no! Please! I'll stop crying!" I stopped and looked back and forth between the two of them.

Nadia stood slowly and put her hand on the bed. "Anaki, I need you to make slow movements now. It appears she has some PTSD."

"What?" My voice rose higher.

"Post-traumatic stress. From her past with her ex. You barging in here while she was crying probably triggered it. I need you to back up. Bear, stay at the doorway, please." Nadia's hand reached out to signal him in a 'stay' position.

I found myself torn between retreating and moving closer to her. I longed to ease her suffering, just as she had soothed me this morning. Yet, what was it that haunted her so deeply that my breaking down the door only added to her distress? I believed she would appreciate my concern, my desire to console her. But instead, I inadvertently dredged up a painful memory, leaving her in turmoil.

Nadia carefully stood up from her seat and rounded the bed. She positioned herself closer to my mate. Her knees bent in a crouch; her posture deliberately submissive. Nadia's movements were slow and deliberate, conveying a sense of caution.

Around the bed, Elena sat with her hand clamped tightly over her mouth, as if to stifle a cry. She squeezed her eyes shut, and tears streamed down her cheeks in a steady flow, glistening like tiny rivers in the harsh light. The room was heavy with tension, each breath and movement echoing in the silent space.

I let out a low, anguished whine that resonated through the air. My scales, glistening and iridescent, began to unfurl and cascade down my arms and across my torso like a shimmering waterfall. An unbearable itch spread through my limbs as they forcefully erupted through my skin.

Pain radiated down my spine. I gritted my teeth when I felt my dragon push himself from my mind to my body. I kept my physical pain silent and pushed the back of my jeans lower as I felt a horrible pain extend to my tailbone.

"Holy fucking shit," Bear whispered. "You cannot shift here. How big do you fucking get?!"

Nadia darted her head to Bear's voice. "I said calm!"

I ground my teeth together, a fierce growl rumbling in my throat. "It's impossible to stay calm when my mate is suffering!" I could feel my tail forcing its way out of my body with a searing intensity. Unlike a lizard's sturdy appendage, mine was sinuous and agile, resembling a serpent, though it never reached the full length of my true form.

"Please, love. It's me," I grated.

Elena panted, her sweat sprinkled on her brow.

"Look at me, Mama. Come on. It's hurting me to stay away from you. Please let me touch you."

I felt tiny scales gradually emerging across my face. My ears stretched and elongated, becoming sharp and pointed, resembling the tapered leaves of a willow tree.

Nadia was closer to her, and my dragon let out a low growl in her direction. In my periphery, I saw Bear move his arm for her to back away. She did so, thankfully, because I don't know what my dragon would do seeing our mate in this state.

Elena's eyes opened, and her hand reached for the sheets of the bed. She grabbed them and held tight to anchor herself.

"That's it, love. It's me. Keep your eyes on me, okay?" I kept my voice light and airy as I approached. She didn't scream, but her eyes still watered. "I'm coming around the bed. I'm going to come closer."

She hiccupped softly, her frail body slumped against the cold, unforgiving floor. Her eyes, a mixture of fear and confusion, lingered on me, scanning up and down before she edged closer to the wall. It tore at my heart to witness her retreating from me like that. Every fiber of my being longed to embrace her, to shield her from harm, but the true battle raged within her, an internal storm from which I could offer no refuge. Helplessness weighed heavily on me, knowing there was nothing I could do to quell the turmoil she faced.

"That's it. There's my love. I'm here. I'm going to pick you up now, okay?" I sat on the floor and scooped her up into my arms. Immediately, she wrapped her arms around my neck and buried her face into my chest. My tail wrapped around her as well.

Yes, this was right. So right.

Nadia stood and pointed to the door as she headed out, closing it behind her. I nodded my head in thanks and took a big sigh.

I petted my mate's hair as I rocked her. "Shh, it's going to be okay. I'm here, I will not let anything happen to you."

This had to be about her ex. A fiery rage surged through me, and I wished he were alive just so I could tear him apart limb from limb, obliterate him into dust, and scatter his remains to the winds. A feral growl erupted from deep within, vibrating through my very core, as Elena whimpered once more. The growl threatened to turn into a roar, but my dragon intervened, releasing a deep, resonant purr—a sound I could never produce on my own—to calm and comfort her.

My mate let out a hoarse breath. "Anaki?" Her hand gripped my tight shirt, and she took in a deep breath.

"It's alright. Everything is fine. You are in the medical room, and you gave us a scare." I ran my hand up and down her arm. "I heard you crying, smelled your tears, and tried to bust down the door." I chuckled nervously and pressed a kiss to her forehead. "I'm so sorry I acted so brashly, my dragon couldn't stand hearing you cry."

She hummed and tried to bury herself further into my hold. I didn't complain, not one bit, especially after the morning I had and the words that Bear had spoken earlier. I felt... emasculated.

"No, it wasn't your fault. I was surprised, and memories from my past flared up and—" she went silent and rubbed her nose against my neck.

I pushed her hair away from her face so she couldn't hide from me. "Do you want to talk about it, or just rest?" I couldn't force her to tell me what happened in her past. It wasn't right, especially since I had yet to scratch the surface of my own pain.

She had hidden hers well. While I knew she had a terrible past, she didn't show it in the short time we had been together. Just the few comments she had made.

Women were both formidable and unyielding, a fact I understood well from observing the bonded mates of the Iron Fang members. Yet, there were moments when I questioned whether this strength was as unwavering as it seemed.

A long, dramatic sigh escaped her lips. She swallowed, nodded, but did not release her hold on my shirt. I enjoyed that she held onto me like an anchor. I knew it was the bond that gave her the courage, and she was truly accepting that I wouldn't go anywhere.

She parted her lips to speak, but buzzing broke our thoughts. I darted my head to the noise to find her bag lying on the floor.

"It's my phone. Probably Emmie."

Elena didn't reach for it, nor did I, not wanting to ruin the moment. It finally quit buzzing, signaling it went to voicemail. We stayed silent until the buzzing returned.

Elena huffed in annoyance. "She won't stop until I answer. She will think I'm in trouble."

I scooted across the floor, not willing to let my mate go. She tried to hold down her giggle when we got close enough for my tail to grab hold of her bag.

I reached inside and found the buzzing had stopped. I turned it on and quickly messaged the annoyed future Luna. *"We're okay. Abuela and Luis have a cold and are sleeping. Try calling later."*

I showed Elena the message, and she nodded into my chest before I hit send and tossed it back into her bag. My tail wrapped around both of us, giving her a tight squeeze.

"It isn't much to tell. Well, a lot that I won't get into anyway. I feel like a lot of the memories are fading, it's been so long, but the big memories still stand out, the hurtful ones, you know?"

I pressed my lips to her forehead and stroked her cheek.

"I was foolish in my younger years when Emm ran off to the States. I was too young to go with her when she left, but as I got older, I thought she would come back for me, take me with her. She didn't. What she did was dangerous, and my health had deteriorated. I had muscle weakness, became clumsy and fatigued. Emm couldn't risk me.

I understood why, but I was still mad at her about it. I rebelled and decided to live away from Abuela for a little while. Gain some independence. I got a job, dated a few guys, nothing serious. The pain was controllable back then, but then I met Cedro," she said his name with distaste.

My dragon clawed inside me; he wanted to rip something apart.

"He was confident, suave, and knew how to woo a woman. With me being so naïve and young, I fell for it. We dated for two months before I moved in with him." She winced. "I didn't see the red flags then, but there were so many. He was overly possessive. He told me what I could and couldn't wear, had to know where I was at all times, and drove me to and from work. I thought, *Hey, he's caring.* Really, he wanted to control me."

As Elena spoke, her voice quivered with raw emotion. Her grip on my shirt tightened, as if grounding herself through the retelling of her painful past. I listened intently, every word she uttered carved a deeper understanding of the strength she possessed beneath her gentle exterior.

She continued in a dull voice. "One night, it all changed. I found out about his dealings with drugs, illegal activities that put us both in danger. When I confronted him, he... he lashed out. The man I thought loved me had become a monster in an instant."

Tears welled up in Elena's eyes, shimmering like diamonds in the harsh light of the medical room. My heart ached for the pain she had endured, for the scars that marred her soul. Gently, I wiped away a tear that escaped, tracing the path along her cheek with my thumb.

"He... he hit me," she whispered, her voice barely above a breath. "He stormed off and left, but when he came back the next day, he told me how sorry he was, that he was drunk and he would never do it again."

My heart plummeted into the depths of my stomach like a lead weight, and I threw my head back, feeling a wave of dizzying dread crash over me.

"I never left. Well, it was on and off. I left a couple of times, only for him to guilt me into coming back. Abuela thought I was crazy with our on-again, off-again relationship, but what she didn't know was... he had threatened her life if I didn't return."

I felt my dragon's eyes surface and glow. "Elena, you should have told her."

She chuckled darkly. "I wanted to prove myself strong. I could be just like Emm. I would save her like she was saving us. Emm kept the cartel away and sent us money to help. I couldn't put that on Abuela." She bowed her head and wouldn't look at me.

"Damnit." I nuzzled into her face. "I wish I was there. I wish I knew you then, I would have stopped it all."

She reached her hand up and petted my face. "I'm sure you would have. That's the sweetness of you." She gave a sad smile.

"I was finally rid of him when he found out I was pregnant. That was what he feared most: a woman officially attached to him with a child and having to actually support them. He accused me of cheating when really, he had cheated on me the whole time. I was a weak woman." Her shoulders shrank into herself.

I pulled her from my chest so she could straddle me. My tail wrapped around her waist, and I put both her hands on my shoulders. "You, my pretty female, are not a weak woman." My nose flared, smelling her salty tears. "You are strong, you survived. You took care of Abuela, your child, and yourself." I let out a sad chuckle. "He's beautiful. He looks just like you, and if he's lucky, he will get his humor from me."

Elena half-laughed, half-cried, as more tears ran down her face.

"You are even stronger for being with me. A dragon. A dragon who has weird customs, and lives at a bar with a bunch of shifters who are fucking crazy. And! And! I cried in your arms this morning, and you are still at my side. You should have run to the hills. Men don't cry in front of their women." Bear's words still rang in my ears.

Elena ran her hands over my chest and sniffed. "I like you how you are. You are open and honest. It isn't what I'm used to, it's refreshing." She licked her lips as her hands rested on my shoulders. "You okay if I'm still a little broken?"

My dragon growled, and I placed my forehead against hers. "Love, we are both broken. We will fix each other."

CHAPTER TWENTY

Elena

My body felt exhausted after the sudden flashback. I didn't want to get into the deeper details of what exactly happened in my past, so I glossed over a lot of it because I didn't want to subject Anaki, or anyone, to what I truly went through.

It was a time in my life I wanted to forget.

When Anaki burst through the door, I was sent back to the very last time he hit me, when *he* caught me crying. It was when I found out I was pregnant with Luis. I thought I would be forever attached to Cedro, and that was when those two pink lines appeared. A wave of sheer terror cascaded over me when that realization hit me.

Back then, when I was trapped under Cedro's oppressive control, I often had panic attacks. I was trapped and had no one to turn to. Cedro was no longer the man I thought he was, too hyped up on the latest drug or sloppy drunk. I'd barricaded myself in a bedroom, heart racing, tears streaming, while he was away to let out my frustration and the panic. The dread of him returning loomed large. If he found me crumpled on the floor, a vulnerable wreck, he'd unleash his fury, striking me until I either stifled my sobs or passed out.

When I missed my period, I had to check. I was in a straight-up panic when I was four days late.

What would he do? His blood, his lineage was within me. There was really no escape now.

I tried to stop the tears when I heard the door slam shut, but he was quick. When he couldn't find me waiting for him at the door like he usually liked, he stomped through the house and called my name.

I didn't answer and prayed he would pass out, or trip and fall.

Cedro kicked the door open, and I begged him not to hit me. I felt a searing pain through my cheek, but I covered my belly to protect the child that was growing inside me.

Even though it was part Cedro, it was half mine.

"The fuck is this?" he shouted when his tall, imposing form hovered over the sink. His eyes widened when he took in the positive results. "You can't fucking have this!" Cedro stepped closer. The veins in his neck pulsated, and my body shook in fear. "Get rid of it!"

"No! I can't!" My voice shook. "I will not. This is one thing I cannot do!"

Cedro's sneer twisted his face as he hurled the test at me with a force that could shatter glass. His finger shot up like an accusing dagger, stabbing the air in front of me, bobbing up and down with the authority of a tyrant passing judgment. "It's not mine," he spat, his voice dripping with venom. "You're a whore. I know you are. Every single time you disappeared from my sight, you were out there, flaunting yourself. That's when you got knocked up, isn't it?"

I shook my head while tears rolled down my face. I held my cheek where I felt the bruise form.

"Ah, you did!" He narrowed his bloodshot eyes. He was paranoid, and it had been happening a lot as of late. I don't know what he was on anymore, but he always accused me of the most ridiculous things.

"Get your shit and leave!" I didn't question him. I hauled myself off the floor and slipped several times, my muscles too weak from the stress. I let out a sob when he tried to kick me.

I left my things, which weren't much, anyway. A few clothes, toiletries, even the phone he gave me had a tracker on it.

I let out a trembling sigh and squeezed my eyes shut to get rid of the memory.

Anaki's tail, which was longer than it had been at the clinic, squeezed around my leg.

We were back in his cave, the walk we were supposed to take, long forgotten. He brought me back here to the security of his cave. He said I needed to rest, and I didn't even bother to fight him on it. I was embarrassed by what had happened in front of Nadia, no matter how many times she said it was okay and told me that many other women had similar backgrounds to mine.

Trauma, lots of trauma.

It made me feel a little better with that information, but my body was exhausted being tense with the emotional pain when that memory came charging back, like a bull.

"I thought you were asleep there for a while, you were so still." Anaki's hand ran through my hair.

It was past dusk. There was no sense of time, with no windows and no clocks anywhere to be seen.

Anaki fed me and dressed me in clothing that he had bought just for me. It was a short nightgown, donned in a deep navy blue with gold threading throughout. It made me smile at how he had us in matching outfits because he didn't come to bed naked either. This was cuddle time, he said.

No taking both holes tonight.

I was slightly disappointed, but Anaki was in his *care mode*. He made dinner from scratch, and I didn't feel like leaving his side. While cooking an amazing meal, he set up a chair in the kitchen. He wrapped his tail around my leg, unable to bear the thought of not touching me.

His tail was very flexible, smooth, and sparkling under the light, even if most of his scales were different shades of blue. It reminded me of fish when you brought them out of the water, how their scales glistened in the sun.

He had changed out of his pants quickly when we came back from the clinic, forgoing the shirt as he put on his sarong to let his tail peek out at the bottom. He appeared much more comfortable that way, and I wondered if he was mostly in this half-dragon form often, or if he just couldn't put his tail away right now.

I hesitated to ask, fearing I might embarrass him and he would try to put it away. I didn't want him to. I couldn't deny the comfort his tail brought me. It was soothing and reassuring, a constant reminder that someone was there for me.

Because, unfortunately, Emm and Abuela weren't. It wasn't their fault, of course.

I'd never told Abuela or Emm the story of Cedro because of my pride. Anaki was the first, and it felt good to get that weight off my shoulders. Especially someone who felt like they knew me, or maybe understood me.

Anaki nuzzled my neck as he held me from behind. He had me stand, and I felt the warmth of his body envelop me. I welcomed his touch and pressed my body into him.

"I'm just a little restless," I said honestly.

Anaki pressed a tender kiss on my shoulder. A shiver ran up my spine and I tried not to push my ass into his cocks. I wonder if his tail could do something, too? Its tip was tapered, and small fins were higher up; I wouldn't mind if he fucked me with it.

I wiggled my butt into his crotch.

Dios Mio, really Elena?

"Love, I don't think that's a good idea." Anaki reached forward and cupped my mound. "I can feel your body is tense, and I know your body will continue to be if I make you orgasm, too much."

"Getting to be cocky, aren't you?" I hummed and rubbed my head into the pillow.

Anaki leaned up on his elbow, and I rolled onto my back so I could look up at him. His eyes held so much sorrow, and I didn't think that my episode this afternoon would hurt him like this. It was like my pain was his, and I didn't like it.

"I'm okay, really. It was in the past."

The back of Anaki's hand tickled my cheek. "I know. I wish none of that happened to you, though. You have gone through a lot and went through it all on your own, but I don't think you have told me the worst of it."

I pursed my lips and shook my head. "Would you want me to know every detail of your past?"

It was Anaki's turn to sigh sorrowfully. "No, but eventually I will have to tell you some of my demons before I officially claim you." He smirked, and his tail wrapped tightly around my leg.

While he was cheerful on the outside, I knew he had darkness inside him. We were more alike than I realized.

Anaki lay back down on the bed, this time pulling my body so we were chest to chest. He kept a firm hand on my back to keep me flush with his body. He took in deep breaths of my hair while I listened to the thump of his hearts.

"Tell me a story," I mumbled into his chest.

I loved the sound of his voice. It was playful, a little sarcastic, and it wasn't deep and scary like most of the men at the bar.

He laughed. "A story, huh?"

"Yeah, like how you got to the Iron Fang."

I felt Anaki rub his chin with his hand. He hummed in agreement and settled closer to me. "Alright, I'll tell you where I came from. How about that? Promise to try to go to sleep, though."

I leaned back and did a crisscross over my chest with my finger. "Cross my heart," I stated.

Anaki rolled his eyes and pulled me back into his arms.

"A menace you are."

I closed my eyes and listened.

Anaki

"My home was nestled around a vast expanse of crystal-clear water known as Mehoen. The glittering surface was surrounded by stretches of white sand, where my clan's dragons basked in the warm rays of our sun. Towering cliffs framed the edges of the water, their peaks disappearing into the clouds. Lush trees dotted the landscape, branches reaching out over the tranquil waters to soak in the light. There were cascading vines draped over the rocky cliffs. I would wake up to this breathtaking view of my home in one of the caves and feel grateful for the magical place I called home."

Elena smiled and nestled closer to me. "Sounds like a fairy tale. Where is this place exactly?"

"Elysian. It isn't here on Earth, love. It's in another realm."

Elena's mouth dropped. "What? That's impossible!"

"As impossible as a dragon holding you?"

She nestled her head closer to my head and rolled her eyes. "Fine, you got me. Only because your tail is holding my leg."

I hummed in agreement. "Now hush. Don't interrupt the storyteller."

Elena pouted and nipped at my skin.

"We didn't live primitively, but we appreciated nature, wanted to preserve it like our ancestors did. We traded with other species such as shifters, witches, and fae. We also went to markets for what we needed, for special clothing and cloth, but we mostly stayed to ourselves. We were an oddity, rare, and we didn't want to bring attention to ourselves.

"You see, according to legends, dragons have been around longer than any other shifter. We roamed both the Earth and Elysian Realms. While there have never been many of us in number, we were strong because of the armor of our scales. They kept us from harm. Unlike most shifters, we could also absorb magic. Unfortunately, we cannot harness or wield it. Our scales are only there for protection."

"You're indestructible," Elena murmured.

I shook my head. "Not quite. While we are strong in our human forms, we can be killed. Dragon forms are harder, but there are weak points. It depends on the type of dragon. I am a water dragon. There are earth, sky, and fire dragons with all their own cultures, but you know water dragons are the best."

Elena hummed, and her body relaxed against me as she continued to listen.

"As I said, the white sand that surrounded the lake was clean, the water fresh and crisp." I closed my eyes as I remembered it like it was yesterday, feeling the fresh air blowing through my hair.

"Dragons set up tents along the beaches. They were just like this." Elena and I gazed around it. I did my best to bring my family home here, to help me remember the good times. "We had lots of places for seating. Our caves had beds and blankets like this, and the tents were the party area."

I chuckled. "The cold walls reminded me of being alone, so I prefer the tent."

Elena's hand stroked over my chest as if to comfort me.

"The tents were always filled with laughter because they were for gatherings of our clan. We all ate and drank together at least one meal, usually at dusk. We would hunt fish, which we mostly ate raw. Equivalent to sushi, I believe. We ate fruit, but preferred the meat mostly. Red meat was a treat, but it didn't do well in our stomachs."

I huffed out a laugh. "I remember the one time I ate my first bite of steak and my mother scolded me for eating the whole thing. The next day, I sank to the bottom of the lake, and she had to fish me out before I drowned. Young children didn't get their gills until they were ten."

Elena made a face of horror.

"You said you were going to try and go to sleep."

"You almost died! How can that be relaxing?"

Oh, honey, just you wait until I tell you the bad stuff.

"Any who... tents served as lively venues for parties, where we held celebrations of all kinds. Under the vast canopy of stars, we gathered for the full moons, paid homage to the goddess, and the joyous occasion of new couples. These new pairings were especially grand, as they were rare and treasured events. These parties would stretch on for an entire week. The adults indulged in so much wine, they'd laugh and forget all their worries, while the fledglings darted around in playful games. Tables were filled with an abundance of sweet desserts, only for special occasions, and we feasted until we could eat no more."

Elena's eyes closed, and she hummed in contentment.

"My favorite part was the dancing, though." I gazed up at the softly glowing lantern above, its gentle light casting flickering shadows all around.

"The dance was an artful display where the males performed for their--partners. Unlike on Earth, it was not the females who were tasked with impressing the males. In my clan, the males had to earn their place before a female, showcasing their worthiness.

As the celebration began, each male, even the mated ones, adorned himself with his most treasured possessions—gleaming gold chains that caught the moonlight, intricately designed bangles that jingled with every movement, and garments of the finest silk shimmered with every step. The rhythmic pounding of drums accompanied by the excited melodies of flutes. The male's dance had always captivated me, ever since I was a child. The fluid and swift movements resembled the surging waters of a rapid river. Their movements were a blend of strength and grace, each step an elegant yet strong expression.

"I practiced in the confines of my cave when I was old enough to have one of my own. I'd dance to the invisible beat of the drums as I moved my body at impossible angles. I'd stretch morning and night, wanting to please my future mate."

And I was going to do it, for Elena.

I let out a sigh and gazed down at my future. Her heart was pounding in her chest, but her eyes were closed. I could smell her arousal. The heat of her body had risen several degrees. I knew she would like the idea of a male dancing for her. I didn't mean to escalate her arousal further.

Whoops.

I rolled to my side, wrapped her into my arms, and placed a kiss on her forehead.

At least I knew she would like it. I just had to find the right time to do it.

CHAPTER TWENTY-ONE

Anaki

Elena's scent had completely flooded every corner of the nest, overwhelming it with her essence. My dragon was deliriously content, thrashing his tail within me with an intense satisfaction that our home was drenched with her scent. It filled us with a profound comfort and a fierce, unyielding calm, a promise carved in stone that she would always be with us, despite the lingering fear of what I had yet to reveal.

My dragon believed in nothing else. It was final. She was ours even if there was no mark on her body.

After I told her last night about where I had grown up and how fascinated she was because of it, I thought taking her to a more magical place, other than my cave, was in order. The fae had brought a little Elysian to a hidden part of the forest where they had colonized and kept to themselves.

It would be the perfect place to take her, to show her a hint of the magic from where I had come.

While the forest that Locke owns had a dappling of moss, vines and trees that do not belong on Earth that the fae had placed for him in thanks, the area the fae had claimed is completely of their home realm.

Elena appeared to be a new woman this morning. Her smile was playful, and yesterday's awful memories were forgotten, thank the goddess. I prepared her breakfast while she bathed in a heated pool in the back of the cave, so she could have her privacy. I felt it was important that she could have time to herself, even if it was hard for me to step away from her.

She needed time, even though the need to claim her grew by the second.

My tail, scales and ears had finally retreated into my body while I slept. I didn't have control over them yesterday, and I was glad Elena didn't ask about it. I would have told her a white lie anyway, too embarrassed to tell her it was because my dragon was agitated. He wanted to have hardened scales, claws, and other ways to protect her if anything physical happened to her when she was in such a vulnerable state.

I knew nothing would happen to her, not in the middle of the club with so many members there to protect the weak, but my dragon didn't understand that. This environment was still too new to him, and he didn't trust it.

Later, she changed into another dress, which she apparently had a lot of. She appeared to have embraced a renewed sense of self when she appeared at the entrance of my cooking area while I finished our breakfast. The burden she carried was lifted, and even a playful smile had taken over her.

It was my turn to tell her what I hid from her, but I didn't have the strength. Not yet.

Coward.

As always, she was stunning, but I knew she would feel a chill since she was so used to the warmer climate. She wore the only sweater she owned. I already anticipated this, and just last night when she lay in my arms while she slept, I had already placed additional orders for more clothing, cozy blankets, and warm jackets These essentials would arrive within the next day or two, ensuring she would soon be enveloped in warmth and comfort.

I wouldn't have my mate going without, but where we were going, she would do well with what she wore. She may even take off that sweater.

I kept her close to my side as we walked, pardoning myself, as I scrolled through the group text messages from Bear and Nadia. Elena took in the surrounding scenes as we traveled down the pathway and seemed to enjoy the silence.

I'm not privy to a lot of information from the inner circle, but when it involved Bear and Nadia, I was told what was necessary. I was ultimately surprised when some of the members were leaving, as well as Tajah and Beretta.

The mansion that held Duke Idris, once owned by Delilah's ex-husband Sean, was filled with women, and more were coming in by the day. Why, we weren't exactly sure, but they had good guesses.

More trafficking.

I wanted to groan in irritation. I fucking hated Idris and had really hoped he had died in the fire, when Grim and Journey had the standoff with him at the warehouse a while ago, but here we were.

I worried for Nadia to go back into that hellhole; I wanted her to stay here, but with Bear and Nadia's bond and it being so fresh, they couldn't leave each other. I hoped her mind would stay straight and that she could handle the situation carefully.

I worried for her, like a sister obviously, and I knew Bear would take care of them. A lot of the fae would be with them as well, including Nadia's parents. It was to be an undercover mission. No blood spilled, just a quick in and out and bring the women back here, but is it ever so simple?

Not once had it ever been simple. Plans never go accordingly.

I pressed my lips tightly together and reluctantly slid my phone back into my pocket. The urge to safeguard those I loved tugged at me, yet I was painfully aware that joining the mission might not be the best choice. Without Elena by my side, I felt incomplete, and she was still human, so her pain would inevitably return. I couldn't bear the thought of her suffering. Yet, staying back gnawed at me; if I went, my strength might falter, rendering me ineffective in their efforts. I was torn between the desire to help and the fear of becoming a burden.

Elena squeezed my hand as we approached the towering trees with dark blue bark, their immense presence casting long shadows on the forest floor. The thick vines coiled around the trunks like serpents, adorned with clusters of tiny yellow berries that glowed softly in the dappled sunlight. The air grew increasingly sweet, a heady blend of honeysuckles, lavender, and ripe strawberries, as we drew nearer to an enchanting area where the vines draped like a veil, concealing a hidden world I eagerly planned to share with her.

Members haven't been this far out into the forest. Locke being out in the wild was a deterrent. Bear and I had been the only ones who have been out here, we could handle ourselves.

I take that back. Bear could handle it. If I got ripped to shreds, I didn't care.

"This is different," Elena said, ripping me from my thoughts.

I pulled her hand up to mine and pressed a kiss to the back of it. Her face heated, and she looked away.

"I wanted to show you something. You were so interested in last night's story about the Elysian Realm, I thought I would let you see a piece of it."

She raised her eyebrow and came closer as I touched the vines. I parted them slightly and paused. "I've only been here a few times. Last time I was here, they were only halfway done building. I'm not sure what it's like now. They work quickly. Especially now that they can work without fear, and it isn't as cold."

"Without fear?"

My shoulders slumped. "Yes, the fae were hidden away in Russia for a long time. They came to Earth for refuge. The Elysian Realm is full of politics. The dragons just stayed away from most of it. We were powerful despite our low numbers, and magic had little effect on us."

Elena frowned and squeezed my hand again. "Fae, certain shifters, even witches, sought power, but that is a story for a different time. These fae, the spring and summer, found Earth and hid for many years, until Locke offered protection to them recently. There is a dome, that Tajah created with her magic, to conceal the territory so no humans flying above can see it."

Elena's eyes widened. "That's amazing. Is Tajah's magic unlimited?"

I chuckled. "Definitely not. She is powerful, and more so with Bram. He is an ancient, powerful warlock who lives here. He is weak now, but he continues to teach her. I don't know the logistics. Tajah can hold so many rune papers, or whatever. You would have to ask them. I know nothing of magic. Just the awesomeness of this body." I ran my hand down my chest.

Elena snorted, shrugged her shoulders, and stepped closer to me. "Well, aren't you going to let me in?"

I bobbed my head back and forth. "Sure, give me your sweater first."

She obeyed, but a questioning face lingered. "You will not need it. Besides, I enjoy gazing at your backside without anything hiding it."

Elena swatted my butt, and I held open the vines for her. She instantly gasped as I pulled her inside the otherworldly domain living inside the forest.

In place of the typically overcast sky that blankets the forest of the Pacific Northwest, the area was bright, bathed in a radiant light that transformed the area. Tiny particles of dust drifted lazily before us, each particle shimmering with golden- and silvery-like glitter, creating a dazzling dance in the air. The bark of the trees, usually cloaked in somber shades, displayed a palette of light grays and whites, mirroring the brilliance of the foliage above. Leaves, tinged with hues of gold, light greens, and delicate pink, caught the sunlight and glowed with an ethereal beauty, casting a spell of vibrant enchantment over the forest.

The grass, thick like moss, sank under us with each step. For once, Elena was silent as she stepped forward, taking in the sight. Once we stepped off the moss and onto the dirt path, rows of homes guided our way.

Twisted branches, vines and trees made up the homes. It didn't appear that anyone had used a hammer or cut any wood. It was all nature that had created the small community.

"Huh." I scratched my head. "They made a little town so damn fast. Kinda neat."

Elena's mouth hung open, with her arms flopped at her sides. "What do you mean, kind of neat? This is incredible! How long did it take to make a place like this?"

"Not long!" A feminine voice came from one house. The tightly woven door shut behind them, and she pranced over to us. She was everything a summer fae should look like. She had golden sparkles on her cheeks, pointed ears, and typical human clothing of jeans and a short-sleeved shirt. More so, she could go into the human town if she so wished. She was, however, barefoot to feel the earth beneath her feet, and her cheeks were a bright red, as if she'd been out in the sun too much. "Name is Meriam. The forest said you were coming. We thought we would give you time to acclimate before we rushed you, since you brought a human."

Several other fae came out of their homes. Most were women, only one male. They all gave us enormous smiles and came toward us.

"I'm sorry, you said the forest told you?" Elena stepped forward.

Meriam nodded. "Yes, we can listen to the forest. Each tree, shrub, and flower is alive; you just have to listen. That is what the spring and summer fae do. There are usually more of us, but many of us left this morning." Meriam gave a small smile, and another female put her arm around her shoulder.

I nodded in encouragement. "They will be safe. There won't be any fighting. It will just be a quick extraction."

"What?" Elena asked. "What's going on?"

A male summer fae stood beside me, his presence as striking as the midday sun. He towered over me, though he lacked the robust build one might expect. Instead, he evoked the image of a tall Japanese Maple transformed into human form, with his elongated, slender frame and flowing deep crimson hair that cascaded down like leafy branches. "Duke Idris," he began, his voice smooth yet urgent, "a stone fae, has taken humans captive, and our kin are assisting the Iron Fang in liberating them. We owe this club our very lives and would go to any lengths to repay that debt."

Elena's eyes now filled with worry. "I didn't know that was going on, Anaki. Why didn't you tell me?"

I ran my hand through my hair. "I just found out before I brought you here. Bear, Nadia, Beretta and Tajah have gone, too. I'm not sure where Abuela and Luis are. I wanted to bring you here before we went to find them. Show you a little of the sunshine you missed, before—"

"Ah, Abuela and Luis? They are here!" Merium interrupted. "They are in my home. I was told to keep them hidden until Tajah and Beretta returned. Come on."

Elena and I exchanged a lingering look before we were gently ushered into the intricately branched home. The light, wooden vines were artfully woven into the structure, their broad gaps allowing sunlight to stream in from above, casting a warm glow throughout the interior. At the rustic wooden table, Abuela and Luis sat, deeply engrossed in a lively card game while savoring brunch-style food. The aroma of freshly brewed coffee mingled with the scent of toasted bread.

"Luis?" Elena yelled.

"Mama!" He jumped up from the table and ran to her, this time being more gentle, and gave her a tight hug. "I got to see the fae! I also got to see Tajah's shop. Mom, I can wield fire!"

Elena's eyes widened. "I'm sorry, what?"

Luis crossed his eyes and stared in front at his fingers. He snapped them together, and a small flame appeared. "See! Fire!!"

"Umm," Merium began. "Let's not do that in the house. The vines don't like fire so much."

Luis covered his mouth. "Lo siento! I will not do it again!"

Elena stood up tall and threw her shoulders back. "Abuela, why can Luis wield fire? What did Tajah do to him?!" Her accent came out thick, and I felt my cocks twitch in reaction.

My mate was hot when she was mad.

Abuela waved her hand in dismissal. "Ah, don't worry about it. It's only fire. It isn't like he can summon the Moon Goddess like I can." She wiggled in her seat in satisfaction as she rearranged her cards. "After that blood test she did, we found out that we do have magic in our lineage, which I suspected."

Elena perked her head up at that.

"I had awakened most of mine, but by doing it myself, I did not come to my full power. But it was enough to do what I needed to in this life." She hummed to herself. "Luis, however, he will have a full life, and with the help of Tajah, has unlocked the first level of magic inside him. She will take Luis under her wing and teach him everything he needs to know. Won't she?"

"Yep!" Luis smiled wildly. "She said I was a little old to be an apprentice, but I will do well since I learn so fast.”

I felt heat radiating off Elena’s body. Her heart raced, and her face contorted like she was eating a piece of sour candy.

Yes, she was mad.

“Hey, love, how about we go outside?” I placed my hands on her hips and pressed a kiss to her shoulder. “Let’s not get mad at Luis. He didn’t know,” I whispered.

Abuela smirked and placed a card down on the table. “Go, listen to your dragon, mija. It might do you some good.”

Elena growled and my cocks ticked in surprise. I pressed myself against her, holding her flush to my body. “Love, come on now. Let’s take a break and come back to this.”

Luis waved to his mother and blew her a kiss. “Bye, Mama! I’m so excited we moved here! I think this place is so much better than our old home, don’t you?”

Elena’s posture softened.

It *was* much better than her old home. More room for Luis to grow, and now that Tajah had awakened his powers. There would be no going back to Venezuela or anywhere else. They were trapped here.

A deep satisfaction rolled over me in waves at that thought.

Was that why she was angry? Or that Abuela invoked his power without speaking with her first?

“We will see you later, Luis. Behave for Abuela and Merium, won’t you?” I asked.

Luis nodded. “Sure thing! Bye!” he said, oblivious to the conflict.

I led Elena outside, and the brightness of the light bore down on her shoulders. She growled into my chest as I turned her to face my body.

“She’s out of control!” Elena banged on my chest. “She didn’t talk to me! That is my son! What if I didn’t want him to have those powers? How am

I to raise him? I know nothing about magic or—"

"Mija," Abuela stepped outside and shut the door. Her face was solemn as she came closer to us.

"You listen here, you old bat!" Elena stepped forward. I grabbed her by the waist and held her back. "You did something life-changing to my son!"

Abuela held up her hand. "I know I did." Her gaze softened. "And it wasn't a decision taken lightly. I came in search of you to ask yesterday, but discovered you had troubles."

Elena stiffened further.

"I left you alone, but sweetheart." Abuela cupped her cheek. "Whatever happened to cause you such distress, I am sad I was not a part of it. That you felt you could not tell me." Her eyes floated to mine. "I am glad you have someone to lean on now, who can help you. Just know that what I did to Luis will help him in the future. So, he can protect himself."

Elena swallowed and shook her head. "I can't believe you did this behind my back." I felt my mate relax further in my arms. My dragon soothed her with a deep rumbling in our chest as she turned and put her head under my neck.

Abuela sighed. "Mija, I know you don't understand now, but hopefully when the time comes, you will. This was the only chance while I was alive to—"

"You aren't dying!" Elena spun out of my arms.

Abuela chuckled. "No, not right now, but—"

"You will not die. You say that all the time. You are not dying or are going to die anytime soon. You will outlive all of us!" Elena slung her arms in all directions until Abuela grabbed them and held them to her chest.

"Don't believe me, do you? After all the wards I have used, after all the magic around you. You still do not believe in me?"

Elena sniffed, but she dared not let a tear fall.

I stood behind her, my hand tracing the lower part of her back to lend her my strength.

She wasn't giving up, but giving in to her elder's words.

"I did it because I wanted to be a part of Luis' awakening. You and Emmie have your soul mates. You will be taken care of and won't need the magic. Luis is young and will be taught in the ways of his ancestors. It would bring me great joy for him to follow in my footsteps until he finds his soulmate one day. This will protect him. Don't you see that? Did you see how happy he was? How accepting he is of Tajah? They are perfect for one another as teacher and student."

I felt my mate's tension loosen.

Although I didn't appreciate Abuela's decision to act behind my mate's back, I couldn't deny the aura of magic that surrounded her. Her voice was steady and sincere, devoid of any deceit, and I sensed no malice in her intentions. She genuinely wished the best for her descendants. Abuela had embraced the Iron Fang from the very beginning because she understood it would ensure their safety. Her wisdom even played a crucial role in helping me earn Elena's trust.

But how did she know her time was so short?

"Luis, knowing magic in this world and living here in the Iron Fang, will benefit him." I managed to say.

Elena let out a huff of annoyance but rubbed my arm that was wrapped around her waist for comfort. "Fine, but anything else, I want a phone call or text message if you do anything to my son."

Abuela smiled and nodded with glee. "Of course, of course. That won't be necessary. I won't do anything else to him."

Elena hummed in annoyance, as if she didn't believe her.

"Now." Abuela gently cupped her hands around Elena's face again, her touch warm and comforting. "Why don't you two go on a stroll? Hmm?

There's a weeping willow just beyond the homes here. It's very romantic." Her eyes twinkled with mischief as she turned away, and moments later, Meriam returned carrying a soft, plaid blanket and a wicker basket that emanated the mouthwatering aroma of freshly prepared food. "You have been so stressed, and this is supposed to be your vacation, Elena. Now, go have some fun for once." Meriam added a playful wink and smiled encouragingly, full of affection.

Elena's shoulders dropped, and she shook her head. "You are a crazy old bat, did you know that?"

Abuela shrugged and wrapped her shawl around her shoulders tighter. "Si. You would find it strange otherwise." She eyed her and held out her arms for a hug.

I released Elena, allowing her to be enveloped in the comforting embrace of family warmth. "Come on, you too, dragon," she called, her voice playful and inviting. I exhaled a soft laugh, stepping in to encircle Elena, keeping her snugly between us. As we gently pulled apart, my eye caught Abuela slyly slipping a tiny, empty glass potion bottle into her pocket. She shot me a wink, her mischievous grin momentarily lighting up her face before it returned to its usual calm expression.

Why did that seem more ominous than it should have?

CHAPTER
TWENTY-TWO

Elena

Anaki was a few steps in front of me, checking the different paths to this willow tree that the fae and Abuela were talking about. The place where the fae stayed was actually quite large. We had only stepped through a small neighborhood where a few homes were. There were other little 'neighborhoods,' the further we traveled deeper into their territory.

I didn't imagine the Iron Fang, a motorcycle club, could also harbor fae in the forest they owned just outside of town.

Go figure.

Anaki ran down one trail while I took my time. It wasn't about seeing the sights or taking in the breathtaking scenery. I was actually uncomfortable. The plug I stuck in my ass earlier this morning was becoming uncomfortable. Each step was a reminder that I hadn't gotten laid in a hot second. I was ready for that double dicking that was promised to me.

Since Anaki was a virgin when he met me, I'm sure he didn't understand about prepping one's asshole, and I knew he would be ready to go when the time came. So being the more experienced one, well more educated, since I'd never had it up the ass before, I took it upon myself to prep.

"Did you find it yet?" I yelled out, nearly panting. I was also very turned on. My pussy was swollen and as it brushed against my panties, it was enough to set me off.

Anaki probably thought I was feeling fatigued after I told him to go find the dang tree, but it wasn't true at all. I was surprised he hadn't smelled me after speaking with Abuela, and having to walk nearly half a mile to this stupid spot.

"Found it!" he called out and rushed back to me. He no longer had the basket in his hand, and the blanket was gone from his arm. He lowered himself and scooped me up in a bridal style position and I screamed when the plug moved suddenly in my ass, to a position that had me wince.

"Easy there!" I laughed and wrapped my arms around his neck.

I was ready to get this plug out, pronto.

With the gentle breeze blowing at us, there wasn't any time for him to take a sniff to smell me. He was walking so fast to the hidden path that he wouldn't notice. That comforted me, but if he looked down at my chest, that would be a different story.

"You're gonna love it. It's big. I don't know if the fae grew it themselves or if a willow is an Earth tree..."

"A willow is an Earth tree, but..."

I fell silent as the willow tree came into sight, gracefully positioned beside the tranquil pond. Though not exceptionally large, its branches created an illusion of grandeur, draping down elegantly with a cascade of vines that enveloped the tree completely. It was as if the tree was adorned with thick, deep red curtains, adding a touch of drama.

"Maybe they adjusted the flowers, because I've never seen a red willow tree."

Anaki walked through the curtain of flowers, and already, there was the blanket set up by the basket. He'd even plucked a few flowers from the branches of the willow and set them down on the blanket.

My heart stuttered, as it grew three sizes too large in my chest cavity, for this dragon when he gently set me down. I winced when the plug dug into my ass too much and leaned on the other side of my cheek. He cocked his head, but said nothing as he sat down.

"This is nice. It keeps out the sound, too. It's like a tent. I don't think I've seen anything like this before," he commented while he continued to look around.

"They don't have willow trees in the Elysian Realm?" I wiggled to try to get comfortable. Pulling my cross bag over my head from where I carried it, I placed it next to the basket. I flipped it open to check the contents inside. I tried to keep my smile from becoming too large on seeing the lube.

This day was panning out better than I planned. Under the willow tree with no one to see, rather than in a forest where a fae or a wolf could pop up somewhere.

It would have been better if Abuela had not unlocked my child's inner magic, or whatever, but I guess that is something I would have to deal with later. I was getting too horny to think about it right now.

"Not where I am from." Anaki rocked his body side to side where he now sat. "I lived on the coastline of a large lake, with rocks and trees that could withstand those elements. When I traveled out of the realm, I didn't pass by any lands that could harbor a willow tree. I also didn't travel through fae territories, mainly shifter ones."

I bobbed my head back and forth. It made sense. Earth was massive, and there were plenty of different climates on it.

I moved my body again to get more comfortable. My body felt hotter than normal, and my nipples pressed against the thickness of my bra. I always liked a thicker padded bra to keep the ladies more secure, but right now, it felt like too much. It was itchy and uncomfortable.

I wanted to take it off.

My pussy also fluttered and the plug in my ass was not enough.

Anaki cleared his throat and adjusted himself over the dark jeans he wore. "Elena? Are you, ah, okay?"

Tension surrounded us, and I realized quickly why. There wasn't a breeze inside the thick curtains, and Anaki's powerful sense of smell might speed things up in my favor...

Why was that both embarrassing and hot at the same time?

I squeezed my thighs together as I tried to relieve the ache between my legs. Everything felt hot. I could feel my heartbeat in my clit. I could even feel the slickness between my thighs. If I slipped my fingers between my legs, I knew I would be soaked.

Was it because of the plug? Had it been too long?

I was no butt plug connoisseur.

I've seen plenty of videos in the past five years and read my novels, but none of them explained the desirous need to be stuffed full while having one inside. A lot of women found it to be a punishment to have one lodged in there. It was a constant reminder that something was in your ass. Not big enough to get you off on its own, just a teasing reminder.

"Is there any water?" I fanned myself and reached out to Anaki. He quickly opened the basket and found a water bottle. He opened it for me and came closer. Before I could grab it, he brought it to my lips.

"Drink." His nose flared, and his eyes shifted into his dragon's.

I stared into his eyes as he didn't even put it to my lips, instead pouring it into my mouth, some dripping down the sides of my cheeks and down my neck.

Fuck, that felt good.

Anaki watched me sip the water, his eyes never leaving my face. There was an undeniable electricity in the air, a tension that hung between us like the thick vines of the willow tree.

As I finished drinking, he slowly reached up and wiped the water from my neck with his thumb. The gentle touch sent a jolt of desire through me, and I bit my lip to keep from making a sound. His thumb traced slow circles on my skin, and I shivered under his touch.

"Elena," he said, his voice low and raspy. "I really, really need you right now."

"Yeah?" I said, hardly daring to breathe as he continued to caress my skin.

"My dragon is going to burst out of me, and I can't promise you what he will do," he said, his voice barely above a whisper. "I want to fuck you so bad."

His thumb moved lower, tracing the sensitive skin at the base of my throat, making my heart pound in reaction. I wanted him to touch me more, to explore every inch of me. I wanted him to take me right here and now, under this willow tree, with its branches offering us privacy.

"Anaki," I whispered, my voice barely more than a sigh as his thumb moved lower still, tracing the edge of my bra. I closed my eyes as I felt... not heat but the coolness of his scales. His body was pushing out beautiful deep blue, silver and white scales over his arms, neck and face, and I hoped they were on his chest. My legs spread on their own accord to let him in.

"Tell me to take you, right here." Anaki pressed his lips fiercely against my neck, igniting a wild surge of heat through my veins. The sensation was electrifying, a tantalizing mix of pleasure and longing that left me craving more with an insatiable hunger. His scales, cool and soothing, provided relief to my searing skin, yet not in the place where the fire blazed hottest, leaving me desperate and yearning for his touch where I needed it most.

I hummed. "More." I pulled at his shirt to get it off him. Scales littered his chest, and my tongue darted out over my lips as I took him in. It didn't scare me seeing those beautiful, dripping diamonds on his chest. My pussy squeezed in on itself, wanting him closer, to be inside.

Anaki didn't waste time with my clothes, while I was dumb struck taking in his physique. He tugged at my dress, his eyes hooded with desire, once he'd pulled it over my head.

"Aw, fuck, I'm not gonna last." He stood up and unbuttoned his jeans. He pulled off the material, along with his compression underwear—it was quite a shame he had to hide those cocks so close to his body.

Both of his appendages bobbed when they were relieved of their confinement. His balls, which I haven't had enough time to admire, were full and heavy.

How in his human form did he not fall over with all that extra weight in his pants?

Anaki leaned over me, his mouth capturing mine. Instead of greeting me with his human tongue, a thicker, forked tongue wrapped around mine. I groaned and ran my hands through his hair.

"Off, off." He chanted and pulled my bra with one hand. The other was holding him up, but something cool tugged at my underwear as I felt the wet material slip down my leg.

I opened my eyes, and they widened when I saw my underwear hanging above me from his blue tail.

¡Dios Mio!

Anaki growled. His cocks pushed up against my pussy. I felt a copious amount of precum slip down his cocks and between my legs.

I was already wet, and I ground my pussy upwards to at least have one of his cocks slip inside me, letting my body have a taste of what was yet to come.

"I need your cocks, right now," I demanded. I breathed against his lips, the words barely coherent as he tore my bra away, and our skin touched for the first time. My nipples peeked in anticipation, hard little buds begging for attention as they brushed against his chest.

Anaki backed away, his cocks dripping. They were sweating, glistening from his come alone. They bobbed when I sat up and turned to bend over, presenting him with my surprise.

Anaki grabbed my hips. His breath hitched as he parted my ass. "Fucking hell, what is this?"

His finger probed around the dark-blue jeweled butt plug. It was in the shape of a heart. I never told Anaki that my favorite color has always been blue. When I found out his dragon colors, I knew he would appreciate this little prize that I had.

I looked around and bit my lip. "Do you like it?" I shook my ass at him and felt my wet pussy drip down my inner thigh.

His claws dug into my skin and gave a sweet sting.

"What is this?"

My sweet summer child.

"It's a butt plug. Do you not know what this is?"

Anaki's Adam's apple bobbed, and I took that as a no.

"I was preparing myself for you, so I can take both of your cocks at the same time. You can't just stick it in my ass, silly. I needed to be prepped. You don't want to hurt me, do you?"

Anaki groaned and twisted the plug. He pulled and pushed it back in, and my body arched as I felt the stretch of it. "I'm a dragon, love. I know how to prep an asshole, Elena," he deadpanned. "But this jewelry here." I felt his thumb run over the fake jewel, and he tsked. "It is a lovely sight. I will have to replace this fake stone with a real one. I can't wait to see you bend over in my cave more often with this in."

That fake stone was enormous. How the heck would he find something that big? Before I could say anything else, I had to bite my lip hard as he dragged it out slowly, and let out a quiet moan.

Anaki palmed my ass, his cocks rubbing against it while he stared at my backside.

"So, are you going to stare at my asshole or are you gonna stuff it?"

Please hurry, so I'm not being paranoid about you staring at that area.

"That butt plug isn't gonna prep you enough, love. I'm bigger than that. I need you to take some deep breaths for me." I gripped the fabric of the blankets, as I heard him fist his cock, the squelching sound letting me know he was getting lubricated.

"H-how do you know all this?"

Anaki chuckled deeply, like his dragon was right there. I didn't know if that was a good or bad thing.

"Dragon males get the sex talk, too, you know. We are taught how to prep females, how to be gentle."

My face heated. "I just thought female dragons would have two—"

"No." Anaki inserted two fingers inside my ass and I groaned as he pushed them further inside. He hummed, his hips pressing against my hips, going at the rhythm of his fingers. "Females have one vagina, just like humans. It takes two male cocks to impregnate a female. It all goes—"

I moaned and pressed my ass into him when he spread his two fingers like he was scissoring me. "In one hole?"

How would that feel? To have both of Anaki's dicks in my pussy? I might need to be stretched there, too.

Anaki hummed as if he wasn't paying attention and slipped his fingers out of me. He saw the cleaning wipes from my bag and quickly cleaned his fingers. "You are so relaxed. I won't have a problem getting inside you, love."

I groaned, feeling so empty with no plug or fingers inside me.

"I've got you," he breathed. "I've waited for this moment, to sink into you, claiming you with both of my cocks at the same time."

Anaki let out an excited breath. His hands shook as he grasped his lower cock. The tip of it grazed my clit and my body buzzed with electricity. My body shook, and sweat gleamed on my skin. If he didn't hurry up and fuck me, I would mount him myself.

Anaki growled as he seated half his cock inside me. "So damn wet. You don't even need my lubricant. Fuck, and tight." His other cock laid on top of my ass, ready to be inserted. He was taking his time, for both our sakes. I was becoming impatient, though, my pussy was dripping ready for him. I wouldn't be fully filled until I had the other inside me.

"Please, Anaki. Put the other one in." I gripped the blanket below me, trying to hold on. I shoved my ass closer to him. His body shook with excitement, and he pulled me closer.

Anaki grunted. I heard squelching come from behind me. I took a quick look to see that he was rubbing his hand up and down his shaft.

"You're slick enough; you don't need any lube," I told him. He needed to get it in me... now! "Please, I need to come," I whined. The heat of my pussy was radiating toward the rest of my body. My breasts felt heavy, my nipples were hard, begging to be sucked, to be played with.

"Wasn't planning on that artificial shit anyway. My dragon and I will give you what you need." He gritted his teeth. "You were made to take this cock in your ass, the other in your pussy."

Where the hell did a dirty-talking Anaki come from?

"Shit, shit, shit," he chanted.

He pressed the tip of his head to my ass. I gasped when he pressed forward. The tight ring stung at first until the head popped through. My body tightened around him, my pussy gripped hold of his lower dick and I let out a low moan of pleasure that jolted through to my soul.

"Fuck!" He threw his head back when he bottomed out.

"Full," I said weakly. "I'm so full, I need you to move."

His hands gripped my hips, pulling me closer to him as he used them to push and pull me onto his cocks. I moaned loudly, each thrust brought a wave of pleasure that washed over me. My body was on fire, every nerve ending alight with sensation.

Our skin slapped together—this wasn't anything quiet—the entire forest would hear the damn noises we were making. It was savage, animalistic and damn it if it wasn't the best sex I have ever had.

My body became putty and I was too exhausted to move. It was too intense, but I loved every second of it. I think what I liked most about it was when he called me...his. Don't get me wrong, the mind-blowing sex was amazing, but the dirty talk, making a future, the idea of being permanent.

I really, really wanted it.

"I can feel both my cocks rubbing against each other," Anaki growled. "They are so close together, rubbing inside you. Goddess!" He lowered himself closer to my body so his torso met my back. The coolness of his scales took away some of the heat.

I cried out when the first orgasm hit me. Anaki's hand came around my waist to play with my clit. "That's it, take them." His voice rumbled like distant thunder, sending shivers down my spine. I could feel the rough texture of his tongue as it traced a path up my back, creating a tingling sensation on my skin. "Mmm, you taste good, female." He continued to thrust in and out of me.

"More." The words tumbled out of my mouth, my voice hoarse with desire.

He let out a deep, rumbling chuckle that echoed around the curtains of the willow tree's branches, as his movements became more erratic and forceful. I could feel the sharp nails digging into my shoulder on one side, while the other hand firmly grasped my breast. "I want you swollen with our fledgling," the deep voice cooed. "Make you ripe with our seed, decorate you in riches. We will take care of you and our son."

My eyes were going cross-eyed at how good his rigid shafts felt on the inside of my body. It felt even better when they were massaging each other with that small strip of muscle separating the two.

Anaki's breath—his dragon's, rather—was coming in ragged gasps.

"Squeeze my cocks, female. Give me more of your pleasure."

¡Dios Mio! I arched my back, and he grabbed my hair to pull me back further. His tail rubbed the lips of my mouth while I stared into those dragon's slitted eyes.

His teeth lengthened into sharp points, and his neck was completely covered with scales. "Mine," he roared, and we both came. My pussy strangled him, his voice choked, his grip loosened on my hair.

His face went into the crook of my neck as I felt the hot ropes of come spilling inside me.

Anaki continued to growl while he hovered over me. He kept my body completely covered, like he was protecting me from the outside. Slowly, he lowered himself to my back and turned us on to our side, keeping his still hardened cocks inside me.

I panted, my skin was still hot.

Anaki groaned and pulled me closer to his body, seating himself deep inside me, refusing to pull out. "Just want to be close to you." His voice was softer, no longer that deep guttural voice I heard earlier.

CHAPTER TWENTY-THREE

Anaki

I had a problem. A huge problem. Make that three since two were my dicks, the other my dragon. He had broken through and used my voice to speak his wants. While no dragon shifter can hear the voice of their reptile inside them, we know their desires. We feel what they want, what makes them tick.

Then, how in all the holy moon did his growls break through, and he use my voice?

My body was hot on the inside, radiating a heat I had never experienced. I was young when I left the clan, had just received my dragon and found out who my mate was. I never went through a delirious rut, didn't know how it felt because my heart and soul were far too broken to make my body produce the hormones for it.

This must have been it, and I think it had to do with Abuela and that cursed empty bottle.

I gritted my teeth. In the process, I gripped hold of Elena. She whined and ground her ass into my cocks once again.

"I could go again," she purred.

Fuck, I wanted that. I wanted it too much. This time I wanted to shove both my cocks inside her pussy and stretch her until she couldn't take anymore.

But I wasn't in control right now, that was for certain. My dragon came out at the peak of my climax, so I had no control of my thrusts and could have ripped her asshole right open. I'm in no way small. My lubricant coated her fine, but I could feel his overwhelming need to claim her.

We haven't even told her about soul mates, the ultimate connection, how permanent it was. We haven't even told her about the claiming, and his wants were just to claim her without her consent.

What if he did... and I couldn't control it?

I slipped my cocks from her body and we both groaned. I felt utterly cold when I backed away from her and rose to my hands and knees.

My dragon roared inside me. His anger radiated through my body. I felt a sharp pang in my stomach and my cocks throbbed. They both leaked lubricant to be put inside her body.

"More," my mouth moved against my will.

Elena glanced over her shoulder; her tanned skin glowed with the sheen of sweat on her body. When she moved her legs, my eyes darted between those parted thighs and watched my come leak out of her body.

Ah, fuck!

I took my fingers and shoved it back inside her cunt. My mate's eyes rolled back into her head, and she spread her legs more.

"Fuck, Anaki, you are freakier than I thought."

Inside, I was cringing because it wasn't me at all.

"I need you to run." I panted while my fingers pumped inside her.

She lifted her head and raised her brow. Her lips parted when my fingers hit a tender spot.

"And why in the hell would I do that?" Her breasts rose and fell. My dragon's tongue swiped across my lips, and then I attached myself to her hardened nipple.

"My dragon," I mumbled against her skin, "is fighting for control, and I need you to go."

Elena cried out; her hips rode my fingers until completion. My hands gripped her hips and lined up both her holes for me to fuck her both in the ass and pussy again.

"Elena!" I barked. Sweat beaded down my brow. "You must jump in the pond, clean your body, and run."

My dragon growled, it rumbled, vibrating my cock that lay over her pussy. She whined and shook her head. "But I want it. Why do you want to—"

"Trust me!" I gritted my teeth and leaned back on my knees. I felt more scales run up my neck, and suddenly, my jaw cracked.

Elena stared up at me with wide eyes and crawled away from me. "What's happening?"

Then I smelled something I didn't want to ever smell from her when she looked at me. *Fear.*

"I won't hurt you. He won't hurt you. Just... don't want him to fuck you."

I pounded my fist into the ground with a force that reverberated through my entire being. My arms swelled with thickly corded muscles, transforming my physique into one that felt unnaturally top-heavy. My fingers elongated and thinned, their form stretching and twisting until they resembled the long, bony appendages of a lizard, overlaying my original human hands with my dragon form.

"I need you to go!" I yelled again. "Now!"

I yelled out, only for it to turn into a dragon's roar.

Elena scooted away from me. Not even grabbing her dress. She jumped into the pond, drenching herself from head to toe.

I didn't care where she disappeared to, as the raging inferno inside me consumed me. The dragon within thrashed violently, clawing and roaring, threatening to break free at any moment. I fought with every ounce of strength I had, desperately trying to cage the beast within.

On top of it all, my body was hot, my cocks pulsing.

I pushed my head into the moss, and my back broke behind me. I let out another scream, which became a roar. I rolled on the ground, my arms and body breaking. This was more painful than the first time I shifted. Was it because it had been that long?

My head felt like it was being split in two as I felt tiny knives nick my skin all over my body. My spine elongated, and the claws on my feet lengthened. Soon, my face had contorted, my yells, growls, more dragon than human.

No, no, no. I chanted in my head. *You cannot take her. Not like this. What the hell do you think you are doing?*

A deep, dark chuckle resonated through the ground beneath us and shook the earth like a low, rumbling earthquake. My body extended with feline grace, our back arching high into the air while our front claws stretched wide and strong before us. The groan that escaped was a low, guttural sound, echoing from my throat as our vivid coral horns brushed against the lofty, whispering branches of the tallest willows, their leaves rustling gently in response.

"You forget we are an animal, Anaki. While your time was short, having me awake within your body before we were rejected, you would have thought to move faster to claim the human female."

I banged my head from within my dragon's body. It was an odd sensation. I had little time inside my dragon's body when he was in control. I only had him for the expanse of a week before I met my mate at the grove, before the rejection.

I was young, naïve, and still trying to learn the ways of the development of my body.

"That's why I have been slow. She is human. You know she's had a traumatic past, you can't just claim her, it has to be her choice," I pleaded.

Our body slunk into the pond and I felt the refreshing water run over our scales. It felt so good as our body became one with the water, feeling the coolness help alleviate the heat within our body. Our cocks still twitched, but soon they were sucked up into the seam where they would be protected just like any other reptilian.

Our head poked out of the water and came out on the other side. "That is where you are wrong," my dragon said. Our firm legs stepped on the soft ground on the other side. Despite our large body, we were silent as we stepped and weaved through the trees. He stuck our nose up into the air and took in large breaths. Our nose flared, and I could smell my mate's scent come in stronger than ever before.

Shit.

"We will not have her reject us; we will not give her a chance to. She. Is. Ours."

He didn't let out a roar like I was expecting, instead, his feet quickened, the fins on our back and tail lowered to our body as he speedily raced through the woods. Our long neck looked behind bushes, around trees. He even dared to climb a tree.

Water dragons don't typically climb trees, our caves are lower to the ground, at least a body length or two high, but he was climbing three or four body lengths up.

There was no fear felt, just determination, when he climbed high to the top of the swaying tree. The sun was touching the tops of the trees, ready to set in the distance. The territory was vast, but Elena was human, and she wasn't used to running. She couldn't have gone far.

"I urge you to stop this," I begged. *"Don't claim her. Give me back control."*

My dragon ignored me and climbed down from the tree. He began stalking through the foliage. He was now concentrating on the hunt. It was a more primitive form of the dragons; it wasn't practiced anymore. Our mates accepted the bond within our clan, but with our history, this had sparked something new and different that I was never taught in the teachings of our history.

I don't know what to do. If I could pull at my hair, I would. The thought of being rejected by Elena was strong in the beginning, but the warmth and, dare I say, love that I felt for her was strong, and how she clung to me made me know she would accept us.

My dragon didn't understand that.

And now he was hunting her because he was afraid of the potential rejection.

The deeper we went into the forest, the more frantic he became. Her scent had faded to near nonexistent, and even I became worried. Where the fuck did she go?

As darkness fell over the forest, our senses heightened, and we could hear the smallest of sounds. Our dragon's nose twitched in the air, still focused on Elena's scent. The tension between us was palpable. Elena was nowhere, and I had no way to call for her or members from the Iron Fang. I was utterly alone with my asshole of a dragon.

Suddenly, a rustling in the bushes ahead caught our attention. Our dragon's eyes narrowed, and he stood completely still for a moment, listening intently. Then, with a sudden burst of speed, he leaped forward quietly when we heard growls and pants.

"So big!" I heard a female whine. "Shit, I'm going to be ripped in half!" My dragon's head perked up and stalked forward. The voice was familiar, and when we peered through the tops of the trees, we saw a sight that will forever be ingrained into our minds.

It was Elena's sister, Emm being fucked by... Locke. I could smell his scent, but I had never seen him like the beast he was now.

His hairy, two-legged figure hovered over her, his breath heaved and was taken in ragged breaths. Emm back was pushed over a log, the moonlight lighting her face. Her eyes were shut while he fucked her into oblivion.

I could have gone without ever seeing this.

"Fuck me!" she cried, her voice hoarse with passion. "Fuck me harder!"

I'm going to be sick. That's my mate's sister.

My dragon shuddered in disgust, and I heard dry heaving come from the other side of the clearing. My dragon's head lifted, and I felt our lips curling over our fangs.

Elena.

"So gross!" she whispered and covered her eyes. Her scent was very muted, and it was because of the mud and the hormones that had surrounded the area. She had run right toward her sister's camper, where she had been staying. No wonder we hadn't smelled her.

While Locke continued to... do whatever he was doing to the Iron Fang's future Luna, we hid in the forest and slithered to the other side. I screamed inside my dragon, trying to warn her to get away, but it was all futile.

He had one desire, and that was to grab Elena. I just hope to the goddess he wouldn't do it right here alongside Locke and Emm.

Elena's eyes were closed, her hands next to her ears. Her body was completely naked, and my heart was crushed to see that she had to be freezing all afternoon out in the open, no longer in the fae's territory.

My dragon chuckled deeply. His nose lowered and brushed the side of her face. She stilled and her eyes opened slowly, lifted her head, and stared back at us.

"Mine," he whispered, and she opened her mouth to scream.

CHAPTER TWENTY-FOUR

Elena

When I saw Anaki in pain, a part of me was desperate to reach out and help him, yet those ungodly sounds he made were terrifying beyond belief. I felt torn between wanting to comfort him and the fear that I would do more harm than good.

My heart raced, and any arousal that had plagued me vanished when I saw his bones break, his neck arch and lengthen. The screams and the roars were unbearable. My body trembled in fear for him, not for my life, but for his.

He was a shifter. I've seen the product of when someone had shifted, but I never witnessed the actual shift. I've heard Bear and Nadia's bones break from behind the tree so they could show us their animals, but this? This was beyond anything I had anticipated.

Nadia and Bear didn't scream in anguish like this.

Anaki roared, the scales pierced through the skin and bled. The long teeth I've seen in his mouth before doubled, tripled in size. Anaki grew into something much larger than what Nadia and Bear did. He was...

otherworldly. I was caught between awe and disbelief, unsure of how to feel. This was wrong. It wasn't supposed to hurt him like this, was it?

Then, when he told me to run, I did without looking back. If Anaki said running was the best option, I would listen. He never let me out of his sight, and if he wanted me gone now, there was a reason.

Was there something wrong with his dragon form?

I did what I was told and jumped into the pond. I'm guessing it was my scent that he was trying to get me to hide.. I didn't stay long and climbed up on the other side of the embankment only to cover myself in mud.

A place full of shifters, they were all animals. They had strong senses of smell, as Beretta mentioned in passing. I would not be found.

I ran, at first not sure where to go other than staying close to the ground. This dragon could be huge. Maybe he couldn't spot me.

The idea of going closer to town would be wise. The dragon wouldn't want to be caught, at least I hoped it wouldn't. I kept running until the beautiful, luscious plants slowly faded around me. I passed through the invisible barrier that contained the beautiful oasis; I knew this because the heat vanished and the more Earthly forest appeared.

The cooler spring night air hit my cold, muddy skin and I sucked in a breath through my teeth.

Great, now I'm naked, muddy and freezing.

I kept moving. My naked body wouldn't last long in acres of forest, but I had little choice. If I kept moving, kept my heart rate up, I'd stay warm. The temperatures weren't even close to freezing.

My adrenaline was the only thing that was going to keep me going, and I prayed my muscles weren't going to ache by the time all this was over.

As my feet pounded against the forest floor, I could feel the crunch of dry leaves, the prickly pine needles, and the soft, springy moss beneath my soles. Birds erupted from the branches above in a flurry of wings, startled by the noise. I watched them jump from the branches in flight, their feathers glinting in the dappled sunlight, and silently prayed they wouldn't give out my location to Anaki's dragon.

My heart thundered in my chest while I continued to run through the late afternoon. I knew he wouldn't hurt me, he couldn't. Not when Anaki was part of the dragon, Bear and Nadia said so, what little they told me. Bear said his animal knew how much Nadia meant to him and would never do such a thing.

Then why is Anaki having me run away? Was he sick? Was there something really wrong? Should I get help?

I half ran and walked for hours until I couldn't anymore. My body was tired, and the breakfast I had wasn't enough. I finally collapsed on the other side of the clearing right as the sun set and curled myself up into a ball. I could hear the road not far from me. If I could just rest for a while, perhaps I could get some strength and find a trail to the cabin where we stayed.

My brain went foggy, my eyelids felt heavy from the run, until I heard heavy footsteps running through the woods. It was a woman's laughter, similar to Emm's. It was that deranged laugh she would get as a child when she would get in trouble for stealing eggs from the neighbors and bringing them home, cracked and broken.

I raised my head from the makeshift nest of pine needles and bark. My body shivered in the cold when I poked my head up, and a snarl came from behind her. She turned with a shriek, and a beast pounced on her and snarled. They spoke, but I missed what they said because the sight shocked me too much.

It was like a damn werewolf. He had a big, long dick between its legs and a ball at the base. It leaked precome everywhere while it ripped off my sister's clothes. I dared to sit up and poke my head out of the bush, but stayed hidden as she moaned and bared her chest to him.

Alright, she wants it, so I'm gonna stay here.

There was more scuffling, like she was fighting. He snarled at her and pushed her over the log and inserted his—

¡Dios Mio!

I gasped and hugged my legs. This was not happening. I've seen my sister twice now get it on with two different guys! Well, technically a beast, or are they the same person?

Does she know all about this? Shifters of the town?

Probably, and was into it. She was kinky.

Runs in the family, I guess.

"So gross!" I whispered and covered my eyes before I lowered my head to my knees again. I rocked back and forth to try and keep those terrible sounds away.

What a family reunion this was.

Suddenly, I felt hot breath fanning the top of my head. I slowly looked up, only to see big, dragon eyes staring straight at me. His body was low to the ground, but by how massive his head was, I knew he was much, much larger.

"Mine," he purred.

I opened my mouth to scream, but his tail wrapped around my mouth. A rough purr sounded in his throat, and his body drew nearer to me.

My eyes darted to the clearing where Emm and the beast that stood on two legs were. They were obviously busy and not paying attention to us.

Emmie, for once, don't think about the cat between your legs and save me!

The dragon's scaly tail coiled softly around my mouth, its texture rough yet surprisingly gentle, as it took its leisurely time enveloping the rest of my body in a serpentine hug. My eyes widened with anxiety. The dragon's lips curled into a smirk—a smirk eerily reminiscent of Anaki's, filled with nothing but mischief.

He was in there, somewhere.

The dragon pulled me closer, and I watched as his reptilian pupils expanded and contracted with an intense focus. His scales were a stunning mosaic of deep blue intertwined with shimmering silver and pristine white. It created a mesmerizing pattern that caught the moonlight with every movement. Unlike the typical menacing dragons with large, curved horns, his head was crowned with an intricate formation resembling strong white piped coral. It was different and beautiful.

The dragon huffed and turned away from our spot. His footsteps were silent as he kept me wrapped in his tail and near his face. He didn't keep me behind him while he walked, but instead with him.

I was surprised by the size and how stealthy he was as he tread through the forest on all four legs. The further we got away from Emm and her monster, the quicker his footsteps became.

"Hmm, you are a smart female covering your scent. You made me hunt for you." His chest rumbled, and I felt the vibrations through his tail. "I will have to train better in case you ever evade me again."

His speaking was different than Anaki's. Deeper, raspier, obviously for how big he was, but also in how he spoke. Anaki was playful. He was not.

The dragon slowly unwrapped the tip of his tail from my mouth so I could speak. I coughed several times and cleared my throat. "What are you going to do with me?"

I wiggled in his hold; the mud I had spread on me earlier had long dried and cracked on my skin.

The dragon chuckled and pulled me closer to his face. One enormous eye looked down at me. "Nothing other than what soulkins should do, little human. There is nothing to fear, unless you plan on rejecting us."

I stopped moving within his grasp and tilted my head. "Soulkin, what is that?"

The dragon huffed and continued to move at a faster speed. We reached the fae's territory within minutes, and the warmth of their home immediately stopped my shivering. He went over to the water and slid inside. "Hold your breath," he said before he pulled me under.

I was under less than ten seconds before I broke the surface. The dragon then held me in his large, clawed fingers and helped wash away the mud.

I winced at the thought of those sharp talons near my head, but to my surprise, the dragon's touch was gentle and careful of his claws. While there wasn't soap, he was rather thorough in washing me. There wasn't a speck left, and I made sure to use the water and my hands to wash any private areas.

He huffed when I slapped his massive caws away when I did so. He would have to get over it. I was very naked and vulnerable. He was an animal, while still part of Anaki, which made him part human.

Then it occurred to me. Did he see Anaki and me doing things? My eyes drifted to the red willow.

The dragon chuckled deeply. "I have seen everything Anaki has seen."

"Can you read my mind?" I spat back at him.

"No, but you are easy to understand."

I stuck my tongue out at him and covered my chest. Bastard!

I was still wary because of Anaki's earlier words. Especially now that this dragon called me a soulkin and said I was his. What was that? And what if I ran? Anaki told me to do it. Do I need to continue trying to get away?

Before I could think further, his tail wrapped around my body, including my arms, and I struggled to free myself. "Isn't this excessive?"

The dragon didn't answer me, instead he slithered with all four of his clawed hands on the ground and went a different way from the town as if not to disturb the fae that were probably already in their homes for the night. I saw lights hung throughout the small town from afar as we climbed back up the trail to the cave.

"Oh, not talking now?" I ground my teeth together. "Better speak now, because it makes you look all the more suspicious. Anaki wanted me away from you for a reason."

The dragon stopped just outside the cave. He pulled me right in front of his snout. His nostrils opened and closed, and his eyes glared at me. "He wanted to prevent me from detecting your arousal. He thought I would take you there in my dragon form."

My mouth fell open in shock.

"He also thought I might claim you there, prematurely binding your soul to ours. I still might do it if you aren't cooperative."

My mouth hung open in astonishment as he crawled into the cave on all fours, his movements fluid and animalistic. A low hum resonated from his throat when he gently pushed aside the tent drapes, revealing the dimly lit interior. He carefully placed me down in the center of the large area. His eyes met mine with an intense glare, a silent command not to budge, before he turned away. With a deliberate stride, he exited the tent, leaving me alone in the quiet, shadowy space.

Being who I was and not taking his shit, I grabbed a blanket and wrapped it around me. Before I could see what he was doing, I heard a loud scraping sound at the entrance of the cave. I stood, hurried to the flap of the tent, and saw on the other side of the cave that the dragon was moving a giant boulder in front of it.

That stupid fuck! Now I will never get out of here!

I stomped in annoyance all the way back to the bed. My hair was wet, my body cold on the outside, but my insides still roared from this afternoon's time with Anaki. Life was not going how I wanted, right now.

I cannot be horny around a damn dragon. That would be insane. He was such a prick, picking me up with his dang tail, telling me I was his. Anaki would never be such a...

I crossed my arms over my chest, and I felt his presence just over me. He was a sneaky dragon. I didn't hear him move the flaps when he reentered. He circled around me on the bedding, and he took his time to get comfortable on the plush blankets.

How long did he hunt me in the forest? Did he make me suffer the whole time this afternoon? Was he punishing me for running?

I balled my hands into fists, my anger already seething the more he stayed silent.

"You are a strong female, I see why the goddess has given you to us."

I scoffed and jerked my head toward him. "What are you going on about?"

The dragon's shoulders shook as he chuckled. "The Moon Goddess, my soulkin. She has paired us. Anaki has been too afraid to tell you, since your relationship with your elder has been strained. I've grown tired of waiting for him to tell you, so here it is. You are ours, female. Ours to have, to hold, to fuck, to breed, to love. For the rest of eternity. And if the goddess dared tried to change her mind, I'd fucking eat her and not let her correct the wrongs she's done to the rest of the world."

CHAPTER TWENTY-FIVE

Anaki's Dragon

The little female was fierce.

She kept her blanket wrapped around her tightly, like it would hide her curvy form from my eyes. I have seen all of her, quite literally. I've felt her as Anaki has felt her, touched, tasted, and *been* inside of her body as he had, and she dared to try to keep herself from me?

It was… entertaining.

I chuckled inwardly to not anger her further. I've never seen her quite like this. It was refreshing. It was stimulating to see how dangerous the tiny claws of a cat could be.

"What do you mean, the Moon Goddess?"

My tongue slithered from my mouth and licked the outside of my lips. Does she really want to waste time playing these games? Ask dozens of questions that she already knows the answers to?

I crossed my legs together in front of me, and leaned forward so my nose came close to hers. She didn't back away. My cocks strained against the seam where they hid. I was ready to take her now, show her that while I may seem in the forefront of Anaki's mind and in this body, that I was in charge.

Anaki was vulnerable. While he was the playful, innocent one of us, I have become his anger and rage that he had suppressed. I took it and harbored it as my own and used it when the time was right. Unfortunately, being asleep for so long, he swirled in darkness, unable to fight the battles within his mind.

No longer.

Never again.

Now that our soulkin was here, he would never have thoughts of ending our life.

I don't see this female rejecting us. She has cared for us in just a short time due to our bond, but I am an impatient beast. I want to claim her now before she has a chance to succumb to human thoughts. Humans, as I have seen in Anaki's mind, are fickle creatures. They change their partners like they change their clothes, and I will not have our human second-guess and need time to *sort out her feelings.*

The bond has become too great.

"The same Goddess your elder prayed to, who blessed you with a soul mate. I know you are not dense. The signs are there, do not be so obtuse." I rolled my eyes in annoyance. She was smart. Why was this so difficult for her? Anaki had been too soft with her. She was strong and independent. The goddess would not have gifted her to us otherwise.

Her mouth opened and closed several times. She stood, still holding the blanket around her body. My nostrils opened and closed, taking in her scent. Her arousal was deepening and my cocks pressed against my seam. While I wanted them free, so she could see my impressive lengths, it was best that I didn't.

She needed a serious conversation, and I hoped my patience would be quickly rewarded.

"Y-you mean to tell me…"—she wagged her finger at me—"that this is what Abuela wished for us? This soulmate thing. With shifters, with dragons and all that?"

Her face turned a flush of red. Her body heated against my scales when she leaned up against my body, which had curled around her.

Mmm, she was accepting. More than my other side truly realized.

"Yes, my little human. And it appears your sister has already accepted her fate."

Elena's mouth opened again, and she gasped. "Emmie? Emmie would never tie herself down." She shook her head. "She would never." She covered her mouth with her hand. "Unless it was some really good dick, and the dude was as crazy as her."

I tilted my head and nodded. "From what I have seen in Anaki's memories, Locke is unwell in his mind."

Locke, the president of this club, has been kind to the members, bringing those who were broken and rejected, while his methods were harsh, brash, and immoral in his dealings with humans. He went as far as to threaten the town's law enforcement to turn a blind eye to what this club did in the darkness of night.

While Anaki and I didn't accept everything this male did, this was home. Our new home, and it would be for our mate as well. It was protection in numbers in this cruel world, and while dragons were mostly independent, there were other darker forces much stronger than a single dragon alone could fight.

My mate leaned against my scales and pressed her hand to her forehead. She chuckled until a manic laugh left her lips. "Insane. I never thought this was what she meant. That any of this could happen."

I leaned my head closer. My hot breath fanned her cheek. "Believe it because it is true. Our soul has craved you since the moment we saw you. Once I looked into your eyes, I knew."

Her eyes softened, and pink lit across her cheeks. "H-how exactly do you both know?"

"Your scent, your looks, but most of all, my soul longs for me to bind you to us. It is an unexplainable force, and I know you feel it, too. You've felt comfortable here with me, and you haven't been able to explain it."

She bit her lip. "That's right. I thought it was strange."

"Because you are ours," I growled, my forked tongue extended, and I licked the side of her neck. She closed her eyes and leaned forward. "The Moon Goddess has declared it; there is nothing more powerful than that. Once we claim you, our bond will remain unbroken."

I gently extended my tongue and traced a delicate path under her chin, feeling the warmth of her skin as it glided to the other side of her neck. Her soft moan echoed in the quiet room, and I noticed her grip on the blanket relaxing, fingers uncurling as she surrendered to our touch.

"Do you accept this bond between us, Elena?" I nuzzled our nose into the crook of her neck. My tail wrapped around the blanket to gently tug it away from her. The blanket had muffled her arousal, but now it bloomed around us.

A guttural growl rumbled within my chest. My body trembled with desire and my slit opened to reveal my hardened cocks. They hung from my body and grazed against the bedding.

"Elena," I hissed and licked between her breasts.

Her knees buckled, as if she couldn't stand. My tongue wrapped around her breast, pulling tight at the nipple on one side, then I did it to the other. The sounds she made doubled my own deep, ancient desires. I wanted to mount her in this form before she had been claimed.

I can't hurt her.

But I could do other things to make her know the want we had for her.

My warm, elongated tongue traced a path to her navel, sliding further down to the intimate patch of hair beneath. A deep groan escaped my lips, delighting in the slickness of her arousal as I gently skimmed over the soft curve of her mound.

"Ah!" She grabbed either side of my face, and I pinned her next to my body, which had wrapped around hers to keep her trapped. "Can Anaki see?"

Is that what she was worried about? That we are two different beings? We are one and the same.

"Do not worry about such trivial things, but he is sleeping inside our mind. He passed out from worry that I might claim you in this form." I took another tentative lick between her thighs, scooping up the slick between them.

She gasped, her hands reaching for my horns.

"Claim me?" she panted.

I hummed, my forked tongue playing with her folds. "Yes. Bind your soul to ours. I said I would wait as long as I remained in this form, for a while." I hummed when I inserted my tongue into her cunt. Her arousal flowed onto my taste buds, and my eyes rolled to the back of my head. "Female!"

She tasted so good, her skin, her liquids. It all fueled my hunger for her. I wanted to bite, I wanted to taste her skin more. We have never felt this sort of need, this possession, this desire. Not even with our previous mate.

Anaki and I were young. I had just risen to the surface when we found the evil male, and I immediately knew something was wrong when I didn't attach myself to him right away. I tried my best to protect Anaki, but the heartache soon caused me to lose consciousness.

This, though, the taste of this female would drive me mad.

My tail whipped furiously against the bed, a restless storm of anticipation. My body maneuvered with a fierce determination and laid her down, presenting her as if she were the most exquisite jewel in existence, one meant solely for my eyes to admire. I craved to see every part of her, to envelop her in our precious treasures, making her the radiant centerpiece of our entire hoard.

Mine.

I slid my tongue deeper into her cunt, and I curled it when she thrust her chest forward with a cry.

Yes, female. Scream for me.

I shook my head while my tongue fucked her. I was becoming feral, and if I wasn't careful, my teeth were going to scrape her delicate skin.

I noticed my tail and smiled inwardly. I removed my tongue as she was pounding the bed and shaking her head.

"I'm not through." I licked my lips where her arousal now coated my snout. I placed my tapered tail close to my cocks, which had leaked lubrication, and I rubbed it along my tail. I would not ruin her cunt, not yet anyway.

As I moved my tail to her entrance, I licked up her body. "My sweet female, soon you will take my cocks in this form."

She panted, her eyes widening.

"Not yet, but soon." I pushed my tail inside her. It was thick enough to match one of our human form's cocks. She muffled a scream with her hand, and I pulled it away with a clawed finger. "No, I will hear your screams."

Her body was light as I lifted her and my flexible tail continued to fuck her. I positioned her so her stomach rested on my torso, her ass raised high in the air, completely exposed and vulnerable. Her sex was slick and hot, gripping my tail as it slid in and out. I leaned over her arched back, my tongue uncoiling from my mouth, hungry and eager as I licked down her back.

"Mmm, what a good female. Now you may scream for me."

I whimpered. No longer able to thrash my tail, I had to keep it calm to fuck her gently. I didn't have a way to let out my stress. My cocks leaked come, and they throbbed for release.

My long tongue tickled the side of her breast until it reached her tit. My cocks felt utterly abandoned so I gripped them together as I used the lubricant they expelled for my pleasure and, I pumped them vigorously.

Ah, fuuuuck!

When I squeezed, I saw stars behind my eyes. My body was completely used. We would both get something out of this, and as soon as I came, I would...

"More!" she cried out, pushing her ass against me.

I twirled my tail inside her, her moans were filthy while she panted. My tongue came up from her chest and slid into her mouth. I wanted to suck both breasts into my mouth and suckle them like they were one giant tit.

Her velvety warmth clenched around my tail, with a pulsating rhythm that sent waves of sensation coursing through me. I mirrored her body's rhythm, gripped my cocks with a fervent urgency, feeling the slick, heated skin against my scaled hands.

A long, languid moan escaped her lips, her breath mingling with mine as my tongue explored the depths of her mouth. Her body quivered when she let out one last cry of pleasure. Her body trembled and her cunt released her grip on my tail.

I continued to stroke my cocks in tandem, my eyes locked onto her face, watching as her eyes fluttered closed, her expression a portrait of pure, unadulterated bliss.

"Dios Mio..." she whispered, and her head lowered, falling onto my body.

I jerked my cocks quickly, seeing how well I had done sating my little human. I felt the tingle in my spine that ran down to my slit and then to my shafts. Thick ropes of my light blue seed spurted out of me, landing on my mate's backside.

She didn't flinch, feeling the warmth of my seed on her body. I growled, happily seeing how I had marked her in my own way. While I did not break her skin, I did scent her, rather well.

Hmm, Anaki will be horrified.

CHAPTER TWENTY-SIX

Anaki

Layers upon layers of blankets cocooned her, each wrapped snugly around her like a protective shell. Our serpentine form coiled gently around her, providing an added layer of warmth. Only her head peeked out from the swaddle, her hair cascaded over our body like a waterfall of silk.

How our body twisted and turned around her reminded me of a cat. What exactly were we made of? A solid? A liquid? We could bend and fold in the weirdest of ways, and this was the first time I really saw what our body could do without worrying myself sick about my animal hunting or hurting her.

Once he caught her, I thought it was over, that he would claim her, but he swore he wouldn't when he caught her scent of fear. Her fear set him straight. Thank the goddess for that, because trying to force myself back in control of the body for so long exhausted me.

I passed out from screaming shortly after he caught her. When I awoke I found ourselves staring down at her in awe. She was covered in our scent from our fucking seed. I was ready to bang our head into the wall, for what all this could mean.

I sighed, and my dragon let out a deep, resonant chuckle that vibrated through the tent. With a gentle nudge of his massive snout, he prodded Elena, who responded with a groan, retreating further into our body.

"What did you do?" I asked in annoyance.

She was absolutely exhausted, that much was for sure. Her eyes appeared glued shut. Not even an earthquake could wake this woman.

"I cleaned and tucked her into bed. I don't know what you mean."

"She smells like our seed. Don't tell me..." I rummaged through our mind. What he could see, I could see. Our memories were one and when I dug through them I saw how he fucked her with our tail, he jacked off our cocks and tongued her mouth like a damn animal.

If I had cheeks to flush with embarrassment, they would. The things he said to her, the vile things he did to her. And she liked it.

Elena's head was thrown back. She welcomed our tongue slurping down her body. Was she okay with all of it?

"She loved every minute of it. I suggest you stop coddling her like a tiny human and have your way with her before I claim her for myself. As you see, she wants us as much as we want her."

She wanted to be claimed. Elena wanted us both.

I just needed to tell her—

Quiet footsteps echoed ominously from outside the cave, growing louder and more distinct with each passing moment. Our hearts shift from a quiet lull to racing with anticipation.

It wasn't an animal, since the footsteps were too hard, and they wanted to be heard. The deliberate approach of two separate sets of footsteps steadily advanced towards our territory. Our heads snapped up, eyes wide with alertness, nostrils flared to catch any hint of their scent.

My dragon instantly went into defense mode, puffed up our neck, and made us appear larger.

Realization dawned on me who they could be. I hadn't had my phone on me in nearly a day, and I should have updates by now. *"It's the club,"* I said quickly. *"They mean no harm."*

My dragon emitted a fierce, guttural snarl and coiled even tighter around Elena, his scales pressed tightly around us with protective intensity. He had no intention of rising; his sole focus was on keeping Elena shielded and concealed from the impending threat of whoever dared to approach.

Seriously?!

He continued to take in the air. The steps came in, louder under the stones of the cave. "Anaki?" The voice was deeper, and immediately I knew who it was, but why was he here?

"Why is this idiot here?" my dragon mumbled, repeating my question. "A shifter should know to remain outside of another's territory with an unclaimed female."

"Bones' is smart, and he wouldn't come without a reason. He's probably worried. You know the club keeps tabs on people. The way he worries, I'm sure he thought we went rabid and Elena was dead somewhere."

My dragon hissed in annoyance, and his claws pierced the mattress.

Another scent assaulted my nose, soot and ash, and I cringed inwardly at what this could mean.

Sizzle.

Another dragon, another species of dragon entering our territory, was even worse. Sizzle isn't one to care, and with him not having his dragon awakened, thought it would be a good idea to come.

It's not. He wanted to die.

My dragon let out another snarl when both of the men pushed the flaps open without a word and came inside. "Holy fucking shit!" Bones stepped back, the flap hitting him in the face. "There is a damn dragon in here!"

Sizzle scoffed. "Duh, man."

He dragged the cigarette from his lips, its glowing ember casting a faint red light. With a casual flick of his wrist, he sent it spiraling to the ground, where it landed with a faint hiss. The sound of his boot scraping against the rough stone echoed softly as he ground the still-smoking stub beneath his heel, extinguishing it completely. "You knew Anaki was a dragon. Did you not think he would actually shift?"

Bones adjusted his cut, the leather jacket that bore the club's insignia, and ran his hand through his hair. Each time I saw him, the contrast of dark grays and stark whites threaded through his once jet-black locks seemed more pronounced. It was as if the weight of each day that passed pressed more heavily on him than on anyone else at the club. Though not the oldest among us, the lines etched into his face and the weariness in his eyes suggested a life of nothing but stress and heartache.

But we all had that. We must show our souls differently on the outside.

"Why are you here?" My dragon puffed up the fins on our back. "Anaki is not present, and you are strangers to me in my territory. My female sleeps. That is the only reason I have spared you.

Sizzle sidled over to the edge of the dimly lit cave, where an old antique desk stood. He carefully picked up a delicate quill, its feather slightly frayed at the edges, and examined it for a moment, the ink glistening on its tip. With a gentle motion, he returned the quill to the glass container filled with rich, deep black ink.

"Oh, so scary." Sizzle raised his hands in surrender. "Gonna get eaten by the big bad water dragon. Not." He pulled another cigarette from his cut pocket.

My dragon sneered and pulled one leg from being wrapped around Elena, as if he prepared to strike.

"Truth is, you don't want to wake up Sleeping Beauty, right there." Sizzle pointed the cigarette toward Elena, who was in too deep of a sleep for any conversation. "You know we aren't a threat because you can feel Anaki's calmness while we are here. He knows we mean no harm. That's why you haven't attacked. I had my dragon a long time before I was rejected. So don't give me this, 'I'm gonna eat you' shit. It would hurt Anaki and, in turn, hurt yourself."

Wow, I guess Sizzle did have a plan walking in here.

Sizzle took out his lighter and flicked the metal piece to light the spark. Once it lit, he took in a deep, long puff. "Fuck, that's good. Alright, Bones. After you, man." He waved his hand in front of Bones, who was still staring at us in awe.

"Yeah, uh." Bones cleared his throat. "Right. We have been trying to get ahold of you since yesterday afternoon. The fae saw you running through the forest, knocking over their trees. They spent most of the night putting them back up."

My dragon opened and closed his mouth in a mocking tone. "My mate ran, and I will fetch her when I please. Are the fae that upset about doing their job?" Our nose buried back into Elena's hair. He used it as a calming scent to keep his heart from racing and lashing out again.

Sizzle gave a look of disgust and sneered.

"That isn't all," Bones said. "Abuela, who is a brilliant woman by the way, also would like Elena to get checked out since... uh, well." Bones rubbed the back of his neck. "Since you chased her naked... through the woods all day yesterday. That can trigger her disease from being so stressed."

Our fins unfurled fast along the length of our arms and tail. They may have looked delicate, but they were sharp as blades. As they expanded, our neck elongated, stretching upward with a fluid elegance, making us appear taller and more majestic.

"Are you saying I do not take care of my female?" Our scaled lips pulled back to show off our menacing teeth.

"You've done it now." Sizzle shook his head. "Now you have a pissed off a lycan and a dragon. You can't win at all, these past two weeks." Sizzle shrugged his shoulders and leaned against the cave wall.

"I am not doing anything!" Bones took the cross-over bag that hung over his body. It fell to the ground with a thump. "I am doing my damn job. I am looking out for a bunch of idiots who can't take care of themselves! Yeah, I do things behind your backs, but it is because you all want to damn die! And you!" Bones pointed to Sizzle and marched toward him. He pulled the cigarette out of his mouth and threw it to the ground. "You are going to ruin your lungs. You will die before you even get your mate."

Sizzle seethed. "I don't want one."

Bones rolled his eyes. *I don't want one.'* He mocked and bobbed his head back and forth. "Fuck off. We all want one. I sped up Locke's healing to help the club. The only side effects he had to deal with were his memories hitting him like a freight train. I do things for others to help because if I don't... people die!"

Bones' face flushed a deep crimson, matching the vivid hue of the extra blankets neatly folded at the foot of the bed. Each breath he took was labored and heavy, his chest rising and falling with the effort. The veins in his neck stood out prominently, thick and pulsing.

Bones leaned forward to Sizzle and whispered, "If I don't take care of the club, who will? Huh? Locke's a damn psycho. No one knows what he's gonna do next, what warehouse he's gonna lead his men into." Bones stepped away and circled around Sizzle. "Who gets blamed for people getting hurt when things fail? I do. You may not give a shit about our life, but I do. I care about everyone in this club. Does it get noticed?" Bones shook his head. "Nah, man. It doesn't. You guys only care when you don't heal according to plan. May it be too much steroids for Locke to get him better or telling someone you are too far gone for this mission, *but go anyway!*" He glared our way. "Damned if I do, damned if I don't."

Bones stepped away from Sizzle, a look of indifference on his face.

Bones shook his head and ran his hand down his face to pull at his beard. His face returned to his normal color after a long moment of silence.

"Alright, Anaki's dragon," Bones scoffed and calmed himself. "I can ask you questions about Elena. I won't touch her. It would make me feel better if I did. If you don't want to let me, and be an ass, that's fine, too. I'll go on with my day. I ain't fighting a fucking water lizard." Bones crossed his arms and leaned on one foot, waiting for a reply.

I tried to force myself through, to talk to Bones. I'd always liked him, never had a problem. Some of the stuff he did I found questionable, but he had the right intentions. With the speech he'd given, I think I liked him ten times more.

My dragon laid our fins down close to our body and stared down at our mate.

"What questions do you have, wolf? I will also answer questions about my species, as well, if you care to know for the future."

Well, color my shit pink.

Bones' face softened, and his lips parted. "You'd do that? Why?"

"Because Anaki holds great regard for you. Dare I say, part of the heart that beats for this future pack."

Out of our peripheral, Sizzle stared at us until he took backward steps out of the tent and to the entrance outside where he waited. We could still hear his heartbeat as he wasn't far.

Bones' shoulders relaxed, and he lowered his body and opened his bag to retrieve his tablet. "Okay, just a few, I won't keep you from your mate.

She appears pretty tired."

CHAPTER TWENTY-SEVEN

Elena

I bolted upright from the bed, the absence of the familiar warmth and tight embrace jolting me awake. I had become accustomed to the sinuous, serpentine coils of a dragon when I fell asleep. Now, I found myself surrounded only by a tangled heap of blankets, their soft folds failing to replicate the comforting, living grip I missed.

Anaki wasn't in the bed, and I couldn't tell if it was night or day.

I haven't slept that well in ages. Each time I slept with Anaki, I woke up more refreshed than the last. Orgasmic-induced sleep was the definition of the way to go.

There was a tray filled with food. Fruits, meats, and pastries were laid out on a large tray we had used before. I immediately dug in because my stomach rumbled. I fell back on the blankets and ate my fill while I hummed contentedly to myself.

Where would Anaki be right now? Or would it be his dragon? His dragon was different than Anaki's sweet soul. Rather demanding creature, more self-assured and knew what he wanted, while Anaki was on the cautious side. I liked both, and I would definitely enjoy the Jekyll and Hyde personalities.

I licked the last of the bacon off my fingers and rose. I let the blanket tumble down from my breasts and gazed around the room. Light music played, and still no one else was in the massive cave.

The wind whispered its way into the tent, causing the delicate tulle hanging from the ceiling to sway gently toward me as they danced in the breeze. I felt the cool touch of the outside air, a refreshing contrast to the lingering warmth that clung to my skin from being cocooned beneath all the layers.

Where was he? Anaki the human and Anaki the dragon?

And did Anaki the dragon have a name? Because he didn't act like Anaki at all, he should have one. I scratched my head. Bossy Scales would fit.

Bossy Scales it is.

"Did you sleep well?" Anaki's voice came from the other side of the cave, where the kitchen was, and just beyond the turn to find the bathroom. I slung my head around to see him, the first time since turning into his beastly form, but he was nowhere to be found.

"Anaki?" I sat up further and pushed the tray away. "Where are you? Why are you back there? Come here."

Was he embarrassed? He turned into a dragon, wasn't anything to be embarrassed about, unless he was upset that he saw how his dragon tongue and tail fucked me. In that case, I should be the one embarrassed.

Anaki cleared his throat and leaned his head around the corner. His hair was a mess, and his cheeks were rosy.

Aw, he was adorable.

I giggled and covered my mouth with my hand. "What are you doing, silly dragon?"

He ducked his head away to hide again. "I thought I could do it, but I can't. I changed my mind." He yelled in panic.

I sprang to my feet, wrapping a silk blanket snugly around my shoulders. My footsteps were as soft as a whisper, scarcely stirring the air as I moved across the intricately woven carpets he had gathered. I reached the shadowy corner of the cave and cautiously leaned forward, peering around the edge. There he was, his back pressed against the rough cave wall, his head rhythmically tapping the chilly stone surface, a steady, muted thud echoing softly in the dim light.

I gazed down at him. He was shirtless and wearing an outfit that was extremely... hot! He'd added a chain to his nipple rings that went from one side to the other. There was another chain that connected in the middle, that went straight down to his navel, which now had a blue spherical stone settled in it.

My mouth watered as I gazed at the intricate dips and bold curves of his muscles. The familiar bulge of biceps and the chiseled outline of his abdomen were human enough, but there were also ridges that seemed to ripple like dragon scales along his forearms, lending him an otherworldly, almost mythical appearance.

The sarong that I usually saw him wearing inside the cave had been swapped for a luxurious silk garment, its fabric shimmering with vibrant hues of deep blues, rich greens, and pristine whites. The edges were adorned with intricate gold trimming that caught and reflected the light like a delicate halo.

Even his feet were adorned with jingling bangles, even his feet were adorned with jingling bangles, matching ones circles his wrists, clinking softly with every movement. He looked like a typical belly dancer at first glance, with the chains wrapped around his waist.

My eyes took their fill of how handsome he looked, how delectable he appeared. Did he get dressed like that for me? Like the dragons back in his homeland for their females? Was he going to dance for me? And was he nervous?

He danced on the bar just fine, days ago, and now he can't?

His eyes were closed, and he panted. The pretty lashes on his eyes fluttered while he counted to ten.

My hand reached out, and the back of my knuckles brushed his cheek. "Aw, sweetie, what's wrong?"

Anaki jumped, and his bangles clinked together. When he looked down at me, he grabbed my wrist and pulled me to his body as he held me tightly. "You can't see me like this, you naughty minx."

I laughed in his chest. "Why not, were you going to change your mind?" I poked his side to make him laugh.

"Maybe?" His voice cracked, and I pulled away to run my fingers through his hair.

"I hope not, I was really looking forward to this." I ran my finger up the chain, from his naval to his stomach, and then his chest. Then I ran to the right side of his chest muscle and gave it a pull. He groaned, and I leaned in and gave it a lick. "Aren't you supposed to give your soulkin a dance before you claim them?"

Anaki's mouth dropped, and he wrapped his arm around my waist to pull me even closer to him.

"Soulkin...how did you know—"

"Your dragon, whom I will now refer to as Bossy Scales, explained what it is." I popped him on the nose with my finger. "Soul mates, huh? And you didn't want to say anything because I was mad at Abuela about all of it?"

Anaki slowly nodded. "I didn't want to force you into anything, I didn't want—"

I covered Anaki's mouth with a kiss. "At first, I wasn't sure. I was a mad, little girl trying to follow in my older sister's footsteps. All I know now is that I found what I want. What powerful feelings I have for you." I caressed his cheek. "You bring out the best in me, the happiness I've been missing, and the magic I've craved. If you say we were always meant to be, I'm going to follow my heart as crazy as it sounds."

Anaki's mouth dropped, and then his whole body did. He picked me up and twirled me in the small space until he brought me out to the main part of the cave.

"You mean it? Really mean it?" he cried and had us fall into a big pile of pillows. The light in his eyes brightened, and I could no longer see the darkness that usually hid beneath. For once in my life, I felt excited, happy with a decision I had made.

I cupped his face and pulled him toward me, giving him another kiss. "Of course, silly dragon. Why would I make it up?"

He peppered kisses along my jawline and down my chest.

"Well?" I moaned when he bit into my breast hidden beneath the fabric. "Do I get my dance now? Aren't you supposed to seduce me?"

Anaki's head popped up, and he bit his lower lip. "You want that, huh?"

Of course I did. I nodded excitedly, and he jumped up on his feet. The skirt he wore was thick around his intimate parts, but had fabric that weaved down to his ankles so it swished and swirled around his feet.

The bangles around his ankles and his wrists continued to jingle when he ran across the cave to where an old record player sat. I continued to watch, trying to figure out exactly how all this electricity worked, when I noticed wires that were neatly wrapped in dark electrical tape leading out of the cave.

Have to ask about that later.

Anaki was on his tiptoes as he danced while he tried to get the right song to work. I got comfortable and crossed my legs. I made sure nothing was showing on my end. I wanted to see him in all his glory. A dance, for me. For no one else, and I was thrumming with excitement.

The song started, which reminded me of a mixture of Middle Eastern and Indian music. It was slow at first, and the movement of Anaki's hips startled me as he quickly adapted to the music.

Did he know the music? The beat already?

I gasped. He practiced??

The idea he had practiced to this song already had my heart pounding. He had practiced for his mate. Me! The person he would spend the rest of his life, I guess eternity, with. He said he loved to dance, but was he seriously that dedicated to dance, like this?

All of his muscles showed as he moved his torso. Muscles that showed in the dim light. Outside, it was dark, as no light shone through. I didn't know if I had slept for a day or if I had woken up in the middle of the same night, but I didn't care anymore. I was wide awake and already turned on, as Anaki began to move his body in ways no man should be able to move his body.

His hips gyrated rhythmically as the pulsing beat echoed through the cave. His eyes met mine, filled with passion and desire. A smirk spread across his face as he moved closer, reaching out to trace his fingers along my cheek. He pulled at my arm, his fingers dragged along my skin, and placed me in a chair that I hadn't seen on the bare floor.

I swallowed hard, my heart pounding in my chest. All playful giddiness fled from me. I wasn't laughing because of how crazy this was; he was hypnotizing me with his body, and I couldn't understand what he was doing to me.

Anaki's smile grew wider, and he took a step closer, his body brushing against mine. The sensation sent electricity coursing through me, igniting a fire within.

He moved away again, his hips swaying seductively as he continued to dance. The way he moved, his hands moving across his body, as his fingers and hands told a story. I felt drawn to him, unable to resist the allure he gave off. He was my sweet, playful Anaki, but he was also the seductive, bewitching male who had put me under a spell. I couldn't look away from him as he continued to glide over the ground with his bare feet, listening to the jingling of his bangles as they demanded attention from me.

Sweat glistened on his skin. Droplets rolled down each crevice of his muscles, between his abs, down to his Adonis belt, and I yearned to lean forward and lick in between all the places where the water droplets fell.

My body heated, and my thighs clenched together. Was it a spell he had put me under? My pussy fluttered, my body was hot, ignited and I wanted nothing more than to touch him, having him touch me, claim me whatever that possibly meant. He had me, stuck himself inside me, even his dragon had done things to me, but I wanted more.

I wanted to be even closer.

I reached my hand out, but he evaded my touch and danced around me. I grunted and followed his every move as he jumped around the chair. He was smirking, knowing that he had utterly captivated me with his movements.

As he danced closer to me once more, he reached out to cup my cheek gently in his hand. His thumb brushed against my lips, and I couldn't help but lean into it, savoring the warmth of his touch. He leaned down then, his eyes never leaving mine, and softly brushed his lips against mine in a feathery kiss. It was so tender and sweet that it took my breath away.

"Do you want more?" he asked quietly, his voice filled with raw emotion.

I nodded eagerly, unable to find words to express the feelings that were churning inside me. Anaki's eyes shone with excitement at my response. "You can't touch me," he whispered huskily in my ear.

"Is that your rule or the dance's rules?"

Anaki chuckled and straddled me as he ground himself into me. He was hard, and I could feel his cocks rubbing up against my stomach. He widened my legs so he could rub up against my lower stomach. I leaned my head back and clenched my fists at my side, trying my best not to touch him.

If he didn't want me to touch him, I wouldn't.

Anaki nipped and bit at my neck. All while moving his hips, rubbing his body up mine. His hands cradled my neck and pushed away the blanket from my body. I felt the fabric fall to my waist until the top part of my body was bare.

I thought he would cup my breasts in his hands, but instead, he backed away and made me feel cold.

"Damn you," I hissed through my teeth and opened my eyes. He smirked, his cocks hard and erected and he danced around me playfully. He went behind the chair, his hands came down to rub my chest, and that was when I couldn't take it any longer.

My arms lifted slowly, fingers weaving into the thick strands of his hair, feeling the softness and warmth beneath my touch. His mouth pressed against my neck, and I felt the gentle scrape of his teeth, followed by the warm, wet trail of his tongue. He lingered at the sensitive spots, alternating between sucking gently and delivering playful nips that sent tingling sensations down my spine.

"Fuck!" I cried when I felt his tail wrap around my leg. It worked its way up between my legs and rubbed at my clit. "Please touch me," I panted.

Anaki growled. I felt the sharpness of his teeth nipping at my earlobe. "You're so wet." Anaki's tail tightened around my leg. His hand reached down and ripped away the silk blanket before he pressed his fingers into my pussy. He hummed. "All this for us?"

I gasped when he stuck two of his fingers inside me. "Yes."

"I wanted to speak with you more about what a bond entails, but I don't think I can last."

"You talk too much," I groaned.

Anaki yanked the chair out from under me with a swift motion, causing me to stagger to my feet. His grip tightened around my arms, his fingers pressing into my skin like iron clamps. Leaning in closer, he inhaled deeply, his nostrils flaring as he took in the scent of my hair. "Is that so?" I heard his dragon's voice double with his. "Then you won't mind the claiming, right here, right now."

Anaki's sharp teeth pierced my shoulder. Instead of feeling pain, it gave way to an intense euphoria of pleasure. Stars exploded behind my eyes, white, blue, and silver light twinkled in front of me. I was pushed onto the bed, furniture clashing to the floor. My body arched on its own accord.

I wanted to be fucked. Thoroughly.

"Nngh!" His teeth sunk further in the meat of my flesh.

I felt his cocks graze my thighs, they were wet, mixing with my own arousal which had dripped down my leg. Never in my life had I ever been so wet before.

"Your body craves us." The deep guttural noise of a growl made me drip even more. "Your soul already has your body weeping for us to fill that pretty pussy. Are you ready to be claimed?"

Those dirty words.

Anaki's familiar voice whimpered, his hand reached around and grabbed my breast in one hand while the other grabbed his cock. I heard the squelch as he fisted it between my legs. "I can't wait to stick both of them inside you," he whispered in his playful voice. "A bite, our cocks buried deep inside. You'll be ours forever. You okay with that, love?" Anaki questioned, his sweet voice made me all the more willing.

I nodded and pushed my ass to his hips to get him to sink into me. He hummed, hungrily, and flipped me over to my back. "No, I wanna see those pretty eyes staring at me when we bind our souls, love. Goddess, I can't believe this is happening!"

I smiled and reached up to cup his face. He fiddled with his cocks, joining them as one. He twirled them around my clit, his come coating my entrance. "Fuck, fuck, so wet. I don't know..."

"You are going to fit," I reassured him. "Like two puzzle pieces that were always meant to be one."

Anaki parted his lips and leaned down to kiss me. I widened my legs and wrapped them around his waist as he pushed forward.

The sting was unbearable, two cocks trying to shove inside me, pushing me, stretching me to a size I have never been before.

He pressed his lips against mine with an intensity that seemed to drown out everything else, and his tongue moved deftly against mine in a desperate attempt to overshadow my discomfort. His fingers dug into my hips with a firm grip, almost as if he was trying to steady us both against the storm of emotions. Inch by inch, he pushed past the tension and resistance until finally his cocks found their place. A sharp cry escaped my lips; a surprising blend of sharp pain mingled with a rush of unexpected pleasure.

The slick that came off his cocks helped ease them deeper inside.

"Ah, fuck," Anaki groaned, his breath hot against my face. "I'm sorry, love. I won't go too deep." He pulled back slightly, just enough to allow me to adjust to the new feeling. The cocks inside me twitched, sending waves of pleasure throughout my entire body. I could feel the ridges of both shafts rubbing against places I didn't know I could even feel.

I clutched at him, pulling him closer.

"No," I moaned, "don't stop. Need you."

Anaki quirked an eyebrow at my sudden change in tone. He pushed forward again, burying himself deeper inside me. My walls tightened around them, pulling him further in with each thrust. His tail trailed up my spine to grab hold of my shoulder to get a better grip on my body.

"Fuck," he grunted, "I can feel your hunger for us, too, now." He started moving more forcefully. His cocks pulsating within me as if searching for something deeper than just my body. Anaki leaned down and bit on my shoulder harder to send a surge of euphoria through the bond that was forming between us.

My eyes rolled back in pleasure as our bodies synchronized their movements - his thrusts matched mine. Our hearts pounded in unison as we surrendered to the passion consuming us both. This was a joining not just of bodies but of souls. I was beginning to feel... *him!*

CHAPTER TWENTY-EIGHT

Anaki

Once I'd poured every ounce of my essence into her, through my bite and my seed, an all-consuming darkness engulfed me. It felt like mere seconds, just the briefest blink, but when I regained consciousness, I was standing amidst the scorching embrace of the sand, surrounded by warm dunes that were hauntingly familiar, as if they held the echoes of my past.

Dusk was approaching, and the warm sands beneath my feet brought on a nostalgic feeling of a happier time. Few fledglings were to be seen, but I saw enough younger dragons that had yet to find their mates come forth from the water.

Friends whom I had swum with over the years, were filled with happiness, with no care in the world as they playfully slung water into each other's faces. Nets filled with fish for tonight's meat, and the mated met on the shore to gather them to scale and prepare for the smoke tents.

My hearts converged, feeling like one giant boulder was in my chest. Why am I here? Why am I back at a place that I had left so long ago?

I lifted my hand to see if it was real until another person ran right through me. I gasped, watching them run away from me without a care.

"They can't see me," I whispered and took a step back into the dune.

"No, they can't," A deep, feminine voice called from behind me.

I squeezed my eyes shut and released a ragged, tremulous breath. This was a disaster, an utter nightmare. Either death had claimed me in the throes of mating, or the goddess herself had descended to pronounce my unworthiness to claim Elena.

My hearts pounded, and my hands shook when I clasped them to my chest.

A warm hand grabbed my wrist and pulled it to hold in hers. "You are one of the sweetest of the group, aren't you, Anaki?"

I finally opened my eyes, but I didn't dare look upon her. I didn't feel worthy to. I knew what she looked like from Journey's descriptions. Long white hair, fair skin, a crescent moon on her forehead. She also said she could come in the form of a dove, but I wasn't about to ask to see her in that form.

I believed everything Journey said. I believed it with all my hearts, because I knew the truth in what Journey told me. I could detect a lie, not by the way wolves could measure heartbeats, but just by how people talked. I learned quickly after my first mate rejected me.

"Anaki," she cajoled. "It's alright, you shouldn't hang your head in shame. This should be a joyous occasion, hmm?"

I swallowed hard and nodded, my throat tight with emotion. Joy was a distant memory, overshadowed by the weight of claiming my mate and being dragged back to this place—my so-called home, where shadows of the past lay in wait, eager to haunt me. Dark memories lurked in every corner, secrets I had not yet unburdened to my mate. Though I was certain of her acceptance, the guilt gnawed at me, a relentless beast that threatened to consume me the moment I revealed my hidden truths.

"Anaki," the goddess giggled and tilted up my chin to meet her eyes. "Tender dragon, in order for this bonding to be complete, all secrets must be revealed. Even Locke's were told to the new Luna."

I tried to hide my grimace from the beautiful goddess before me, who had graced us all with a new chance at a second mate.

While many blamed her for the problems we all had with the rejections, I did not. Every soul was given a choice, and while our souls were best matched with who she thought we would be with... we could reject the pairing.

Unfortunately, she could not see what would happen when a soul was rejected. That the person left in the cold without a mate would die. She wasn't an all-seeing goddess. That was where everyone blamed her. Call me an idiot, but after Journey explained it, I didn't blame the goddess any longer and quickly begged her for a mate for myself.

"I know, I know." The goddess turned us away from the scene over the lake. The clan was creating fires, preparing food, and there was not much else to see but laughter and screams of joy. Not that I didn't care to see it, it's just that one terrible memory ruined all the joyful ones. "Emm did a wonderful job accepting it. She understands Locke and will be capable of keeping him calm." She tapped her lip. "However, she will need her sister to help keep her grounded. While I know Grim will be the pack's beta, Elena will be Emm's right hand and protector."

I jerked my head toward the goddess, and she smiled. "Yes, Elena will be the one protecting the Luna. Isn't that a turn of events?" She held out her arm for me to follow, and I did so willingly, as she guided me toward the forest that lay behind the tents.

My footsteps became heavier the more we traveled. My memories came back stronger than they ever had in the dreams.

This was too real.

"I don't want to be here," I stated, and put my hands on my knees. "I don't want to venture into the forest anymore."

The goddess placed her hands in a praying position and turned back to me. "Your mate has almost completely forgotten the abuse of her past, you know."

I looked up at her, and my breath came in small pants.

"She doesn't remember she was beaten, she just remembers she was in an abusive relationship, just like—"

"Journey's pain," I grunted and straightened to stand next to her. "Why are you telling me this?"

"Because it will be the same for you, Anaki. Already, your memories are fading. It will get worse before it gets better. You do not feel pain because of the rejection; you feel pain because of the lies. Your strong empathy is something you've likely already discovered. You feel with your heart, your soul. You love everyone in this future pack. You are this club's heart and soul. You see what others don't."

My chin wobbled, and I took my hand to rub it to keep it away.

You can't cry in front of the goddess, you twat.

My dragon grumbled in agreement, and I got the courage to take a couple of steps closer to her.

We traveled deeper into the forest. It was to a secret place where Caelen and I would go.

I winced. How long had it been since I thought of his name? Decades. So many years since I even thought of the name that had haunted me. I referred to him as a *they*, just a person in time. He no longer existed, so why even think of his name now?

But he was a person. We grew up together in the same clan, which was unheard of. Dragons were not fertile creatures, and fledglings were few and far between. One fledgling born every ten to twenty years from a mated pair. There weren't many pairs to begin with, and not many fledglings in my time. We were a small, water dragon tribe, and when Caelen and I were born just a month apart, our parents saw it as a blessing.

Two fledglings to play with one another.

We became close. While we were young, we were the best of friends. Where one went, the other followed. As we grew older, in our pubescent years, it wasn't friendship we held for each other, but something deeper. We had developed feelings. We didn't know if it was due to lack of females, to hormones, or to the idea of wanting to express ourselves, but we knew we could do nothing about it.

Male to male mated pairs were unheard of, but if the goddess gave it to us, why would it be banned? That was my thinking. That was my hope.

I was more open with my feelings and ideas, hopeful that we were mates. Caelen, not as much.

One evening, long after many had gone to bed, we sat at the shoreline. We often did this, as it was our time alone to contemplate what we wanted to do once we had received our dragons.

We both wanted to travel, beyond the large lake, find larger bodies of water to swim in, and find other clans to speak with. Even dare to find other clans of dragons, such as fire and air.

This night was different. Caelen was distant. He wasn't laughing, not his usual playful self. Normally, he would have me pinned to the sand and playfully kissing my cheek. This night he was stoic, rigid. Nervous.

His birthday was a week away. I felt it in my bones that he was meant to be mine. I couldn't be sure, I've never had a mate before, but surely he felt something if I felt it, too.

"What if we are mates, Caelen? Wouldn't that be amazing?" I laced my hand with his. "Then we wouldn't have to fight our feelings anymore. We could go where we want, when we want. We wouldn't have to worry about anyone else or what they say. The goddess put us together, and that is all that matters."

Caelen said nothing and stared over the water.

"And we find our own cave together and curl up to stay warm. We wouldn't have to hide to cuddle." I snorted out a high-pitched laugh and laid my head on his shoulder.

Caelen brushed me off and stood up.

"Hey, what's wrong?" I stood up with him and put my hand on his shoulder. "Is something the matter?"

"My birthday is next week." He rubbed the back of his neck. "Father wants me to go with him to the market."

I bobbed my head. It was a tradition when you came of age that you get to go to the markets with other shifters to see how to trade. He was old enough to go, so it wasn't anything out of the ordinary. "That's great. Are you leaving soon? That's quite a journey on foot."

Caelen cleared his throat. "Yeah, tomorrow. Sorry, I didn't tell you." He didn't look me in the eyes, but Caelen could be like that. He was shy at times, but only near other shifters if I showed possessiveness. I understood his request to keep our friendlier side a secret. Unmated were not to touch anyone but their intended.

Caelen would always sneak into my cave later and curl around me to tell me he was sorry when he had brushed me off in front of others. He was only looking out for us, as he was our protector. He had big feelings now. Especially since his dragon was approaching.

I still had a month to feel mine. I felt possessiveness over him, but Caelen was much stronger than I was. More muscular. He would be a great protector and, most of all, a great mate. I thought he had so much weight on his shoulders.

"Were you worried I would get upset? Is that why you didn't bring it up?" I asked.

Caelen nodded, still not looking me in the eyes. "I won't be able to come by later, we are leaving early. Before sunrise. I'll miss you, though." His cheeks turned pink. His skin was a beautiful olive, and he had dark hair with salmon-colored streaks running through it. I couldn't wait to see his dragon.

"I'll miss you, too." I smiled widely at him and grabbed his hand. "And if someone else is your mate, I'll be happy for you. We will still be the best of friends. Alright? I care for you and want you happy."

Caelen took a deep breath and nodded.

And I meant it. If the goddess gave him to someone else, then I would have been happy.

Jolted from my thoughts when I heard Elena call. She came out from one of the massive trees that shaded an area almost completely. Her eyes were wide as she took in the unfamiliar foliage that was vastly different from Earth. "Anaki?" Her hands intertwined with themselves, knotted around her stomach, while she steadily stepped to the next tree as if to hide herself from anyone else's view.

She was here, in the very heart of my world, where I had spent my formative years. My throat constricted painfully, parched and raw as I struggled to summon her name. A surge of panic suffocated my words. I knew the inevitable was upon me. She was about to uncover everything, and the thought clawed at my insides. If only I hadn't been so reckless, so consumed by the feverish urgency to claim her, I could have told her all of this. She wouldn't have to have seen—

"She still would have had to." The goddess stepped beside me. "In order for her to fully understand what Locke has created, for the broken souls of his club and to help her sister, she needed to see."

I gritted my teeth to keep my mouth from biting back. This was just embarrassing.

Elena scanned the forest and, spotting us, her heart raced as she sprinted over. Her plain dark blue dress didn't do justice to her beauty. She quickly embraced me, ignoring the goddess by my side.

"Where are we, and why didn't you say anything when I called?" Her head darted to the Moon Goddess, her eyes widening. "And who is she... oh." I watched her eyes widen, and her arms tightened around me. "Is she?"

I nodded. "Yeah, this is the goddess your abuela prayed to."

"Do I bow, pray, or something?" she whispered to me.

I chuckled. "Probably, but I'm still in shock myself."

The Moon Goddess smiled and shook her head. "No, let's forget the formalities. I think there is enough repairing on my part that warrants no formalities."

Elena tilted her head in question.

The goddess let out a sigh. "While I have given your dragon the ability to speak Anaki, even he could not speak to your mate about the true purpose of the Iron Fang. Instead, he used his tongue for pleasure and not what I had intended him to use it for."

Both of our faces turned a bright red. Elena buried her face into my chest while I had to regard the goddess with my own.

The Goddess smiled until she laughed and waved her hand. "I understand, you both are caught up in the bond, it is understandable, but now our time is short, and dangers are coming. Now walk with me."

Elena and I both looked at one another while the goddess gave us her back.

"But we just bonded, aren't we supposed to be on a honeymoon?" Elena whispered. "Like I'm still sore."

"I can carry you," I whispered back.

"But what about round two?"

"Are you coming or not?" The goddess turned with her eyebrow raised.

Elena's shoulders slumped. "We can do more later. I guess upcoming danger trumps more sex."

CHAPTER TWENTY-NINE

Elena

I grabbed Anaki's hand and laced our fingers together. The world we walked through I knew was not of Earth. I stayed quiet as we walked barefoot together and kept my thoughts to myself.

Anaki's emotions were like my own. I felt his worry and guilt. It was strange to feel someone else's emotions; it was very separate from mine.

Before I opened my eyes and woke up in this world, an onslaught of Anaki's memories flooded me. Anaki, with a boy named Caelen whom he had grown up with. They appeared to be best friends and the only children close in age.

Anaki was the spunky, charismatic boy everyone loved. Everyone smiled because of him. He played jokes, he danced and sang to make those around him laugh. He spread love wherever he went. I smiled at that because he was still that same person today.

My Anaki.

Caelen, however, was more reserved. He was the silent observer and took his tasks seriously around the clan. He had desires to reach an elder position for others to see him as a leader.

Since they grew up together, Anaki took it upon himself to do every-thing in his power to make Caelen smile, and it appeared he did. Once they got older, Anaki's obsession to make him laugh grew, and I saw how Caelen returned those feelings, but there was hesitation.

There was jealousy when everyone greeted Anaki first, instead of Caelen. They enjoyed his lightheartedness and ignored the hard work that Caelen tried to do for the clan.

Yet Caelen was still drawn to Anaki. I saw visions of them together and how they held one another in the forest's darkness. It was Caelen's doing, hiding them from the world. Anaki's memories revealed that relationships before mating age were frowned upon, but the intensity of those feelings that these two had was strong. Caelen was determined to keep his affection for Anaki secret.

Even putting him down in public.

Anaki was wild and free, and any time he was too loud or boisterous Caelen would scold him to be calm and compose himself. Anaki would brush it off, but I could see his young self with the hurt in his eyes. The same hurt I saw when I first met my dragon.

This was the pain that Anaki had hidden all this time from me.

I squeezed his hand as we came to a large stone that jutted from the soil within the forest. The sun was now high in the sky and a younger Anaki sat cross-legged on a boulder thirty feet away from us.

Anaki slicked back his hair. The sarong he wore draped around his thin waist, its rich, deep blue fabric shimmering like the scales of a dragon, a nod to his signature color. His muscles were well-defined.

Around his neck hung several gold chains, each one catching the light with every movement. More gold adorned his hips in a delicate chained belt, and his ankles and wrists jingled softly with every step, encircled by intricate bangles that I'm sure would dance when he walked.

Anaki had dressed to impress. My heart sank a little when I saw it. He had dressed to meet someone special.

"Caelen is supposed to return after being at the market. It's been a month. He was supposed to return weeks ago. I haven't shifted here yet. I'm close, though. Before you are blessed with your animal, your entire body changes," he said to me.

I squeezed his hand. He appeared a little different from what he looked like now. Maybe a few wrinkles around the eyes, slightly tanner from being out in the sun. He was definitely wiser. "You looked handsome," I commented. "All dressed up." My voice was low, jealousy tinged within it.

"Caelen was my mate."

I stiffened.

"Caelen was supposed to be my mate. I felt it for a long time. As I felt my body change, my smell heightened while he was gone, and I knew. When I sniffed his clothes, the overwhelming possessiveness came over me. I asked my parents what it meant, and they explained. They were... happy for me."

I pressed my lips into a thin line and said nothing. This was Anaki's story to tell. He needed to let it out, even if I was a second choice.

Anaki turned to me, both of his hands on my shoulders. "I'm sorry you are finding out this way. It was painful for me to tell. I didn't want you to think—"

I covered his mouth with my hand. Before I could speak, the goddess interrupted me. "Every soul has a choice to accept or reject. However," she raised her finger, "I never expected souls to reject such a gift. I should have had a plan for an event like this, but I didn't." She sighed. "Even gods make mistakes. However, I will tell you this: if I knew then what I know now about bonding human souls to supernaturals, I would have bonded you to Elena. Even if that meant you would have to have waited eighty-seven years to find her." She didn't look at us as she stared at the young Anaki. "I've made mistakes, and I am doing my best to rectify them for those who have suffered."

"You are eighty-seven years old?" I gasped and slapped his chest. "I'm dating a dragon daddy?"

Anaki's mouth dropped. "You seriously picked that up, out of all of what was just said? Not the whole, 'I had a mate before you'?!"

The goddess covered her smile with a hand and shook her head.

I grabbed him by the hips and pulled him to me. "Last I checked, I took your virginity, so that means you're mine. Right?"

Anaki's shoulders visibly relaxed, and he placed his forehead on mine. He chuckled. "Yeah, Mama, that means I'm yours. You still have to bite me, though."

I pushed and pulled on his hips to make them wiggle for me. "You can count on it, grandpa."

Distant laughter echoed through the air, immediately capturing my attention. The Anaki clinging to me remained still, but my head swiftly turned toward the young Anaki who had risen to his feet. A broad, infectious grin spread across his face, and he leaped up with enthusiasm, his excitement palpable upon hearing the deep, resonant voice that unmistakably belonged to Caelen.

"He will be happy to have you," Young Caelen said. "I'll know he's taken care of and get to see him often, as a friend, of course." A male chuckled near him.

Anaki brushed my hair from my face, but I didn't look away from the scene unfolding. Caelen came into view with a woman on his arm. She had fair skin and hair. Her voice was soft and gentle when she laughed at something he whispered in her ear.

Oh shit! This wasn't good.

Young Anaki, being the sweet, innocent dragon he was, still had hope in his eyes when he strode over to them. Caelen kept his arm around the woman and hardly looked Anaki in the eye.

Anaki's head tilted, and a thunderous growl left him. "Who is this?" He reared back his head. "Why is your scent all over her? You must know—"

Caelen lifted his hand to silence Anaki. "Anaki, I'm glad you got my letter to meet us here. I know it's been some time, and I haven't returned."

Anaki stood his ground, and I could see his blue dragon scales ripple down his back.

"But it is because I have had both of our interests at heart."

I growled on my own accord and tried to leave Anaki's arms to storm over. How dare someone try to break my man's heart? How dare anyone try to reject such a sweet and wholesome, caring man such as him?

Anaki pulled me back and held me in his arms. I grunted and tried to remove myself. "Love, it's alright." He petted my hair. "It's okay." I shook my head.

"You see, I realized we were mates before I left for my journey to the market. While dragons have issues with producing more fledglings, it is only proper that we put our bond aside to try to produce more of the dragon species. Besides, a same-sex bonding is rare, almost unheard of." Caelen chuckled to himself and stroked the female's cheek.

Young Anaki's mouth dropped, and a whimper escaped him.

"And only growing up around you, Anaki, my body just grew accustomed to a male. Now that I have been around Desani, I prefer a female. They smell nice, especially since she is an air dragon. She smells of wildflowers." He lifted a lock of her hair to sniff it.

"Bastard!" I whispered and gripped my fingers onto Anaki's biceps.

Anaki chuckled. "He's lying, you know. At the time, I didn't realize he was. All I thought about was the betrayal. He didn't truly care for the female."

"How do you know? Why would he do this?"

"He cared what others thought of him. He wanted status, to be looked up to. A male mating wouldn't put him where he wanted, since it would be considered different. He wanted his cake and to eat it, too.

Me with a male, or a female, it doesn't matter. I care for who I care for. The emotional connection, the bond, is what I long for. That is why I had never done it with anyone else. I'm not even sure if Caelen had kissed this female. He had only scented her to anger me."

I ground my teeth. Caelen doing this to Anaki was damn terrible. Soul-wrenching. Caelen lied to a bond for his own selfish reasons. He didn't deserve Anaki, anyway.

"This"—Caelen waved his hand to the side—"is Armeleo, Desani's eldest brother. He has been without a mate for many years and grows impatient. I've told him about you and your preferences and he wishes to keep you as his."

I didn't think things could get worse, but they just did. I let out a gasp of horror when Armeleo stepped forward. Though not overly muscular, he was tall and shared features with his younger sister. He gave a wide, fanged smile, and the blue sarong he wore matched young Anaki's.

When Anaki saw the sarong, he sneered. "No. Absolutely not. And how dare you!" Anaki took a step back and pointed to the wrap around Armeleo. "Those are my colors. That is my wrap, I gave it to you!"

I watched in horror as Caelen frowned and let go of Desani. He stepped closer to Anaki, his voice low when he approached. "You really thought we would have a happily ever after? That we could be mates, Anaki? You're delusional to think that this would actually work. It's funny how you were a water dragon, with your head always in the clouds."

"You, your actions..." young Anaki's voice broke. "You would come to me, we held each other in the night—"

Caelen backhanded young Anaki in the face, and I screamed. He fell to the ground but stood up quickly.

Anaki held me tight and kissed my forehead to keep me still.

"You told me you loved me," young Anaki whispered.

Caelen, flustered, looked back at Desani. She tilted her head and gave a small smile. "Her father is a clan leader; I've been given a title to help with their food resources. I'll be able to hunt in their waters on their territory. As for you, I've secured your protection since I do hold some regard for you."

Anaki held his hand to his chest, like a knife had been pierced through his heart. I have never seen such betrayal in all my life. The betrayal broke his heart and soul. I felt tears well in my eyes and my body nearly collapsed, feeling his past.

"Elena," the Anaki who held me in my arms whispered to me. "I never loved him like I love you. I didn't know real love until I had you. You see me. You accept me. I hope you know that. I don't even feel him anymore."

"He hurt you, it makes me want to..."

Kill him. I wanted to murder him in cold blood.

A feral growl erupted from my throat, a resonant and thunderous roar that seemed impossible for my human form to unleash. My fingers burned with a searing pain, and the sharp, metallic scent of blood invaded my nostrils, overwhelming and raw.

"Love, be calm, the memory isn't over yet," he hissed. Anaki pulled me to standing, and when I looked down at my hands, I saw that my fingernails were no longer human, but long white opaque talons, blood dripping off the tips.

"¡Dios Mio! What the fuck?!"

Anaki wiped away the blood from his arms.

"Let go of me!" young Anaki yelled. Armeleo seized Anaki's arm with a vice-like grip, twisting it mercilessly until it was pinned behind his back, eliciting a sharp gasp of pain. His hand traveled down Anaki's abdomen with deliberate force until he reached the chains on Anaki's hip. A deep, guttural groan escaped Armeleo's lips, a sound filled with a primal satisfaction.

"I've always had an appreciation for the water dragon mating dances. I can't wait for you to do one for me." His long, serpent tongue ran up the side of Anaki's cheek.

Desani giggled and reached out for Calean. "I told you my brother was ravenous for males. You sure you are alright with him having your mate? My brother isn't allowed in the clan, he has to stay on the outskirts. Anaki will be alright with that?" She twirled her finger around Caelen's nipple.

Caelen didn't look over at young Anaki and shrugged his shoulders. "As long as he offers protection and gives Anaki what he wants, I have no issue."

Young Anaki struggled against Armeleo. "What are you doing? I will not be hidden away! I will not bond with anyone else! No one! Do you hear me?"

Caelen rushed forward, and Armeleo let go so Caelen could grab young Anaki around the neck and push him to the tree. Anaki grabbed Caelen's wrist to let go, but was not using his full strength, I could see it. His eyes were pleading as Caelen went closer to whisper into his face. "Do this," Caelen warned. "Do not make a fuss. If you behave, I will visit you. Just like old times." Caelen's eyes softened for a fraction of a second before the look vanished.

Caelen let go, and Anaki fell to his knees.

Caelen wrapped his arm around Desani. "Desani and I will bond tonight. You and Armeleo will as well. I'm doing you a favor, Anaki, you should thank me. This way, perhaps your soul will be saved." He took one last look over his shoulder.

Armeleo approached him with deliberate steps, his shadow stretching long across the ground as he leaned down to pick him up. Anaki let out a low, menacing snarl, a sound that rumbled deep in his throat like distant thunder. The scales on his back, which had previously sliced through his skin, glimmered with an even fiercer intensity, catching the light like shards of polished sapphires. As if responding to his rising anger, more scales erupted from his arms and legs, spreading like wildfire across his body, creating an impenetrable armor of gleaming, jagged edges.

"Get away!" young Anaki roared, and a fin from young Anaki's forearm flipped open. Armeleo, not ready for the sudden shift in Anaki's demeanor, was sliced across the face with the sharpened fin.

"Holy shit!" I shouted. "I hope you keep going." I kept egging on a fight that had already happened and gripped onto my man's arms, making sure I didn't pierce his skin again.

So much was happening right now.

Armeleo roared, his hand to his face. Blood pooled down his face and neck. He pulled his hand away to see the damage, and it was a lot. A flap of skin fell from his cheek, and I could see his teeth inside his mouth.

Glorious!

Anaki continued shifting, with more fins sprouted from his body. He screamed, his eyes glowing with rage. His fingers broke, and talons elongated in their place. He swiped at Armeleo, who appeared to be too shocked to do anything, and sliced across the bastard's chest.

Armeleo's eyes widened in terror as the jagged edge of Anaki's talon sliced through his skin, leaving a deep gash that was bleeding profusely. He stumbled backward, clutching at the wound, desperate to stem the flow of blood.

As I watched young Anaki continue to shift, still swiping at Armeleo, I knew one thing was for certain. My mate was no pushover, not the weak dragon that Caelen thought him to be.

Anaki was a badass, and I was getting turned on at the sight of it.

CHAPTER THIRTY

Anaki

I didn't know one could smell arousal in a dream-like state, especially one when the goddess had willed it. Yet my mate was determined to push every boundary.

My younger self was currently in the middle of pulverizing a male who dared to touch me and tried to claim me as his own. I never condoned that sort of violence but touching me was a hard fucking 'No'! I hated people touching me unless I welcomed it, and of course, this forced my first shift to be quick, painful, and violent.

It had turned my mate on watching me destroy an enemy. Now I don't feel as bad. I smiled into her hair and chuckled softly.

"Anaki, look at you go!" she whispered, but it rang in my ears like a yell of praise. I closed my eyes and reveled in it.

"You little praise-kink slut," my dragon snorted at me.

I let out a puff of air through my nose, rustling Elena's hair. Yeah, she knows of my praise kink, and she will probably realize a lot more about me now she can enter my mind. I'd take her love anyway I could get it.

I turned my head and lay my cheek on her head. Her chest rubbed against mine as I felt her nipples pucker against the thin fabric of the dress she wore. Even in the dream, she felt like heaven to me and while the chaotic scene unfolded, I wanted to rip off the dress and eat her pussy like a starving male.

"The goddess is right there," my dragon hissed. *"Have some respect."*

What I really wanted was for my mate to disrespect me. I supposed I should wait for that until the entire event was over.

A roar ripped through my younger self when my dragon came into its full shift. The fins on my back and on the lower part of the arms flipped open and sliced more pieces of skin off of Armeleo. Dragon shifters' humanoid forms were weak compared to the dragon's scaled armor. He tried to shift, his scales trying to protrude out of his body, but with one snap of my jaw, I crushed his skull with one bite.

"Mierda!" Elena shouted and turned her face into my chest. "You bit his head right off!" She turned her head back to the scene where my dragon spat his head onto the ground toward Caelen and Desani.

I held onto Elena even tighter as she watched Caelen's face morph into shock.

"I lost control of the shift," I told Elena. "It was my first time, but when any shifter shifts for the first time out of anger, it can be... disastrous. There isn't any control on the human side, and I had no control over my emotions. He was too strong."

Caelen shifted as Desani backed away from him. Her salty tears were nothing compared to the coppery stench of blood that filled the air. "You killed him!" she screamed at me, but even her voice was weak as she backed away.

Caelen was now fully shifted into his stained-red and salmon colored dragon. His teeth were long, his fins similar to my own, and the rounded coral on his head made him appear to have a large battering ram ready to run me into a tree.

My dragon stood its ground. I remembered not having any fight left in me to fight my former mate. I knew he wasn't mine, that he had rejected me for a female who had also rejected her own mate somewhere.

How dare she hurt someone else too?

I remembered my dragon's feelings at the time on the matter. He was furious with her for agreeing to such a thing.

While our dragons had no ability to speak to each other, even to us, I had felt with every fiber of my being what he was going to do. Kill them both.

I had never killed, never had the desire, but my will to live anymore after that heartbreak was bleak. I didn't care what my dragon did.

I let my dragon unleash his animalistic side. He jumped forward, and Elena, the goddess, and I, watched the chaos unfold.

My dragon opened his mouth wide, the sharp teeth of his fully shifted form scraping the air as he charged towards Caelen's dragon. The two beasts collided. Caelen's blunt head hit my dragon's chest while my claws raked down his back. The roars shook the ground, our shorter legs rolled us into the dirt, hitting the thick trees of the forest and making them quake.

Our bodies weren't designed for soil, since we were meant to fight in the water. I could remember vividly the bark and rocks that brushed up against our scales, and my dragon craved to be in the water to fight this battle.

There was none, but his anger was still too strong to stop.

Elena gripped me tightly, her heart pounding against my chest as she watched the battle unfold before her eyes. The goddess stood aside, observing the scene with calm detachment. We both knew how this ended.

As my past fought in front of me, I couldn't help but feel the burden being lifted. Elena knew about my past. She will know it in its entirety, and I don't feel any resentment or anger from it.

I held Elena close, feeling her heartbeat synchronized with mine. I realized that amidst the chaos and destruction she's who I was supposed to be with. While the goddess is a being with power, fate ultimately had different plans.

My dragon lashed out with its tail, striking Caelen's dragon on the side, causing it to lose balance. He recovered quickly, sunk his talons into the dirt and pushed forward to get up under our body. My dragon faltered, and the razor-sharp fins sprouted from Caelen's dragon's back, slicing us into our underbelly. My dragon yelped and crawled behind a tree to assess the damage.

Caelen's dragon licked its tongue across its mouth and wiped the blood away. I remember feeling my dragon's anger and the finality of his decision about what he wanted. Caelen's blood smeared all over our body.

We slithered away from the tree and stayed low to the ground while Caelen's dragon puffed up to appear larger. His dragon swiped across my face when we grew close. My dragon roared but ignored the pain and leapt on the coppery dragon with all its might. We had him pinned. My clawed foot pushed his head to the side, a claw pressed into his ear.

The dragon body beneath me slithered and squirmed. Caelen jerked its body like a snake with its head cut off. He tried to whip me off of his body, move me so he could be free of my weight. My dragon pinned our body to his torso. His tail whipped and tried to slash me in the face. I ignored the slashes of his fins; they only superficially scratched my scales.

Caelen's dragon hissed, and my dragon didn't think twice, sinking his teeth into the long neck. My teeth pierced through the scales like butter, and my dragon pulled with all his might at his neck. The sinews of the meat, tendons, and muscles took time to rip. The strength of any dragon was powerful, but mine was determined to take out our former mate with one blow.

As we looked on, I watched blood spurt from Caelen's wound. I held my breath. I once felt sadness at what I had let my dragon do. I let him kill our mate.

I no longer felt that way.

Not with my love holding onto me tightly, right now, exuding that sweet-smelling scent.

I gritted my teeth when I heard the gurgle of blood rise from Caelen's throat. It was almost over; it would end at any moment.

"That bitch!" Elena pointed and watched as Desani ran off into the woods. "She didn't stay to save her new mate? Didn't even shift?"

The goddess made a tsk noise and shook her head.

I smirked, no longer interested in the scene. My mate was so engrossed, I found it utterly adorable. Would it be bad to take her behind the tree, where I once hid, and fuck her there?

The goddess hummed a chuckle when we saw Desani trip and fall.

"Aren't you going to get her?" Elena snarled, my cocks immediately stood to attention and pressed against her hip. She stilled and bit her lip when she looked up at me.

"Does that turn you on for me to chase down another female?" I raised a brow.

She pressed her chest against mine. "Only if you are going to kill them for hurting you."

My dragon lashed his long, sinuous tail, sending it crashing into the towering trees with a resounding crack. The mighty trunks trembled under the impact, and a cascade of shattered branches and scattered debris rained down around Desani. She tumbled to the ground once more, sprawling over the jagged rocks and splintered limbs that fell like a chaotic shower around her.

My dragon snarled, slithered across the ground with expert precision. He gripped her by her waist with our maw and lifted her. She screamed, our teeth piercing her stomach. Her body tried to shift from instinct to protect herself, but it was too far gone.

This is where I felt the most sick, killing a female who had done nothing to me.

Elene grabbed me by the chin with one hand and made me look at her. "You don't feel guilty! She tried to have her sicko brother rape you," she said fiercely. "Don't you dare feel guilt over killing any of them. You are too sweet and kind for this world. You stopped them from doing it to anyone else." She pulled me into a fierce kiss and missed, where my dragon flung her into the air to swallow her whole.

When Elena let go, my dragon had already begun to work on the other bodies. I tried to keep her face away, but she was an insistent woman and watched in fascination. "You ate them!" She gagged and turned away, so we were both facing the goddess.

The goddess smirked and folded her arms in front of her. "It's what saved his life for so long and ensured he had not gone rabid sooner. If he didn't, he wouldn't be here with you today."

Elena tilted her head in confusion.

I sighed and rubbed the back of my neck. "Rabid is a term we use at the club for rejected souls who have no control over their human selves. Their animal takes control. They go crazy and ultimately harm everyone in their path."

The goddess nodded for me to continue.

"The Iron Fang was created by Locke and Grim. Rogues are those who are rejected by their mates but still have the ability to keep their animals contained. The shifter world will not accept us because we are a liability. We have no packs or clans, and no one to care for us. We are meant to die alone."

Elena wrapped her arms around me and shook her head.

"After the club's creation, rogues of all kinds arrived. Not everyone gets in, it's a process. Some that were rejected needed to be. Only the good ones get in." I winked.

"Rogues who stick together lengthen their survival, we don't go rabid as fast. Bones is even working on some meds that can help keep rabids calm enough to keep them locked up, so we can do something with them in the future. Before we... have to put them down." I hung my head.

I was never part of that, and never wanted to be.

"Your sister is the only one who has pulled a rabid shifter out of their funk. Emm has given everyone hope. Once again, Locke has given people a reason to live longer, even if they go rabid. He created the Iron Fang to help those who were suffering, to help us live a little longer and not be... completely alone."

Elena's eyes glistened with unshed tears. "Were you close to becoming rabid?"

I blew through my nose a little too hard and bowed my head.

"Oh, my sweet dragon."

I pulled her to me, and her face planted into my bare chest. "It's alright, love. I've got you now. I'm not going anywhere."

"Mierda," Elena whispered. "I need you right now."

CHAPTER THIRTY-ONE

Elena

In the blink of an eye, we were back in Anaki's cave. While many things had come to my attention about the Iron Fang, I already knew they were a bunch of broken men and women, but I didn't know to what extent. Now I knew.

All had been rejected by someone who was supposed to be their mate. It was horrible, damn devastating, and now my sister got caught in the middle. I knew one thing was for sure: my sister would love this Locke guy fiercely and would be a great leader alongside him.

And I would love and protect Anaki with all my heart.

From the visions I had seen of Locke from Anaki's perspective of him... I decided my brother-in-law was a straight-up lunatic, but he cared for his people. My sister would keep him straight. She's as crazy as he is.

Anaki, however, was my perfect match in every conceivable way, and there were depths within him I was desperate to explore. Upon waking, a sharp ache throbbed on my shoulder—a vivid reminder of the bite he had given me earlier. It seared with an intoxicating burn that coursed through my entire body. It ignited a fire deep inside me, all the way down to the memory of the intense, double penetration from before, which still lingered. It left me breathless and yearning for more.

My pussy wept to be fucked, and thoroughly again, but this time, I was going to fuck Anaki and not the way he was probably thinking.

Anaki let out a soft groan as I straddled him, his voice mingled with the gentle rustle of the blankets scattered around us, which created a cozy, intimate nest. Now that I understood his culture more thoroughly, I realized how significant it was for him to maintain such perfection in his surroundings. Every detail of his home—the textures of the fabrics, the harmony of colors, the thoughtful arrangement—reflected his dedication and care, all thoughtfully curated for his future mate, for me.

My heart wanted to explode. I wanted to give him all the compliments, and that was what I was about to do.

Anaki gently raised his hands, his fingers brushing against my sides before settling firmly on my hips. He gave a reassuring squeeze. As his eyes fluttered open, they met mine. "Well, aren't you a sight for sore eyes?"

I hummed and lowered myself to his lips and gave him a loving kiss. "You made me a beautiful nest. I was thinking about giving you a reward."

Anaki's face turned a bright red. His hands stilled on my hips. "I, er, what?"

I bit my lip and ran my hands over his chest. The chains were still attached to his nipple rings. They crossed over the plains of his pectoral muscles, and I gave them a little tug. He groaned as his nipples pulled against the rings and my pussy fluttered against his already engorged cocks.

"You heard me, little dragon. I want to reward you for making me such a pretty nest and for claiming me. Do you think I can do that?"

Anaki's chest rose and fell rapidly, like he didn't know what to do. There were times I noticed when his confidence soared and others, when he was a shy, little dragon. I concluded that when he was more bold his dragon had taken over to push him. This time, I could feel his dragon sitting back, letting Anaki take the driver's seat.

I was here for it.

"Uh, yeah?" Anaki blinked a couple of times, and I trailed my finger up his chest, his neck until I bopped him on the nose.

I grabbed the sarong that he ripped off before he marked me. I smiled when I placed it around his eyes and tied it behind his head. "Are you going to be a good boy for me and wear this blindfold?"

"Oh fuck!" Anaki licked his lips. "Yes, Mama."

Goddess, this was going to be fun.

I kissed him again with a fervent urgency, our lips crashing together. My tongue darted across his lips, insistently pressing between them. The air around us seemed to ignite, and I clasped his head in my hands, feeling the heat radiate between us. "Good, now stay here and don't move."

I quickly jumped off his lap and ran to where my bag was. Abuela had packed my bag, which magically arrived here at the cave. Along with the butt plug that was in here, which embarrassed me to no end, because I don't even know where she got that thing, there was my dildo and, believe it or not, straps for said dildo. Which I did not pack originally.

His poor asshole.

She obviously knew something I didn't at the beginning of this, and we were going to need a serious talk later.

I grabbed all my supplies and practically skipped back to the enormous bed. He stayed perfectly still, didn't move an inch.

Perfect little thing.

"Anaki, what a good boy you are for staying in the same position." His cocks jerked and my mouth watered wanting to swallow them, but I refrained. This was about Anaki.

The pain he went through, holding in his inner struggles because he was worried about what I would think, broke my heart. He was so sweet and caring toward my past that he didn't want to burden me with his. My dragon was far too thoughtful, and I was going to make him feel like the best dragon of all.

Even Mr. Bossy Scales.

I crawled toward him. His cocks were already leaking with precum and that tasty lubricant. I wouldn't need any lube. It was great to see how women didn't have to do all the work, getting excited and providing the lubricant, the men could, too.

So freaking hot.

"Is my good boy ready to play?"

"Fuck, fuck, fuck."

I slapped the side of his thigh, and he yelped in surprise. "No cursing. I want you to use your words and tell your mate how you are feeling."

I could totally do this Domme stuff.

He groaned and rubbed the sting from his leg. "Yes, ma'am. I'll do what you say."

Giddiness erupted in my chest. "Are you okay with light spankings? The blindfold? What about a little bondage? Can I tie your wrists together?"

Anaki nodded eagerly, and he squirmed on the bed. I slapped his thigh again. "I said words, little dragon, or I'll slap that plump, muscular ass!"

Anaki groaned and rolled over onto his stomach. "I don't think that really is a punishment, Elena. Here it is, spank it." We both laughed, and I slapped it more firmly this time. He screamed and rubbed his hand over it. "Too hard!"

"Yeah, well, it's supposed to be a punishment. It isn't supposed to feel good all the time."

Anaki grunted and buried his face into the pillow in front of him. "You can never tell the club this. Don't you ever tell Bear or Nadia either."

I snorted. "Never. This is our private time." I rubbed my hand over his heated cheek. "You will say red if it gets to be too much. Can you do that for me?" I leaned over his shoulder next to his ear. "Because I want to hear you say 'don't stop,' I don't want to get confused."

"Damnit, what are you gonna do to me, female?" Anaki raised his head from the pillow and tried to roll over. I pushed his shoulder back down.

"All the good things. Now, stay on your stomach because you are right where I want you."

"My dicks are on the other side, though," he whined.

Are they now?

I ignored him and grabbed a soft scarf that was in my suitcase, wrapping it around his wrists. I tied them tight enough not to leave marks but to keep them together. In my mind, I knew he could break free, but this just made it so much more fun.

I bit my lip and straddled his lower back. My hands wrapped around his shoulders, and I gently massaged them. His shoulders instantly relaxed, and a soft groan of appreciation escaped. I pressed a kiss on his neck, and his body lengthened to get more of my touch on his skin.

"You know, I can smell you really well now."

Anaki hummed and nuzzled his head further into the pillow.

"Like fresh water. Clean, refreshing. I just want to bury myself in you. I want to absorb all of you."

I trailed fervent kisses down his spine, my hands exploring every inch of his skin with deliberate intent. Each touch ignited a fire within me, a damp heat pooling between my thighs as an involuntary reaction. It wasn't about my own release; it was about uncovering the hidden depths of his secret desires. I yearned intensely to delve into the uncharted territory of his pleasure, a mystery he had kept veiled, now desperately waiting to be revealed.

My hands wrapped around his hips, massaging the muscles there. His body was soft but firm, and I took my tongue to lick up his spine. He shivered against me, and his hips pushed into the mattress.

"Mm, you taste so good, too. I want to put you in my mouth and taste you."

"You can," he said quickly. "I can flip over and…"

I pushed his body back down into the mattress and he landed with a *humph.*

"Who is in charge, little dragon?" I hummed.

He whined, and his fists tightened around his restraints. "You are."

"That's right. Now, I want you to get up on your knees."

Anaki's head shot up and turned his head toward me, even when he couldn't see. "What?" His high-pitched voice made me laugh.

"Do as I say, unless you are saying red."

Anaki grumbled and slowly got up on his knees. He raised himself on his arms as well, and I tsked. "No, lower your arms. I want your chest on the bed, ass up."

Anaki gasped but still obeyed. His fingers grabbed at the blankets and pulled. His whole body had turned red. I could see his cocks twitching from underneath him, precum continuously dripping from them.

He was absolutely turned on, and my nose caught a strong whiff of his scent. "Wow, now I understand how you can smell me when I'm aroused. I can smell you."

It must be from the bond we shared.

Anaki groaned and shook his head into the pillow. "I never thought that would be embarrassing."

"You said it to me!" I countered. "See how it feels?"

I glided my hand over his ass, and he flinched, but the tension soon filtered out as I palmed his ass. I leaned over him and felt the front of his thigh and grabbed hold of his cocks. One for each hand.

"You are positively hard, Anaki. Are these for me?"

Anaki nodded into the pillows, and I took my hands away to give him a swift smack to the ass.

Anaki jerked his head up. "Yes! Yes, they are for you!"

I leaned over on his back and placed a kiss. "Mmm, good boy. Good job for answering." I grabbed hold of his cocks again, gripping them tightly and jerking them slowly. I let his lubricant slide over his shafts, hearing the slick glide through my fingers. He panted, his hips pushing against me, fucking my hand.

Anaki was a panting mess and when I felt like his cocks were getting even harder, his groans becoming too much, I let go and he let out the most pitiful whine.

"No, please!" He pushed his ass back into me. "I was close!"

"Oh, no. Poor baby. Did you not get to come?"

Anaki groaned and pulled at his restraints.

"No, no. I'm just getting started. It will be worth it. Trust me. I needed you nice and hard, begging for me, for this."

I wanted Anaki relaxed He was nervous, so jerking him off, and him begging to come was the perfect way to be more receptive for what I had planned. In the back of his mind, this is what he wanted, but exposing himself like this to me was scary to him. To me, it was instinctive; I wanted to please him the way he had pleased me.

I never took my hands off him. I ran my hands down his thighs and back up to his ass cheeks. He was still groaning, whimpering and my pussy fluttered with excitement at how much he wanted me to touch him there.

My mind had other plans. Dirty plans.

I spread his ass cheeks and his head popped up from the pillow once more.

"E-Elena? What are you—"

"Shh," I cooed. "Be a good boy and let me make you feel good."

He was completely still as he waited. I was taking a rather long time, not because I was second-guessing myself, but because of how shocked I was.

His asshole was completely bare. He had the cleanest asshole I'd ever seen. Not that I had seen many, but he was squeaky clean.

I mentally slapped myself. Get on with it. It'll make him feel good, and you've always wanted to try it.

I leaned forward and licked the side of his ass hole. Anaki whimpered, and I took it as encouragement to keep going. I took slow, tentative licks around where he needed it. I knew there were so many nerves there but teasing it as you would a clit seemed like the way to go.

Anaki panted and whined like a pitiful little dragon until he pushed his hips slightly back. I gave in and slowly licked from his heavy balls up, up, up, and finally swiped ever so slowly right between the center of his cheeks.

CHAPTER THIRTY-TWO

Anaki

She was licking my ass.

Fuuuuuck! She was licking my ass.

I'd never whined and groaned like that in my life. I gripped the sheets so hard, the restraints would rip if I kept putting more stress on them. I wanted to turn around and fuck her but I'm also wrestling with having her stick her tongue—

Shit. She did!.

Her tongue swirled around the most sensitive parts. It darted inside for a second and I groaned loudly like the whore I am for her.

Shit, shit, shit!.

Her hands kept me perfectly spread. My head was buried in the sheets. I couldn't move, couldn't do anything. I was at her mercy, and my body was quaking. My dicks were so damn hard and leaked so much I wouldn't have any seed left to fill her up.

I was going to come and when I did, it would be so much, I wouldn't have anything left in my balls.

She hummed, her mouth vibrated, and I let out a shout when my cocks jerked. Is it possible to come while someone was licking your ass? I'm no expert, obviously, but she must be because she was eating me like she was licking the bottom of an ice cream bowl.

"You're doing so good." She backed away, and I immediately missed her heat. I was also grateful because I was about to spill my load. I didn't know if that was the intention or not, as I was in uncharted territory.

Was I supposed to like that? Because I did, I liked it way too much.

I panted and wiped my forehead from the sweat. I adjusted my body position and wiggled side to side on my knees. Where did she get the fucking audacity to even do that?

"She knows your mind," my dragon purred inside me.

Ah, hell. Now that my dragon could talk, he was going to talk to me often. I heard about wolves and their animals talking to them all the time. I thought it was awesome when I heard about it, but I was starting to think it was a curse. Hawke would talk aloud at the bar all by himself and I swore I thought he was going crazy when he called his wolf a crazy fucker. Now people are going to think I'm crazy.

"What does that mean? Of course she knows me and my mind. We are mated."

My dragon had the audacity to chuckle. *"Even the thoughts about what it would feel like to be with a male?"*

I paused and lifted my head slowly. *Fuck!*

I heard rustling behind me and a moan. When I turned around, I heard my mate rubbing something... and her arousal came in strong. There were clicks and movements that sounded like straps, and immediately my jealousy was lit. Was she playing with herself in front of me?

That's my pussy.

"What are you doing?" My voice was gravelly when I rolled over.

My cocks swung in front of her. I could imagine her nipples hard and cheeks flushed. I went to sit up to take a bite, but she pushed me down. "Not done with you yet, little dragon. Be a good boy and stay still."

Her hands went straight to my cocks, and took long, deep strokes. She hummed, and I just tried to imagine how her breasts swayed behind them. It was a beautiful, heated sight, thinking about watching them sway.

Immediately, I groaned and lifted my hips for her to do what she wanted with me. "Mmm, please, more."

I imagined Elena smiling and biting her lip. Her thumb ran over the heads and gave them both equal attention. When she abruptly removed her hand, I gave out a long sigh. "You keep edging me. I'm going to die," I whined and rubbed my hands down my face.

She giggled, and I heard the bedding rustle. "Because good things are yet to come." She crawled up toward me and leaned the side of her body next to me. "Now kiss me."

I didn't hesitate. My arms were still restrained, and I fervently sought her mouth.

"You are so eager. It turns me on so bad when you want me this much."

"I've always wanted you. From the moment I saw you." I groaned and tried to put my restrained arms around her neck. She allowed it while I plundered her mouth. She let me do as I pleased, then retreated when I overstepped. She was in charge, and she let me know when I was being too aggressive with a bite on the lip. "More?" I begged.

She smiled into the kiss. "Are you ready for more?"

I nodded excitedly, and she grabbed one of my cocks. "I think you are ready for your next present." She kissed me down my cheek and along to my neck.

I let out a breathless moan as she gripped one of my cocks tightly. It was like she was trying to milk me of all my lubricants, and I fucking loved it.

"Spread your legs for me. Nice and wide."

More ass play?

My hearts raced and I widened my legs. The blindfold made it easier, not seeing her reaction but I was still scared shitless.

"I want you to take deep breaths for me. Be a good little dragon." She pulled on my leg to widen me even more. My cheeks heated with embarrassment and she tickled my asshole. She inserted one finger slowly. I felt the burn and gasped. "That's it. We are going slow. Going to prepare that asshole before I fuck the hell out of it."

I gasped when she reached in with the first knuckle. My ass squeezed her, and she bit down on my nipple. The pain of my nipple caused me to release, and she slipped inside. "Let me finger fuck you, little dragon. Then we are adding a second."

The lubricant from my cocks aided in her sliding inside of me. It helped me relax, and soon she pushed in another finger. I whimpered, unable to control myself as her fingers continued to tease and probe me.

She smiled against my neck, her lips brushing against my skin in the most sensual way. "You're such a good boy," she murmured, her fingers working their magic on my prostate. "I'm so proud of you."

I gritted my teeth and shook my head on the pillow. "I'm gonna come. Please let me come."

She bit my cheek. "You are making such a mess, leaking all over your stomach with your seed, little dragon. I think we are ready for something bigger. You can come then."

She removed her fingers, and I whimpered at the loss, but then I felt something cold and hard against my entrance. "Are you ready?" she asked, a note of mischief in her voice.

"Yes," I whispered, my voice barely audible. "Please."

I felt something blunt probe me. I lifted my head up in question. "It's alright. It's a dildo. I used to use it all the time." I could almost see the smile on her face.

She was using her dildo, to fuck my ass.

The head pressed against my entrance, and then she pushed forward. The sensation was intense, but I tried to relax as much as possible, taking deep breaths as she slowly entered me. Her movements were deliberate and calculated, each inch deeper driving me wilder with desire.

"Your lubricant worked so well to coat it. We won't ever have to buy any lube."

When she was fully inside me, she paused, allowing me to adjust to the feeling of being filled in a way I had never experienced before. "Good boy," she praised, her voice low and sultry. "Now we're going to fuck."

And we did. Her movements were erratic. She pulled almost completely out before thrusting back in with enough force to make me cry out in a mix of pain and pleasure. She leaned forward. Her stomach grazed my cocks again, stroking them in time with her soft stomach. "That's it," she whispered and pushed my arms above my head. "Take it all."

I did just that, moaning loudly as she took control of our bodies and brought us closer to release. Her movements became more erratic, her breaths shallower as she neared her own climax. I could feel the vibration at the base of the strap-on dildo. She was panting, getting herself off at the same time.

Fuck, so damn hot.

Her body tensed, and she cried out. Her orgasm sent waves of pleasure permeating through the air and my cocks leaked more come onto my stomach.

"Come for me," she ordered hoarsely. "Show me how much you want me."

It was all the encouragement I needed. Elena ripped off the blindfold, and her body towered over me. Her face was flushed, her tits swung in front of me.

"Anaki." Her hips moved and I looked down to watch my cocks bob beneath her. They continued to drip and leak with arousal as she pumped into me.

"Please!" I begged. "Please."

Finally giving me relief, she gripped her hands around both and tightly squeezed, rubbing my shafts up and down. It didn't take long as she fucked and stroked me until I came with a strangled cry.

"Ah fuck!" I whimpered and came and came until my balls ached. My vision swam for a moment before clearing up again. Sweat, come, and arousal covered both of us, and I was damn spent.

"Look at you, all covered in seed." Elena took her finger and played with the arousal on my stomach and swiped it up, putting it into her mouth. She sucked on her finger and let it go with a pop.

Goddess, have mercy on my soul.

Elena slowly pulled the dildo out of me. I sobbed at the loss of feeling so full. She smiled and placed a kiss on my hip while she unbuckled herself from the strap and took it off her hips.

She crawled to my side and carefully undid the restraints and made sure to rub my wrists where I had pulled them too tight. Shaking her head, she rubbed my skin to increase circulation.

"How did you like that? Scales told me you have had thoughts about doing something like that before." She leaned down and gave me a quick kiss. My body stiffened at her words.

"Scales?"

She nodded. "Your dragon. That's his name. I need something to distinguish between the two of you. Somehow, he got in my head and said you needed this side of you sexually satisfied. He didn't have to twist my arm.

I've always wanted to try."

I opened and closed my mouth, then wrapped my arms around her to pull her to my chest. Yes, I was really regretting ever wanting to have my dragon speak.

Elena nuzzled into my neck. "You are still hard," she vibrated. Her leg slipped over my waist, her pussy was wet, and I could smell her arousal strengthen. "And I haven't bitten you yet."

My voice shook when I let it out. "Elena?" Her hand ran up my chest.

"And I really, really want to bite you."

She leaned her head back and grabbed my cocks to stroke them. She lifted herself over my hips and rubbed the heads of my cocks over her hips.

Oh shit, she was going to take me again.

I braced myself by grabbing her hips and slowly having her settle her pussy on both of them. She was right, I was insanely hard, and the ridges were really pronounced. "I don't know if it is wise..."

"I need you!" she growled, and my eyes snapped to hers.

Holy fuck! What the hell is happening?

She impaled herself on my cocks, her pussy gripping me like a red-hot vise. I jolted upright, my face buried in her breasts, hands clawing up her back like a man possessed.

She moaned deeply, her breaths ragged as she moved. The feeling of filling her up in one hole was my favorite damn thing. I felt her muscles tightening around me. Her hands gripped my shoulders as she leaned forward, our bodies becoming one.

"Fuck, yes," she gasped, her voice muffled by my skin. "Fuck me."

I thrust upwards, relishing in the feeling of her body enveloping me. The more intense it got, the more her eyes darkened, and she bared more of her teeth.

Mark me. Goddess, please mark me.

"Anaki," she groaned, "Bite. I want to bite."

My eyes widened for a moment before my expression softened, and her eyes bore into mine. It wasn't a want. It was a need. She was desperate, her hands clutched my shoulders, her nails, no claws had protruded. Her dragon was seeking the deeper connection. "Do it," I whispered. "Mark me as yours."

And with that permission, she did just that. Her fangs extended, and she bit down on my shoulder. It was euphoria. The sensation sent a thrill through me, a mixture of pain and pleasure.

Elena tensed and cried out, her pussy pulsing around me. My dragon's vibration of satisfaction, her pussy milking me were too much for me to handle, I couldn't take it anymore.

"Now," I growled, grasping her hips tightly. "Come again for me now."

And with those words, we both reached our climax together. Her pussy clamped down on me so hard it was almost unbearable, as she cried out. My body trembled and convulsed as I shot my seed deep inside her, my dragon's essence mingling with hers.

Finally spent, we collapsed onto each other, panting heavily and covered in sweat and come. Both of our eyes fluttered. I barely had the strength to pull her close to me. But I kept my dicks still buried in her pussy as we both just lay there to catch our breaths.

CHAPTER
THIRTY-THREE

Elena

We both woke up several times. Either he or I nudged the other for more mind-blowing sex. I didn't know sex could be like that, honestly. I knew women could keep going at it for hours. We didn't have a refractory period like men do. It was usually a one-and-done sort of deal, but not with Anaki. It must be a dragon thing because he was coming once, twice, and sometimes three times before he passed out from exhaustion.

His dicks had to be chafing, because my pussy was delectably sore after the fifth round of who knew how many hours. We were a panting mess, and both of us noticed the small headaches appearing, which he thought was strange.

I was no stranger to pain. May it be my muscles with my disease or just the general aches and pains, but it unsettled Anaki. He'd never had a headache in his life, and I could hear Scales grumbling on the other side of his mind, saying something was happening but wouldn't elaborate on what.

We took a break by eating and drinking, believing that too much sex was the culprit. We hoped that wasn't the case and prayed to the goddess that it wasn't. We were both still very much in the touching and honeymoon phase of whatever this was called, the beginning of our bonding?

Anaki had to break a few things to me that I'd not searched for in his mind. One of them was to come to terms with… me becoming a dragon.

I dropped a carton of eggs on the floor when he casually blurted it out, like it was the most natural thing in the world. He stared at me with not one ounce of regret on his face, and cleaned it up like it wasn't a big deal.

"How else will you carry our fledglings?"

Who the hell did he think he was?

After some yelling, more of me cursing at him in Spanish, and pacing around the room, he would follow me, always touching me and ensuring I was okay. He eventually fucked me into the mattress, double penetrating as always to ensure I got pregnant sooner.

That was another conversation to be had because, obviously human birth control doesn't work on the supernatural.

Because, of course, it didn't. The other shifters had super sperm, and they wanted to impregnate everything that they could!.

He told me not to worry because when Bones was here—I never recalled Bones ever being here—he said that I wouldn't get pregnant until I had my full shift. It could be a while, because the texts he'd collected from Beretta said dragon females took a long time to fall pregnant.

Which was true to the story he told me. Dragon females don't fall pregnant easily because male sperm was not potent.

Hence the double dicks, I guess.

Somehow, I don't believe that will be the case for us. Call it a woman's intuition.

Bones also hypothesized that once we mated, my pain would go away since I would soon change into a dragon. Although becoming a dragon and enduring excruciating pain the first few shifts would be daunting. It would be worth it to have my chronic disease magically disappear. I'd had no pain in my muscles, only my poor, dear pussy being stretched to the max each time.

Mary and fucking Joseph!

Anaki lay back down on our mess of a bed and checked on Bear and Nadia with his phone while I pulled out mine. Anaki rested his head in my lap, and I played with his hair as I texted Abuela.

She snapped back really quickly with a text message, saying to leave her and Luis alone as they were with the spring fae.

I was sure Luis was having a fun time with all the magic around them, but I couldn't help but miss my little man. He was so happy to push me away to go have fun in this new place, but he was all I had for so long.

Anaki's arm lifted, and his fingers curled into the back of my hair. "What's wrong, Mama? You got all sad on me."

"Thinking about Luis. He hasn't wanted to see me." I sniffed.

Anaki pulled the phone away so I could stare down at his face in my lap. "Love, he's a kid, and he's in a new place with all this cool stuff. It isn't because he loves you less. Plus, Abuela is being, well, Abuela. She wanted you to find me. You have been taking care of her and your son for so long. I'm sure she's keeping him distracted."

I nodded. It was true, and keeping a young child like that distracted wasn't hard to do. Was I wishing he wanted me more? That he was a level five clinger? He was never that sort of child, always independent. Very much like Emmie. I wouldn't be surprised if he started taking lessons with Tajah, lessons I wouldn't approve. I scowled and balled my fists.

"Oh, there is my sexy, angry Mama. Are you gonna punish me again?" Anaki bit his lip and wiggled his butt on the mattress.

"Do not distract me. I'm still upset they performed a ritual on my child without my permission and opened up some inner magic inside him."

Anaki shrugged his shoulders. "It was fate. And really, the best tutors for him are right here at the Iron Fang. Tajah is the best, and Bram was a professor at some big-wig magical university thing. He's in excellent hands. I'm not worried, and we are bonded, which means you shouldn't worry."

I narrowed my eyes at him.

"You shouldn't." He pulled me down and met me halfway for a kiss. "Now I'm giving you vibes. Vibes of calmness through the bond." He wiggled his fingers at me and made a ghostly noise. "I know it was wrong that they did that, but what's done is done. We will work on it together to establish boundaries. In fact, we can go right now if you wish."

I hummed and leaned back on my hands. "Maybe in a bit. I am really enjoying myself."

Anaki smiled. "Yeah? I'm not that bad to be around?"

I giggled and shook my head. "Nah, you are alright."

Our moment was broken when my phone rang beside me. Anaki turned and buried his face into my lap. His tongue slithered out of his mouth and licked close to my pussy.

I let out a long sigh. "Stop, it's Emm!" I slid my finger across the screen to answer.

"Hello?" I said in a breathy moan. It was right when Anaki slipped his tongue right over my clit.

Naughty dragon. I slapped my hand over his naked butt and he squeaked and pulled away.

"Hey, sorry I haven't called," Emm began.

Not that I cared that she hadn't called. Anaki had told me why Emm didn't call. Emm and Locke were mating just like we were, and more than likely, she was in heat. Warm blooded animals go into heat, and had ruts where they have uncontrollable sexual desires to fuck.

Which was hot.

Journey was the first human to transform into a wolf in the club. She experienced a nesting period where her body was slowly changing. So far I haven't had those instincts—yet.

Dragons do have heats and ruts, but since I am a human about to change into a dragon, there will be complications. Since the goddess has willed this to take place, I'm putting trust in her. Something I'm not sure is wise or not, but I don't have a choice. I'm scared to death about the change, even more scared that I will have animal instincts.

Rutting, heat, nesting, falling pregnant. Having a baby with Anaki—that is something I wanted. The way he got so excited at the mention of another child, and he already loved Luis. I could feel it between us already.

I cleared my throat. "So, how have you been?" I prodded. "Has anything interesting happened to you in the past few days? I bet it has been—exciting." Anaki snorted in my lap and kissed my stomach.

"Yeah, it's been something. I have something to tell you."

"No, no, no. Let me guess!" I said giddily. "You stopped pursuing Locke as a bounty and fucked him into oblivion. In the forest, no less." I raised my finger and pointed at her invisible self like she was in front of me.

She was silent.

This was too good.

"And, and," I screamed excitedly, "you took that big nasty knot and let him come all up in you raw."

Anaki gasped and bit my leg to cover his laugh. "Mama, what are you doing?" he nuzzled into my thigh.

"Elena!" she screamed. "How the hell?"

I cackled. "Emmie, I am fine! Just a headache, though. So are Luis and Abuela. We are all doing great. Better than ever."

"Then, how did you know? About a knot? How—"

I continued to laugh hysterically. "I'm sorry. It's just that I've never been so happy for you. Have you bitten him, yet?"

I ran my fingers through Anaki's hair. He was smiling up at me. I've never felt so loved before. This never felt so right, so inevitably right I just had to let go and let it happen. Why did I fight so much?

"Elena, what's going on?" Emm growled into the phone.

"All the things Abuela told us as children are coming true, Emmie. We have soul mates. I'm just so happy for you. That you are letting this happen." I could almost hear the wheels turning in her head.

"But you guys are still in Venezuela. Our family is apart, and now that I am with Locke, I can't leave. I don't know how I'm going to get you all out of there. I'll raise the money. I'll work at the bar here in town. I'm not hunting or doing bounties."

I was silent for a long while. Emm was always unapologetic. She was brash, thought of herself, and did what she thought was necessary for the family. This was her way of showing love. No matter what I said or did, she would never really listen. It was her way of showing love. She would hurt or kill anyone who stepped in the way of us. No remorse. "Emmie, are you feeling guilty?"

"Yes. And I think that was why I haven't bitten Locke, yet, to complete the madness."

"It's so hot. You should have done it already," I whispered.

"You act like you know everything that has happened to me!" Emm snapped. "Do you know about wolves, knots, biting, where have you—wait. Like you have been through it?"

I rolled my lips inward and bit them. I guess I wasn't really supposed to tell her yet. I just got so excited. Does this mean Locke was going to kick my ass? I really doubted it.

"Where the fuck are you?" she screamed into the phone. I pulled it away and squinted my eyes.

I smacked my lips. "I can't tell you that right now. You are in the middle of your mating thing, and you are in heat. Which—let me tell you—"

"Shut up! What the fuck! Where is Abuela? You two monsters have kept secrets from me!"

"Emmie, we had to. You were still coming to terms with Locke, and—"

"Don't Emmie me!" I shook my head even though she couldn't see me. "You knew things were weird and said nothing!"

Like she would have believed me.

"Because I couldn't!" I screamed back. "Locke wanted to keep it from you. He wanted to tell you himself. You wouldn't have believed me. And, anyway... I needed my time, too."

I looked down at Anaki. His eyes were soft, his hands roaming my body, teasing me with those fingers and claws. I got what I wanted, now Emm needed to let go and get what she wanted.

I probably shouldn't have said anything, but I was high on my own love. Emm would see it through and fall for her man, in time. I wish she had stayed on the phone for longer so I could have told her I found my mate, too.

CHAPTER THIRTY-FOUR

Anaki

I had flicked through my phone at the messages, when Elena looked through hers, of which I had a lot.

Bear and Nadia kept me updated, despite keeping my phone on silent during my time with Elena.

I asked Bear to do it, so when I could take time to break away, I read them. I only checked to see if they were sending messages. That let me know they were safe.

The Iron Fang's mission to Duke Idris' mansion, formerly Sunshine AKA Delilah's douche bag ex-husband's place, was successfully infiltrated. Almost too easily. They had rescued women and some men and brought them back on the stolen plane we had used to bring Elena and her family back. The fae would be returning soon as well, by their own means, just as quickly.

They were runners, diggers or something or other. I don't ask questions.

According to the timing of the text messages, they should arrive back at the club any minute.

What struck me as strange was that they were having head pains as well. And it all started around the same time that Elena and mine started. Were they connected? Most likely because things like this in the supernatural world were not coincidences. It all happened for a reason.

I glanced over at my mate, who had just gotten off the phone with her sister. She had just wrapped herself in a thin red linen. Her hair was wet, dripping with water and my cocks instantly sprung to life, ready to claim my female over again.

Unfortunately, it was time to tell her of another danger that the Iron Fang might have to deal with, sometime soon.

Duke Idris.

He strikes, we strike. It's a terrible cycle, really.

She stood up and slipped her phone into her bag, done with the contraption for the moment. I extended my hand towards her, inviting her to return. With a warm smile, she instinctively moved onto her knees and gracefully crawled over to me, positioning herself to straddle my waist. The water droplets, glistening like tiny jewels, trickled down from her damp hair, cascading over her chest and tracing a path along the curve of her cleavage.

I hummed, took my long tongue and slipped it between her breasts. "You taste so good."

She leaned her head back and pressed her chest toward me. "I'm feeling really warm, actually." She placed her hands on my shoulders. "Usually, I'm always cold. Is the temperature outside changing?"

I reached around her back and gently laid her on the bed. Previously, I hadn't noticed her scent. I knew if I took in her scent too much, I'd want to fuck her while she was on the phone.

I wasn't that kinky.

She sighed and settled herself into the sheets. I remembered when I was young, my father would lie my mother in our cave in their soft nest, and he would sniff between her legs when she complained about being too hot or uncomfortable.

My parents never explained any of this to me, maybe they didn't feel like they needed to and knew who my mate was all along…

When I parted her legs, Elena went to push my head away, but I grabbed her wrists and held them. "Let me smell you," I growled and pressed my nose to her pussy.

My eyes instantly rolled into the back of my head.

It wasn't potent yet, but it was oncoming. I didn't know how many hours or days we had, but judging from what my father did, I do remember spending time with the clan jumping from cave to cave while it happened.

As a fledgling, I thought it was the greatest thing spending time with everyone, but I never understood. Now I know why.

"Fuck, love, you are going into heat soon."

Her head perked up. "Huh?"

"Not right now, but soon. We need to talk first. There are stirrings at the club, and I'm concerned."

Elena wrapped the linen around her body and sat up. "One thing at a time." She held up her hand. "First, the club. What's wrong?"

I liked how she put the club before herself, but I could feel the tension tightening her body.

"It's alright. Things are going to work out." I pushed a wet strand of hair behind her ear. "Bear and Nadia are back. Along with the other mated couples. They all have head pains like us."

Elene tilted her head in question.

"They are in pain, too? Are they okay? What about Nadia?" Elena scooted closer, sitting on my lap and wrapping her arms around my neck.

I enjoyed this bond we shared. She knew how close I was to Bear and

Nadia, and I was glad she understood I only saw them as family. Especially with Nadia's history with head pains, this was a step back for her.

"She's going to be fine. They are finishing getting the rest of the humans in the right placements. Some are coming here, to town. They will stay at the apartments we have set up, and we will figure out jobs for them. Others are being sent back home where they wanted to go."

Elena nibbled on her bottom lip. "We should go help." She tried to rise from my lap, and I laughed as I grabbed her hips and pulled her back down.

"Easy there. You are not going anywhere." She landed on my lap with a 'humph'. "I can't have you going into heat around any males. I won't. I'm unsure what Scales would do, and frankly, I'm unsure what I would do. The last time I got pissed off, bad things happened." The playfulness fell from my voice, and I leaned forward to whisper in her ear. "I might eat people."

Elena gasped. "No, you don't think you would do that again?!"

I shrugged my shoulders. "I prefer not to find out. It would probably be worse since we are mated. So, no going near any shifters. Fae, yes, since they can't smell as well. I think that will appease both sides of me."

I could see Scales nodding in my mind.

"Yes, he agrees. Fae are fine. We can go to the fae village and see if they need help, if you want to. Otherwise..." I cupped her breast, and she slapped my hand.

"We need to help do something besides fucking. What are Locke and Emm doing?" my mate asked.

I shook my hand and pouted in defeat.

"Fucking, like I want to be doing. Bear sent a message, and now Hawke is going to try to intercept it and steal his phone or something. They don't want to let Locke know that all of us were having head pains right now. Because,..." I sang. "That's dangerous and tedious work trying to get a damn lycan to break away from fucking your sister."

Elena gagged. "Not to add more pressure, but Emm doesn't like to be interrupted during 'private times' either."

"Mama!"

Luis raced through the bustling crowd of weary fae, and collided with us. Elena, unfazed, enveloped our son in her arms, pressing her nose against his neck. The noise of the crowd faded around us.

While my soulkin didn't know it, she was scenting Luis as a dragon mother would do to her fledgling, and I think my heart grew two sizes.

One day, I hoped to give her another.

"Anaki! You bit her!" Luis ran his finger over the slightly raised bite mark on his mother's shoulder. She winced and pulled his wrist away.

"Aye, you know what that means? Has Abuela been talking too much?" I chided.

Luis shrugged his shoulders. "Just means you are married now. We are a family now, right?"

I gently placed my hand on top of his head and felt the soft strands of hair between my fingers as I ruffled it. The smell of his shampoo filled my lungs. My scent was coming in stronger than ever ."That we are. I'm not going anywhere. Ever."

"That means, I call you Papi now? Or Dad? What do you want most?"

The sensation was akin to trying to swallow a huge chunk of food that simply refused to go down. My chest constricted, and a wave of heat enveloped my entire body.

My mouth hung open, and I tried to get the words out, but they never came. "I.. I... uh..."

Luis waved his hand in front of my face. "Does this mean I get to choose what I get to call him, Mama?"

Elena held back a laugh and buried her nose into Luis' hair. "Maybe you should give him time to process. I think your Papa isn't quite ready."

Luis looked back at his mother. "No Papi then?"

Elena shook her head. "You call me Mama, which is more of an English term. Papa would be more appropriate, or Dad would fit well. Even Daddy." Elena bobbed her head and pressed a kiss on Luis' cheek.

Luis nodded and reached for me. I immediately grabbed him, and our bodies connected in a hug. "Okay, you are Dad, then. I don't want to call you Daddy because that sounds like it's for babies."

I snorted and hugged him back.

I have a son. A genuine son. Both of them belonged to me, completely and undeniably mine.

Scales purred for the both of us, happy that we had a family. I nearly forgot where we were until I saw Abuela step onto the path and walk towards us.

She didn't look like the happy woman I once knew. Her step showed determination. She spoke to herself, and she was holding onto her bag like her life depended on it. The crowd of fae broke away from her as she walked. She was too busy in her own world.

"Something is wrong," Elena said. "Abuela has only had that face a few times before."

I stepped closer to Elena, my dragon already puffing up inside me.

"Once, when Abuela took me away, after Emmie murdered her fiancée and fled the country. She wanted to protect me from being taken and married off later."

I growled, and my teeth lengthened. I had seen enough of what Elena went through. Her father was a bastard. Using his daughters to pay off debts, with arranged marriages and selling their bodies. The male didn't even help raise his own children after their mother had died. Abuela took them in and raised them to be strong, independent women, as she tried to make up for the sins of having such a terrible son.

"And the other, well, when she finished the moon ritual the next morning. Emm said she swore Abuela must have seen the face of God that day. Now I'm guessing it was the goddess. But why would she fear her? She was nice to us." Elena looked up to me for answers.

"I don't know, love." I wrapped my free arm around her.

Her tight-lipped smile revealed a mix of emotions, conveying both warmth and a touch of sadness. "Elena, I'd like to have a word with you."

Elena's anxiety soared, and there was nothing I could do. I would know through her emotions what was happening due to the bond.

"Alright. Anaki, will you take care of Luis?"

Luis' head was resting on my shoulder. I rubbed my hand up and down his back. "Of course. Do what you need to do."

"I've already talked to Luis," Abuela said. "One more kiss, mijo?"

Luis turned slowly, his gaze briefly meeting Abuela's before she planted a lingering kiss on his cheek. He then turned away, burying his head back into my neck, finding comfort in the warmth against me. Oh shit!

I worriedly rubbed his back until my fingers found his hair and stroked him gently.

"We'll take a walk. Come, mija." Abuela turned and started her walk. Elena stalled.

"Go on, I'll know where you are. We will come get you if I feel you spiraling." I pulled her toward me and gave her a kiss on the side of the head.

Elena quietly followed, and with each step my soulkin made, I wanted to race after her. Unfortunately, I knew she had to take those steps alone. Something was wrong, but obviously she needed Elena alone.

I stood there, watching them disappear into the distance. The sound of their footsteps gradually faded away. I felt a comforting warmth through our bond. Beside me, Luis's breathing slowed, eventually lulling into a soft, peaceful rhythm as he drifted off to sleep in my embrace.

Great, I couldn't ask him what was up then.

"Hey, stranger." Bear strode up next to me with Nadia in his arms. Nadia was asleep as well, but she was being carried in the popular bridal style, how all the women around here liked to be carried in.

"How's she?" I nodded to the bundle in his arms.

"Her head hurts. Traveling to the place where she was trapped for two years also did a number on her. Beretta said she'll help with a memory-blocking spell when this is over, but we got other problems."

I pinched the bridge between my nose. There was always something. "What is it? Is it Idris?"

Bear huffed in annoyance. "Not sure. We got the humans out without a problem. That is what I find strange. Didn't even see Idris, and the guards were... obtuse. Easy in, easy out. I worry about that, but what I really wanted to tell you is about the head pains. It's the link trying to get established."

"Link? What wolves have? That is a mammal thing. Reptiles don't have those." Reptiles didn't have voices, was what it was. We didn't need to have a link because we were not pack animals. Dragon shifters came together because the human side needed it more.

Bear grunted. "Looks like you're getting one. You are part of the pack, the Iron Fang. It looks like the goddess is giving everyone one. Don't look at me for answers. You said you had head pains, so that's what I'm telling you. I've got strict orders to head to the pack house for a big ceremony to speed up the process. Tajah said she is going to shift Emm into a lycan."

My eyes bugged out of my head.

"Do the fuck what?!"

Bear shook his head in confusion. "That is all I know. The pack is forming, tonight. Any other information, I don't know. I'll text you if I get any more info. I will tell you this: be on the lookout for Idris. I got a bad feeling. It would not surprise me if he and his ass hats popped up. I tried talkin' to Hawke, but he's in dad mode, worried about his mate and pup feeling pain."

I ran my hand through my hair. Fuck, fuck, fuck!

I just let Elena and Abuela walk away from the village, and right into the forest where danger could be.

I felt my scales sliding through my skin, my ears elongated, and my fins ripped through the tunic I wore.

Bear stepped back. "I'm gonna go. All mates are required to come."

I shook my head. "My mate is approaching her heat." I felt my eyes shift from human to dragon. "No way I'm going down there with a bunch of shifters. We will stay with the fae. You don't want a feral dragon."

Bear shook his head quickly. "Nope, don't want that. I'll let them know. Elena would be a distraction for Emm anyway."

I grunted in reply and headed in the direction to go find Elena and Abuela. Watch out Spiderman because my dragon senses are tingling.

CHAPTER THIRTY-FIVE

Elena

Once I caught up to Abuela, the silence was deafening. I could only hear birds chirping and bugs crawling on the forest floor. That was something I should not have been able to hear, but did anyway. I rubbed my ears, trying to muffle the sounds.

Abuela stepped closer and put her arm around me.

"I see you took your relationship to the next level," she began. "Tell me about it."

For the next few minutes, I told her, in not so much detail, how I had come to fall in love with Anaki in a short amount of time, despite fighting it at first. How I met the goddess, how I let the bond happen on its own. All the while, her tight lips turned into a broader smile. It relaxed me, and soon we were walking in an easy stride along the border of the fae territory.

"It's weird about all of this. It's real." I waved my hand in front of her. "I can hardly believe it. Still can't wrap my mind around it, actually." I did an involuntary skip.

Abuela hummed and stopped before a tree that wasn't from Earth. Its bark was light, almost white, with hints of gray that swirled around the knots. This tree had light turquoise leaves, and it immediately made me feel like we were in a fairy world that had no problems in it at all.

"I knew you would accept it, eventually. Both you and Emmie. The bond did that. That is what *she* told me."

I stepped closer to Abuela, who was running her fingers over the velvet-covered leaves. "The Moon Goddess?"

"Si. She explained a lot to me that night. Over the years, she came to me in many dreams once I made the deal with her."

My fists were clenched tightly at my sides, my jaw set in a determined line as I turned away from Abuela. The view before me was breathtaking: a deep ravine with thick trees cascading down to a shimmering blue lake. The sun filtering through the leaves created a green and gold haze around us.

"And what exactly did it all entail? This deal." I knew parts of it. What could a mortal give a goddess?

Abuela came beside me. Her warmth enveloped me even though we didn't touch. "Once you both fell asleep, and I bared myself to her, she took me to a place inside my mind I have never been to before. The Moon Goddess was there, and explained to me only what I had read and dreamed about was possible: soulmates between humans and supernaturals. She was in the process of fixing her past errors, and she found both your and Emmie's souls to be the perfect match to two shifters who would work together in a pack."

"The Iron Fang?"

Abuela nodded. "She was predicting fate, but she was sure that both of my granddaughters' souls would align perfectly. I had to prepare you both and lead you on the path here. I had to keep it in your heads that there was something better out there, and keep you safe. Of course, you both had to make things difficult.

"Emmie ran off, away from my reach. She was always so stubborn." Abuela pouted. "Then, I failed you. Kept you hidden too much. You left me as soon as you could to explore. You'd come back every once in a while, more broken than the last time. I never could get you to stay."

Abuela's eyes filled with tears.

I never wanted her to see me as a burden when I was younger. Emm was strong. I was getting sick. I yearned to prove to her I was resilient and capable of standing on my own. Torn between these emotions, I turned away, clutching a nearby limb for support, unsure if I was ready to face her.

Abuela continued. "I never knew what was wrong, and you wouldn't tell me. I held off finding out until I couldn't take it anymore. When I knew you were with *him*." Abuela's arm shook and wrapped around mine. "I know what he did to you." Abuela's voice shook. "Why didn't you tell me? Did you think of me as a weak woman, mija?"

I shook my head quickly. My voice trembled. "H-how?"

Abuela rummaged through her large bag and pulled out a ragged doll. It didn't look like one a child would play with. It was perfectly stitched with dark brown hair, real hair by the looks of it. It had a pair of jeans and a ripped white collared shirt. Blood was splattered on the shoulder.

My eyes widened. "Is that a voodoo doll?" I grabbed it from her hand, looking it over.

Abuela scoffed. "I killed the bastard, Elena. It was slow and meticulous. I made sure that he lost everything before the final blow was delivered, and I made sure it was my face he saw before he closed his eyes and was sent to Hades himself."

¡Dios Mio!

"Abuela, what,... I don't understand. I didn't think you were capable of this kind of magic. What happened to your rocks, your mushrooms? Your quirky personality? Are you on mushrooms right now? Oh goddess, are you on heroine now?"

My hands were waving in the air. I couldn't believe she would do such a thing. I turned to walk away, but suddenly I was hit on the back of my head. I turned and growled. "Did you just hit me with a chancla?"

Abuela stomped toward me and slid it back on her foot. "I did, and there is a perfectly good explanation why I could do such things." She wiped down her blouse like she took great effort to even throw the damn chancla at me.

I crossed my arms and raised a brow.

Abuela sighed dramatically. "The reason I was able to do the voodoo doll..."—she stalled and shuffled her feet—"was because I have lied."

I stood up straight and pressed two fingers to the bridge of my nose.

"Aye, Abuela, you will have to be more specific." I slapped my hand on the other. "There is a lot going on. Lied about what?"

Abuela tipped her head back and ran her hand down her face. "I have much more magic than I let on. The goddess told me we are descendants of great wizards and sorceresses. My great-great-grandparents immigrated to Earth to get away from Elysian, due to the council slowly becoming corrupt. They then locked their magic away, along with the future generations, so we did not become any part of their realm."

My mouth hung open. "You gave Tajah your blood... she should know..."

Abuela chuckled. "That sorceress is powerful, but an old magic binds our blood. Even she doesn't know. It will appear as a weak Wiccan magic. My power is much, much more."

I looked down at the voodoo doll in my hand. "And what else have you done?"

Is she some serial killer?

Abuela stepped closer to me. "Took care of your ex. That is the only life I have taken. I gave Emmie the strength to run from her ex-fiancée. I didn't know she had it in her to kill the man, but she did." She smirked. "Damn proud of her for that."

Her smile faded. "No, mostly I used my magic for frivolous things." Abuela walked over a log and beckoned me to follow. I didn't hesitate, too absorbed in the lavish lies she had told over the years.

Secrets she kept from us.

But were they really secrets? She took us into the woods and showed us what she was doing. Played with her crystals, told us there was more than met the eye.

"I remember," she began. "When you both went through a phase where you both absolutely hated storms." Abuela chuckled and put her hand on my knee. "Somehow, they only happened at night, and you both would scream and wail. It was very inconvenient for me." She shook her head, and I snorted and covered my mouth. "You both would run to my double bed and jump on me. It scared the magic out of me once."

I perked my head up. "Like when the lights turned on and off and you said it was the electricity acting funny?"

She nodded. "Yes, that time. I swear I messed up so many times, and none of you even saw it." She bumped her forehead against the side of my temple.

"There was one storm that was particularly bad. The wind howled, and the thunder was loud. I think Emm's cries were louder, but don't tell her that."

I lay my head on Abuela's shoulder and laughed.

"So, I just hummed until I pushed the clouds away."

There were many nights when there were thunderstorms, the particularly bad ones, I did remember Abuela humming, and soon after the thunderstorms would depart. I never put two and two together because I just thought it was a coincidence.

"I didn't do it every time," Abuela stated. "Because each time you use magic, it drains your manna. I was constantly using my reserves, always using my magic to keep the protection around us. That was why your father didn't bother us much. I tried to tell Emm, but you know her."

Yep, Emm was stubborn like that.

"And this magic is buried inside you. You both have mates who are shifters, now. This magic we hold in our bloodline is powerful. Too powerful. I don't know if you can truly awaken any magic inside you along with your animals, but I suggest not." She raised a brow. "You would need years and years of training, and when you let it out, it will all come at once and spill yet another secret."

"Mierda! How many more secrets!?" I yelled, Abuela was faster than lightning, taking off her chancla and slapping me across the leg.

"You do not cuss in front of your elders! How dare you!" She smacked me several more times, and I rose from my seat to get away.

"Okay, okay! What is the other secret?"

"It's with your son, Luis."

My face instantly paled.

"As you know, his magic has been brought to the surface. I was there when they did it, for a reason. I made sure that his magic would slowly come to him and not all at once. Unfortunately, there will be a time when he reaches his full potential, when he is an adult. He will surpass the teachings of Tajah and Bram."

I wrung the doll in my grasp.

"His power will be great. So great, mija His blood, our blood, must remain a secret; our family's name must not be repeated or be known. The name we came with from the Elysian Realm. Do you understand me?

Luis will be the catalyst to humans and supernaturals getting along here on Earth, in the far future."

Back. The. Fuck. Up.

Before I could speak, she spoke again. "The goddess told me all of this. Citlalli, that is our ancient family line. You can't tell Emm."

I put my fingers into my hair and pulled at the roots. "This is too much pressure! I can't do this! What do you mean I can't tell Emmie! I tell Emmie almost everything! Why can I not say that name?"

"You can't! Swear it!"

My heart pounded against my chest as if trying to escape, and a thunderous roar echoed from beyond the horizon, reverberating through the air and sending shivers down my spine.

Anaki.

I felt fear explode in my chest. Panic, rage.

Luis.

I jerked my head to Abuela, who stood tall. The panic that she might have had displayed on her face when she told me about the ancient family name, was gone.

"Listen, Elena."

I shook my head. "I don't want to," I whispered. There was more shouting in the distance. "I have to go help. I have to—"

Abuela grabbed my arm. "When I unlocked my magic to its full potential, I was ordered to keep my lineage, my granddaughters and my grandson, safe. You will all have mates now. I have done my part, and with unlocking my magic so late in my life, it has damaged my body, mija. I only have enough manna to use one last spell. In doing so, I will forfeit my life."

My knees wobbled and threatened to buckle beneath me. My chest felt as if a weight had settled firmly upon it. A raw, wrenching sob tore through my very being, shaking me to my core. Hot tears streamed freely down my cheeks, blurring my vision as I reached out for her, drawing her closer to me. Her familiar scent enveloped me, a comforting blend of sage and burning ozone.

"No, please. What are you saying? You can't go, you are all we have."

Abuela petted my hair. I felt her kiss the top of my head. "You both have your mates, you have the Iron Fang now. I have warned you, my sweet child, that I would be departing soon. Especially since Luis has been born."

Tears streamed down my face, and my voice cracked. "I didn't believe you."

Abuela chuckled. "Mmhm I thought as much. I leave you with much, but our time is up, Elena. I want you to know I love you very, very much. Luis knows how much I love him, and I will be watching his training."

I sobbed in her arms as I fell to my knees. The pounding in my head grew, and I wailed.

"Emm knows how much I love her, but please tell her it was not her fault. None of this was. My death was on my own terms, and she's not to blame herself."

My body shook, and I felt my heart was about to explode, like the worst heartburn ever.

"No, no! Please do not leave!"

Steps from behind us caught my attention. They were stealthy, but they were loud in my ears. It was like, an instinct that I didn't understand. A chilling emotion crawled up my spine like frozen ice, stopping at the base of my neck.

The person behind me let out a sardonic chuckle. "Isn't this just a lovely scene?"

I twisted my head and saw black, shiny shoes. They were completely out of place in a forest like this. As my eyes roamed up dark, dress slacks, a three-piece onyx black suit, along with a cape. His skin was borderline gray and white with dark flecks of black and silver on his cheeks. He was a fae from the looks of it, with pointed ears and a near cat-like appearance with his slitted eyes and sharp fangs.

I gasped when he pulled off his leather gloves and saw the dark black claws that came from them. He crossed his arms and raised one finger to twirl a long, black piece of his perfectly straight hair.

"Lovely evening, isn't it, Elena?"

The fae wasn't looking at me on the ground, on my knees in front of Abuela, though he was looking at Abuela.

Confused, I turned my head to look at her, and it wasn't her at all... it was... me!

CHAPTER THIRTY-SIX

Anaki

Before I was able to get too far out of the village, silence fell behind me. My ears immediately perked up, and I stuck my finger in my ear to shake it.

The birds stopped flapping their wings. The bugs that crawled on the forest floor stopped moving. Luis groaned in my arms, and I shook my head, trying to listen for the all too familiar sounds of the forest.

"Dad, what's wrong?"

Damnit, he called me dad.

"Focus," my dragon growled inside me.

I whined. *"But he called me dad."*

"He won't keep calling you dad if something comes out and kills all of us," he snarled.

Yeah, I did not like having a talking animal. I much preferred them staying quiet.

His growl of annoyance didn't deter me, and I hugged Luis tighter. Scales was right, though, we needed to find out what was going on, and my gut told me it was happening back at the village. "Luis, I need you to do something for me."

Luis tilted his head in curiosity. His eyes were red-rimmed from crying at whatever Abuela had told him earlier. He was a strong kid. I could feel it radiating off of him. He left me and his mother alone to bond, like he knew it was important, and now he has to deal with—well, this.

"I need you to stay here." I rubbed my cheek against his, letting my scent radiate off my body. It was thick and heavy, not to mark the scent of a mate, but for a fledgling. It was to help hide the human scent he had and to have him blend into the forest.

Nothing would find him. Even for a shifter's nose, it would be near impossible. That meant I had to come back for him. I wasn't even sure Elena could find him with her slowly emerging abilities coming to the surface.

"Stay? But why?"

I carried him off the path and to a nearby tree. It was large, like most of them, but there was a crevice, enough for him to sit inside. Luckily, he was small for his age, and he fit inside nicely. I pulled several bushes and branches away for a place for Luis to hide, and pushed them back in front of him.

I continued to let my scent penetrate the area, keeping everything covered in it. "Do you hear that?" I moved the branches around to keep him hidden.

He shook his head. "Don't hear anything."

"That's right. Something is wrong. Not even the animals are moving." I stared up at the sky. The clouds were thick, and thunder rolled in the distance. Darkness had taken over. I didn't even remember what time it was, but I didn't recall it being that late.

Did time mean anything anymore?

"Promise me something, Luis." I grabbed both of his hands. "Promise me you won't leave. No matter what you hear. If your mother calls, if I call for you, do not come out. I will come to you."

Luis' eyes were large, concerned.

"Why—"

I put his hand on my chest. "I need you to trust me. I know we have spent little time with each other, but I've got a bad feeling. Magic, dark magic..." My instincts went into overdrive, and I felt my scales cover my back. "Do not come out. Bad people..."

Luis reached out and wrapped his arms around my neck. "I won't leave. I promise."

I hugged him back and rubbed his messy hair. "Thank you. I'll be back for you. Remember what I said." He nodded, and I prayed to the goddess he did what he was told.

As I raced back to the village, the silence broke with an earth-shattering *boom.* I tumbled and fell to the ground. I let my claws extend, as my scales continued to ripple to cover my back and chest to protect me. I wouldn't shift into my full dragon—yet.

I didn't need the fae worrying more and thinking I was the enemy. They didn't know I could fully shift yet.

As I sprinted to the edge, I looked around the corner of the first home and onto the pathway to see the commotion. Fae were on their knees, most of them bound with a muting and bonding spell because they were unmoving and silent. They were bleeding, bloodied, and bruised.

There were rows of them, and I didn't hear any of it. There had to be a silencing spell or something.

Damnit, surely the cameras caught all of this. With our luck, Idris turned them off or put them on some sort of loop. Idris was a sneaky bastard.

Dark, hooded figures stood by, while men who appeared to be human, but there was a tinge of other smells that were shifter and vampiric blood mixed together. These must be the men Idris had experimented on and who remained loyal to him.

Hybrids.

Idris promised them power and strength if they stayed with him after Delilah's ex-husband's timely death. He gave it to them, alright. Some were in crouched positions, ready to strike, while others' eyes glowed red, and they licked their lips as if they were hungry from thirst.

"Put them away and deal with them," A towering, hooded figure exuding an aura of authority spoke, its voice cutting through the air like a blade. Instantly, I recognized the person by their distinctive gait—an unwavering confidence in every stride as they emerged from the crowd and disappeared into the depths of the forest with an air of undeniable control.

I couldn't go to Elena, not yet. I had to save these people, but delicately. Scales was ready to obliterate, but one wrong move and this could all go to shit.

There was a reason I liked to stay behind the bar.

Two hooded figures–they appeared to be magical entities–had them all rise. They were being led single file to a cage that flickered gold, and was out of the way of the town, near the hidden entrance where Elena and I usually frequent.

I watched the crowd follow the magicians' orders.

If the fae got into the cage, it would give them protection while I shifted and took out all the hybrids before any harm came to them. So, I waited and stripped out of my clothes until the final fae was in the large cage. The door was barely closed before I fully shifted.

Scales unleashed a thunderous roar that echoed through the air, seizing control of our body with a powerful surge. With a swift, graceful motion, we leaped into the heart of the town, landing amidst the hybrids with a force that sent vibrations through the cobblestones.

The hybrids that Idris had created seemed nearly uncontrollable. Their moves jagged, their claws and fangs unable to descend quickly enough as they raced toward me.

Scales smiled at them as I backed off and let him take the lead. I wasn't about violence, though I had the overwhelming urge to protect those I loved, but this was his thing.

He knocked the first wave of hybrids from in front of me with one swipe of his long neck. Our tail swiped behind us, knocking hybrids to the ground. The snarls, the guttural growls, and the smell of blood filled the air as I stood my ground, facing the advancing horde. The hybrids lunged at me, their eyes filled with rage and hunger. Scales reveled in the thrill of the fight, every move calculated and precise as we deflected their attacks.

But amidst the chaos, a flash of movement caught my eye. A figure darting through the shadows, moving with a grace that seemed out of place in the midst of battle. They were swift, like the wind pushed them along. They were fast, the white braided hair behind them flowing, smacking tree limbs as they went by.

They stopped behind a hybrid vampire who was about to leap for my neck, not that it would be able to penetrate my scales, they grabbed it by the forehead, took their dagger and slit it across its throat. Once it fell to the ground, they decapitated the head and kicked it away.

The hood fell back revealing a feminine face I had seen a few times before.

Her skin was as white and pure as freshly fallen snow, creating a stark contrast with the vivid, crimson blood of the hybrid that stained her. The droplets glistened like rubies against her alabaster complexion. When she lifted her gaze to meet mine, her identity was unmistakably clear.

A winter fae.

The white and silver snowflake-like sparkles in her cheeks were tainted with blood when she looked up at me. Her amethyst eyes glowed with bright determination as she rubbed the blood that dripped from her dagger.

I'd seen her at the club before. She was a prospect. Normally, she sat in the corner and stayed by herself. There weren't many females who joined, but when they did, they tried to prove themselves as much.

This one was a mystery to me.

The winter fae nodded her head over my towering shoulder. My dragon turned and snapped its mighty jaws, immediately biting a hybrid shifter in half. Screams echoed into my still-sensitive ears, and I shook the body away.

The fae joined me in the fray. Her stealth, along with the massive swipes of my body, created a symphony of destruction against the enemy.

A terrifying scream came from the gilded cage behind me. Scales' eyes dilated, and he let out another roar in its direction. One of the magical entities held up a rune, a golden parchment that held a spell, and had begun chanting. A dark smoke had risen from their hands and was seeping through the cage.

The fae on the inside backed away, the smoke had already gotten hold of Meriam, the fae who took my family in so willingly the day we came to visit the territory the first time.

Scales let out an ear-piercing whine, our tail knocking over the hybrids continuing their pursuit. The wind picked up behind me, but it was nothing to move me.

I lunged forward. The two magical entities in front of me didn't see me coming, too involved in their spell-casting. I ripped one away from the cage, their rune flying into the air, the spell cut off. The smoke dropped, but it was too late for Meriam, who was still screaming in pain.

My dragon, not yet finished, swiftly lunged forward catching the cloaked figure with his claws, sending him sprawling to the ground." My dragon's massive foot came down with force and pinned them beneath. The sickening sound of cracked bones surrounded us.

The gilded cage flickered and dissipated like there was no cage at all. The fae dispersed and cried out a fearsome cry, ready for battle. They picked up their weapons to fight. When I turned to Meriam to check on her, another fae kneeled next to her, weeping and shaking their head.

"She's gone." Her face was wet as she stared back up at me. "She's gone."

The thick, acrid smoke that had wrapped around Meriam had curled upward like a relentless serpent and was now gone. It left a trail of blisters where it didn't have time to eat the other half of her body. Her flesh still bubbled and sizzled, the rest of her body still slowly eroding away, just like the other part of her body that had already been eaten.

My stomach churned violently, revolting against the nauseating sight and stench. My dragon let out a half-whimper, half-roar.

I failed.

"You need to go find Elena," the winter fae ran up to me, a bloodied dagger in her hand. "The rest of the fae have this."

The pounding in my head came back with a force and distorted my vision.

I failed. I didn't save her in time.

"Anaki, you need to go!" The fae tapped my leg with the flattened part of her blade and brought me out of my stupor. "We've got it from here. They're retreating."

I snarled as I watched the fae who went to fight the hybrids returning. They were all wounded, bleeding. Some even coughed up blood.

But the hybrids were retreating? That's not right.

The fae who were less injured were running into houses and pulling out their medical supplies. I didn't want to stop to see if there were any more fae dead. My heart couldn't take it.

My throat closed up with emotion. "They are retreating because they are going to attack the pack house. That's the only reason they would leave. Go warn Locke."

The winter fae eyebrows rose in surprise. "You can talk?" she squeaked. "Dragons can't—"

"Goddess blessing. Now go," my dragon grunted and turned away from her, ready to barrel through the forest. We stopped and turned. "What is your name again?"

She stopped mid-crouch, ready to run as well. "Nefeli."

The wind picked up and brought a chill to my scales. When I blinked, she was gone.

The village was a cacophony of cries and wails, but nothing compared to the blood-curdling screams of my mate, which tore through the forest like a savage beast. It was a sound so chilling and raw, it seemed to rip apart the very air around us, drowning out every other noise.

My hearts broke for her as an intense emotional pain took control.

We leapt forward and followed the bond, straight for her.

Once we got closer, I could smell the saltiness of her tears, the dampness of the earth in which they fell. I scrambled closer to her once I found her, not caring if there was danger, but Scales didn't seem to scold me either.

"Elena!"

Our voice thundered through the forest, the trees quivering under the impact of our commanding tone. Her body, curled tightly in the fetal position, was pressed into the dirt. With a sudden movement, she sat up and reached out desperately for me. I swiftly gathered her into my arms, and she clambered up my neck with a frantic urgency, seeking the safety and closeness near my head.

"They took..." she sobbed, "... her. They took Abuela." Her cries were desperate. "She turned into me and told that fae she was me!"

Nothing of what she said made sense.

I pulled her off my neck. "Love, take some breaths. I know this is hard. Tell me. I'm here, listening."

She took in three large breaths and stared into my eyes. "Abuela can do more magic than we thought." She hiccupped. "She was protecting us. She said she was dying. She had enough manna for one more spell, to keep her promise to the goddess. She used it to protect me one more time. She made me look like her, I looked like Abuela. Then Abuela looked like me. The fae took Abuela, thinking it was me!"

Tears ran down her face. I took my claw and gently wiped them away. "But why? Why would he take you?"

Elena shook her head. "Collateral. He's trying to stop Emm and Locke from making a pack to help rogues. If Locke makes a pack—"

"We're stronger. We can destroy him, rise up and defeat him. Idris wants to make Earth his realm and become all-powerful. He can't when the rogues who actually have a conscious band together and beat him."

Elena wiped away her tears. "He knows about my father. He knows about the cartel that is after Emm, and some guy wanting to marry her? Why is he still holding a grudge like that?"

Her cries pierced the air once more, now laced with fury. She clenched her fists so tightly that her knuckles turned white, and her brown eyes blazed with an intense, fiery pink that seemed to burn with the heat of her rage.

Oh shit!

I pleaded, "Elena, you are going to have to calm down."

Elena snapped her head to me and snarled. "You don't tell a woman to calm down!" Her voice changed, darker. Her breathing picked up as she hyperventilated.

This wasn't a case of her just being upset, but something entirely differ-ent. She was going to force a shift, just like Journey.

CHAPTER THIRTY-SEVEN

Anaki

"What the fuck is wrong? Is she hungry?" Scales panicked, and, for once, I was dumbfounded by the dragon.

"You think she's hangry? She just lost her grandmother..."

"When females are upset, aren't they usually hungry?"

I internally groaned.

Dragons are idiots. Maybe Hawke had a point.

I pulled Elena closer to me. Her heart was fluttering as fast as a hummingbird's, and if it went any faster, I feared it would just stop.

Can a human's heart stop?

Scales took over for a moment and thumped our tail. *"Most likely! And they only have one! Fix this!"*

I cradled Elena in my arms, gently swaying her back and forth. A low, rumbling sound resonated from my chest, a mix between a growl and a purr, filling the space around us. My tongue traced a slow, deliberate path down the curve of her neck, while she squirmed slightly, her body pressing closer to mine with each movement.

"Please, please don't. You can't die. You can't shift, you can't do it. I don't know if you would survive shifting into a dragon right now!" My voice cracked.

The dense foliage rustled ominously behind us, and I instinctively let out a low growl in sync with hers. Her sharp claws, tense with alertness, pressed against my scaly hide, sending a sharp twinge through me that made me flinch.

"Mama?"

Luis' head popped out of the bushes.

That boy was in trouble. "I thought I told you to—"

"Mijo! Come here!" Elena wailed and held out her arms while I kept her tight within mine. He ran as he wailed, his hair sweeping back from his forehead.

"Mama, Idris took her. He really took her!" He buried his nose in her chest.

Her heart rate slowed, and I swore under my breath in relief. He was calming her. At least one of the men in her life could calm the Latina.

Both of my loves pressed heavily on my stomach, leaning insistently against my chest. I forcefully pulled them away, determined to get a good look at them. My chest still vibrated with a deep, resonant purr, and I felt my eyes blaze with an intense glow. Elena had sprouted light pink scales that shimmered brilliantly under the light of my eyes.

Scales' anger radiated out of my voice. "How do you know about Idris, Luis?"

Luis showed no fear when he looked at me. Just determination. "Abuela told me that Idris would take her. She told me the whole plan."

Elena's voice caught as she wrapped her hand around her throat.

"He's going to be pissed when he gets down there to try to take Emmie. It won't work, though." He shook his tiny head.

Elena sniffled. "If I wasn't so upset, I'd scold you for cursing."

Luis clung to Elena's neck in desperation, his grip fierce and unyielding. She held him with the fervor of someone grasping a lifeline in a stormy sea, and I entwined myself with them both, anchoring us in our shared grief. This was not how I envisioned our family bonding time—entangled in sorrow, mourning the loss of their grandmother.

"I could go down there," I said with determination. "I can stop it all, I can leave now." I slid them off my body and rose.

Luis kept his body wrapped around Elena and shook his head. "No, you can't. Abuela says you have to go to the lake."

A relentless pounding throbbed in my head once more as jagged bolts of lightning tore through the darkened sky, illuminating the chaos above. Beside me, Elena clutched her forehead, her fingers pressing into her skin, and let out a cry.

"Mama, what's wrong?"

She rubbed her temples. "This headache is getting worse!"

I shook my head in disbelief, my tail instinctively curling in on itself, coiling tightly like a resting snake. Elena sat on the ground, looking pale and weary, while Luis hovered over her, tending to her with gentle care. Meanwhile, Scales, the fierce presence within me, was roaring with a ferocity that echoed through my being. Suddenly, a sharp, cracking sensation erupted inside my mind, as if a colossal tree had splintered and shattered within the confines of my skull.

The wind picked up, and Elena and I both stared at each other.

"Pay attention; reinforcements are coming," Bear grumbled. *"Hawke to the west, and the fae are approaching."*

Scales and I stood up on all fours. This was unbelievable. There was no possible way that I was in a link. Dragons don't establish links. Links were for pack animals, but they somehow did it. They included me, a reptile shifter, in the pack.

That means Sizzle and Surkash would be a part of the pack, too? Or would they need to be mated? Too many questions for right now.

"I-I can hear you?" Elena touched her temple. "I can hear you thinking. I heard Bear speak in my head. How—"

"Don't ask me how it works, I'm not exactly sure. But the fae—"

"Go." Elena closed her eyes. I didn't think it was possible for someone to cry as much as she had. Elena took her shaky hand and pointed to the forest. "Go help them. Save who you can." Her lip wobbled, and she grabbed onto Luis. "We can go back to the village, and we can—"

I cleared my throat, but mind-linked her instead. "Go to the cave, don't go to the village."

Elena stared at me for a long moment before she nodded. She must have looked inside my mind, for she knew what had happened.

"And try not to get upset. I can't have you shift." I stepped forward and rubbed my neck along them both to conceal their scents. My tongue slithered out of my mouth and slowly ran up her neck. "Stay safe, stay hidden."

Elena rubbed her head against mine. "Don't tell anyone what Abuela did. That she could change herself."

I stood still and searched through her mind. While we could see each other's memories before, with the bond, it felt so much easier to comb through. My eyes widened in shock the more that was revealed.

Abuela was a fierce female.

"You have my word, love. No one will know."

Before Scales could persuade me from leaving and taking care of only our immediate family, I slithered into the forest with speed.

It didn't take me long to reach the lake. Voices were constantly going through my mind. Bear, Hawke, Locke, I could hear them all. Where they were and how I could find them. The link was strange, and Scales didn't know what to do with it. We were not programmed to hear other people's thoughts, only emotions.

I wasn't supposed to have a dragon speak to me, but here we were.

The lake enveloped me with a soothing embrace as I plunged into its depths. It felt inexplicably right—not to my physical self, but as if I had found the place where I truly belonged. Slowly, I descended to the bottom, where the world above faded away, and I waited, nestled into the soft, cool embrace of the sediment that cradled me like an ancient, welcoming bed.

Only weeks ago, I thought I should stay down here forever as a human, and let my life be taken from me. Thank the goddess I hadn't.

As I gazed upward, the moon boldly pierced through the heavy clouds, its luminous glow struggling to reach the earth below. The silvery light danced delicately across the surface of the lake, shimmering faintly amidst the gentle ripples that disturbed the otherwise tranquil water.

There was a commotion on the shore, and with the link, I tried to pinpoint who it could be. It was two powerful entities, and Scales immediately recognized it as the source of our mind-linking abilities.

Alpha and Luna.

Locke and Emm.

We propelled ourselves upward, slicing through the water with powerful strokes until our eyes and nose emerged into the open air. The cool surface of the water kissed our skin as we hovered there, barely allowing our ears to rise above the surface. From this position, the muffled cacophony of the battle reached us, a chaotic sound of bullets whizzing, animal roars, and shouted commands. Every fiber of my being was poised to surge out of the water and join the fray, yet a persistent whisper in the recesses of my mind urged patience, forcing me to bide my time.

It was a battle for Emm that she must do on her own. I listened to it, and it seemed familiar. I only listened to it for so long until I couldn't take it anymore.

There was more fighting and yelling. Locke struggled into a position where he couldn't move. He was yelling, then grunting, but again, it was like I was frozen in place.

If Locke knew I was there, he would've had my head.

But again, I watched.

Scales was pounding in my mind to go, and I was holding back as hard as I could, but slipping.

"*Wait.*" The voice called to me.

I squeezed my eyes tight as I watched my new Luna take a hit that would hurt later. I somehow know she needed this pain.

"*Almost.*" The voice was the goddess. I was listening, waiting. If it were any other member of the Fang, I was sure they wouldn't listen. No male would listen to her, but I did. She gifted me a mate, and I would do what she said. A mate, a son, and my dragon's voice.

I owed her.

I watched for what seemed like forever, as I witnessed the pain and destruction that all parties seem to do to each other's bodies. I didn't look away, I watched it all. Scales' anger rose, while my worry for my friends grew.

Until the final word tickled my ear. "*Now!*"

Scales took over.

I was utterly powerless over my own body, as if I were a puppet on strings. We surged up from the lake, the water cascading off of us in shimmering droplets, and there he was—the imposing figure of Duke Idris himself.. The shoreline was a gruesome scene. It was splattered with crimson streaks of blood. Emm lay sprawled on the ground, motionless and vulnerable, while Locke stood poised, every muscle tense and ready to deliver the decisive blow to the Duke.

Idris was unmoving, cackling like a madman, ready to die.

Locke would want to kill him, slowly and painfully. But Scales and I could smell Abuela on his clothes, and in my hearts, I knew she was already gone.

Scales lunged forward with a swift, menacing grace, his massive jaws opening wide to clamp down on Idris's torso. Idris's body stiffened in our grasp, a tense rigidity taking hold of him, and just as abruptly as we had surged from the water's surface, we yanked him back into the dark depths below.

Scales shook him violently, thrashing with a relentless force that drove our sharp teeth deeper into his abdomen, tearing through flesh and sinew. The water churned around us, a chaotic dance of bubbles and blood, as Scales ensured his suffering would be prolonged. His struggles grew weaker with each passing moment, his eyes wide with terror and pain. We could sense his impending doom, knowing that soon he would succumb to the watery depths. Only then, once he had drowned in the murky embrace of the water, would we feast upon his lifeless body.

At least Scales would eat him. I'd ignore him.

The thought sickened me, but it was the only way to be sure he was dead. Once his movements ceased, we released him to eat him headfirst, but as soon as we did, black smoke surrounded his body and dispersed into the water.

We shook our head and searched in the water for his body, but there was none to be found.

We continued to search as I sank to the bottom to see if he had escaped us. We kicked up the sediment, and the fish swam away in panic.

"Anaki?" My name came in loud and clear in my head. Locke was trying to reach me, and I winced at what this could mean. Pissed he didn't get his shot to kill Idris or just straight up wondering what the hell was going on.

I rotated my body and swam to the surface. He was patient as I slowly emerged from the water, thankful we had a mind link. I'm not sure if I was ready to speak in my dragon form to him. He would have more questions than I wanted to answer.

I was ready to get back to Elena and Luis. They were my priority, now that Idris was no longer present. Dead or not.

"Alpha-" Scales used his voice through the link. He was doing it to protect me. My voice would have shaken if I did. *"I apologize. It's been a while since I've had to control my instinctual side."*

Locke stood on the shoreline, staring right at me like I was the enemy. He has never seen a dragon in his life, so I won't fault him for that. "I get it. But where the hell is Idris? He better be buried underneath a rock in the deepest part of the lake," he sternly said.

I curled my body and looked back at the vast emptiness of the lake. *"His heart stopped beating, and I held him in my mouth, but he disintegrated. Is that how the fae die?"*

Because hell if I knew.

Locke snarled and ran his claws through the fur between his ears. "I don't know. We will have to speak to Bram. He knows more. Where are your mate and her son?"

I took my long forked tongue and wiped it across my lips. *"Safe within my cave. Her grandmother ran off and said she must fulfill her destiny. I tried to stop her—"*

I hated lying, I really did. Because I absolutely sucked at it.

Scales tutted in my head. *"He didn't even ask for that information. Why are you giving it?"*

"I'm so nervous!" I snapped. *"It makes me antsy."*

Locke shook his head and held up his hand. "She fulfilled it. But she is no longer with us."

I slumped my shoulders and turned away. *"I failed her,"* I told him.

"No—" He shook his head. "It had to be done. It was her destiny, and I'm sure the goddess will bless her in the afterlife."

I'm sure that was true. The goddess had kept up on the promises she had given thus far. Unfortunately, the result of Abuela being gone will leave heartache on both of her granddaughters.

CHAPTER THIRTY-EIGHT

Elena

I took Luis to the cave. Our home now.

We would have to figure out a separate room for him. I'm sure there were other tunnels or parts of the cave that we could use. Anaki was very mindful that he was going to be a father, and while he has spent little time away from me, he's been thinking of having Luis here. I was sure of it.

"Mama?"

My arms encircled Luis from behind as we paused at the tent's entrance, the canvas flaps rustling gently in the night. We peered inside, where shadows flickered against the dim light of a lantern. Luis tilted his head back to look at me, his eyes wide with worry, eyebrows knitted together in apprehension.

He was so young, and he was here having to deal with the death of a grandparent, and finding out about all this shit. Soon he would know his aunt was a damn Luna and a freaking huge, monster dog-thing was his uncle.

"Are you okay? You have this weird look on your face?"

I let out a shuddering breath and shook my head. "That's a loaded question. Let's go."

I led Luis inside, his eyes wide as he took it all in. He was exhausted. Hell, I was exhausted, but I didn't think sleep would come anytime soon, for me at least.

Luis was covered in dirt and leaves. I showed him briefly around the cave to get him familiar with it. It kept both of our minds off of what had just happened, a brief time for our minds to reset from the day.

I guided him to the bathroom, and after he assured me he felt comfortable showering and tending to himself, I quietly withdrew. I decided to go on a hunt for something clean for Luis to wear.

To the right of the narrow hallway leading to the bathroom stood an ornate dresser, its wood intricately carved and polished to a sheen. Expensive, it looked expensive. This part of the cave was unfamiliar to me; I had always dashed in and out of the bathroom, ready to get back to Anaki and more fun times.

He had the body I wanted to explore...

I rubbed my forehead. Probably need to chill on that while Luis is here. I chuckled and opened the drawer to see if I could find one of Anaki's old-school tunics that looked like they were from the 1800's but when I looked inside, I found clothes that were for Luis.

Well, cover my tits with peanut butter.

I pulled out the first drawer and found shirts, shorts, pants, all in Luis' size. There were even shoes, socks and other accessories. Everything a child would need was within this massive dresser.

I sniffed, trying not to cry when I got to the pajama drawer.

The first one was with Transformers, Pokémon, and more cartoon characters. Usually, I just gave Luis a large t-shirt to wear from the men's clearance rack. For our son to have actual pajamas and in so many designs was unbelievable.

I move them all aside, just trying to pick one for Luis to wear tonight, and curious of what all Anaki had bought. Once I reached the bottom, I found a blue fluffy material. When I pulled it out, my lip wobbled, and I nearly cried when I realized what it was. It was a blue dragon pajama onesie.

When I pulled it to my nose, and it fucking smelled like him.

Did he get me one? He'd better, because I want one, too.

"Are you going to cry again?" Luis was wrapped in a towel, water dripping on the floor behind me.

"Yeah, but they are happy tears. I found you some cute pajamas?" My voice cracked as I held up the onesie, half ready for him to dismiss it. He was getting too old for them, and he was mature for his age.

Instead, he smiled and nodded. "I like it. Looks just like Dad's dragon."

Damn it. My eyes were going to be red for days.

Once he was dressed, I led him back into the main room. The large bed was made, with fresh sheets, thank goodness, and I put him in the middle. He turned his head to either side of the mattress and looked at me. "Why are there so many pillows? And blankets? And why is the bed so big?"

I carefully tucked the soft, warm blanket around Luis, ensuring he was snug and comfortable. Not stopping there, I gathered an array of fluffy pillows, placing them meticulously until we were enveloped in a fortress of cushions, each one strategically arranged for maximum coziness.

I bustled around the bed, adjusting and rearranging, determined to create the perfect haven for my son, for myself, and for Anaki when he returned. With each motion, I huffed and fluffed more pillows, their plush textures yielding under my touch. Finally, Luis sat up in the bed, surrounded by our cozy creation.

"Mama?"

I perked up and turned to him. "Oh yes, sorry, what?"

Luis smiled and lay back down. "Is it because you are becoming a dragon you are doing this? Making a... nest?"

My face reddened, and I nodded. "Is that what I'm doing?"

Luis yawned again and buried his face in the pillow. "Yeah, Bones said you would do that. That you will act more animal once you guys got shifter married. But why the big bed?"

Luis closed his eyes, and I crawled up next to him. I brushed his hair out of his face, but he pulled on his hood to show off the tiny dragon horns and the big googly dragon eyes that went with it.

"Because Anaki would want to lie in here as a dragon, so he made the bed big enough for his bigger form, and so we can fit in it, too. But don't worry, we will make you your own room."

Luis hummed. "Good. I don't need to hear dragon noises all the time."

I didn't know how to take that. I turned my head away and rubbed his back until he fell asleep.

At least my little man wasn't crying. He wasn't sobbing over Abuela, and he wasn't in a fit of overwhelming disbelief.

Unfortunately for me, I could see right through Anaki's mind and see what he had done to protect Luis and me. He and Scales fought those creatures and still weren't able to save everyone.

Not even Meriam, the sweet fae who'd invited Abuela and Luis into their home.

I snuggled closer to Luis, too tired to get up and clean myself off. I couldn't bear the idea of leaving him right now. What if one of those things came into the cave? He would be left unprotected.

What could I do to save him, though?

I tried to push the claws out from my fingers. My hand shook as I tried to extend them, but to no avail.

We were sitting ducks here if I thought about it. I didn't have a way to protect us.

At that very moment, Anaki was down there, fighting against a fae who had cruelly snatched away the one person I had shared most of my life with. The woman who had been taken from this world far too soon, leaving a void that could never be filled.

I should have listened to her words more intently, and cherished each word she spoke. I should have believed wholeheartedly in everything she had ever told me. I took her presence for granted, and I failed to shower her with the love and appreciation she so deeply deserved!

I held back a sob and dug my fingers into my hair.

"Abuela, why? Why did you leave? You didn't have to do this."

Then she abandoned me with nothing but a name. A family name that feels like a curse on my tongue, forbidden to ever be spoken aloud. Why would she do that? Didn't she understand the torment of carrying this burden alone. Surely she knew I must eventually share it with someone? Secrets between sisters are a volatile flame, always ready to ignite into chaos.

Just look at the destruction I caused before!

"What have you done?" I whispered into the darkness. "Do you want my insides to explode? Do you really want me to tell? What mind games are you playing?"

Luis stirred beside me.

"Damn you. Damn the magic, the secrets, and our ancestors."

I must have dozed off, despite being afraid someone would come inside the cave. The nest surrounding us made me feel safe. Anaki's scent was strong, and I felt nothing could penetrate this fortress of softness.

When I awoke to the faint sound of light footsteps echoing outside the cave, my heart pounded wildly in sudden panic. The soft shuffle was loud through the stillness. Beside me, Luis remained peacefully asleep, his small form snugly curled beneath the layers of blankets, his breaths steady and rhythmic. Carefully, I disentangled myself from the cocoon of pillows and blankets, making a concerted effort not to disturb him.

I moved towards the entrance of the cave, I peered outside and saw that dawn was nearly approaching. Morning light filtered through the trees, casting eerie shadows on the forest floor. And then I saw movement near the edge of the clearing.

My breath caught in my throat as I recognized the silhouette of a figure approaching the cave.

The figure drew closer, and I could make out the familiar features of Anaki's face, drawn in concern. Relief washed over me when I saw him. He was completely naked, but that didn't deter me when I jumped on him and wrapped my legs around his waist.

"Hey, love, I'm glad you're safe." His warm hand ran up and down my back. "I was worried about you—"

I shook my head into his neck. "Stop, just stop and let me smell you."

Anaki chuckled softly, a warm, infectious sound that danced through the air. His hand glided down my spine, a gentle caress that lingered at my lower back before traveling upward, weaving its way into my hair. The sensation was both comforting and electrifying, sending a shiver of delight through me. "It's been a rough night, I promise it won't always be like this."

"What happened?" I whispered into his neck. "Is she..."

Anaki hugged me tighter. "It was quick, love. She didn't feel a thing."

I took in a sharp intake of breath.

"You can't think about that, love. You can't. It is what she was destined to do. I'm sure she talked to Tajah about it, too. We can talk to her, okay?"

I nodded silently. "What happens now? What's happening down there?" When I tried to listen, I couldn't hear much. My hearing would come and go. My body was exhausted, and the few scales that had appeared on my skin had faded away.

A dragon, I was going to be a dragon.

"They're cleaning up. Once the mind-link was established, it was over. It appears only the mated have a mind-link, but with that alone, we can communicate much better. Mated couples are stronger and feed off each other for strength. Tajah's power grew. She was able to shield the Fang, the prospects and the unmated members got in some good fights, but a lot are wounded."

"We need to go help." I stepped away from him so we could get dressed.

Anaki grabbed my wrist and pulled me back. "They will be fine. We will rest. We are still recently mated. I don't want you around a bunch of unmated males right now. You still haven't gotten your dragon yet."

I stomped my foot. "I'm not going after anyone. I've only got eyes for you."

Anaki smirked and wrapped his arm around my waist to lead me back to the cave. "I know that, Mama, but you just lost family. You and Luis are tired and need to process. Locke has given me orders to keep you safe and do what is necessary."

I let out a low grunt, trailing behind him as he moved to the entrance of the cave. He grabbed my hand when I wasn't paying attention, and he suddenly moved me in front of him and pinned me against the cave wall. The cool, jagged rock pressed into my back as his eyes locked onto mine with an intensity that made the air feel heavy. "Even if that means rubbing your pussy to make you compliant," he breathed into my neck.

Butterflies fluttered in my belly. When I felt grief, I knew my Anaki would make me feel better. That was what I wanted right now. A release, a break from all the pain.

"It's like you know me." I moaned.

He hummed. "That I do." He cupped my pussy on the outside of my dress with his palm.

"If I rub your pussy like a magic lamp, do I get three wishes?"

I pressed my lips into a thin line, trying not to laugh. "Maybe."

He touched my forehead with his. "You wanna know what my wishes are?"

I bit my bottom lip.

"One would be, you would come shower with me. Right now."

I raised my eyebrows at him and smirked.

"The second you would let me fuck you there. Not sure what way, though, and I think I would have to ask nicely if you would call me a good boy when I do it."

I snorted and banged my head on his chest.

"And the third would be to let me transform into my dragon and let me curl around both you and Luis while you sleep."

My eyes softened.

"So I know you are both protected, safe, and warm. Then after, I will make the biggest breakfast casserole you have ever seen and try my best not to feed you too much in front of Luis, because it does gross him out. I can't make many promises on that, though."

I giggled. "And these are your wishes?"

My fingers gently combed through the soft strands at the nape of his neck, twirling them absentmindedly as I nestled closer. "Then I guess you better rub my lamp then."

CHAPTER THIRTY-NINE

Anaki

Elena would not have time to mourn for Abuela while Luis was here. I knew it when she ran up and wrapped her arms around my neck.

As pathetic as it was, I was elated she found me as her safe space. I was jealous she calmed so quickly when Luis stopped her from shifting, but maybe she needed two men in her life. At least it was her son and not another male.

My dragon scoffed at that. He still thought we were enough, and in time, we would have calmed her down. He was cocky, but I figured most animals were as much.

Elena had sorrowful dreams as she slept. It was strange how this mind-link worked. It was like I could go into her mind at any time. It was invasive and could be way too much at times. I tried to stay out of it as much as I could, but she was very loud, and the cries in her dreams for her Abuela to come back to her were heart-wrenching.

Idris towered over them, his eyes fixed intently on their faces. His index finger traced a slow path down his cheek, as if he were deep in thought, while his tongue flicked across his lip with a deliberate, contemplative gesture. "You are much better looking than your sister. I'm surprised everyone is putting up such a fuss over that cunt."

"Don't speak of her like that!" Elena said as she sat in the dirt. The only way I could tell it was actually her, and not Abuela, was in her eyes. The pleading, the desperation. She knew what was about to happen, and there was nothing she could do.

Idris sidestepped Elena with a swift movement and reached out to seize Abuela, who was standing in Elena's place. His fingers clamped down with a firm, unyielding grip, causing Abuela to flinch with a pained expression crossing her face. "Now, I could see the appeal in this one. You look soft and compliant. Much better material to work with."

Elena growled from the forest floor, but Abuela said nothing as she was pulled away. "No! You let go of her! It's me who you want, not her!"

Idris scoffed. "I think not. You can't even stand. Consider yourself lucky I haven't done away with you. A tender mercy."

"Bastard! Stop!"

Elena's voice pierced the air as she screamed and stretched her arms toward Abuela, her fingers trembling with desperation. She attempted to inch her body forward, but her legs looked as though they were trapped to the forest floor. Abuela stood a few paces away and gently shook her head. Her eyes were soft yet firm, and a subtle movement of her hand, discreetly hidden behind the folds of her dress, signaled Elena to remain where she was.

Elena wailed again. "Please no, please no!"

My heart broke as I watched. I didn't like seeing this and feeling her pain. Nevertheless, I would pick up the pieces and put her back together.

Elena slept while I took care of Luis. He was tired and still felt the effects of the night before. I couldn't blame him, he was suffering, but being young, he would recover faster than his mother, after the death of his elder.

I had a feeling that his grandmother had cast a spell for him to understand her part in all of this, and he would understand far more the significance of her death. However, I wanted him to know that the Iron Fang and I would be here for him.

We were all family.

We made breakfast quietly while Elena slept. He was inquisitive about dragons and where I came from. He also wanted to know everything about what would happen to his mother. Bram and Tajah had told him as much as they knew about Elena's transition. Maybe too much.

Mostly, that she may be out of the picture for a while, and he would need to spend time at the Iron Fang with Tajah and Beretta.

Scales growled at that. He felt it was our place, and ours alone, to tell Luis what was best for our female and son.

That was something our dragon would have to get over. We were part of a pack now, and we were family. If he wanted to rut our soulkin during her heat, which was approaching quickly, we would have to have Luis stay with others. Not only that, but once Elena's dragon surfaced, she would want more, sating as well.

My cocks twitched and my body shivered in anticipation. I remembered stories about females gaining their dragons and their sudden desires. Males didn't have such a desire until their mates wanted to claim what was theirs.

It was going to be like marking her all over again.

Throughout the rest of the day, Luis and I attended to Elena. She stayed wrapped in the blankets of her nest and slept. Much like her sister, who was being attended to by her mate, Locke. Elena often asked how her sister was, and both sisters were asking to see each other.

Unfortunately, the alpha refused.

But my dragon felt the same, so win-win?

Locke was being a bastard about it, while my dragon, well, he was being a bastard as well. Through the link, Locke was sating her through sexual advances, while I had Luis with us and couldn't do a thing. So, we force-fed her, played board games, forced cuddle piles, and I brought out the large movie projector, and we watched movies.

Luis had a great time, laughing and giggling, which brought a smile to Elena's face as she ran her fingers through his hair. There was still guilt hovering over her that she should have done more, but I constantly used the newly formed link to tell her how much I loved her and how brave she was.

None of this was her fault.

Abuela had her own agenda, and she should be grateful she had all this time to spend with her as she did. Emm did not.

It took Elena only two days to finally rise from her nest and shower. Part of it, I think, was Luis who made her get out of bed. He was worried and continued to ask her if she was alright. She did it for him, and if it weren't for him, I'm not sure how long she would have lain there.

Scales would have fucked her until she left the bed and was out of the cave. Luckily, he had some sense. Toward the end, Scales kept putting erotic scenes in her mind to make her uncomfortable. She shot daggers at me during movies that should not warrant any sort of lust, and I couldn't help but smirk at the debauchery Scales was sending her.

The scenes of fucking her with his dragon cocks in her pussy and ass was so real looking, it was... tempting. I was fucking hard. I ground myself into her backside while Luis was innocently eating popcorn and watching his movie.

"You're going to hell," she whispered to both of us.

"It's not me, it is him. I'd never do such a thing in front of a child."

When the movie was halfway over, she'd had gone to shower and, of course, she was touching herself in there, sending me visions of her pumping three fingers into her juicy cunt.

Scales growled in my head. *"She's getting her ass spanked for that."*

"Think she would spank me, too?" I replied when I pounded my head into the pillows.

I had blue balls from hell, and to top it off, when she orgasmed, I swore I felt my shafts squeeze like they were inside her. It wasn't fair, not at all. I whined and curled up into a ball, then heard the chirp of my phone. Luis' feet padded across the carpets, he grabbed the cursed contraption from the table and ran back to the bed. "Dad, your phone!"

I groaned and held out my hand, but ended up swiping it.

"What's wrong? Is your stomach upset?" Luis' voice, laced with concern, hovered over me. I wrapped the surrounding blankets around us both. Although I knew Luis couldn't smell, sense, or know what was wrong with me, I felt embarrassed.

"She is a vengeful female," Scales groaned.

"It's all your fault. Ever since you showed up, she's been so feisty," I snapped back at him. *"She was so lovely until you started all this."*

I cleared my throat. "I'm fine!" my voice squeaked. "What does the message say, Luis?"

Luis tapped the phone. "It's from Bram. He says he wants to speak with us. Do you want him to come here or us to go there? Bones would like to meet with Elena, too."

I grumbled to myself. I preferred neither.

"I don't wanna." I groaned.

Elena came out from the cave hallway. She had a towel wrapped around her chest and another wrapped around her hair. "Luis, go shower and get dressed. We will go to the club. Think you'd want some of their cheese fries you like so much?"

Luis perked his head up. "Heck, yeah!" His fist pumped the air. "I love their cheese fries."

I pulled my head from the covers. "What's wrong with the healthy stuff I've been feeding you. You are a growing dragon."

Luis' eyes grew wide. "Ah, nothing. I just need some grease, is all. So, it all slides down nice."

Elena made a face. "That's disgusting. Go get dressed, you nasty dragon. You can't wear those pajamas another day."

Luis groaned. "But I have a tail." He pulled it around his body and waved it. "I have to show everyone."

"It smells like popcorn." Elena shivered. "With a mix of Anaki and my scents all over it, it's gross. I'll put it in the washer, which is weird that you have a washer and dryer in a cave, by the way." She looked over Luis' head and smiled at me. "Then, I'll have it dried by the time it's bedtime."

Luis slumped his shoulders, nodded his head, and headed down the hallway that he had become familiar with. I couldn't help but feel happy that he was so accustomed to our home. Still, I needed to get an extra room ready for him. Perhaps a more private den for my soulkin and me, as well.

My balls were going to explode.

Elena strolled toward me, her towel slipping from one side of her chest.

"How does it feel to put naughty thoughts in one's head, huh, Scales?" Elena gracefully sank onto the bed, her presence commanding and intense as she leaned closer to me. Her tongue unfurled from her mouth, no longer resembling anything human. Instead, it took on a dragon-like form, sinuous, as it slithered up my neck. My breath caught in my chest, a mix of anticipation and surprise, while a flood of arousal surged through me, leaving me trembling with desire.

"Fuck, Elena, you aren't just punishing him, but me, too." I grabbed myself and buried my face back into the pillows.

The shower in the bathroom turned on, and I screamed into the fluffy textures. "You are going to kill me, female!!"

Elena giggled.

She damn giggled!

She pushed me over while I panted. "Please, no edging. I can't take it. You have been upset. I'm trying to be a good little dragon for you. It was all Scales, not me."

While I complained, she was unwrapping me like I was a goddamn present. I couldn't understand what was going on, speaking a mile a minute, until she spread her legs over my hips and put my lower cock into her pussy.

Sweet fucking relief.

"Good dragon. Let's get you some relief."

I whined and reached for her hips. "Yes, please, Mama."

Elena dropped the towel to expose her breasts. "You only get one cock wet because Scales was being bad."

One hand gripped her ass tightly, and I bucked up into her pussy.

"Be good, Scales, or I'll just get off and finish myself."

He growled. "No, please."

Elena's hand gripped my shaft.

"Alright, alright." I panted, my eyes locked onto her beautiful face. "I'll be good."

She smiled, her eyes sparkling with mischief and desire. "That's better. Now show me what it means to be good."

With that, she began to move her hips, setting a slow, steady rhythm. I matched her pace, each thrust propelling me further into her warm depths. Her breasts bounced with each movement, sending waves of pleasure through me. I gripped her ass tightly, feeling the familiar heat building deep within me.

"Yes, Elena," I groaned. "Yes, so good."

Elena moaned in response, her hand never faltering on my shaft. Her other hand came up to play with one of her nipples, making her gasp and arch her back ever so slightly. It was a sight to behold—her body responding to our lovemaking as she stroked me relentlessly.

"I'm gonna come. Can I come?" I whispered, my voice rough with need. "I'm gonna come so hard..."

"You want to come?" she urged. "Come inside me like a good boy." Instead of pinching her nipple, her hand ran up my chest and cupped my neck. Her eyes dilated and my cocks grew harder.

Fuck, fuck!

"Yes." My eyes rolled back in my head. "Please, please," I begged.

She squeezed the sides of my neck, just enough. I saw spots floating in my vision.

Her grip intensified, her fingers digging deep into my flesh. I could barely breathe, and the pleasure-pain mix was unbearable. My heart raced and my cock twitched, ready to erupt. I felt like I was on the edge of an abyss, about to fall headfirst into oblivion.

"Now, Anaki," she hissed, her eyes burning with desire. "Now!"

And then it happened. My orgasm hit me like a freight train, hurling me into a world of pure ecstasy. It was as if every nerve in my body was singing.

I cried out, unable to hold back my lustful cries as wave after wave of bliss coursed through me.

Elena's eyes widened in delight as I came inside her, spurt after spurt filling her completely. Her voice rose with mine as she, too, reached her peak, her body trembling beneath me. The feel of her muscles contracting around me sent me over the edge once more, milking every last drop from my exhausted body.

We lay there for a moment, our hearts pounding and our breaths ragged from the exertion. Slowly, our bodies relaxed, returning to their normal state. Elena pulled me close, wrapping her arms around me as we caught our breaths.

"That's what I like to see," she whispered, her voice soft and contented. "A defiant dragon learning how to be good." She licked the side of my neck, then kissed me softly on the lips.

CHAPTER FORTY

Elena

Bones carefully lifted the stethoscope from my chest, the cold metal leaving a brief chill on my skin, and unplugged the earpieces from his ears with a soft click. He draped the stethoscope around his neck where it rested against his white coat, then reached over to the sleek tablet on the table beside him. The screen flickered to life as he picked it up, his fingers poised to scroll through my medical records. "Your heart is beating faster than a normal human. It isn't just anxiety. I'm guessing it is because your body is preparing itself for changes, or it could be from your impending heat arriving."

I wrinkled my nose and looked away from him.

"It's hard to say, I've never dealt with a dragon shifter before. I can only give you my best guess."

Anaki surprisingly took us upstairs to the clinic when we arrived at the bar. First, we had Luis looked over for any cuts or bruises. Of course, he was fine after the entire ordeal. Nadia, who was under Bones' training, was in the room as well. She was there more so for the emotional side of the visit and asked Luis a lot of questions about what he had seen.

Luis saw more than I realized, including seeing a fae strangle an enemy with their vines. My motherly instincts instantly took over as I ran from across the room and held him as he told us what happened. Not that it would do anything to take the memory away. It was just too soon for my son to see death, but here he was.

Luis held a brave face while he explained. It was the whole reason he left his hiding spot in the first place to come find us, because the danger had come too close to him.

My brave little mijo.

I was a terrible mother.

He didn't even want to call me mama anymore. He said since he feels like he has grown up so much, he wanted to call me Madre now.

Oh, Goddess!

I drew in a shaky breath, trying to steady myself as Bones continued talking about how baffling my symptoms were to him. Anaki was instantly by my side, his presence a force of nature as his scent filled the room. My head instinctively sought refuge on his shoulder, pressing into him with a desperate need for comfort. As if his very essence could ward off the spiraling thoughts of my son growing up too fast because of the world we were a part of now.

Bones pulled away the glasses that sat on top of his nose and gave me a concerned look. "Is it something I said? I'm sorry, I don't have a lot of information about your condition and what is coming. I've asked Bram to give me as many text books as he could about dragon anatomy, there just isn't a lot—"

Anaki shook his head. "No, it's not that. She's worried about Luis."

Bones stared at the door where Luis had left minutes ago. "Ah." He pulled up the rolling stool from behind him and sat down next to the exam table. "I'm going to tell you something right now, Elena. Your son is strong. Even though I am weak, with no wolf to help me, I can tell he is meant to do great things. Your Abuela told me so."

I sniffed and nodded in reply.

"He has an old soul." He laced his hands together. "Luis will grow up well around people like us. He was born in the right family and will be raised by the right mom and dad. You have done nothing wrong, you've done everything right."

Anaki reached out and put his hand on Bones' shoulder. Bones flinched.

"Not gonna hit ya," Anaki chuckled. "I'll leave that up to everyone else. You're a good wolf. Thank you."

Bones studied Anaki intently, caught between a desire to smile and what appeared to be the need to remain cautious. "I do what I can. Now..." Bones stood and cleared his throat. "What I need you both to be aware of, what I have learned about dragons, is that your shift will take time. You are lucky you didn't force a shift. A wolf forced to shift was dangerous, a forced dragon shifting, I would think, would be fatal. You need time alone. Your dragon, Anaki, should help coax Elena's."

Anaki stood up tall and straightened his back.

"Does this mean he will need to speak to her?"

Bones leaned on the counter and crossed his arms. "After seeing what our alpha's lycan did for our Luna, I believe that to be the case. Locke said it was like two separate parts of him. He could command the pack, while his wolf took charge and helped Emm shift."

My heart pounded. Emm forced shifting? "Is she okay? Why did she have to force a shift?"

Bones rubbed the back of his neck. "It was required to form the pack. She had to be of equal power as the Alpha, and Locke is a special wolf, well, Lycan. Can walk on two legs, speak through his muzzle. Not just a wolf. Emm had to skip from being a human to Lycan to create the pack and the link. She went through a lot of pain to do that."

I gasped. "How is she? Can I see her?"

I was worried about Luis, and I hadn't even seen or heard from her. Locke was keeping her away from me, and I hadn't had my phone!

"Our Luna is fine. Alpha is taking good care of her. She is very depressed and needs time alone. The mind-link is a mess right now, as you can imagine. How are you both doing with that, by the way?" Bones picked up his tablet again and began typing again.

I leaned into Anaki, and he hopped onto the exam table. "Dragons never had one. I don't know what's normal. Sometimes there is static, and sometimes, I'll hear Elena's thoughts, or see her past when I don't want to. I try not to listen or watch past memories."

Bones hummed. "Yes, dragons didn't have that sort of communication. You had emotional connections. Since you are able to speak with your dragon, and he with you, you can dig through each other's memories now. You will both need to set boundaries with each other, along with the link, and when you want to read each other's thoughts."

I bit my lip and buried my face into Anaki's chest.

Bones chuckled. "I'm guessing you both have already done something I don't need to know about."

Anaki coughed into his fist. "I can't answer that."

"Oh gods, are you reading our thoughts right now?" I slapped my hand over my mouth.

Bones laughed sadly. "No, I do not have a link. I am still not technically part of the pack."

I sat up straight. "But why? I thought with Locke and Emm doing all that stuff, you would automatically be in the pack?"

Anaki's fingers ran through my hair. "Doesn't work that way, love. His wolf is weak. He needs him to help establish a link. His wolf is too far gone. We need to get him his mate."

Again, I felt my eyes filling with tears. "Let's go then. Let's go through the town and find some women he can meet. We can't just sit here." I went to stand up, and my medical gown rode up to the top of my thighs. Anaki pulled me back onto the table, and a growl escaped his throat.

"Hold on there, you aren't going anywhere." Anaki bit down on my shoulder.

I groaned and leaned back into him.

Not cool.

Bones cleared his throat. "And with that, I will conclude this exam. I suggest you find someone to watch Luis for a couple weeks, maybe even a month, while you undergo your transformation and your, uh, heat." Bones turned his back on us and walked to the door. "Someone you trust, I know you would prefer Emm, but with her still under her depression with Abuela's death and still realizing this new role she will take on, I suggest someone else. Do you know of anyone? Perhaps Bear and Nadia? They watch Hawke and Delilah's child often."

Anaki and I looked at one another and immediately knew who would be the best.

"I think we know," I replied and gave him a small smile.

Anaki gently rested his hand on the small of my back as we descended the staircase. The bar was far less crowded than the bustling scene I recalled from my initial visit. The atmosphere had changed; there were no men perched up on the bar, gyrating energetically while women eagerly stuffed bills into their waistbands.

The music hummed softly in the background as we stepped inside, a gentle murmur of conversation could easily drown that out. Luis was instantly noticeable, perched at the bar with a generous plate of fries in front of him. The fries were a golden cascade, smothered in melted cheese, crispy bacon bits, and accompanied by a side of the special ranch sauce.

While I wanted to tell him that was completely disgusting, a little bit of junk food was okay right now.

We strolled leisurely over and took a long, careful look at everyone gathered there. The air was thick with stories of struggle and resilience, as each person bore physical marks of their bravery. Some people were still nursing severe injuries; bandages were wrapped tightly around arms and legs, while others sat with limbs in splints. They were seated at tables, deep in conversation, recounting the battles they had endured.

Bones off-handedly said some will heal faster than others, all depending on how far their animals had gone rogue or when they were rejected. Some souls' healing was down to a human's pace.

My heart ached for them, knowing they were unjustly rejected and cast aside, yet part of me couldn't help but question how they ended up in this club. They were not at fault, yet many remained angry with the goddess. I felt a powerful urge to protect them.

My jaw clenched so tightly I could almost hear the grind of my teeth, and my fist curled into a tight ball. Heat surged through my body, and beads of sweat gathered and trickled down my forehead. Suddenly, Anaki's firm grip closed around my wrist, pulling me back with a swift motion. He spun me around to meet his intense gaze.

"Hey, love, take a deep breath for me."

I grunted in reply and shook my head. "It isn't fair to them. It isn't their fault."

Anaki smiled and pulled me into his chest. He released his scent yet again. I cursed him inside my head and I could hear the most cocky laugh of Scales. *"Feisty one aren't we, soulkin?"*

I stomped my foot.

"Mama, they are going to get their chance. They have been loyal to the Fang."

"What if it's too late?" I linked.

Anaki laid his cheek on the top of my head. "Bones has a serum that helped Locke. No one is going to be put down anymore. We will figure it out, don't know how, but we will. Just keep that feisty spirit, okay?"

I hummed and pulled away to find Luis staring at us from over his shoulder. Ranch dripped at the corner of his mouth.

"Hi, mijo." I came up behind him and gave him a hug. In the process, I took one of his fries and popped it into my mouth.

Anaki sat beside him and gave him the side eye. "Enjoying your grease, so you can have better bowel movements?"

Luis shoved another fry into his mouth. "Si, I feel my gut moving as we speak. I can't wait to put a load down the only toilet in the cave."

I gasped. "Mijo, NO!"

Anaki laughed and rubbed his chin. "You know, he's right. We don't have great ventilation. I think I need to get a hold of the bear shifters and see if we can extend the cave for another bathroom while they are working on the pack house. It would be beneficial."

"The pack house? What's wrong with the pack house?" I asked, panicked.

"Destroyed." A dark-haired man said with an emphasis on the s. The man had a snake tattoo on his hand that crawled up his arm. He had been working behind the bar the night Anaki was dancing. He set down a glass of milk next to Luis and pointed to him like he was to drink it. "At least not all of it, but most. A lot of cabins were messed up, too. The bear shifters were called in to take care of it."

"This is Surkash, Madre. He's a snake shifter. Isn't that so cool?"

Anaki shuffled from side to side. "But dragons are cooler, right?"

"Of course!" Luis said, but gave an exaggerated wink to Surkash. The stoic face of the snake shifter's lip curled only slightly until he walked away.

¡Dios Mio! what did I just witness?

"I feel betrayed. We can't leave Luis alone, Elena. He might start calling Surkash dad. I can't have my title taken away from me!" Anaki pulled on my arm.

Luis barked out in laughter, and Tajah walked up behind him. "I told you it would tear Anaki up. Isn't it fun pulling pranks on people?" Tajah smiled while Beretta shook her head behind her.

"Tajah, you cannot teach the boy those kinds of tricks. Not when Anaki is still trying to fill in his new role as a father. Luis, don't play tricks like that unless we say it's okay. We can't have a cranky and emotional dragon in the bar, or he might squirt water all over the flaming shots."

Tajah snorted and slammed her hand on the bar. "That I would love to see!"

Anaki relaxed and ran his hand down his forehead. "You both are asking for it. Next time you ask for a drink, I'm putting laxatives in it. Stronger than the last time I put anything in there."

I cringed. Maybe he deserved it.

CHAPTER FORTY-ONE

Anaki

Elena stood at the mountain's edge, her eyes tracing the winding trails that snaked through the lush green valleys below. "Are you sure he's going to be okay?"

I gently lifted Elena off the back seat of my motorcycle, steadying her as she found her footing on the gravel driveway. I reached up, fingers deftly unclasping the strap that secured her helmet, lifting it to reveal her wind-tousled hair. We had just returned to Bear and Nadia's rustic cabin nestled among the towering pines back in the forest. The ride had been fun, my sleek and streamlined bike slicing through the air with ease, a far cry from the bulky machines that everyone else liked so much, which rode like big clunkers.

I don't know why everyone likes those big ones, because the smaller Kawasaki Ninja H2R was where it was at. The ladies have to hang on tight like little backpacks. Elena's tits were pressed right on my back. It was like a tease riding all the way up the mountain.

I hit every pothole I could, just to feel her chest drag up and down my body.

Would she be okay if I drove back down?

"Mama, Luis is going to be fine. In fact, I bet he won't want to come home after it's all said and done."

Luis was going to stay with Beretta and Tajah for the time being, not that he minded. Tajah and Beretta were using him for their own entertainment. He was, for all intents and purposes, their child, too.

Elena had mentioned earlier at the club about them becoming his godparents. That didn't make sense to me because how could they be godparents, they weren't gods? However, it was a human term, referring to a tradition where they would act as second parents to him.

Humans were strange in their customs, and I wouldn't question it.

As long as Surkash would not be a godfather, that was all I cared about.

Earlier, when Elena spoke with Tajah about Luis' future schooling with his magic, I pulled Surkash aside at the bar. Scales made our eyes shimmer under the dim light, casting an eerie glow in our eyes that seemed to pierce the darkness. I could feel the heat of his jealousy rising, a palpable tension that crackled in the air. With a deep, guttural snarl that resonated through the room, I asserted my presence, causing onlookers to retreat in fear.

Yes, I am a dragon.

Surkash stumbled backward, colliding with the bar behind him. The impact sent bottles toppling from their shelves, shattering on the floor with a sharp, chaotic crash that echoed through the now-silent room.

I was nose to nose with him as I whispered, "You stay away from my son. Do you understand me?"

I'll never forget the way Surkash's eyes widened, his pupils dilating in sheer terror. His scales shimmered under the dim light, and I could almost see the fear emanating from the subtle tremors that coursed through his body. A musky, sharp scent of snake pheromones wafted around him, unmistakably signaling his distress. I pictured his tail tucked tightly between his legs, had he possessed one.

I felt powerful.

"Because you are, you are a dragon. Do I need to spell it out?" I asked. I could see Scales rolling his eyes in my mind, but I ignored him.

Then Elena had to step in and calm me down. She pulled me away before I could threaten Surkash to not even look at Luis.

I didn't want any chances that my son would become too close to anyone else, until we bonded more.

Elena secured the helmet on the bike and wrapped her arm around mine. "You are thinking so loud I can hear it. Are you only worried about Luis and Surkash? He just has a thing for reptiles. He will like dragons more. You know that, right?"

I pulled Elena's hand, leading her to the path that led to the cave. "I can't help it. I've got a son, and I don't want him to like any male but me. I want to do all the things my parents didn't do for me. I want to be like one of those family dads on those TV shows in the '90s and 2000s. They were wholesome and played catch and helped their kids. I want to be a *cool* dad."

"You sound ridiculous."

Elena made a face of disgust. "You know that is TV. It isn't real. Most father figures aren't like that, and there is no perfect parent. If there were, they would make bank on a *How To* book right now."

I huffed in annoyance. "No, I understand. I want him to have a happy childhood. In the dragon clan, fledglings were passed around a lot. We were taught to be independent. I don't want him to feel alone, and now we are leaving him."

Elena stopped me and grabbed my hands. "I feel the same. Very much so, right now." She cupped my cheek with my hand. "You didn't want to be passed around like that?"

I shook my head and pouted. "Not really. I felt disconnected from my parents, but I knew they loved me. It was the culture, I later realized. Dragons are a hard species to understand, and it was because we didn't communicate well. Heats, ruts, and our transformations can be dangerous, and we just didn't talk about it much."

Elena nodded. "Luis understands that. He's been told by many. Abuela, Tajah, me, and even the other Iron Fang members. This is for his safety, and it isn't because we love him any less that we are away from him. We are a phone call away. I don't enjoy being away from him any more than you do. Did your parents not explain this to you as a child?"

I shook my head. "No. Communication is not a dragon's strong suit. That is probably why there aren't many texts about our species."

Then the goddess did us a favor by having my animal speak.

"See, having me was for your benefit."

I'm still deciding on that.

Elena moved a messy curl from my forehead. "Do you miss them? Your parents? Did you ever have a proper goodbye? That had to have been so hard."

I huffed out a breath. "Yeah, I did actually."

Elena gasped and pulled me closer. "You didn't tell me that! That wasn't part of the memory! What happened, please tell me!"

I didn't dare tell her that it would have all been in the memory we shared after the big battle, where she got all horny and wanted to jump my bones. Not that I was complaining or anything.

My parents actually saw the whole betrayal. They were so excited for me and my soulkin to get together that they secretly followed me into the forest. They did not intervene because they knew it was part of my own life journey, to do what I had to do. Destroy the male who had hurt me. I don't think they were expecting me to eat them, but nevertheless, I did. My poor mother had thrown up several times in the bushes before my father emerged from the forest and approached me. I had shifted back into my human form in a heap, and was a sobbing mess.

That night, we made camp, far from the scene of the crime, and they told me they loved me but that it was no longer safe for me to stay. My mother stayed with me while my father ran back to the clan and got me as much coin and clothing as he could carry, so I could leave. They were the ones who told me to leave the realm, all those years ago.

I'd tried my best not to think about that day, and perhaps it was good that my family and I did not have the close familial bond that most humans have with their children, for that reason alone. They cared for me, gave me what I needed, and told me they would pray to the goddess that I would be safe and would not succumb to the darkness.

I've never seen my mother cry like that before. But then, I'd never heard of a dragon rejecting their mate before me, and neither had my parents. There was always a first time for everything.

I unfortunately could never return. One for not having a mate and being a threat of losing control of my dragon and causing harm. And two, I ate people. That is a big no-no.

Yet we continue to do it...

"We do it because it's tasty."

Elena frowned as I pulled her back to the cave. Her arousal was perfuming, and I knew her heat was near. It had grown over the days, but now it was at a point where it would become uncomfortable for her. Her stress was declining, and her sorrow for Abuela was subsiding the slightest bit.

And it would become more uncomfortable for my dicks. My poor dicks were constricted in fucking compression underwear.

I ran my hand down the side of her hip and pulled her close. "My parents would be happy for me. My entire clan would," I said as I kissed her temple.

"Can we send them a letter? To let them know? Is there some sort of correspondence between realms?"

I rubbed my chin and shoved my hand into her back jean pocket. "Maybe. I could ask Bram, since he would know best. He's the all-knowing voodoo magic dude. His magic is waning, but that seems simple enough. I think that would put them at ease to know I was happy."

Elena hummed. "Or, or!" She clapped. "We could go visit them." She pointed at me and then to her nose playfully. "We could go visit them!" She said again excitedly, as she skipped down the path. "We could go! It would be so much fun, just for a couple of weeks."

She kept going on and on about how fun it would be while I shook my head. Sure, yeah, it would be fun to take her into a realm that she has never been to, but I haven't been back in ages. I didn't know what it was like there. The Royal Council could have spies watching all over the portals now. The one where I appeared in Ireland so many years ago was so small I could barely get through it.

The one near the Canadian border was still wide open, but... it was dangerous.

"Elena." I ran to catch her as she pranced up to the cave. "So, can we go? After I shift? I have to be a shifter to get in, right?"

I panted and put both of my hands on either side of her face. "As much as I would love to take you to a place you would find so magical, I think it would be best if we didn't."

She frowned. "But why? I want to see all the things."

I chuckled. "Yes, but all the things may be dangerous now. When I left, many years before most of the Iron Fang members got here, it was mostly at peace. As members started to cross, the Royal Council was taking over."

I further explained about the Council: the head supernaturals of each species who came together to discuss topics for the betterment of the realm. The creation of it was a farce. It was all about titles, who had more magical power, money, and physical power. It was barter and trade. Who were the weakest countries? The only people who benefited were the rich, while the poor suffered.

Bonds were breaking, and the practice of worshiping the goddess was ending. It was more dangerous there now.

There were a few rules that kept everyone on their toes here in the Earth Realm, and it was the minimal use of magical powers and mixtures of species. If it ever got back to the Royal Council, it would risk their coming here. We didn't want that, because wanted to stay free for as long as possible and never come up on their radar.

As far as we knew, they didn't even know that rogues crossed over and had integrated into a lot of the territories of Earth.

"Well, that's no fun." Elena pouted. "There really is no good, anywhere?"

And there may never be. There will always be evil, no matter where you go, it's just a matter of how you deal with it.

I nipped at her bottom lip. "I think I can put two good things into something really good, right now, though."

Elena gasped and slapped my chest. "Naughty dragon!"

I carefully slid my hand beneath her shirt, gently lowering the cup of her bra as we moved together. I guided her backward, expecting her to come into contact with the rough, cold surface of the cave wall. Instead, we unexpectedly stumbled into something soft, and the surprise of it caught us both off guard.

"You are out in the open, are you trying to defile her out here?" The husky voice had us both screaming like children.

I pulled Elena's shirt down and pushed her behind me.

"Not even your dragon sniffed me out; that is disappointing." The dark-cloaked figure pushed back his hood to reveal Bram's white and gray bearded face.

Scales took over my body. He made us stand up straight. "Because I don't find you threatening, old man."

I gasped, regaining control. "Oh my gosh, I'm so sorry. He did not mean that." I slapped my hand over my face.

Scales uncovered my mouth. "I most certainly did. Not even his magic could penetrate our skin with our mate bond. It's why I said nothing. Besides, I like when our mate gets embarrassed, she tastes much sweeter when she comes."

"¡Dios Mio! shut up, Scales!" Elena cried out.

CHAPTER FORTY-TWO

Elena

"*You enjoy a bit of taunting, don't you, little human?*" Scales hissed mischievously inside my mind, sending electric shivers down my spine. I swear to the goddess, my nipples practically pierced through my bra with a jolt of pleasure.

If I wasn't careful, my tits would cut right through the fabric. I have been on the edge for most of the day. I had done my best to think of other things. Like getting my son set up, and worrying about Emm. Also, about how this newly-formed pack was doing. So many people were still healing. It had only been a few days.

Now that we were deep in the forest, with Anaki's warm body so close to mine, I had let my walls down. The moment his claws raked down my chest, it was like a surge of electricity shot through me. Desire ignited within me, an overwhelming blaze that consumed every inch of my being.

I was experiencing the scorching heat I'd been warned about. It wasn't just the usual monthly pangs of ovulation, where a few good orgasms and a satisfying encounter would suffice. This was something else entirely. An insatiable craving consumed me, demanding to be filled immediately and relentlessly.

"I'm not really a human anymore. You can't call me that." I took a deep breath in and let it out slowly.

Why was Bram even here? Luis had gone back with Taja and Beretta. The second floor of their holistic, witch-crafty store held two apartments. Luis would stay with the women, while Bram had his own, and we were told he was resting.

"Your body temperature has risen, your cunt is dripping in front of another male. I'm not sure if I appreciate that," Scales taunted.

I ripped my head in the direction of Anaki's body. Anaki was speaking to Bram, but I was too busy being distracted by Scales being an idiot. *"Then, stop talking to me all growly like and maybe I won't get so turned on."*

"Ah, does my voice alone turn you on? That's good to know. You will enjoy what I have planned for you and that juicy cunt of yours when we get inside."

This fucking dragon!

"Elena, are you alright?" Anaki cupped my neck and leaned my head back with his thumb. "You're eyes are dilated and your nose is flaring. Fuck, you are burning up."

Did he not realize?

Scales chuckled darkly. *"See how I can close his nose so he can't smell you? You are all mine, human. He has no idea. He's so pathetic without me."*

"Take it back!" I said out loud.

Anaki tilted his head. "Wha—"

"Your dragon," Bram interrupted, "is taunting your mate. He wants her to fight him. Your dragon likes her sass, and he wants to fuck it out of her. She's in at the start of her heat."

Anaki sniffed around me. "I can't smell—"

"You can't smell her because he blocked your ability to. Now pay attention." He snapped his fingers at the both of us.

Anaki snarled, but Bram didn't take any offence.

"Locke had a feeling about Idris and him not being dead, so I am here to tell you in person since you will not be present during the next meeting. I am confirming to you that Idris is indeed not dead."

I wish I could say my pussy dried up like the Sahara Desert and I no longer had the pounding need in my clit, but that wasn't the case. Anaki's tail coiled smoothly up my leg, its sleek scales brushing against my skin in a gentle embrace. The tip of his tail came to rest over my crotch, like a soft, protective shield.

"Anaki, doing what you did, drowning him in the lake, did partially kill him, however." Bram stared into Anaki's eyes. "If Locke had ripped into his body with his claws we would have been one step back from ridding the damn nuisance. Trust me, Anaki, you drowning Idris has put us ahead."

Anaki's shoulders slumped in relief. "What do you mean, doing what I did helped? I didn't kill him. He's still alive?"

Bram nodded. "He's taught himself to be a necromancer. What do you think those forbidden magic beings do?"

I parted my lips. "Necromancers in video games help others come back to life. Is he doing it to himself?"

Bram smiled. "Exactly that. First, he died by fire when Journey and Grim wounded him enough at the warehouse, then you dragged him into the water to drown him."

Anaki gasped. "The elements? He's living off the elements? So, what's next? Earth and air? How the hell do we kill him with air?"

Suddenly, an agonizing cramp seized my stomach with an unforgiving grip. It was as if my insides were twisting and knotting violently, the sensation crawling from my core all the way up into my abdomen. A guttural moan escaped my lips as I doubled over, writhing in excruciating pain that threatened to consume me entirely.

"You need some good dragon cock, don't you? Fill up that greedy little cunt."

"Arrgh, shut up, Scales!"

Bram shook his head. "Shifters, you are an interesting bunch."

Scales took over Anaki's body and leaped forward to try to get a hold of Bram. He stepped away easily, and Anaki's body fell to the ground.

"I'll be going."

Bram turned sharply, causing his dark, flowing cape to sweep dramatically across the ground, whispering through the fallen leaves that carpeted the path. The fabric rustled softly, stirring the crisp, autumn-hued foliage into a gentle swirl around his feet.

I unbuttoned my jeans and shoved my hand down my pants. If I could just get off, just one quick orgasm, that would give me enough relief.

"Just a little flick, just rub one out, right here," I whispered.

That was the wrong thing to say because Scales, and it was Scales by the way Anaki's eyes were glowing, their bright blue, jumped toward me, his long tail growing longer by the second, pinned me onto my back with my hands over my head.

"No!" I cried and crossed my legs. I tried to hit the seam of the jeans, just to rub my little bean, crush it until I came and found relief.

"Your come is mine, your orgasm is mine!" Scales' nose ran up my neck, and I let out a pathetic whine.

"Yes, yes, please." I tried to push my pelvis into his raging erections.

Footsteps came closer to us, and we heard the sound, like a cork coming out of a bottle. "Pardon, I forgot to ask. Do you mind giving a sample? Female dragon come is very rare, and it would really help with complicated enchantments."

Anaki's face transformed more into the features of his dragon, more reptilian than human now. His head moved with deliberate slowness, accompanied by a growl. His entire body seemed to hum with an intense, primal energy, and my own body, driven by an insistent need, instinctively aligned itself to where the sensation was most vibrating. A deep groan escaped me as the vibration hit where I needed it most. I dug my nails into the remaining patches of skin on Anaki's back, feeling the textured surface beneath my fingertips.

"Back away, old man, before I slice you up for good." Scale's deep, guttural voice made me shiver. I pulled his head toward me and forced my tongue into his mouth. Scales groaned, his cocks pushed against me.

"Take off my pants, please," I begged.

Bram tapped the glass with his finger above us. "Just a bit? I swear I would not use it for my own pleasure, just for magic. That's all."

Anaki tore himself away from my lips, rising to his full, towering height with a fierce growl. His shirt shredded into pieces, unable to contain the explosive transformation into his dragon form. His cocks, exposed in their full glory, dripped with come.

He was one angry, horny dragon.

Ugh, why isn't he paying attention to me?

I snarled. "Anaki, Scales, I need you, please!" I rolled over to my stomach and crawled toward him. I didn't care if I looked like a desperate horny, feral cat, I was going to get what I needed.

It was only natural in a state like this, right?

Bram brought up his hands in surrender. "Come on now, easy there. This is for the need of the club, for protection."

"Fool, how dare you test me?" Scales circled Bram like a predator sizing up its prey

This was why men didn't live as long. They asked dumb questions, did dumb things. It apparently went across both species, both human and supernatural.

I cried out and clutched my stomach as I trembled. I kicked at my jeans. So hot, I was so damn hot. I needed all of these clothes off. Bram was going to get a view.

As soon as I felt the cooler air hit my bare legs, my pussy fluttered in relief. Arousal coated down my leg when my mate growled again.

Damn, that growl would have me chest down and ass up in a second.

"Female," Scales snarled and left Bram in an instant. He surrounded me, coiled his body around mine, and pushed me up on all fours. I groaned, my body hot, and I pushed my shirt and bra off as I tried to steady myself.

Scales' nose forced its way between my legs, and I felt the big suction of wind soak up the scent of my arousal. "Mmm, you are in heat. My sweet female, this is my time to impregnate you."

My body shivered in anticipation. "Quit talking about it and hurry up!"

Scales let out a deafening roar, his dragon form fully unfurled as he wrapped his tail around me, pulling me closer. He positioned himself behind me, his shaft throbbing and pressing against my entrance. I could feel the power radiating from him, the animalistic desire, and I couldn't help but be drawn to it.

"One cock to start, then the other," his voice trembled with excitement. "Take what I give you."

I arched my back, my eyes closed, ready to receive, but then my eyes burst open at realization. I'm about to take dragon dick.

"That isn't going to fit!" I screamed and tried to crawl away.

Scales chuckled darkly and wrapped his tail around my ankle to pull me back. "You cannot escape me. Your male is about to breed you. Don't you want to sate your heat?"

"Not when you break me in half! Let me talk to Anaki!"

Scales continued to drag me in the dirt and leaves, pulling me toward the entrance of the cave. "He cannot save you now. He is blinded by lust.

Ready to fill that greedy cunt. If he's lucky, I'll let him take over when I need a break, and you can use that double-headed dildo he had delivered as a surprise for you both."

Oh gods!

Scales relentlessly dragged me through the rough dirt, and I welcomed every scratch and bump with increasing ecstasy. When he roughly flipped me onto my back, I pinched my nipples hard, savoring the pain. The icy cave floor, slick with moisture, sent a shockwave through me, making me cry out with a mix of agony and pleasure.

"Goddess, stop teasing."

Scales groaned, watching me all the while. His cocks bobbed and continued to leak an absorbent amount of come, as he backed his way into the tent. His eyes never left my body while he dragged me in and tossed me to the bed.

He circled me, like I was his prey now.

And I really, really liked it.

"Look at the mess you made." His nose flared. "Your slick has dripped down your thigh and onto the nest. I did not give you permission."

His tongue licked up my thigh, cleaning me of my slick. Only more came from me, the more he touched, the more my body heated.

"I can't take it, please." I rolled over and the first thing that came to mind was to give him a view of my ass.

"Mm hmm, you are ready to be bred, aren't you, sweet female? Showing me your slit, dripping and wet for me. Look at those folds." His large, clawed hand gripped my thighs and pulled them apart, much wider. His tongue slipped between my folds, then up between my cheeks. "You can take me, we've bonded. Don't worry about that. I won't hurt what is mine."

Yeah, I wasn't worried anymore. All I felt was empty. He could rip me open and I wouldn't give a rat's ass.

"Tell me, soulkin, tell me you want your dragon's cock to fill you." His cock prodded my entrance, the head large and pulsing against my clit.

I pushed against him. He growled, and that growl alone made more slick travel down my leg.

"Give me your words, soulkin. Tell me you want my seed to fill your womb, fill your belly with my fledgling."

I fisted the covers.

"P-please. Please fill me," I whined.

Both of his claws held my hips, his massive body hovering over mine. "Speak, Female. Tell me you want this giant, dragon dick."

"Give me that giant dragon dick and fill me up until I feel it in my throat!" I screamed.

He hummed. "Close enough."

With an overwhelming, primal force, Scales drove himself deep within me, eliciting a cry that tore through the air—a raw, unrestrained expression of ecstasy. The sheer, untamed power of this male consumed me entirely.

"Fuck yes," I moaned, my body writhing beneath him. "Fuck me harder, dragon., Fill me!"

Scales' growls became louder with each passing moment, his grip on my hips tightening as he surged forward again and again. The air was thick with the scent of our lust, my body coated in a sheen of sweat as he used my pussy. My breaths came fast and shallow, each one filled with the sound of Scales' feral grunts. His scales and my skin slapped together.

"I'm going to breed you," Scales snarled, his voice rough with need. "I'm going to fill you full of dragon cock until you're bursting at the seams."

The thought sent waves of pleasure coursing through my body, and my core clenched around his shaft in response. "Yes," I whispered hoarsely. "Breed me hard, make me your fuck toy."

My words seemed to be the catalyst Scales needed, for he began to thrust even more furiously into me. His tail wrapped around my waist tighter, holding me close as he slammed into my core again and again. The sensation was overwhelming, but I welcomed it, craved it, as wave after wave of pleasure crashed over me.

"I'm going to come," I gasped, the excitement building within me like an uncontrollable force. "I'm going to come all over your cock."

Scales roared again, his thrusts becoming erratic, in their intensity. "Yes, give me your pleasure," he growled lowly into my ear. "There are higher chances of conceiving if the female is satisfied."

His hand reached around and grabbed my breast. "And I shall satisfy you to ensure you carry our young."

CHAPTER-FORTY THREE

Anaki

While Scales took control, every nerve in my body was electrified with want. I was consumed by an insatiable hunger for her, a desperate craving that left me paralyzed at what to do with her heat. I was thankful that Scales handled the conversation, because I sat in the back of my dragon's mind, utterly overwhelmed.

Her body, her intoxicating scent, her absolute submission to us had me salivating uncontrollably, my senses overwhelmed.

I didn't want to mess up.

My dragon knew what to do, and while I was annoyed and still trying to comprehend my animal having a voice, I was grateful now for him.

"Do you see this perfect ass. Her hips were made for breeding. Look at her."

Damnit, he was addressing me now, too? The audacity! I could feel the searing heat radiating from her, the electrifying touch of her skin with every deliberate thrust he made into her cunt. He wanted to attempt the impossible—trying to ravage her with both of our dicks. It was destined for failure, but he was relentless in his determination.

"No, it's not going to fit. We can't hurt her."

But my body wasn't mine right now to control. The sick part of me wanted it to work, to shove our second cock into that perfect pussy, to impregnate her even if the chances were so slim. It could take centuries to impregnate her. Sperm count was low for dragons, did he not know that?

He hummed and prodded his declawed finger along the cock that was in her hot pussy. She automatically pushed against him, trying to welcome the extra stretch. Her body was accepting, thank the goddess, and it was only because of the bite that was slowly changing her.

"Mmm, more," she moaned, as more of her arousal gushed from her.

Fucking hell, that was the hottest thing I've ever seen. It wasn't a squirt; it was continuous fluid, like her body knew we were there to impregnate her.

Scales let out a deep guttural growl. His patience had worn thin. Mine had, too, as I scraped at the surface. I could smell her, feel everything that Scales did.

Was this a rut?

Scales shoved another declawed finger into her. Immediately, panic rose inside me when I thought I saw blood. Instead, Elena groaned and cried out as we felt her pussy tighten around us and nearly had us spill our seed.

"You're ready, sweet female. Ready to take both of our cocks and fill you to the brim."

Our hearts pounded, excitement ran through our bodies, as he pulled our fingers away and brought them to our mouth. The taste of her arousal was ten times sweeter. Our cock slipped from her body, and she cried out in protest.

"No, please don't." She turned her body, her big brown eyes looking up at us pleadingly.

My voice came to the surface as Scales grabbed his cocks and situated her more comfortably on the pillows. "Shh, love, it's okay. We are gonna put both our cocks in you and take the pain away. Make you feel real good," I whispered.

Her ass was in the air, and she sighed in relief. "Anaki, so you're still there?"

Scales flinched, and our hand ran up and down her body as he said, "Anaki is here, I am here. Always. Do you not trust me to help you with your heat?"

Elena shook her head. "No, I want you both here. It's hard, and I'm scared. I don't know what's happening to me."

"Shh," I cooed, and Scales let me take control of our body to pick her up. Her body was hot, and I felt her tense when another cramp made her contort in on herself. "It's okay to be scared, your body is changing into something beautiful and different. It craves me and it makes me so hard, and makes me feel wanted."

Elena panted. "It does. You don't find it weird? It's just—"

"No, love. It's hot, I like it when you get all needy. Haven't you noticed I'm needy? I want to touch you all the time. Scales just wants to fuck you."

"Not true. I want these cuddles as well," he snapped.

Elena leaned into me, the tips of her nipples hard as she rubbed up against our scales. "I trust you both. I'm not myself, I want... everything. To be filled, and fucking defiled. And by a dragon, no less. That is not normal."

"This is our normal." I slid her down my body, so her pussy sat on my cocks. "And no one can tell us different."

Scales' fingers grazed her clit as he whispered, "Let us take care of that need, Elena. Let us show you what it means to be loved by a dragon."

She shivered at the touch, a delicate tremor coursing through her body as her eyes fluttered shut, lashes casting shadows on her cheeks. Her hips began to rock gently against him, a movement born of instinct rather than intention. Our cocks throbbed in unison, a silent plea for entrance. With deliberate slowness, I guided our other hand to her face, letting a finger glide down the soft curve of her cheek. It paused at her lips, teasing them apart with a gentle nudge before I whispered in a low, inviting tone, "Open up for us, love."

Elena complied, wide eyes darting between us as she took our finger in her mouth. Her tongue danced along the tip while a soft whimper escaped her lips. We moaned in delight, our hands gripping the back of her head, as we thrust our finger deeper and deeper into her welcoming mouth.

Scales chuckled lowly, "See? You do trust us. You don't want this to stop." He leaned in to whisper in her ear, "I want to come in your greedy little mouth."

Our cocks twitched and a surge of desire shot through me at the thought of our dragon seed being swallowed within Elena's body. "Fuck yes!" I growled, imagining my appendage filling her throat.

Elena's eyes widened in surprise at my response, but she quickly recovered, focusing on the task at hand. We didn't stop stroking and fucking her pussy with our fingers as she lowered her head onto one of our shafts. She did the best she could, licking the engorged head, trying to suck it into her mouth.

She increased her pace, sucking and bobbing on the top cock as she stroked the base of them both with her hands. The sensation was overwhelming—I knew it wouldn't be long before we lost control.

"That's it..." Scales panted, his voice rough with desire. "Take what you want from us. Show us how much you crave these cocks."

Her body stiffened and her pussy gripped our finger as she orgasmed.

With a renewed vigor, Elena sucked harder while stroking faster, causing us both to groan loudly. Her eyes locked onto ours as she eagerly accepted more and more, her jaw dislocating just like it would be able to in her dragon form.

"Fuuuuck," Scales and I gasped, barely able to keep still amidst the chaos of sensations coursing through us. "Are you ready for them?"

Her response was muffled by my cock but clear enough: "Yes! Give them to me."

Instead of letting us finish in her mouth, we moved our hips away from her and turned her body. We couldn't waste our seed, not now, not when she was ripe. We set her up on all fours to shove it into her womb.

"Oh, fuck... fuck... fuck!" We cried out simultaneously as we slowly pushed our fully lubricated cocks into her pussy at the same time.

Elena screamed as they mercilessly stretched her, her body yielding to their relentless invasion. She came hard, her pussy convulsing around their tips. They weren't even fully inside her, and she was already pushing them to their limits, her body demanding more than they were prepared to give. Her climax was a storm, a brutal test of our control, as she writhed and bucked against them.

More. We wanted more.

Our body convulsed violently as we pushed forward, her slit convulsed as it tried to milk the seed from our shafts. Our tail whipped around the bed, disturbing the nest she had made.

Again Elena cried, trying to push more of herself onto us while we flooded her with our hot seed, filling every nook and cranny within that tight pussy until there was nothing left but blissful oblivion.

"Mmm, you take us so well. Look how wide that pussy stretched," Scales groaned as he grabbed her hips. He pushed and pulled her body on and off our cocks. I could see our cocks swell and her pussy pulse. Her lips stretched wide around us. "Rub your clit, give us one more orgasm, and suck our seed right into your womb. Fill you up so good."

Our chests heaved as a primal vibration surged down to our abdomen and culminated in a throbbing urgency within our cocks. Her screams pierced the air, and we seized her, impaling her on our shafts with a feral intensity. We unleashed a torrent of seed into her, claiming her with each pulsating jet. We gripped her stomach possessively, feeling it swell with our invasive presence, our essence flooding her completely.

Great satisfaction filled me as she mewled and grabbed her breasts as we filled her.

We didn't stop there. We continued to fill her until it spilled from her slit.

We couldn't stop, we continued to pump into her, as she clawed at the sheets below, moaning and writhing with pleasure. Her eyes rolled back in her head as she came again, her pussy pulsing around our cocks in rhythm with her orgasm.

We grunted and groaned, feeling the ecstasy building within us once more. The sensation of her pussy clamping down on our cocks was unlike anything we had ever experienced before, and it only served to drive us closer to another wave of release.

"Fuck, you feel like heaven," Scales gasped, his voice strained with desire. "I'm gonna fill you up again."

As we neared our breaking point, we slowed our movements slightly, savoring the feel of her tight pussy, milking us for every drop of seed. Her moans and whimpers filled the room, urging us on as she begged for more.

Suddenly, a surge of intensity washed over us both, and we knew we were about to reach our climax again. From our last release, she was so wet, so full, we slid in and out of her effortlessly.

We thrust deep into Elena one last time before unloading our seed deep inside her. Our body shook as wave after wave of pleasure washed over us, filling her with our essence.

"Yes, female. Take all of me," Scales cried out as he spilled his seed into her. "I'm going to fuck this pussy so much that just at the sight of my cocks will have you ready."

Elena slowly pumped her hips back. "More," she panted. "I need more."

She just came like three times. How much more?

Scales panted. It was his body we were exhausting. I was just along for the ride, not that I was complaining. *"She's in heat. This could go for days."*

Oh, well, I'm here for that.

Two days of hot, sweaty sex.

I didn't know there were so many positions, but here we were, and I didn't know that Elena would want to peg me while she was in heat, but she did. I had fully gone into my rut as well at the same time, which I guessed was normal.

I'd been as hard as stone.

Scales was exhausted. He had passed out in the back of my mind for hours, and it was nice not to hear him telling me what to do. It was just Elena and me, and letting her do whatever she wanted to do with my body was hot as fuck.

She had my hands tied above my head to a circle hook I used to hold back the curtains in the tent. She had my legs spread, and was currently licking my nipples. She liked to pull the nipple rings, and hell, I was leaking so much come, I was surprised my balls hadn't completely shriveled up.

Bear and Nadia had dropped off food the past few days. It was the only way we had survived. When Elena slept, I ate what I could, and then when Elena woke up, I fed her with my tail while I ate her out.

She was insatiable.

Thankfully, she did sleep. It wasn't for long, and it wasn't a surprise when I would wake up to her sucking my cocks trying to get it ready for her.

Elena was in a playing and edging stage of the heat. She would suck my cock, my nipples, then ride me before I came and get herself off before she would suck me dry with her mouth and deny me filling her pussy.

That would upset the primal part of me, making me break free of my bindings and fuck her into the mattress like an animal.

She loved it when I would go feral for her in my human form.

"Maybe I should get my nipples pierced?" She nipped at my ear. "You can pull on them like I do yours, too, huh?" I whimpered when she lined up her pussy against the head of one of my cocks. Her slit fell onto the head and I gasped.

I whined. "Please, I want both of them inside you."

She giggled and sank a little deeper. "Do you think you deserve both of them inside me?"

I nodded eagerly and tugged on the restraints, knowing full well I could pull them from the wall. "Yes, I helped you with your heat. I made you come a lot."

Elena sunk fully onto my cock and we both gasped. "You are right, you did. You also got to come a lot, too, didn't you? Filled me up so good, trying to get me pregnant."

I leaned forward and rubbed my face into her neck, letting my scent cover her.

"Please, please, Mama, fuck me with both. I'll be your good dragon."

Elena ran her fingers through my hair and tugged. The sting felt so damn good.

"I know you will be a good dragon. You are always my good little dragon."

I smiled and bit my lip.

"Now, suck my tit and I'll give you what you want."

Oh goodie!

I greedily sucked her nipple into my mouth as she lined up my second cock with her pussy. She bounced vigorously and I sucked harder. I swore the harder I sucked, the sweeter it tasted. I groaned and pulled at the restraints. I wanted to hold her closer to me. She still felt too far away.

"Damn, I'm going to come already." She pushed her breast forward and smashed my face into her chest. I pulled on the soft restraints, the fabric that kept me tightened, ripped and fell around me, and I wrapped my arms around her.

I hummed, and sucked the other breast. "Yes, come on my cock, love," I mumbled around her tit. "Please, please!"

She threw her head back. "Ugh, it's so hot when you beg." She slammed down on my cock once more and let out a strangled cry. Her body tried to lift up again, but I flipped her over onto her back and rutted her into the mattress. "More, please more!"

And I gave her more.

I gave her so much that I came in her twice more before I stopped. My body depleted of everything in me, hovered over her and planted kisses up her neck until I reached her mouth.

"I love you. Fuck, I love you so much."

Her hands ran through my hair, and my chest purred along with hers. More excitement built through me, and I wanted to make love to her all over again. Every day, something new was happening to her. Another step closer to her becoming a dragon.

I wasn't going to be the only water dragon anymore, and it excited me to no end.

"I love you, too, Anaki, and Scales." She giggled when a deep growl resonated through my throat. "Love you both, so, so much. Thank you for helping me with this heat. I think it's almost over." She yawned. "I'm getting more tired now."

I buried my face into her neck and peppered kisses down to her mark.

It was unlikely, but I wouldn't tell her that yet.

"Let me wash and feed you. Then we can get you to sleep."

She groaned and shook her head. "No, I will sleep here. I can't move. I think my lady parts are broken."

My cocks, which were still buried inside her, begged to differ. They were still clenched by her vagina vacuum and there was no sign of her letting us go.

I needed some fluids.

"Just a small nap. Then, I'll clean you up. How about that, love?" I trailed a finger down her face her eyes fluttered and she nodded.

My soulkin was out before I could say another word, my cocks still inside her with no signs of her letting me go.

Not that I minded. I got to keep her forever.

CHAPTER FORTY-FOUR

Elena

A guttural scream tore from my throat as my chest heaved and expanded grotesquely. It felt as though my ribcage was shattering from within, each cracking bone a new torment. I howled, my voice raw and desperate. My spine stretched unbearably, each vertebra popping and snapping as if rebelling against me.

Previously, relief from my heat pain came through orgasms, semen, and Anaki's touch. But now, I found myself in a state of agony that nothing could alleviate. It felt as if my body was falling apart in the most dreadful way imaginable.

"It's alright, love, you got this," Anaki's soothing voice, meant to be comforting, was anything but.

I snarled, a voice not of my own snapped at the one person who had always been kind.

"I'm sorry!" I cried out, collapsing into the dirt. The earth felt cool against my skin, which was now covered in hardened, light pink scales. The damper the soil, the better it felt, and I found myself inching ever closer to the lake.

Anaki edged closer, disregarding my sharp remarks. Dressed only in his boxer briefs, he reached out to seize my arm. I tried to pull back, but he maintained his grip and drew me into his embrace. "It hurts, love, I know. Just know I'm here."

I panted heavily, my breath coming in ragged gasps as my body stiffened in his arms, a tension overtaking me. My legs straightened out with a sudden, uncontrollable force, and before my eyes, they transformed, sprouting sleek, glistening fins. Blood gushed down my legs in a warm, crimson stream that painted my tanned skin. I squeezed my eyes shut, overwhelmed by the intensity.

"It's alright, don't look. Just stay with me." Anaki turned my head away.

"This is worse than labor. Oh goddess, fuck! Why does it hurt so bad?" I grabbed onto Anaki's arm. My fingers had sprouted claws, not of my own volition, and pierced his skin. He didn't say anything. He only winced as his scales gathered around the wound to try to protect himself.

"It's almost over. You've broken almost every bone, and soon you will shift. I know it's slow going. You are doing so well. It won't be like this every time."

Static fizzled in my head, and I heard Locke's voice come in, clear as day. *"Is she dying? Emm is about to have a damn conniption, and I can't keep her away for much longer."*

I cried out again when I felt my ass damn near explode, then heard a thump as something hit the ground. When I looked back, a long tail had emerged, pale-pink with a white, feathery fin.

"I just shit out a tail!" I whined.

Anaki held his lips in a pursed, thin line, trying not to laugh. "Let's get you in the water, it will cool you off, and make this better."

"Alpha, Elena is fine. She's in the final stages. I'll keep you updated."

Locke groaned on the other end. *"Be quick, my Luna is getting fucking antsy and I can only keep my dick in her mouth for so long to keep her quiet."*

I tried to laugh, but my jaw dislocated, and I winced.

Anaki picked me up. "Easy, easy. That's it. Let's get you in the water, and the rest of these clothes off of you." I closed my eyes again and let him do his will with me.

Anaki ripped the rest of the clothes off me, which were nothing but strips of cloth. He took me deeper into the water, and my body was almost completely submerged except for my head. I felt tiny pinpricks over my body as the scales covered me. Anaki was shifting, too, and I felt his chest rumble in comfort.

Scales' voice came out, and he hummed. "You're changing, look. You are no longer my little human."

As I gazed down at my transformed self, my skin shimmered with a stunning, pale-pink hue that seemed almost otherworldly, interlaced with ethereal, white iridescent tones that danced across the surface like sunlight on water. My fins, more like delicate, translucent feathers than traditional fins, gracefully extended behind my legs and adorned the top of my tail and its tip, adding an elegant flair to my silhouette. Although I couldn't glimpse my own face, the sight of my body was nothing short of breathtaking. It was a vision of feminine grace and serpentine elegance, as if this exquisite form had been crafted precisely for me, perfectly embodying my essence rather than requiring me to adapt to it.

I swished my tail, and I cut effortlessly through the shimmering water like a blade through silk. Anaki had released me, and I was now swimming independently, feeling the thrill of freedom coursing through me. I continued in a graceful circle, observing how my body naturally buoyed and flowed. Each muscle rippled beneath my skin, scales glinting in the dappled sunlight, and fins fluttering harmoniously, as if I were a part of the water itself.

And most importantly, the pain was gone!

Dios Mio.

"You're beautiful," Scales and Anaki said simultaneously.

I stared at them and then touched my face with my webbed, clawed hands.

Could I speak, too? Did I have a voice inside me?

"I..." I said, and then a giggle rose in my throat. "I can talk like this, too?" I sat up and rubbed my chest. I was in control, all of it. "What about... do I have a voice inside me, too? Like you have Scales?"

Anaki swam closer to me. His body circled mine, and he intertwined our tails. "I've spoken to the other mated members about this while you have been sleeping. There is a pattern with humans that gain animals. It can take time for them to speak. It is like they are born within you. They are understanding the world around them. Give her time, she will speak soon, then she will never shut up."

"*Hey,*" Scales said. "*I am relatively quiet. I only speak when deemed necessary. Like to correct you.*"

We both rolled our eyes. Our bodies continued to coil around each other on the surface of the water.

I heard footsteps from the shoreline, and my head perked up. Anaki chuckled and shook his massive head. "I knew they wouldn't stay away for long."

When we both turned our heads, there was a small crowd. Luis, Tajah, Beretta, Bear, Nadia, Locke, and Emmie all stood on the shoreline. Everyone was smiling, Luis was on his tiptoes with a camera in his hand and Emmie looked like she really had been sucking cock somewhere in the woods; her hair was a mess.

"What... what is going on?" I tilted my head and held onto Anaki tighter.

I hadn't seen anyone in almost four weeks. It was odd seeing everyone gathered, and to be honest, I was ready to see them, but I wasn't sure if I was ready to be seen, like this. A dragon.

I wasn't the same person anymore. I wasn't a weak, sickly human. I had undergone a change that stretched myself hormonally and physically. I had become extremely possessive since the bonding and the heat, and I couldn't let Anaki out of my sight for a long while.

I called Luis almost every day after my heat. We video called constantly, and I missed him so much, but the thought of even my son touching Anaki brought feelings of horrible jealousy. I would never hurt my son, but it made me feel like a terrible mother that I didn't want him to be near the only father figure he has never had.

Nadia and Bones' video called as well, trying to help explain my feelings, that it was normal for shifters to be possessive. However, they hadn't had a child before meeting their mate, and while it was normal to be possessive, I shouldn't have been so possessive as to keep my own child away. It was a new guilt that I would carry with me for a long time.

Now that I had my dragon, I didn't feel as possessive. Maybe it was because I felt like I was more of Anaki's equal, that I was a dragon, and good enough for him.

Which was a silly thought, but... who knew with these dragon's hormones, thoughts, and desires that ran through me.

"Better now, right?" Anaki rubbed his head close to my cheek. I half purred, half growled as he did so and nodded.

I swallowed heavily. "I was so scared. I don't know why I was so obsessed with you. I was scared to share you. I felt so—"

Anaki chuckled, a deep, resonant sound that seemed to vibrate the air around us. His long, serpentine tongue slithered up my neck with a slow, deliberate motion, leaving a trail of warmth in its wake. "Again, natural.

That is why I told you it was best we spend time away from everyone. Now that you have your dragon, things will be much better."

Luis jumped up and down by the shoreline. "Madre! Hurry up! We need your picture for the bar!"

Anaki perked his head up. "Yes! I can put our picture up on the bar now, just like the other mated couples I have up there." He pulled me along so I didn't have to swim. I laughed as he swam so quickly. Waves pushed up onto the shoreline as we crawled up onto the sandy shore.

Anaki nudged me further onto land. "Quickly, come on, love. We have to pose. Luis, get in here. This is a family picture."

Luis screamed and tried to run over, before Tajah ran forward and grabbed him by the shoulder. "Is that wise?"

I snarled and stood up on two legs. "Give me my son!"

Everyone stood back, and Luis beamed at me. "See, she's fine." He moved his shoulder away from Tajah and ran up to me. I lowered myself to all fours, and his little arms tried to wrap around my torso.

"Madre, you have two hearts now. I hear them thumping all crazy!"

I tilted my head and gazed up at Anaki.

He smiled, showing his bright white teeth. "Yes, two now. It's why your chest hurt so much." He came closer to me and linked. *I'm so jealous of your hearts right now, because they are pounding inside of you and I'm not.*

I gasped and blinked in surprise.

"You're terrible."

Locke cleared his throat. "Smile for the camera."

Instead of looking straight into the camera, I nuzzled under Anaki's neck, and he rested his head on mine.

Once the picture was over, Emm sauntered over and put her hands on her hips. "Well, look at you. You became some bad-ass bitch, didn't you? Don't think I can't whoop your ass." She nudged me with her elbow.

I huffed in annoyance and lowered my head to whisper. "Yeah, we will see about that. I think I got you beat in the sex department this time. Instead of lycan dick, I can take two dragon dicks."

Emm's eyes widened and stared at Anaki. "No, damn way. Are you serious?" She looked at Anaki and then between his legs to look for his slit. I growled and stood in front of him.

"Keep your eyes away from him," I snarled.

Locke came behind Emm and kissed her on the shoulder. "Easy there, princess. You want two dicks? I'll get a mold of mine and shove it in you at the same time. How about that?" He ran his hand down her stomach and cupped her pussy.

I groaned and turned away. I tripped when I got closer to Anaki, and he used his body to prop me up.

"Love, I'm going to show you how to shift back, it's been too long. Then, we are gonna go feed you."

Once shifted back, we found ourselves in the cozy warmth of Bear and Nadia's cabin. I was sprawled out on the plush couch, my head resting comfortably in Anaki's lap. The soft glow of the fireplace painted the room in a warm, flickering light. Luis was sitting cross-legged on the wooden floor, carefully feeding me. Anaki watched Luis with a discerning eye, ensuring that he offered me a generous serving of freshly cooked fish and vegetables.

Anaki was a stickler about the food I should be eating.

My eyes were on the verge of closing, but I wanted desperately to stay awake to see everyone. It wasn't because I was lonely staying in the cave with Anaki for a month, but this pack had watched my son, and I was grateful to them. I wanted to show my appreciation.

We also missed a lot while we were gone. Anaki might have reached out, through the link or a phone call or two, to find out what was going on, but I was still very much behind.

The pack had been established, mainly by mated couples. There were a few single shifters who were able to join with a link but were still on the watch list. The only reason they were able to join was that they had only recently been rejected.

More prospects were being admitted into the pack. Those who had proven themselves in the battle with Idris were instantly approved. Where Idris was currently, no one was sure. The mansion on the East Coast was empty, and now that Idris knew where we resided, we would have to be more vigilant. We were pack now. We had an Alpha and a Luna, and we were stronger; we were what Idris didn't want us to become.

That didn't mean he was weak, however. Far from it; he was desperate now, and Switch had all eyes and ears open on the web. Even searching the dark web in a hunt for any bounties that he may put out, like he did for Emm to out Locke .

So far, there was nothing, fortunately or unfortunately, depending how you wanted to look at it.

"The bear shifters are ready to work on your cave, Anaki, if you are willing to stay here at Bear and Nadia's for a few days while they fix it up. They might put a scent-clearing bomb inside to clear the stench."

I growled lowly, but everyone ignored me.

Anaki waved his hand in dismissal. "That's fine. I will go retrieve our bedding and things I don't want touched and bring them here. Are you guys fine with that?" Anaki turned to Bear and Nadia. "I don't want to take her to the bar apartments."

Nadia shook her head. "We would love to have you here! I'd like to check both of your mental health if that's okay. You both have been through a lot. I'd also like to check on you, Elena. Any weakness? Pain?"

I shook my head. My cheeks turned pink. "No. No pain at all."

Nadia smiled widely and clapped her hands together in excitement. "Wonderful. I had a feeling. Sorry to ask so openly, it's just great news. Abuela felt so guilty about that."

I sat up on the sofa and lifted an eyebrow. "What do you mean?"

Nadia came over and sat beside me. "Abuela told me in private that she wanted to cure you, but it would cost her too much manna, and she had to save it to hide all of you. She felt so guilty she didn't have enough stores to rid you of your illness." Nadia brushed back a wet tendril of hair from my forehead.

I gave her a solemn smile. "That didn't even cross my mind," I told her. "I wouldn't expect someone to heal me. It was my own sickness, just dealt a bad hand. Just because someone has magic doesn't mean they owe me anything to heal me."

Tajah's brows furrowed. "No magical entity would have been able to cure you, Elena. It would take an extreme amount of manna, a very powerful entity, to do such a thing. Not even my manna stores could touch you. It would take potions, enchantments, and the cost of those would be far too great. All magic comes at a price. The pain would be gone, but another ailment could have replaced it."

We were silent for a time as I pondered her words. Tajah didn't know what Abuela was capable of, and I needed to keep it that way. I was sure Nadia didn't really know what she was talking about, unless Abuela purposely let that slip. I believed that Abuela could have helped me, but keeping us protected was what was more important.

Besides, being with Anaki was what healed me. I didn't need her magic. Locke settled himself onto the plush, inviting cushion of the La-Z-Boy rocking chair. Emm followed and nestled comfortably onto Locke's lap. His fingers gently traced through her hair, each stroke soothing and deliberate, while she instinctively snuggled closer, seeking warmth and solace in his embrace. "Speaking of Abuela and her abilities to protect us. The running and hiding are over for our family."

Luis giggled and pushed another forkful of food into my mouth. Anaki high-fived him and pointed to the plate to get another scoop of food.

"Wait, what?" I pressed. "What do you mean?"

Emm smirked and ran her finger across the rim of the glass of wine she was drinking. "Our sperm donor is dead, and most of the cartel's men. We are no longer in hiding, and we can expect them to leave us the hell alone." She winced. "Sorry, mijo."

Luis stood up. "That's twenty bucks in the cursing jar!"

Emm cursed again.

"Forty!"

Locke snickered. "The jar is back at the bar, and I swear, to the fucking goddess, there has got to be a grand in it by now."

"Twenty!" Luis laughed.

Journey put her hand on her hip. "Serves you all right. There are children at the bar now. Soon, Deliah's baby is going to be talking, and she would be so upset if her baby's first word was something bad."

Grim chuckled and rubbed his beard. "That would be funny as fuck." We all stared at him. "Aw, dammit."

Anaki threw his head back and laughed, then pulled me closer.

That may have been the most unconventional family dynamic I had ever encountered, but it was really, really growing on me.

EPILOGUE

Anaki

I jumped down from the bar, my chest soaked with sweat. The place was bustling tonight, and I was relieved that my shift had finally ended.

I wasn't going home alone now, I had my soulkin waiting for me, with our son tucked away in his own section of the cave.

He had been attending school with Tajah and Bram. Now that his powers had awakened, and Elena and I knew what sort of power Luis held, we knew it wouldn't be wise to send him to regular school.

Besides, the children who grow up in the Iron Fang wouldn't be normal either. They would need to be taught here in their early years, to know they were different and to keep themselves hidden until they knew their strength. This was for their sake and for the safety of the humans.

In a few short weeks, Luis went from snapping his fingers to create fire to wielding it and throwing fireballs. This concerned Bram at first, but Luis' ability to control it in such a short amount of time put him at ease.

Bram would continue to keep us updated on Luis' progress without letting the others know of his strength. We would still worry about Luis' future and safety, especially with a power that would be greater than Abuela's ever was.

Pushing my way through the throng of bodies in the packed bar, I caught fragments of heated conversations about the alarming attacks on the fringes of the Iron Fang territory. Idris' rogues, along with those outcasts expelled from the club, were growing dangerously audacious, brazenly invading our land without a shred of fear or concern for the imminent retribution.

We didn't know if Idris was behind these rogues, trying to make us feel trapped, or if these beings were doing it on their own.

Tajah's ward around the territory kept us safe, and our families could roam freely within, but there were always shifters and prospects taking shifts now. It brought the normalcy of what a pack should be to protect our land, at least, to the wolves who were used to pack life.

Lately, Locke and Emm had been on edge. There had been attacks of hybrids, fifty to a hundred miles away from town. With still limited resources, we hadn't been able to travel to check it out ourselves, but word had gotten around that humans had seen creatures they couldn't describe. Half human, half animal with fangs, fur, and claws. Old legends like Bigfoot, Moth man, vampires, werewolves, and other unexplainable phenomenon that humans used to obsess about resurfaced because of these disturbances.

Were these the Idris hybrids?

All of that brought on worry that the Royal Council would get involved and bother us here in the Earth Realm. Or would they even care? They had their own realm to bother and to rule? I thought the latter.

I grabbed my jacket and slung it over my shoulder.. I didn't do clean up much anymore, not when I had a family to go home to. Surkash nodded at me when I made for the back of the bar to leave.

Sizzle sat hunched over his beer, the amber liquid barely touched, as he gazed across the dimly lit bar. His eyes rolled with a mix of boredom and envy, watching as the rest of the inner circle entwined with their partners, sharing whispered secrets and stolen kisses. He fiddled with the unlit cigarette between his fingers, tapping it rhythmically on the weathered wooden bar, as if weighing the decision to light it or not. Eventually, he stuffed the cigarette back into his jacket pocket with a resigned sigh and tilted his head back, draining his drink in one swift motion. With a heavy exhale, he pushed himself away from the bar, the stool scraping against the floor, and strode toward the exit, his pace slow and deliberate as he headed for the door.

Bones sat by the door, the chair tipped back on two legs, his gaze fixed on nothing in particular. His eyes were dull, like glass marbles. Slowly, he leaned forward, the chair legs thudding softly onto the floor. His hand disappeared into his worn leather jacket, fingers searching with a practiced motion. A faint rustle of fabric was followed by the emergence of a syringe, its barrel glinting faintly in the dim light.

I adjusted my jacket, pulling the collar up against my cheek as I watched him from a distance. With a quick glance around to ensure no one was watching, Bones removed the cap from the syringe and carefully rolled up the sleeve of his worn-out hoodie. His hand trembled slightly as he discreetly jabbed the needle into his leg. He lowered his head, his face contorting briefly in pain, and then he swiftly withdrew the needle. After capping it with practiced ease, he tucked it back into the inner pocket of his jacket, his movements precise and deliberate.

I blinked several times, but before I could link the Alpha, he was already in my head.

"Leave him. I'm watching it."

I turned to see Locke behind me, and he put his hand on my shoulder.

"Go home to your family. I've got it from here." Locke continued to stare at Bones.

I nodded, my heart pounding, and cast one final, lingering glance at

Bones, who lay slumped and lifeless on the table. Nadia approached, draping a blanket over his still form and whispering something urgent into his ear. A chill ran down my spine; something was seriously wrong with Bones, and I hoped to the goddess it wasn't what I thought it was.

As I returned to the cave, I was already peeling off my clothes. I appreciated my human form, but after a long day of bartending, I was eager to unleash my inner dragon.

Elena had been practicing during the day, with her animal self, while Luis was at school. She was constantly at the lake trying to coax her dragon to speak with her. She also started up her editing business again. Many of her clients came back to her after her few-month-long hiatus, and she was ready to dive back into it.

While she didn't have to work, and I had plenty of gold to sustain us, we all needed something to fulfill our lives, and if she wanted to do it, she was by all means more than welcome.

I continued to strip out of my clothes as I pushed the flap open. The main area of the cave no longer held our nest. It was now a living room with carpets, a large screen tv with video game consoles, a board game cabinet, and even shelving for all of Abuela's crystals.

Who knows, maybe Luis could use them one day.

The cave was dark as I passed through. Luis was most likely in bed, and

Elena could be for that matter. She had been tired the past few days and was falling asleep before I even got home.

I let my dragon out, my scales rippling down my body as I did, and went down the hallway, pushing back the thick drapes of our den chamber. It was large. The bear shifters did an excellent job creating an area big enough for both of our dragons to lie. I even got new bedding, and it took a while for Elena to get the nest the way she wanted. I thought she had gotten even more picky about how she wanted things situated in there, but it really turned me on how she would get all growly about it.

"Elena?" I poked my head inside and didn't see her there. I then backed away and decided to check on Luis.

I slithered down the dimly lit cavern hallway, the cool stone brushing against my skin, until I reached his room. Gently, I moved the soft, thick blanket aside, revealing a large bed. A small nightlight, shaped like a crescent moon, cast a soft glow across the room, splashing stars onto the walls and ceiling, creating a celestial canopy. The tranquil quiet was almost perfect, yet the absence of a window left the room feeling slightly incomplete, depriving it of natural light and the view of the world outside.

Children loved sunlight, and the ability to see the sun's rays in their room, but I couldn't allow it. My precious family lived here, and I didn't want any enemy to get to them. I showed Luis the secret way to get out of the cave, which ended up at the lake. He was appreciative of that, and the window issue didn't seem to bother him as much as it did me.

I just wanted him happy.

I was quiet when I went inside and nuzzled my nose into his neck to take in his freshly bathed scent. He groaned and petted my cheek. "Hi Dad. Nothing's on fire right now," he mumbled before his soft snores took over the room again.

I chuckled softly, leaving him to his own devices and turned back towards my our den. As I approached, the warm, inviting glow emanating from our den was noticeably brighter, casting a gentle, golden hue over the stones. The air was filled with the delicate notes of soft music.

My cocks jerked in my seam and I groaned.

She must have a surprise.

A good surprise.

I pranced on my claws up to the den, trying not to giggle.

Scales groaned. *"Goddess, pull yourself together."*

I disregarded him and cautiously threaded my head through the blanket, where I was met with an incredibly breathtaking sight. My soulkin stood there, adorned in a vibrant red silk dancing outfit that shimmered in the soft light. The fabric clung to her form, her breasts provocatively spilling over the top, while intricate gold chains, glinting like light, wrapped elegantly around her waist and cascaded down to drape perfectly around her thighs. Each movement sent the chains jingling in time with the music, creating a symphony of sound. Her gaze was fixed on me with an intensity that made me feel as though I was the very force that kept the moon suspended in the sky.

Her hands beckoned me to come over, and I stumbled over the pillows to get closer.

"You are a fucking idiot," Scales hissed as I got closer to her.

"There's my little dragon." Elena reached up, pulled my head down, and kissed my nose. "I don't think I've ever danced for you, so I tried to practice. It's belly dancing for humans, I don't know if it's the same—.

My cocks instantly fell from my slit. "This is perfect, keep going."

Elena laughed, and I curled up behind her as I watched. My tail reached for her, petting her leg as she rotated her hips, moved her soft belly, and twirled her hands and arms around themselves. I was memorized by her as she continued, and I wanted to pounce on her and give her the dragon cocks she so desired.

As she danced, she smiled. "You know, I have something to tell you." She came closer to me, and her body rubbed up against my neck, her scent permeating the air.

I groaned and let my scent pour over her. "Yes, what is it?" My tongue rolled out of my mouth, and I licked down her neck. I was near panting, ready to have her body.

She leaned closer and brought her mouth to my ear. "I'm pregnant."

"Yes, I'd love to lick your pussy and later take it in the ass," I replied, pinning her into the sheets. She squealed while I tried to claw off her top, my tongue wrapping around her nipple.

Scales screamed. *"You are so dense! We have impregnated our female!"*

I continued to lick down her chest, then her stomach until I reached between her thighs and spread them wide. Then I paused, and my head rose in panic.

"I'm sorry. What?"

Elena's face was red, with a large smile. "Anaki, we are going to have a little dragon baby." She began to cry.

I felt her panic and immediately shifted. By the time I was back in human form, she was full-blown sobbing, and I pulled her into my lap, petting her hair. "Goddess, love, it's okay. Are you upset? I'm so sorry, I didn't think you would get pregnant so soon. I'm sorry—"

Elena took in a deep breath. "No, I'm happy. It's just happening so fast! Are you okay with it?"

I beamed and cupped her cheeks. "This is the best day ever! Besides finding you, and Luis. And bonding you. And... fuck this is all amazing. I'm going to be a dad, again!" I wrapped my arms around her and fell into the nest. I peppered her with kisses, both of our chests purring around each other.

"Sure, we can handle this? I mean, this is kind of a big deal?" Elena raised her hand and chewed on her nail.

I tucked her hair away behind her ear. "Of course. I'm here. I'll be here every step of the way. I don't know much about dragon babies, since there have always been so few, but... I'll be the best, I promise. I'll keep all of us protected. Especially in this cave." I nuzzled into her neck.

Elena relaxed into my arms as we settled into the nest. "Um, Anaki? I'm not going to have to... uh, lay an egg, am I?"

I pursed my lips together, trying not to laugh. I really was trying, but instead I boiled over with laughter.

"No, a normal human pregnancy. Except, humans bake humans for nine months, right?" Elena nodded. "Dragon pregnancies are actually longer—"

Elena's body stiffened. "How much longer? Nine months was terrible—"

I sucked in air through my teeth.

Scales chuckled. *"Good luck."*

"Fifteen months," I winced.

Elena sat up and growled. "What do you mean, fifteen months?! For what? For the thing to cook in there? How big does my stomach get? I already have stretch marks!" Elena started speaking in Spanish and I had no idea what she was saying. She stood up and paced around the room.

The only thing I could think about was how sexy she was going to look with a rounded stomach.

We put a baby in her.

Our first try!

I couldn't wait to see if we could do it again.

BOOKS BY VERA

<u>Iron Fang MC Series</u>

Grim

Hawke

Bear

Locke

Anaki

Bones— coming soon!

<u>Under the Moon Series</u>

Under the Moon
Clara and Kane's Story

The Alpha's Kitten
Charlotte and Wesley's Story

Finding Love with the Fae King

Osirus and Melina's Story

The Exiled Dragon

Creed and Odessa's Story

Under the Moon: The Dark War

Clara, Kane, Jasper and Taliyah's story

His True Beloved: A Vampire's Second Chance

Sebastian and Christine's Story

Alpha of her Dreams

Evelyn and Kit's Story

The Broken Alpha's Princess

Melody and Marcus' Story

Twinning and Sinning From Mutts to Mates

Dax, Dimitri, and Seraphina's Story

Under the Moon: God Series

Seeking Hades' Ember

Hades and Ember's Story

Lucifer's Redemption

Lucifer and Uriel's Story

Poseidon's Island Flower
Poseidon and Lani's Story

Thanatos' Craving
Thanatos and Juniper's Story

Saving Zeus—Coming soon!

<u>Under the Moon: The Promised Mates of Monktona Wood</u>

Thorn

Valpar

Simon

Sugha —-Coming soon!

Visit authorverafoxx.com for updates and future books!